REA

D0330343

BUFFALO
MEDICINE

AUG 1 2 2004

ALSO BY APRIL CHRISTOFFERSON

After the Dance
Edgewater
The Protocol
Clinical Trial
Patent to Kill

BUFFALO MEDICINE

APRIL
CHRISTOFFERSON

TOR®

A TOM DOHERTY ASSOCIATES BOOK
NEW YORK

NOTE: If you purchased this book without a cover, you should be aware that this book is stolen property. It was reported as "unsold and destroyed" to the publisher, and neither the author nor the publisher has received any payment for this "stripped book."

This is a work of fiction. All the characters and events portrayed in this book are fictitious or are used fictitiously.

BUFFALO MEDICINE

Copyright © 2004 by April Christofferson

All rights reserved, including the right to reproduce this book, or portions thereof, in any form.

A Forge Book
Published by Tom Doherty Associates, LLC
175 Fifth Avenue
New York, NY 10010

www.tor.com

Tor® is a registered trademark of Tom Doherty Associates, LLC.

ISBN 0-765-34419-X
EAN 978-0765-34419-9

First edition: August 2004

Printed in the United States of America

0 9 8 7 6 5 4 3 2 1

For Mike,
my peaceful warrior

ACKNOWLEDGMENTS

Over the past few years some extraordinary people have come into my life, many of whom figured in the writing of this book. The day I first visited the Buffalo Field Campaign's headquarters outside West Yellowstone, Montana, I knew immediately I had to write about this group of activists. Megan Fishback, my BFC liaison and now dear friend, provided not only inspiration, but also insight into the passion that drives these lovers of the wild bison. To Megan, Mike Mease (cofounder of the BFC), Clark and Heather, Justine, and the rest of the BFC volunteers, my deepest respect and gratitude for your tireless fight.

Other kindred spirits, and champions to the bison, are George, Crystal, barb abramo, and the late Phil Morton. I also want to thank barb for her insightful comments on my manuscript, as well as her support.

In Natalia Aponte, I have an editor willing to put matters of the heart and conscience ahead of more practical matters, for which I am touched and grateful. Tom Doherty, Linda Quinton, Paul Stevens, and Jodi Rosoff make writing for

Forge a pleasure and privilege. I'm also thankful for the talents of Seth Lerner and Aimee Seeram.

Thanks to my terrific literary management team, Ken Atchity and Michael Kuciak. Also to the wonderful Charlie Peterson, Steve Linville, Monte Ahlemeyer, and Laurie Bohall.

To Joan Coffey-Dietrich, a class act, brilliant publicist, and the best kind of friend. To Jeff Barry and Suzy Lysen, I can never thank you both enough. To Darrell Oldham, another lover of the buffalo, for the spiritual strength he's given those dearest to me. To my dear friend, Lynn Stringer, for her exceptional company and motivation to hit the trail. To Dr. Robert Bush and Dr. Stephen Lindsay, for their input. To John Kokinis for high-tech advice. To Ranger Michael Leach for reading my manuscript with a keen eye toward keeping my depiction of the world he so loves accurate and true.

Joe Stringer, of the Forest Service, provided insight and information about the allotment process. He also happens to epitomize the integrity of mission that our governmental agencies should strive for.

To my delightful mother and dear, recently departed father, who started my annual trips to Yellowstone as a young child and instilled in me a love of the West and its wildness that today is one of my greatest cornerstones.

To my grandfather, Floyd "Doc" Carroll, Wyoming rancher, cowboy, and dedicated veterinarian who regularly rolled up his sleeves to save the most hopelessly ill cattle and fought to eradicate brucellosis long before I was born.

To Steve, my champion and partner in life. *My* Houdini.

To Ashley and Crystal, my conscience, my inspiration, my purists, my delights. To my beloved Archie.

And to the bison.

May you live wild and free. And without fear.

What is man without the beasts?
If all the beasts were gone, man would die from a great
loneliness of spirit.
—*Chief Seattle (c. 1784–1866)*

PROLOGUE

SWIPING AT THE river of sweat that poured down his fore-head with a damp, stained bandana, Reed Jones straightened and eyed the Montana sky to the north. Directly overhead all was a fading blue, but north a bit—no more than five miles or so, by Reed's calculations, just about over Pony—huge black clouds had rolled in. As was usually the case in early summer, the clouds were accompanied by a thunder that rumbled its way across the valley, as well as the occasional bolt of lightning that briefly connected cloud to earth.

"Better get this stretch finished up and call it a day," Reed told his ranch hand, Manny Darby.

Reed turned to survey the eighty-some yards of barbed wire the two men had strung that afternoon, to replace a section of fencing left tattered by a spring stampede that Reed blamed on a duo of wolves that had broken loose from the Chief Joseph pack in Yellowstone. Reed hadn't actually seen the pair, but several of his neighbors claimed to.

"That storm's movin' fast," he said, "and we've still got the whole summer before we bring this herd back."

"I still say we could drive them cows back here from Horse Butte in September and save you a whole bunch of money," Manny replied over his shoulder as he snipped the wire and began looping its end tightly around the new post they'd just sunk in ground made rock hard from lack of rain.

"The days of drivin' cattle across Montana are gone," Reed replied. "Too many goddamn fences in the way, put up by millionaire assholes tryin' to play like ranchers. Hell, real ranchers stick together. Between those new bastards and the fucking environmentalists, us old-timers are gonna be put out of business."

"Ranchin' used to be more fun," Manny replied. "That's for sure."

Reed allowed his usual bravado to give way to a moment's introspection as his eyes scanned a portion of the five thousand acres that made up the Bar Z, a ranch he'd worked as a child alongside his father and grandfather, who'd homesteaded it.

"Worked my whole life to build something I could turn over to my boys," he said quietly, "and now that they're educated, neither of 'em wants anything to do with this place. Hell, even my wife's sayin' she's had enough."

The boss had never spoken to Manny about his personal life before and Manny seemed uncertain how to respond.

He remained silent.

The first drops of rain began to fall.

Embarrassed by his spontaneous display of vulnerability, Reed turned away from Manny, picked the coil of remaining wire and his leather gloves off the ground and glanced around for the little blue heeler that rarely left his side.

"Where'd Missy go?" he said gruffly.

"Probably caught the scent of a deer," Manny replied.

Sticking a thumb and forefinger between his lips, Reed let loose with a piercing whistle, but it was mostly lost to the wind the approaching storm had kicked up.

A small plane appeared in the sky just to the east, flying ahead of the storm.

As he and Manny headed toward the pickup, which they'd parked on the scrub grass alongside the fence, Reed cursed, "Damn dog." He handed Manny the coil of barbed wire and turned toward the swell in the pasture, just twenty yards away, to look for Missy. Manny continued on to the truck.

Reed had almost reached the crest of the hill when it hit, a bolt of lightning so explosive and deafening that Manny turned, expecting to see the plane had crashed in the pasture.

Instead he saw Reed stumble to the ground into a boneless heap. Smoke rose from his body.

With a yelp Missy came running from a stand of trees off to one side of the pasture. She and Manny made it to Reed's lifeless form at the same time.

"Boss!" Manny screamed, turning Reed over as Missy whimpered, nudging her master's hands, then arms.

Reed's hair and eyebrows had been burned, patches of both scorched right off his skin. One cowboy boot lay several feet away.

Manny put his ear to his boss's chest, then mouth, then nose.

No heartbeat. No breathing.

He'd never learned CPR, but he'd seen it administered on *Baywatch* more than once.

He began pounding on Reed's chest, then, after thirty or so seconds, gave that up to blow into his mouth.

The rain pelted the ground.

Manny worked furiously, occasionally glancing toward the sky, fearful of another strike.

Missy had decided that Manny was responsible for her beloved owner's condition. She backed away now, growling, showing her teeth to Manny. Warning him.

When blowing his breath into the boss didn't produce results and Manny went back to pounding on Reed's chest,

Missy lunged at him, biting him first on his heels, and then on the back.

Manny didn't let it stop him. He knew Missy was just trying to protect her master.

He also knew it was too late.

CLAY KITTRICK LIKED to stare out his fourth-floor window while he talked on the phone. He was a man of action, and sitting didn't come naturally to Kittrick. Gazing out across the plains that extended south of Butte, as far as the human eye could see—hell, as far as a soaring hawk could see— helped him tolerate the hours he spent chained to a desk.

It reminded him that, in the opinion of many, including Clay himself, Clay served as a kind of "king" of all that open space. Its protector.

Of course, technically speaking, his job was to protect the cattle that grazed it, but everyone who knew ranching, everyone who understood the dynamics, knew that the Montana Department of Livestock's real mission was to ensure that none of the open range that stretched across the state—not a fucking acre of it—would be lost to what Clay thought of as "outside forces."

While Clay had used his position to attain not only an inordinate amount of power, but also a sprawling ranch along the shores of one of Montana's blue-ribbon fly-fishing rivers, the Blackfoot, he liked to view himself in nobler terms, as the last defender of a people, and a way of life, being threatened from all sides. He approached his job with a cowboy mentality— that sometimes in the name of what's right a lawman has to break the law—capitalizing on the cows-versus-condos myth, the modern-day ranchers' mantra to justify bargain-basement grazing fees and other government subsidies by claiming their necessity to keep out urban sprawl.

The way Clay saw it, he was the guardian of the West's last open spaces. And no one was going to fuck with that.

"You're the state veterinarian," Clay said now into the phone. "It'd be better coming from you, not me."

He fell silent, listening.

"All I'm saying is that you make one call. Something for the record. You let Whittaker know what that latest study found. That two of those cattle tested positive for brucellosis."

Another pause.

"Hell, yes, I know that doesn't mean they're actually infected. I know that fucking test shows false positives all the time. But just do it, damn it. Make the call."

He hung up the phone, exasperated. Unable to stand another minute at that desk, he reached for the cowboy hat that sat on its corner.

His secretary's voice over the intercom caused his hand to freeze in midair.

"Cyrus Gibbons is on the phone."

Cyrus never called unless it was important. Clay reached for the phone.

"What's up?"

"Bad news. Reed Jones was struck by lightning yesterday."

Clay leaned forward in his chair. "Killed 'im?"

"Yep."

Clay fell silent.

"Have you talked to his wife?" he asked after several seconds.

"Spent most of last night with her," Cyrus replied.

"And?"

"She wants out. Says she's moving to California to live with her sister."

"She's just upset. She'll calm down."

"Not this one. Reed told me half a dozen times these past years that she's had enough of that ranch."

"What about his sons?"

"They were both on their way to Montana last night, one from Chicago, the other from Portland. I left before they got there; but Reed's wife told me that neither of 'em could be dragged back to this area with anything short of a noose. And she said that's fine with her, that she'd rather see them livin' on the streets in the city than come back and take the Bar Z over."

As if Clay didn't have enough problems to deal with.

"Papers get wind of it yet?"

"Nothing in today's *Gazette*."

"You know anyone works there?"

"Sure. Just about everyone."

"Make sure they don't print it."

"Gotcha."

"And you better set up a meeting for me with the wife. I'll need to talk to her right away."

"She's pretty busted up right now. You should probably wait until after the funeral."

"We can't afford to wait," Clay said. "Get it done. And get back to me right away." His mind shifted to their other problem. Hopefully just a fly in the ointment, but Clay prided himself on his diligence, and in being proactive. "Have you worked something out with the girl?"

"Yes. She's on board. I knew she'd go for the idea."

"It wasn't just a rumor, then?"

"No. He's on to something. And he's no dummy. I had a friend of mine at Washington State check him out. Graduated at the top of his class. Was involved in some groundbreaking research even when he was still in school. It's the real deal. Don't worry, though. I've got it under control. Shouldn't be a problem for long."

"That's good. I don't have to tell you how much you have at stake. What could happen if he succeeds."

"No, you don't," Cyrus answered. After a pause, he added, "I suspect you've got a bit of a personal interest in it, too."

The comment infuriated Clay. Cyrus was fishing, like he always did. But Clay was too smart to give him anything. Cyrus—and all the others, for that matter—could speculate all they wanted. Clay had his own back covered.

But hell if he'd take this kind of crap to his face.

Pressing his mouth to the phone, looking as though he might just eat it for a mid-morning snack, his voice came out low and mean.

"It's my job to protect the livestock industry in this state. And I take that job pretty fucking serious. Do what I have to do. You have something to complain about, take it up with my boss. The governor. You hear? Otherwise you keep your fuckin' mouth shut about how I do my job."

"Whoa, Clay. Take it easy. You know I think you're the best thing ever happened to ranching in the state of Montana."

"All right. Just take care of this Reed Jones thing."

"I'll get right on it."

ONE

NOW THAT THE seed of distrust had been planted, Jed Mc-Cane felt it gnawing away at his insides like a maggot on dying flesh. Even the brilliant sunset over the Gravellys—pink cotton candy swirls against a blue that only Montana skies could deliver—failed to work its usual magic on his tired soul.

He glanced at his watch.

Nine o'clock. It would be well past eleven by the time he drove by the Double Jump. Too late to drop in unannounced on Rebecca, who, during the summer months, rose by four-thirty to put breakfast on the table for over a dozen ranch hands.

Or maybe it wasn't too late. Maybe dropping in unannounced . . .

A flash of anger—not at Rebecca; but at himself, for the way his mind had been working recently—brought Jed's fist down hard on the padded steering wheel of his pickup.

In the next instant, his truck lurched violently to the right, careening off the two-lane highway, toward a deep, empty creek bed; and in that nanosecond when Jed first realized he was in deep trouble, he blamed his temper.

But then he realized that the truck tilted dramatically toward its right front end. He'd blown a tire. Struggling to retain control, fighting his natural instinct to stomp down on the brake, Jed eased off the gas and used his considerable strength—a result of wrestling thousands of pounds of flesh on a daily basis—to keep the truck from flipping. As it veered crazily toward the upper crust of the creek bed, which dropped off into a black void several yards from where the asphalt ended, Jed braced himself for the inescapable roll.

His mind flashed briefly on the thirty-gallon tank of gasoline he kept in the back of the truck—a hazard made necessary by the long days he spent on the road, far from any gas stations. He'd become careless about it. How long had it been since he checked the straps that held it against the wall of the truck bed? If that tank broke loose, the impact when he flipped into that creek bed, then smashed into its other side, would likely blow the truck, along with Jed, sky high.

Using every fiber of muscle in his body, Jed fought the wheel, trying, with no success, to turn it back toward the center of the highway.

Suddenly his headlights picked up a huge, dark form. Just ahead, lying on the side of the road. It took just an instant for Jed to recognize it.

A steer. Dead, its body bloated twice its size by the summer sun.

Fixated on the carcass, sweat now pouring down his face, Jed gave the steering wheel one last, explosive effort.

Miraculously, the truck's course straightened—by no more than a few degrees, but enough to delay its meeting with the creek bed by seconds.

Enough to send it directly toward the dead steer.

The impact—a surreal explosion of metal and blood and

rotting flesh—threw Jed forward. His head smashed the windshield, shattering it, and, as the truck entered a strangely silent roll over the massive carcass, Jed's world went black.

SLOWED BY THE cushion of bloated flesh, the pickup rolled onto its roof, slid across gravel and dirt and scrub grass toward the drop-off, then flipped—almost gently, like a pair of dice tossed by a loving hand—into the creek bed, miraculously landing upright.

When Jed came to, he had no idea how long he'd been out, how long he'd sat there, strapped into the truck. His head felt like it had been used by the gods in a game of squash. He sat quietly, drifting in and out of consciousness, a crescent moon and the crude field of diamonds in a sky of ink providing just enough light for him to see a coyote slink across the creek bed twenty-five yards up ahead. It moved like liquid gold up the bank and disappeared across the road.

That—the coyote's presence—told Jed he'd been there a while.

Suddenly, the hum of a motor pierced the night's silence.

Jed craned his neck forward, and looked up, through the shattered windshield, toward the road.

Lights! An approaching car.

Jed pulled the door handle, then let out a grunt as he hoisted his upper body against it. It didn't budge. Frantically, he reached for the light switch on the dashboard, flipping it on and off, but the impact—either with the steer or the ditch, he could not know which—had broken the headlamps.

He tried the horn, twice, but each time with no luck. The impact must have loosened a wire.

He could not signal for help.

But then, something amazing happened.

He heard the whine of poorly maintained brakes. They'd seen the truck and were stopping to help.

3 1833 04671 2573

Through his veil of grogginess, Jed leaned out his side window—the glass of which had crumpled into a thousand jigsaw-puzzle pieces and now coated both the ground and Jed's lap—and heard footsteps.

Help was on its way.

A true modern-day cowboy, Jed waited patiently. Silently.

After a brief silence that indicated his rescuer had stopped for some reason, he heard a female voice. Even in his haze, he thought it one of the most unusual voices he'd ever heard; almost like the sound of the newborn calf he'd delivered the day before—bleating for its mother as it tried to rise on stick-thin, unsure legs.

"Damn, K.C.," the voice said. "Looks like it's been here for days. Whew! Get a whiff."

Confused by this discussion of the dead steer—why on earth had she even stopped to look at it?—Jed strained to hear the reply from the car, which still sat, motor idling, in the middle of the road.

A man's voice. K.C.? "Okay, then, hop in."

Incredulous, all his reactions slowed by his head injury, Jed heard the sound of footsteps running back across the road's pavement, before he could react. *They were running away from him.*

The slam of a car door followed. They were leaving!

Even in his fog, Jed knew this was a bad thing. A very bad thing. He leaned out the window.

"Wait."

The car's motor shifted in pitch as the car lurched forward.

Jed lifted a hand and brought it down again, harder this time, on the truck's horn.

The blast pierced the night. Jed felt his head begin to throb, in long, sadistic pulses that kept time with the horn.

Still, he did not let up.

The other vehicle had already covered at least fifty yards,

but now, Jed heard it braking. Then it began backing up. They must have heard the truck's horn.

"What the fuck was that?" Jed heard a man say.

"Down here," Jed yelled, once more struggling to open his door, which the impact had crumpled. "In the ditch."

This time, two car doors opened, then slammed shut. Footsteps again, running toward the ditch.

"Oh, my God," the woman called from somewhere above. Jed still could not see her. "A truck. Someone's in it."

Rocks and gravel ricocheted noisily off the truck's hood as she scrambled down the incline, into the creek bed.

A mass of long, dark curls appeared behind Jed's shoulder, filling the gaping hole that had housed the window on the driver's side.

"Are you okay?"

That voice. A blend of silky honey and metal grating against metal.

The moon's light, reflected off the hood of the truck, revealed eyes the color and warmth of hot chocolate in a pale, narrow face. The unmistakable concern in them made Jed wonder how bad he looked. Aside from the slow reactions, and the headache, he didn't feel all that bad. But he also knew that shock was likely.

"I think I'm okay," Jed answered. "But I can't get out. The door's stuck."

Jed literally left his seat when, without warning, the metal toe of the woman's hiking boot drop-kicked the door at his elbow. She looked about the size of one of those calves her voice reminded Jed of, but that leg packed a hell of a wallop.

"Open, dammit," she ordered, yanking angrily on the door.

Suddenly, something stopped her cold, her hands still frozen to the door handle.

She lifted her nose—a small, perfect ski jump of a nose—into the air and sniffed. She turned and yelled over her shoulder.

"K.C., quick. I smell gas. We've got to get him out."

"Here I come," K.C., obviously the slower of the two, yelled from somewhere behind her.

In his first moments of coherency, Jed hadn't noticed, but now he could smell it, too. The unmistakable odor of gasoline.

He struggled against his seat belt, fumbling in the dark to find its release, but the locking mechanism had become jammed against the caved-in door.

For the first time, Jed realized that the car's motor still hummed quietly.

Slowly, he reached for the ignition, but a man with hair even longer and curlier than the woman's had appeared on the seat next to him and he beat Jed to it, flipping the key to the off position.

Then he directed his attention to getting Jed out of his seat belt.

The woman had gone round the other side and stood watching over his shoulder.

"Hurry," she urged.

"We're gonna have to cut him out," the man declared. "Megan, run back to the car and get my bowie knife."

"You loaned it to Bear the other day, don't you remember?"

"Shit," K.C. replied. "You're right."

"In the back," Jed said. "There's a scalpel in my medical bag."

The woman, Megan, turned to go.

"Wait," Jed cried, realizing what he'd just suggested. "There's a can of gasoline back there. That's what we smell. The back of the truck's rigged with lights. They go on automatically when the door's opened. They could spark a fire."

His two rescuers looked at each other briefly.

"He's right," K.C. said.

"We have to get him out of here," Megan replied. "I'm getting the scalpel."

Without further discussion, she disappeared.

"Stop her," Jed directed the man.

K.C. lifted calm eyes—were they drugged? How else could they remain so serene?—to meet Jed's.

"You don't know Megan. There's no point in trying to stop her."

Megan reappeared. "It's locked. Where's the key?"

Jed felt like he was moving through thick molasses. Megan had already jerked them out of the ignition by the time he'd reached for them.

"Stop her," Jed ordered again.

K.C.'s only acknowledgment was to call after her as she disappeared again. "Be careful, Megs," K.C. said. "Please."

All it would take was a spark. If the fuel had spilled and splattered all over the back of the truck, even turning the latch could ignite a fireball big enough to be seen a hundred miles away, in Ennis. Jed held his breath as he heard the keys jingling in the dark.

K.C. too had turned to look toward the back of the truck. Jed sensed K.C. felt more fear than he let on.

Seconds passed, then a minute. Finally, lights from the back of the truck parted the darkness.

"Man, you smell something burning?" K.C. asked, his eyes now wide.

"Yes," Jed yelled. "You two get the hell out of here. *Now.* Do you hear?"

K.C. disappeared toward the back of the truck, in search of Megan, but like a ghost suddenly materializing out of nowhere, she reappeared at Jed's window.

"Got it."

She stood triumphantly holding the surgical scalpel Jed had used just hours earlier on Cyrus Gibbons's mare.

"Give it to me, then go," Jed ordered. "Quick."

Ignoring him, Megan reached inside. Moonlight flashed

briefly off the blade as, with one quick, fluid motion, she sliced through the top strap of the seat belt. Next, without regard for the shards of broken glass, she grabbed the strap that ran across Jed's lap.

In another second, Jed fell free.

He could see the blue-jean-clad rear end of K.C. as he scrambled up the side of the ditch.

Megan remained at his side, pushing him through the window, toward the open passenger door.

"Hurry."

Jed scrambled out the passenger door. He glanced over, to make certain that Megan was heading toward the road, then ran to the back of the truck.

The minicooler was lying on its side. Deeper inside the truck, permanently affixed to the wall behind the truck's cab, was a generator-operated refrigerator he'd had installed. The impact had swung its door open. Broken glass vials, mingled with blood, littered the back of the truck.

Megan had turned and now stood at the top of the ditch.

"What are you doing?" she screamed. "Get out of there!"

Jed grabbed the cooler and sprinted toward her.

As he did, a large black form rushed by him, heading toward the truck.

A dog.

"Pie," Megan screamed. "Don't go down there."

She started down after the dog, but K.C. suddenly appeared and stopped her, grabbing her by the arm.

"No, Megan. You can't go after him." He cupped his free hand to his mouth, screaming, *"Pie."*

Tossing the cooler toward them, Jed yelled, "Take this."

Then he turned and headed back toward the truck, his eyes searching the dark for the dog.

* * *

THE EXPLOSION ROCKED the night. Megan felt it coming at her, a wall of heat so intense and thick that it lifted her off her feet and threw her, facedown, onto the asphalt.

Heat seared through the back of her blue jeans. She lifted her head to look for K.C.

He lay dazed, several yards away, shielding his eyes as he stared back toward the ditch.

"Megan?" he screamed, blinded by the fireball.

"Here."

K.C. ran to her, crouching beside her.

"Are you okay?"

"Yes," she said, rolling into a sitting position. "Where's that guy? Where's Pie?"

"There."

Megan looked in the direction K.C. pointed.

Silhouetted against the white-hot flames, several yards behind her on the side of the road, the man was rising from his belly to his hands and knees. Flames had taken hold of the scrub grass and now licked at his clothing.

A dark form, completely still, lay next to him.

Pie.

K.C. ran to them. Sobbing, Megan raised herself up. As she stumbled toward them, Pie suddenly sprang to his feet, tail wagging despite a dazed expression.

"Pie," Megan cried, bending to give him a quick hug. The dog whimpered, then, tail dropped, stole back toward the safety of the car.

Together, Megan and K.C. pulled the man onto the asphalt. He was big. Not fat, but even through his green overalls, Megan could see he was as muscled and rugged as her beloved Houdini.

Once they got him clear of the fire, Megan beat at his smoking overalls with her bare hands.

"Your dog okay?" he mumbled.

Megan nodded. "Yes," she said. "Thank you. Thank you so much."

His eyes had a glazed look, but scanning the scene, they apparently missed nothing. He rose to a sitting position, nodding toward the car.

"Do you have any blankets in there?"

Rising to his feet with a shaky urgency, he shrugged out of two wide straps and, with his overalls hanging around his waist, began unfastening the buttons of his long-sleeved shirt. Impatient, he ripped them apart, never taking his eyes off the flames by the roadside as he removed his shirt.

Across the creek bed, for ten or fifteen yards beyond, the ground was lit up by dozens of tiny fires.

"Grab whatever you have," he said. "We have to put the fire out."

K.C.'s mouth dropped open, his eyes glued to the sight of the truck engulfed in flames that shot at least twenty feet into the air.

"You're crazy if you think we can put that out."

"Not the truck. It'll be okay in the creek bed. But we've got to stomp out the grass before a wind spreads it. Hurry."

Megan opened the back door of the Subaru and grabbed the sleeping bag she kept stashed there. She threw it at K.C.

"Here, use this."

She turned back to the car and bent over the back-seat floor, scooping odds and ends (a box of dog biscuits, empty bottles and cans bound for recycling, a stack of newsletters) out of the way, her thin arms flying like a dog digging for a long-buried bone, and emerged seconds later with a pad of carpet, about two feet by three.

One folded paper fluttered to the pavement, disappearing under the car.

Calling to Pie, she ordered him inside the car and shut the door.

The man had already started across the ditch, running up the road several yards, far enough to stay clear of the fireball. He jumped down into the creek bed. From how wobbly he looked, Megan wondered if he'd ever emerge from the other side, but then she saw him scramble up its bank, waving his shirt at the flaming grass, using his big booted feet to stomp at the clusters of burning scrub grass.

He was right. Had the truck landed anywhere else, they'd have no chance of stopping the devastation a fire would wreak. It would start with the prairie, parched dry by a month of unseasonably high temperatures in the nineties, then move its way up toward the hills, where the trees—lodgepole pine, Douglas fir, quaking aspen—would give it new life and take it to another level. Just a little wind and it would roar like a runaway freight train in either direction: north, along the Madison Range, perhaps even jumping the mighty Madison River to shoot over to the Tobacco Roots, and south, toward Yellowstone National Park.

Megan had grown up in Boise, where the National Park Service's Wildfire Prevention Unit was headquartered. She knew from years of watching the local news just what was at stake, how even a careless cigarette butt could change an entire landscape—killing everything in its path, including dreams like hers—for decades to come.

The dry creek bed appeared to be containing the heart of the fire, providing a perfect fire pit in which to burn, but Megan recognized the danger that the small, spotty patches of scrub grass represented. Not just to the ranchers nearby, but to the untold thousands of domesticated and wild creatures that lived within a hundred miles in either direction.

She joined K.C. at the side of the road, lifted her rug pad and began beating at the flames with something akin to a primitive rage.

Within minutes, pickups began arriving, driven by cowboys carrying shovels and blankets and various containers filled with water. One beat-up 1959 Chevy backed toward the fire. When its owner dropped the tailgate, Megan saw an old cast-iron bathtub filled with water in its bed. Without a word, the old-timer, she would guess his age to be near eighty, stood on the truck bed, scooping a black rubber bucket into the tub time and time again and tossing water (futilely, as it had no chance of reaching the fire) toward the flames shooting out of the ditch.

At least a dozen figures beat at the flames on either side of the road in silence.

They did not stop until every last ember had gone black.

When the fires were out, Megan slumped to the ground. Exhaustion and fear had drained her. She stared at the now contained fire, burning itself out in the creek bed, her chest heaving with each breath.

The men had begun talking among themselves.

"Helluvan explosion."

"I was just leavin' Del's when the whole fuckin' night lit up. Took me a while to figure out which road it was on."

"Me, too. Someone said Doc was down at Cyrus's place, stitching up one of his mares. Must've been takin' the back way home."

"Good thing Jennie forgot to buy me that bottle of Johnnie Walker today. I would've been half in the bag by now. Wouldn't't've been worth shit."

"Hell, Monty, you ain't never worth shit."

Hearty laughter.

They seemed either not to have seen Megan and K.C., who had plunked down at her side, or not to know what to make of them.

"Doc okay?"

"Yeah, just a little beat-up, I guess. Look, here he comes now."

Megan turned. The flames from the creek bed had shrunk to little more than an oversized campfire. It provided just enough light for her to recognize the man from the truck. Despite what he'd been through, he now moved more steadily, even with the hint of an athletic grace.

"Howdy, Doc," one of the cowboys called out in a drawl worthy of the best Randy Travis tune.

"Jed," another said, this one a little lighter on the twang. "Sure glad you're okay."

The others quickly joined in.

"Too bad about your truck, Doc."

"Damn shame."

"Lucky you hit that fuckin' steer before you went in the ditch," one particularly grizzled old-timer said. "Looks like one of Ozzie's black-faced steers, don't it?"

"It's Ozzie's, all right. Triangle C brand on it."

When Jed, or Doc, or whatever his name was, stopped in their midst, they closed around him, swallowing him until Megan could no longer see him. But she recognized his voice.

"The truck's insured," he replied. "And I got some of the samples out."

"You mean for your research? That brucellosis vaccine that you can actually spray on?"

"Yeah," he answered. "Earlier today I sampled three herds in Madison County. And a couple dozen park bison. But I lost the samples I took yesterday from Reed Jones's herd. They were in the refrigerator in the back of the truck."

Wide-eyed, Megan and K.C. looked at each other. Had they heard him correctly?

"That a big setback?"

"It's a setback, all right. Reed's herd was the one I was most interested in and I won't be able to resample them. I took those samples as they were being loaded for transport to slaughter."

"Ol' Reed'd turn over in his grave if he knew that woman of his sold that whole herd. They were his pride and joy."

Murmurs of agreement circled the group.

"What about all those records you keep, Doc?" Another voice, this one even deeper and with a twang so pronounced that it struck Megan as artificial. "'Spose you lost them, too."

"No, thank God. Probably lost all my hard copies, but I left my laptop at Rebecca's last night. It has all my data, all my research. Speaking of which, I'd be much obliged if someone could either drive me up to the Double Jump, or loan me a truck. Rebecca'll be frantic when she gets wind of what happened."

"I'd be happy to, Jed," one of the cowboys said. "Gotta meet Emma's parents at the train station in Ennis tomorrow morning anyway. I'll just sleep in the truck."

"Hell, Tom," Jed replied, "Rebecca wouldn't let you do that. You can bunk with the hands."

"I hear she's already got a full crew on hand. Truck's fine with me, Jed. No worse than the couch I've been sleepin' on for months now."

A new voice chimed in. "Hey, Tom. Emma still tryin' to decide whether to give you the boot?"

"Somethin' like that."

The conversation quickly turned to the late-summer cattle drives to bring herds down from summer ranges in the high country. Still two months away, it was the highlight of the season for most of these cowboys, the closest they came to living the romantic dream that had brought young men west a hundred years earlier. During the discussion, two of the cowboys quietly took their leave.

K.C. turned to Megan.

"Let's get out of here," he said softly.

As they were walking away, they passed the two men who'd just left. They were putting their shovels and pickaxe into the bed of a beat-up, lemon-colored pickup truck. Huddled together, the men did not see them.

Their conversation, part of which Megan overheard, made little sense.

"This could be our lucky day. We better make tracks, before Doc leaves."

She recognized the voice, the one with the fake drawl.

"We can always call ahead," the other said.

"No cell coverage between here and there."

One of the men glanced over his shoulder and saw Megan and K.C. They fell silent.

As Megan and K.C. climbed into the car, the truck roared past them, heading north, toward Ennis.

K.C. had just turned the key in the ignition, bringing the Subaru sputtering halfheartedly to life, when the driver of the truck came running up.

"Wait. How can I thank you? You saved my life."

"And you saved Pie," K.C. replied. "That makes us even."

Megan could only see his well-muscled chest—now streaked with soot and dried sweat, giving it a camouflage look—as Jed stood at the window on the driver's side.

"I'd at least like to know your names."

"I'm K.C., and this is Megan."

Bending low, he stuck his large hand in the window, and grasped Megan's.

"I'm Jed McCane." The soft light from the dashboard revealed a face unremarkable but for its eyes, which were the color of late-summer wheat and had the same trusting, straightforward quality Megan usually associated with highly intelligent animals. "I don't know what I would've done if you hadn't come by and stopped. You risked your lives for me. I'd like to do something to thank you."

Tail wagging to beat the bush, Pie's nose suddenly appeared over the back of the seat.

"Hey, big fella," Jed said, patting the top of the dog's head. An easy smile made stark contrast of his tanned face, still streaked with soot, and his perfect white teeth.

"We're just glad you're okay," Megan replied. She glanced in the direction of the group still gathered around the nearly spent flames—flames which would now be easy to extinguish, if the group were so inclined, which it wasn't. There was nothing a ragtag bunch of cowboys loved better than shooting the breeze around a late-night fire. Even if fueled by a mangled truck instead of timber. "Looks like you won't have any trouble getting a ride."

With that, K.C. shifted into gear. And as soon as Jed Mc-Cane pulled his hand back out of the window, they drove off.

TWO

JED STOOD WATCHING the Subaru go, totally perplexed by its occupants.

The only thing he knew about these two people, who had saved his life, then stayed to help put out the fire, were their first names: Megan and K.C. In Jed's world, such selfless acts dictated some reciprocal gesture: a meal, a bed, help with the next haying, or barn raising, or, at the very least, a round of drinks at Del's. Some means of acknowledging the kindness, or perhaps, just evening the score.

The knowledge he would not be afforded the chance to thank them properly no doubt explained the unsettled feeling Jed experienced as he stared after the compact, beat-up car, which took off so fast he caught only a fleeting glimpse of a bumper plastered with stickers, the kind that pretty much told the world the driver's outlook on life. In Jed's neck of the world, these ran toward CHARLESTON HESTON IS MY PRESIDENT, THE ONLY GOOD WOLF IS A DEAD WOLF, and the new one he'd seen just the day before, in West Yellowstone: I LOVE EXPLOSIVES. Jed felt pretty certain the Subaru's stickers painted an entirely different picture, but he couldn't say for sure because he had no time to actually read any of them.

At the last second, he strained to see the issuing state on the license plate, but the blackness had already swallowed all but the single, left taillight, which glowed like the tip of a cigarette for half a minute or so before being snuffed out by the night.

He turned back toward the group in the creek bed.

A light breeze had lifted a piece of paper from the road, dancing it across the asphalt in front of him, to a patch of still smoldering scrub grass.

As Jed strode across the road to join the others, the center of the paper suddenly ignited.

Jed quickly stomped out the flames, then bent, crushed the half-burned paper into a ball with his fist and stuck it in a pocket of his overalls, avoiding the possibility of another such mishap.

With a sideways, soccer kick, he booted several inches of loose, sandy dirt on top of the grass, extinguishing it once and for all.

By this time, Tom Barton had joined him.

"Wanna head toward Ennis?" Tom asked. "The guys here say they'll keep an eye on the last of the fire. We all think it'd be a good idea for you to get some rest, then get yourself checked out in the morning."

Jed's eyes surveyed what was left of his truck. His nose had grown numb to the pungent, unpleasant smell of scorched metal and melting rubber, but now, as the light breeze shifted, it picked up the scent of burned grass, which actually had a sweetness to it. Though he could not have foreseen a blowout—his tires had less than twenty thousand miles on them—Jed still felt responsible for the fact that he'd almost started a wildfire that could have devastated everything in its path for miles.

"I can't leave, Tom, not until it's all out, and there's no

chance the wind'll get it goin' again. But thanks. I'll catch a lift into Ennis or West Yellowstone later. You go ahead."

Tom Barton shook his head in mock frustration, then cupped a four-and-a-half-fingered hand to his mouth.

"Monty, Jed says he won't leave till the fire's burned out."

By now, two six-packs of beer and a bottle of Johnnie Walker had materialized in the creek bed. Most the men had either settled on the bare ground, or sat crouched low on their haunches, swigging from the Johnnie Walker before passing it along. At Barton's words, a giant-sized figure rose, took off his mangled straw cowboy hat and swatted the air in their direction.

"Hell, Jed, get out of here. Whaddya think we are, a bunch of incompetents? We can handle this little shit of a fire. Now git."

A chorus of voices seconded Monty's sentiment.

Jed stared up the road one last time, in the direction the Subaru had disappeared.

Now that the adrenaline had run dry, his entire body shouted with pain; beginning with his forehead, the knot on which had grown to the size of a golfball, down through his shoulders, diagonally across his chest and lower abdomen, where the seat belt's violent restraint felt like he'd been sucker punched, twice for good measure, with a tire iron.

He wiped the back of his soot-blackened hand across his forehead. "I have to admit. It would sure feel good to get to Rebecca's and get some shut-eye."

"That settles it," Tom Barton said. "Let's go."

They headed toward the row of trucks parked haphazardly along the roadway. The rear end of Tom's 1991 Ford Bronco angled out sharply from near the end of the line. Jed had just opened the door on the passenger side, when he heard shouting.

"Doc, wait."

In synchrony, Jed and Tom turned toward the creek bed.

Pulling his long leg back out of the Bronco, Jed started back along the side of the highway, limping now, toward the group. When he'd left, the men had been sitting in a loose ring around the burning truck, but now all of them stood, clustered together, at the front right bumper.

"You better see this, Doc."

As Jed slid down the embankment, the group parted for him.

Crouched within twelve inches of the smoldering ruins of Jed's pickup, seemingly oblivious to the smoke that still billowed from it, Monty Payton pointed toward the truck.

Jed waved away the smoke, which smelled of burned rubber, squinting to make out the target of Monty's rapt fascination.

"You said you blew a tire," Monty said. Even in the half-light, his grin exposed teeth stained brown by years of chewing tobacco. "Hell, Doc, it wasn't a tire you blew. The whole fuckin' wheel's gone."

"That can't be," Jed said. "Wheels don't just fall off brand-new trucks."

"Well, this one did. Take a look."

As the men stared through the smoke at the gaping hole in the wheel well and discussed this new development, Jack Hamlin—known locally as "Dead Man," in recognition of the Fourth of July he'd spent passed out on the floor of Del's, until someone finally thought to check if he was still alive—dropped down on both knees and produced a flashlight from his overalls.

Following the light's beam, Dead Man stuck his head right into the wall of smoke.

He coughed and spat two or three times, then finally cleared his voice to speak.

"Hell, Doc. That wheel didn't just fall off," he said, his voice echoing faintly against the hollow shell of burned-out metal. "Somebody loosened the fucking lug nuts."

* * *

INSIDE THE SUBARU, Megan turned excitedly to K.C.

"Did you hear that? Reed Jones is *dead*."

"I heard," K.C. replied, his brow scrunched in confusion. "But how could we not know that?"

Megan's mind raced, trying to give meaning to everything she'd heard, as she stroked Pie's forehead and ears.

"It makes no sense."

"None."

"And that vet," Megan said, her voice rising excitedly. "He's working on a brucellosis vaccine that's *aerosolized*."

K.C. glanced sideways at Megan, flashing her a smile. K.C. wasn't much for clothes, or grooming, but he had the prettiest, whitest teeth Megan had ever seen.

"Yeah," he said. Several black tendrils danced and bobbed in front of his eyes as he shook his head in excitement. "Can you believe it?"

They both fell silent for a minute. Megan looked over at K.C. again.

"Wow," she said. "Maybe we better drive up to the reservation tomorrow and visit Colleen."

K.C. met her gaze briefly.

"That's what I was just thinking."

Megan turned to look for Pie, who'd disappeared.

He now lay with his head propped against the back of the back seat, looking into the darkness behind them.

"You liked him, didn't you, Pie?" she said softly.

THREE

WHO THE HELL was that?"

White darts of pain shot through Jed's neck. The trauma of the accident had caused its muscles to seize up, making any movement excruciating, but that didn't stop him from craning to get a look inside the light-colored pickup that bounced and rattled past them at a speed the narrow gravel road was never meant to accommodate. Between the truck's speed, the cloud of dust it kicked up, and Tom Barton's ratty old Stetson blocking most of the view out the driver's window, all Jed could make out were two silhouettes inside the truck's cab. That two people were inside, instead of one, helped ease the knot that had grabbed his gut the moment Tom's Bronco had rounded the last curve to the main house and they'd seen the two headlights snap on, then come heading hell-bent in their direction.

Under the hat, Barton's brow furrowed into three distinct rows of flesh.

"Probably one of the hands," he answered. "Or one of their girlfriends. What's the big deal?"

Jed straightened in his seat, staring forward, toward the

house, and did not answer. Through the stand of cottonwoods that danced in the breeze, Jed could see several lights blinking ahead.

He glanced at his watch. Nearly two A.M.

Barton slowed for the suspension bridge that led up to the sprawling log structure Rebecca Nichols had had rebuilt three years earlier, after the death of her father, the infamous Buck Nichols, great-grandson of the founder of the Double Jump Ranch.

One of southwestern Montana's oldest and most profitable ranches, the Double Jump sat snug up against the foothills of the Gravelly Range, with Highway 287 forming one border, the Madison Mountains due east, and the mighty Madison River bisecting it into two long stretches of mostly flat, fertile pasture.

Cattle heaven, that's what Buck used to call it.

He'd passed his intense pride in the place down to his only surviving child. And when it burned down shortly after Buck's death, no amount of persuasion could deter Rebecca from having it rebuilt, log for log, stone for stone, precisely as Rebecca's memory, aided by box after box of photo albums, dictated. The architect had suggested moving the ranch house east, across the narrow bridge and closer to the highway, for convenience and safety's sake. The bridge had always been tricky, especially in winter. In fact, a liquored-up ranch hand had once gone over it in the early morning hours. Buck had found him the next day, still strapped in his truck, head underwater in the overturned vehicle. The architect, as well as friends concerned about Rebecca's refusal to let Buck go, urged Rebecca to update the house's look and feel. Rebecca would hear none of it. So intent was she on re-creating the house of her childhood, the house Buck Nichols took unending pride and comfort in, that she even had furniture custom made to replicate that destroyed in the fire. When an artisan from Jackson Hole delivered a replica of

Buck's favorite easy chair—the original of which had hand-tooled leather—and the bucking bronc rider on the chair faced left instead of right, Rebecca had sent it back, refusing to pay for it until the chair as Buck knew it was delivered.

As Tom and Jed approached the house, tucked into the cottonwoods at the base of the foothills, the bridge groaned softly under the Bronco's weight.

"Looks like somebody's up," Tom said, echoing Jed's own thoughts.

Jed scowled. The barn windows stared back at them, black squares in the night. A single light glowed in the bunkhouse. But nearly every window on the first floor of the main residence, and several on the second, blazed with light.

"Looks like it," he replied, still thinking about that truck.

They'd barely rolled to a stop when the front door opened.

Rebecca Nichols stepped onto the porch, her white cotton nightgown flowing in her wake; the light behind her, from the door, outlined a body gifted by genetics and toned by grueling ranch work. A riot of strawberry-blond locks, half pinned up, half cascading over her fine-boned shoulders, gave her the illusion of an angel dropped suddenly to earth.

Jed could not look at Rebecca without catching his breath.

Nor could any other man in Madison County, including, right now—Jed could feel it, he didn't even need to look—Tom Barton.

Jed stepped quickly out of the truck.

"Jed, is that you?" Rebecca crossed the wooden porch, skimming down its three stairs. "What's going on? Why are you here?"

Jed's appearance stopped her cold . . . Her hands went right to the gash on his forehead.

"You're hurt."

Was it Jed's imagination or did his gash stop throbbing the moment those fingers, calluses and all, touched it?

"I'm fine."

"You're *not fine*," she said. "What happened to you?"

When Jed did not respond, she grew angry.

"Tell me right this instant. Do you hear?"

"Truck blew a tire," Jed answered. "Down past Cameron. I was on my way home from Cyrus Gibbons's. Truck's totaled. Tom offered to give me a ride up here, on his way to Ennis."

"Didn't blow a tire," Tom Barton offered from the station he'd taken up, close to the open car door. "His whole wheel came off. Jed could've been killed."

"The wheel? How could that happen?" Rebecca asked. "That truck was new."

Jed felt acutely aware of the blood and soot staining his clothing, face, and hair as Rebecca now studied him with heightened concern.

"I don't know how it happened. Maybe some screwup at the factory. But I'm okay. Just a little sore."

"Dead Man says someone deliberately loosened the lug nuts," Tom said, continuing his offerings from the safety of his Bronco.

Jed snapped, "Shut up, Tom," but it was too late.

"Deliberately?" Rebecca echoed. "You can't be serious."

"That's what Dead Man says," Tom replied, "and he's pretty good at car stuff."

Jed lifted a palm in the air, silencing Tom.

"That's nonsense. Of course it wasn't deliberate. Dead Man loves stirring the pot. It just happened. And I'm fine. Enough said, okay?" Holding his voice steady, trying for nonchalant, he turned to Rebecca. "So what were you doing up at this hour?"

In the half-light off the porch, Jed saw the corners of her mouth tighten.

"It's Peyton, Jed. He looks awful. I left him out in the pasture all day and when I went to bring him in, just before dark, he could barely walk a straight line. He must've stumbled four times before I got him in his stall. I've been out with him for the last hour. I'd just come back in when you arrived."

Jed should've left it at that, but instead he asked, "Why didn't you call me?"

"You just said, you were at Cyrus's."

The answer didn't appease him.

"Who was that leaving just now?"

"I don't know," Rebecca replied. "Must've been one of the hands, or one of their pals. I didn't see. But that's not what we're talking about now, Jed. This is about you, and what happened tonight. Not about me. I want to know who would do such a thing. Who would deliberately loosen your wheel."

Jed stepped forward and took her chin in his hand.

Calmly, his voice steady, his eyes locking with hers, he said, "No one did it deliberately. You hear? Whatever happened, it was an accident. Now let's go inside."

He nodded back over his shoulder. "Tom needs a bed. I told him we'd set him up in the bunkhouse."

Rebecca held Jed's gaze a moment before replying. Jed could not read her thoughts, could not tell whether that defiant jut of her jaw reflected concern at what Tom Barton suggested, that someone had tampered with the wheel, or—if she'd picked up on Jed's suspicions about the pickup he saw leaving—anger with him. She could be one hardheaded, hard-to-read girl.

He did, however, know one thing, and that was that when they finally retired to her bedroom, Rebecca would either turn an ice-cold shoulder on him, or give him the night of his life.

After one last steely look, Rebecca turned and addressed Tom.

"Bunkhouse is full. Come on, Tom, I'll set you up in the guest room."

Jed felt a keen disappointment. At that moment he wanted Rebecca and the house to himself more than anything he'd ever wanted in his entire life.

Tom must have read his thoughts.

"Thanks, Rebecca, but I'll just sleep here in the car."

Rebecca picked her way, barefoot, across the gravel to the Bronco. Hands on hips, she walked right up to Tom, nose to nose.

"I will not take no for an answer, Tom Barton. Do you hear?"

Ashamed of what he'd just been feeling, Jed seconded her. "She's right, Tom. You drove me all the way up here. We're not about to let you sleep in the car."

When Tom was slow to reply, Rebecca said, "I mean it, Tom. You're sleeping in the house."

Eyes downcast, Tom finally said, "Well, I'd be much obliged, then," and allowed Rebecca to take him by the arm and guide him, childlike, into the house.

Jed shook his head in amusement as he followed them inside.

More than once, he'd heard it said, in reference to Rebecca, that it wasn't right for a woman that good-looking to be in the ranching business. That it played with men's heads. Changed the whole complexion of things. Made idiots of otherwise predictable, competent cowmen.

Rebecca both appreciated and resented that fact. She'd become adept at using her appeal to get her way. But it was that same appeal, and the effect that it had on men, that made her greatest desire impossible. Buck Nichols had served for years as president of the Montana Cattlemen's Association, and Rebecca was determined not only to follow in her father's footsteps, but to be the first woman to do so. But, as Jed had not so diplomatically pointed out on one of their first dates, Montana ranchers wanted to bed Rebecca Nichols, not vote her into an office of authority.

With the touch of her hand, coupled with the idea that he would be sleeping under the same roof as she, Rebecca had just managed to reduce the normally macho Tom Barton to a marshmallow.

The moment Jed entered the house, something struck him as odd. But his first reaction—a flood of relief—was so welcome that it wasn't until later that his thoughts came back to it and still could make no sense of it.

Lights blazed throughout the house. The huge living room, with its exposed wood beams, a rock fireplace that took up an entire wall, the hallway, lined with trophy heads and Indian rugs; the kitchen, just off the living room.

Light from the upstairs hallway also drifted down the broad central stairway, with its hand-carved oak banisters.

Hardly the setting for an intimate midnight tryst.

Unless Rebecca had been messing around with not one, but two men, in a well-lit house, Jed could discard his suspicions about the men in the truck.

With a sense of ease, Jed's thoughts returned to Rebecca's explanation for being up at that late hour.

"I'll go check on Peyton," he said.

Then he remembered the cooler. Maybe his head wasn't so clear after all.

"I left my samples in Tom's Bronco."

"You didn't lose them with the truck?"

"Some, but not all. Not the ones I took in the park."

Rebecca's smile warmed him. "That's wonderful, Jed. What a relief. Let me get them for you. I'm so worried about Peyton. Please just hurry out to him."

Jed hesitated. "I'll get the samples first."

"Jed." That's all she said. Just his name. But the look in her eyes told Jed Rebecca felt insulted.

"You'll put them in the fridge?"

"Of course, Jed. I can handle it, Just go."

JED HEARD PEYTON'S soft knicker the moment he stepped inside the barn and flipped on the lights.

The chestnut Thoroughbred's sculpted head hung over the

stall door, his white blaze and intelligent eyes as startlingly beautiful as ever.

From this angle, at the sight of his magnificent head, Peyton appeared healthy.

Jed walked up and stood stroking the big head as his eyes traveled over the body that kidney failure had, over the past six months, pretty much decimated, reducing it to little more than a skeleton.

"You must be feeling better," Jed said when Peyton put his nose down and began using Jed's sore shoulder as a scratching post for his forehead.

Jed lifted the latch and stepped inside for a closer look.

He pinched an inch of skin from the horse's shoulder between two fingers, then let go. Like a designer dress on a wire hanger, Peyton's fine coat hung over his frame, draping it, accentuating each rib.

Still, the horse's pinched skin rebounded quickly enough, indicating Peyton wasn't overly dehydrated.

Jed had been sure, from Becca's description, that dehydration had set in, which had then caused Peyton to have another one of his episodes where he stumbled, and had difficulty walking, a common complication in late-stage renal failure.

But while the time it took for the pinched skin to return to place indicated perhaps a low degree of dehydration, it definitely wasn't enough to explain the behavior Becca described. Last time that had happened, it had taken forty liters of IV fluids to rehydrate Peyton, to bounce him out of his state of near shock.

When Becca described Peyton's behavior earlier in the evening, Jed had felt certain he'd need to administer fluids again—though he had no idea how, since his supplies were gone with the truck. Either that, or do what he'd been gently telling Becca was in the near future.

Put Peyton down.

But with a sigh of relief, Jed decided that neither alternative appeared necessary right now.

Before leaving the barn, Jed gave Peyton a handful of oats. He could hear the big gelding munching contentedly as he stepped out of the barn, into the dark. To the east, just over the Tobacco Root Mountains, a ribbon of light sky contrasted sharply with the blackness above.

Becca would be rising before long to feed the hands.

Hurriedly, Jed reentered the house. He noticed all but a single light in the hallway had been turned off.

He suddenly felt it again. That same sense that something was wrong.

Why had all those lights been on in the first place?

If Rebecca had been out in the barn with Peyton, why would it have been necessary for the entire first floor of the house to be lit like a runway waiting for a plane that's just radioed a Mayday?

Sometimes Jed hated himself for the way his mind worked. For the fact that he had to make sense of even the most insignificant observations. It wasn't just related to his suspicions about Becca—that was an entirely new phenomenon for Jed, a side of himself he'd never before experienced, and one he hoped would be short-lived. But his mind had always worked like a cheap detective's, or perhaps, more accurately, the scientist that he was at heart. Some people floated through life paying little attention to the details, but Jed was not one of them. And he had a compulsive need to understand those details. Like the fact that so many lights had been on in the house when he and Tom arrived unexpectedly.

He climbed the stairs to the bathroom, where he took a quick shower, then headed for Rebecca's bedroom with a question on the tip of his tongue.

But when he opened the door to her room, the sight that greeted him zapped that question—and any others that he might have been tempted to ask—out of Jed's consciousness.

Becca's white cotton gown lay on the floor next to her side of the bed.

So did her bikini panties.

She was already settled under a lightweight yellow comforter, but when Jed opened the door, Rebecca threw it aside.

She'd left the light on in the master bath, and the door cracked open just enough for a beam to fall across the bed, spotlighting her there, as she lay propped up against a cloud of down pillows.

With a smile that declared she knew exactly the effect the sight of her had on him, she waited for Jed to come to her.

Jed stood at the foot of the bed, with Rebecca watching him strip. His arousal soared to an almost unbearable level.

Any pain he'd been feeling from the accident dissolved when he climbed on the bed, into her open arms.

"Thank God you're okay," Rebecca whispered, pulling his mouth to hers, wrapping herself—her tanned arms, legs at least a mile long—around his big, naked frame.

Jed could only groan in response.

It was the night of his life.

FOUR

IF IT WEREN'T for the pain, Jed might have slept the day away. But when he sleepily tried to roll onto his side it literally surged through him, jerking him awake.

He lay, eyes open, wondering what time it was, but hurting too much to turn and look at the clock on the bedside table. Becca no longer lay beside him.

A breeze that carried the first hint of moisture in a month parted the sheer bedroom curtains and Jed heard her voice. Outside, in the driveway.

He could not make out what she was saying.

Slowly, he threw his long legs over the side of the bed. He knew the second day after a trauma was always worse than immediately after it happened, but this beat anything he'd expected. With a low groan, he stood.

A hot shower might help.

He padded to the window. Becca was talking to someone in a pickup. She glanced up, toward the window, and waved at Jed.

It embarrassed him that she'd seen him. Rebecca might think he was spying on her.

He headed for the bathroom.

He'd been standing under the hot stream of water for several minutes, wondering who was in the truck, whether it was the same vehicle he'd seen leaving the night before, when she came into the bathroom.

"How are you feeling?" she asked.

He pulled his head out and looked at her through the glass shower door. She was dressed in her standard uniform—Levi's, T-shirt, worn cowboy boots, her hair tied back in a ponytail. She looked sensational.

"Like my truck rolled into a creek bed with me strapped into it," he replied. "Who was that?"

Becca placed her hands on her hips, cocked her head, and stared him down.

"Jed, why do you do this?"

Avoiding her gaze, he stuck his head back under the spray without answering, let it pour down on him. She was right. Rebecca ran a full-sized ranching operation, had reason to deal with dozens of different parties on any given day, most of whom, given that it was Montana, drove pickups.

He pulled back, out of the spray, and said, "I apologize."

She'd turned to look at herself in the mirror above the sink.

"That's okay," she replied, quick to forgive. "In exchange for that apology, I'll tell you. Just this once. That was Joaquin Coleman. He came by looking for work. Guess Mike Russell sold his place. He just told Joaquin and the rest of the guys."

"That explains why Mike called Clancy and canceled his annual vaccinations."

Through the foggy glass door, Jed watched as Rebecca smoothed moisturizer over her face, then pursed her lips to apply a light shade of lipstick.

Sometimes he wondered if she had any idea how appealing she was. Watching her now, he saw the satisfaction the image looking back gave her.

"He's been struggling for a long time," she said, running

her hand over the top of her hair, then pulling the ponytail tighter. "Maybe it's for the best."

"I doubt he sees it that way."

"Who knows?" She'd turned her attention back to Jed. "Listen, would you mind if I use your laptop for a couple minutes? My computer just crashed. I'm worried it could be that virus everyone's talking about. I thought that's what that program I got was for. To protect me from viruses."

"Have you been updating it every month, like that guy at Radio Shack told you?"

"Not really."

"You've got to do that. There are new viruses all the time," Jed said. "Go ahead. Use mine. Should be in the library."

"You sure?" she said, her tone casual.

"Of course. As if I'd mind you using my computer."

"No, that's not what I meant. Are you sure you left it in the library?"

"That's where I always use it."

"But I already looked there. I didn't see it."

Panic struck Jed. All the way to the Double Jump the night before, he'd thanked his lucky stars that he'd left his computer at Becca's. What if he'd been wrong? Could the culmination of two years of research, and data and just plain old conjecture, now be lying in a ditch, reduced to scorched metal and ash?

He reached for the shower's knob.

"Here I come."

The force of Becca's response surprised Jed. "No. You stay there. That shower's good for you. I'll find it. Just tell me where you think you might have left it."

His heart beginning to trip wildly, Jed punched the faucet's knob in, stopping the water.

"I told you, stay in the shower, Jed," Rebecca said, almost angrily.

Jed brushed past her, grabbing a towel off the rack.

"My research . . ."

"Just stay calm, Jed. We'll find it."

With Becca close on his heels, he headed down the staircase for the library.

Rebecca was right. He usually left his laptop propped up against the desk, but it was nowhere to be seen.

His head pounded, whether from the accident or the possibility he'd lost all his research, Jed could not tell.

Rebecca stood directly behind him.

Suddenly he pivoted and turned on her. "Who did you have over here last night?"

Stunned, she drew back. "What are you talking about?"

"Who was driving the truck that Tom and I saw leaving at two A.M.?"

"I told you, I never even saw that truck. It must have been someone visiting one of the hands."

"I thought you were up with Peyton, who, by the way, wasn't even dehydrated when I checked on him. Why the hell were the library lights on in the middle of the night? Who was here, Rebecca?"

The sting of Rebecca's hand across his left cheek took him by surprise.

"How dare you?" she practically hissed. "What? Do you think that before I made love to you last night, I fucked some cowboy down here, in the library? Is that it? Then, after we were done, I gave him your computer? As a thank-you?"

She stared at him with what Jed took to be pure loathing, and Jed, in his agitated state, glared back.

"Listen to yourself, Jed. What's happening to you?"

Suddenly they both felt a presence.

Simultaneously, Jed and Rebecca turned toward the door to the library, where Tom Barton stood.

The look on Tom Barton's face made it clear he'd heard the entire exchange. It was also clear that he would have given anything not to have.

"I just wanted to say thank you," he said, stumbling over the words, his eyes anywhere but on Jed or Rebecca.

"God, Tom," Jed said. "I'm sorry . . ."

Tom's presence was not enough to silence Rebecca's fury. "What about me, Jed?" she cried. "Where's *my* apology?"

Jed turned then to Rebecca. "Do I owe you one?" he asked, locking eyes with her.

Barton cleared his throat.

"Uh, Jed, uh, your computer . . . I think it's up there, in the room I slept in."

Rebecca appeared every bit as surprised as Jed.

Jed felt the color start to rise in his face as it came back to him. Two nights earlier, the night before the day of the accident, he'd wanted to check for an e-mail before going to bed. He hoped to have a response to some questions he'd sent the NIH scientist who'd pioneered RB51, the brucellosis vaccine currently considered the standard protection against the disease. Rebecca, however, had been on the main line, in the library, for well over an hour. When Jed stuck his head inside to ask how much longer she'd be using the phone, she'd been quick to stop her conversation, place her hand over the mouthpiece, and inform him that she needed privacy. Later she would explain that she was talking to her banker, which Jed thought odd at that hour.

Frustrated, Jed had started up the stairs to go to bed, but as he passed the guest bedroom, he'd remembered the extra phone line Becca'd had installed to that room, when Virginia, her college roommate, had sent her daughter Chelsea out the previous summer, to get away from Seattle's Capitol Hill drug scene.

Jed had gone online in the guest room and, as was now apparent, left his laptop there. Which explained why he hadn't noticed it in its usual place the next morning.

Thank God, because if he had, it would now be lost with his truck.

However, this recollection made the clearly implied accusation he'd leveled at Rebecca even less acceptable.

Silently, Rebecca slipped out of the library, passing Tom without a glance.

When Jed returned from walking Tom to his truck, he went directly upstairs, to the guest room.

Sure enough, there sat his laptop, on a chair in the corner, its modem line still connected to the jack in the wall.

He was down on one knee, packing it into his carrying case, when Rebecca entered the room. Jed did not look up. He could not face her right now.

He felt her standing there, watching him.

"What have I ever done to deserve your distrust?" she said, her voice quiet, but strong.

Jed raised his eyes to hers briefly.

"Nothing." He sighed, then dropped his head into his hands. "I don't know why I'm doing this to you. Or to me. Maybe I love you too much."

"I love you, too, Jed. But that doesn't seem to make a difference."

"I don't know what it is, Becca. It's just this feeling I can't shake. Sometimes I wonder if I'm going fucking insane. You've done nothing to deserve it. I think . . . maybe . . ."

"What? Maybe what?"

"Maybe we both need some time. To sort things out."

"That's not what I want, Jed."

Jed thought back to the previous night, making love to Becca. How tender, and giving, and mind-blowingly erotic she could be, and instantly wanted to take back his words. But the rational side of him told him it was the right thing to do.

"It's not what I want," he said, raising his eyes back to hers. "It's what I need."

She stood, meeting his gaze.

"I washed your coveralls," she said. "They're down on the dryer."

Then she turned and left the room.

It took Jed several minutes to gather his odds and ends from the bedroom and bath.

After he'd thrown it all into his duffel bag, he stopped by the laundry room, on his way out of the house. Rebecca was nowhere to be seen.

The sight of his work coveralls on top of the dryer, washed and neatly folded, almost caused Jed to break down. To go looking for her and beg her to forget everything that had happened that morning.

As he turned to leave the laundry room, a crumpled and charred piece of paper in the otherwise empty wastebasket on the floor next to the dryer caught Jed's eye.

He recognized it from the night before. The paper that had blown across the road, then caught fire on the smoldering scrub grass. Rebecca must have checked his pockets before throwing his overalls into the wash.

As if trying to delay the moment he actually walked out of Rebecca's house, or perhaps simply to distract himself, he stooped and picked it up, studying it as if it held the answer to how all this had happened.

As he unfolded what was left of it, its ashy center turned his fingers black.

An image of a lone buffalo filled the top one-third of the front page. Then, in bold print, the words "Buffalo Field Campaign."

He recognized the name. They were a group of widely hated, hippie-type activists that lived just north of Yellowstone, known for their willingness to do just about anything to stop buffalo that roamed outside the park from being hazed and slaughtered.

The paper he'd retrieved from the side of the road was their newsletter.

Below the graphic and title, a collage of photos filled the rest of the page. One of buffalo grazing peacefully in the shadow of snow-covered mountains. Two others were partially burned, but even so, Jed could see that they contrasted dramatically with the tranquility of the first. In one, buffalos were being chased by snowmobiles; another showed a man holding a club in the air like a baseball bat, the inference clear, despite the fact that its victim had been obliterated by the flames.

Jed stared at the paper, wondered briefly how it had come to be out there on the road, and why the people behind it did what they did.

Then he crumpled it up, tossed it back in the wastebasket, and walked out.

CLAY KITTRICK'S MOOD went sour as he stared at the e-mail.

> Jed McCane had an accident last night. He survived and he managed to save all his samples but the ones from Reed Jones. I say it's time to make the call.

Kittrick began rummaging through stacks of paper on his desk, looking for his address book. Not finding it, he opened the top drawer. Again, he had no luck.

"Robin," he yelled, leaning toward the open door, "where the hell's my address book?"

When she did not respond he angrily picked up the phone and dialed directory assistance.

"What city, what state please?" a mechanical voice prodded.

He sighed in frustration. He hated these fucking automated systems.

"Hamilton, Montana," he said, each word coming out in an angry huff.

"Listing?"

He opened his mouth to answer when a voice at his door stopped him.

"Jim Pritchard's here."

He looked up to see Robin, his secretary. With unseasonably cool temperatures hovering in the seventies she wore a thick, cowl-necked sweater that reached halfway to her knees, and fit too tightly across her round belly and broad hips.

"I'm in the middle of an important call."

Robin's eyes widened. She said, "Well . . ." In the next instant, Clay saw the Forest Supervisor over her shoulder. Tall and stooped, dressed in a Forest Service uniform, Jim Pritchard stood behind Robin, hat in hand.

Clay gave Robin a scathing look, and said, "Come on in, Jim."

He had mixed feelings about Pritchard. The guy was a little too squeaky clean for Clay's taste. Still, they seemed to share many of the same ideas about the future, and because of both men's positions, working together was a necessary evil.

Slowly, moving like an aged greyhound, Pritchard entered and lowered himself cautiously into the chair facing Clay's desk.

Clay knew the head of the Forest Service's Western Montana District wasn't much for idle chatter. Pritchard cleared his throat and reached into the front pocket of his dark green shirt for a set of folded, stapled papers. Extending the hand with the papers, he got right to the point.

"I think we have a problem, Clay. With the Horse Butte allotment."

If he'd wanted to catch Clay's attention, he'd succeeded.

Clay's hand shot out for the papers.

"What's this?" he said, immediately beginning to unfold it.

"A grazing application."

Kittrick's eyes skimmed the filled-in portions of the application. When they reached the signature at its bottom, he threw the papers down on his desk and met Pritchard's gaze with a steely look.

"I don't see what the problem is, Jim."

Pritchard straightened in the chair.

"Now that's not the response I expected to hear," he said. "I thought you'd be mighty upset."

"What's to be upset about? You can't tell me you're giving this application consideration for Reed Jones's grazing permit?"

"I don't see how I can *not* include it. Fact that it's from the Northern Cheyenne doesn't change that."

All it took was this—mere hint of resistance on Pritchard's part for Clay's outrage to boil to the surface.

"Hell it doesn't," he said. He picked the papers back up and shook them in the air. "Talks to Sky's a Cheyenne. You know she's behind this, and that she's the head of the Inter-Tribal Bison Cooperative. This is all about protecting those goddamn buffalo, and you know it."

Pritchard remained unruffled. "The Cheyenne run a cattle operation. That's all the rules require for applicants for grazing permits. I've given it a lot of thought, Clay, and I just don't see how I can avoid including this application."

A look of pure madness crossed Clay's face. He swiveled a quarter-turn in his chair. Holding the papers away from Pritchard, he tore them in half.

Pritchard shook his head, but made no attempt to stop him.

"Now why'd you go and do that, Clay?"

With Pritchard watching, Clay placed the two halves on top of each other, then ripped them in half again, and then again.

"Dammit, Clay. You know I'm just gonna have to tell them to submit another application."

"What are you thinking? The Department of Livestock

and the Forest Service have always been on the same page on this, Jim. Hell, everyone knows there are plenty of ranchers who'd jump at the chance to get that allotment! No one can make any accusations when the Cheyenne don't get it."

"After all the scrutiny we've had recently, all the lawsuits those damn environmentalists have filed over the bison, I can't afford not to handle this by the book. I'm already getting accused of keeping Reed Jones's death a secret."

"I'd like to know how the hell that news got out."

"Folks don't die in these parts without other folks knowing."

"Well, if you'd just hurried up and awarded that allotment to someone else—someone legitimate—we might've gotten this thing resolved before those fucking Indians got wind of it."

"Rules said I had to have a thirty-day open application period."

"That's what's wrong with you, Jim. Rules don't mean shit when it comes to what we're charged with doing. Do you know what'd happen if the Cheyenne got that grazing permit on Horse Butte?"

"Of course, I know, Clay. But more and more people are seeing the logic in what the tribes want to do. Hell, the government gets twelve hundred dollars a year from that grazing allotment. And it's costing them almost two million dollars a year to test and slaughter the buffalo that wander onto Horse Butte, which wouldn't be necessary if we didn't allow cattle out there. How long you think you can pull that arithmetic off?"

This brought Clay out of his chair. Red-faced, he planted his feet and glared across his desk at Pritchard.

"You accusing me of something, Jim?"

"Now settle down, Clay. You're right. We've always been on the same side, and that's not changed. You're just doing your job. But you can't blame me for wanting to play by the rules, not when every goddamn environmental organization in this country—and now a federal judge, too,—is watching me like a hawk."

"It's just one application, Jim. One application in many. Everybody knows that. It's not gonna raise any eyebrows if the Cheyenne don't get the Horse Butte allotment."

He cautioned himself silently to stay calm. As mild mannered as Pritchard appeared, Clay knew that he could not afford to push him too far.

"The Forest Service and ranchers have always been friends," he continued. "Ranching's the most powerful force in this part of the country. Do you really want to get on the wrong side of the Cattlemen's Association? 'Cause that's what'll happen if that grazing permit goes to those fucking Indians."

"Is that a threat?"

"All I'm saying is I wouldn't want to be you if the Horse Butte allotment ends up setting a precedent that weakens the traditional role of grazing allotments in the cattle industry. That's all I'm saying. This is cattle country. You know that. People are willing to fight for that. Hell, they're willing to die to protect that. If you know what's good for you, you'll issue that permit to a true cattleman. That's all I'm saying."

FIVE

JED HAD ALWAYS liked that his job called for spending most of his time on the go, crisscrossing the back roads of rural Montana to serve far-flung cattle ranches—mostly small affairs, but also plenty of big spreads, owned either by giant corporations or families like Rebecca's that had been ranching for generations. And then there were the nouveau land barons that continued to flock to the land of Big Sky as if it were some religious mecca, a chance at redemption. But never did Jed appreciate his job more than now, when staying bone-tired busy offered his only hope of keeping his mind of Rebecca.

If Jed had his way, he'd spend one hundred percent of his time in the field, but he could not escape an hour or two a day at his clinic in Ennis to tend to finances, paperwork, and calls needing to be returned, which kept growing in volume due to West Nile. The virus had reached Montana now, killed two champion quarter horses—a barrel racer and a stud—that Jed had been treating ever since he opened his practice ten years earlier, and he'd been flooded with questions about the vaccine.

Some of the newer vets that had moved into the area simply refused to hang a shingle anywhere. They functioned out of their cars, using a cell phone and laptop as a virtual office, trying to save the overhead of owning or leasing a building and hiring help; but Jed couldn't see ruining the best part of his job—his time in the field—that way.

Besides, Clancy had been with him from the start and she needed the work. Her son, Lance, had just turned five and had recently been diagnosed with juvenile rheumatoid arthritis. Jed had cringed when Clancy came home from a Spokane, Washington, hospital with the diagnosis. He was fond of the boy. No way Clancy could find another job with insurance benefits that would cover the expensive medications necessary to control Lance's condition, or a job where she could bring Lance with her to work.

And time each evening at the clinic had become all the more important when Jed began his research several months earlier. He now kept half a dozen steers quarantined in the barn out back, animals used to research his innovative concept for a brucellosis vaccine. Some nights he would spend hours running tests and recording observations. Others, he simply checked each animal's condition, threw out hay, and mucked out their stalls.

He'd declared the building off limits to everyone but himself.

The accident with his truck had been a setback. It had taken him three weeks to resample the cattle. All the ranchers had heard about what happened, and not a single one of them balked at his request to come back out and draw blood again, but for almost three weeks, it added an extra two hours to his workday. Thank God he hadn't lost the blood he'd taken from the bison. It had been hell trying to get approval to draw it from that Clay Kittrick at the Montana Department of Livestock. While the bison belonged to Yellowstone and hence came under the domain of the National Park Service, due to the brucellosis issue, once they left the park grounds, the Montana Department of Livestock assumed authority. Kittrick had been difficult to deal with from day one. Jed had had to drive to Butte to meet with Kittrick face-to-face in order to get the authority he needed to sample the bison rounded up at Horse Butte.

Horse Butte was a now infamous piece of land adjacent to Yellowstone's northwest border that park bison typically spilled out on to during harsh winters and in spring. In the summer, this same land was leased to cattle ranchers by the U.S. Forest Service.

Bison were known to carry brucellosis, and despite the fact that there had never been a documented transmission of the disease from bison to domestic cattle, the fear of it happening had caused one of the most explosive and divisive battles in Western history, pitting environmentalists against the ranching industry.

Cows infected with brucellosis aborted their fetuses. States protected their "brucellosis-free" status with a vengeance, knowing that to lose it would cause untold economic damage in cattle country. Because of the shared use of Horse Butte, despite the fact that the bison occupied the land months before cattle were moved on to it, a facility had been built to test park bison who wandered outside park borders for the disease. Over loud and vehement protest by environmentalists—protests which in recent years had received more and more media attention—those buffalo that tested positive were destroyed.

The way Jed saw it, Clay Kittrick ought to have been damn eager to encourage work like Jed's, which could eradicate the fear of transmission once and for all. But nothing seemed to be going as it should these days.

Little did Jed know when he first came up with the idea for the brucellosis vaccine how difficult his research would make life. Never in his wildest dreams had he expected it to affect his relationship with Rebecca. Had it not been for his thoughtless—and unfounded—accusations about his laptop's disappearance, he might be going home to her tonight, instead of to an empty apartment.

In most other respects, in the three weeks since he'd last seen Becca, Jed's life had settled pretty much down again.

But he still hadn't received that reply from the NIH researcher, the one he'd asked to help Jed interpret his most recent findings.

After stopping to check in with Clancy and hearing that his car dealer had called him that morning to tell him that the check he wrote for his special-ordered new truck had bounced, Jed headed for his office.

It was located at the back of the clinic, adjacent to the hallway that led to the small apartment Jed called home.

Jed flipped the lights on in the small, bare-walled room, then plopped down into his chair and logged on to his laptop.

Five new e-mails had arrived.

He recognized the senders of four of them—three clients, plus the one he opened first—a notice from the bank that they'd been unable to electronically pay one of his bills due to his overdraft.

But the sender of the fifth, an innocuous name—BS169— did not ring a bell.

Probably junk mail.

Or maybe one of those porn messages. Ever since he'd visited that one Web site—he'd only gone there once, that night he'd invited Rebecca to his place for dinner and she never showed up—he'd been getting them. The kind of e-mail that a family man wouldn't exactly be eager to have his wife or kids come across. But for now at least, Jed wasn't a family man, and the way things were looking with Becca, he wouldn't be any time in the near future. And the truth was he actually found this porn version of spamming amusing. It was so beyond the bounds of good taste that he had to wonder what kind of guy actually got turned on by what the subject line described as "Do you Like Watching Girls . . . with their Animals?" Or "Sorority Sisters LOVE Their Mascot."

Maybe they knew he was a vet.

This one must really be bad. They couldn't even come up with an uncensorable tease line.

Mildly curious, Jed clicked on the blank subject line.

There was no salutation, no name attached. Just:

Be careful. Someone is trying to sabotage your research.

Jed stared at the single line.

It had to be some kind of joke.

Then it hit him.

Tom Barton. Tom must have told some of the guys about the conversation between Jed and Rebecca that he'd overheard that day in the library. Some cowboy with a sick sense of humor must be trying to get under his skin.

Jed did not find it funny.

He clicked on the reply button and typed just three words: "Who are you?"

He stared at his own message for several seconds, debating whether to dignify this prank with an answer, then clicked send.

Troubled by his recollection of the last time he saw Rebecca, he scrolled down to the next e-mail and opened it. A question about a chronic founder case. He wrote a quick reply.

As he started reading the third e-mail, Clancy interrupted him.

"Sandy Beeman is here," she said from his doorway.

Jed turned to her and scowled.

"I'm in no mood for Sandy," he said. This caused Clancy's eyes to grow wide and her eyebrows to shoot up dramatically.

Jed still didn't get it.

"Tell her I'm busy."

In the next instant, a familiar face peered around Clancy's shoulder.

Perfect features, perfect makeup, perfectly styled hair—chin length, black, with spiky bangs—all contrasted dramatically with Clancy's tired, no-frills look; all trademarks of Sandy Beeman, the Seattle-based sales representative from Manson Cline, one of the veterinary industry's largest pharmaceutical companies.

Jed had dated Sandy before he met Rebecca.

"Don't I deserve better than that?"

Jed felt his face flush.

"Sorry, Sandy, it's just that I'm swamped. And we're in good shape for samples."

"I left some oxycytin," Sandy replied good-naturedly. "Just in case. But I also wanted to say hi."

To her credit, Sandy hung back, behind Clancy, as if she were resigned to—even half-expecting—this inhospitable reception. Jed suddenly felt ashamed of himself.

Half-rising from his seat, he managed a weak smile and said, "Please, come in. Sit down."

With an almost shy smile, Sandy stepped into the office.

Once settled, however, she wasted no time getting under Jed's skin.

"So how's Rebecca?"

Jed avoided her stare. "I don't know."

One of her perfectly shaped eyebrows rose into a sharp arch. "You're kidding."

"No, I'm not. We're not seeing each other right now."

"You broke up?"

Jed finally met her gaze. "I don't know, Sandy. I hope not. Becca's the best thing that ever happened to me."

He saw the flicker of hurt. But just a flicker. Sandy wasn't Manson Cline's top sales rep in the country for nothing. She could handle herself in uncomfortable situations.

"Rebecca Nichol's a lucky girl," she said. "Big successful

ranch, surrounded by horny cowboys. Dating the best-looking vet this side of the Mississippi. And believe me, I'd know. That's my territory—the western half of the country, not horny cowboys. Though I wouldn't mind learning a thing or two about them."

Jed kept his expression neutral, refusing to let Sandy get the rise out of him she was working so hard for.

"Like everything else," he said, even now feeling the need to jump to Rebecca's defense, "it sounds a lot better than the reality. Running a ranch like the Double Jump is backbreaking work, and Becca's out there doing it right alongside those so-called horny cowboys. And as for dating a vet, while it has its advantages, it's no picnic, either. My hours don't give us much time together. Especially these days. I've never been busier."

Or more paranoid, he thought, but he kept that to himself.

It was just the segue Sandy was waiting for.

"I hear you're doing some interesting research."

"I've got some theories I'm working on."

"On brucellosis?"

"Yes."

Manson Cline hadn't developed the brucellosis vaccine RB51, but they'd bought up the rights when it first came out in 1996, and they'd made a fortune on it since.

"How far along is your work?"

"Not far," Jed lied. "It's pretty much conceptual at this point."

"That's not what I hear. I hear you've been sampling. That sounds like lab work. Serious research."

"What is this, Sandy, an inquisition?"

"Of course not. It's just that you know you can't do this alone, Jed. I mean, what are you thinking of? It takes millions of dollars to research and fund a new vaccine. I could talk to Manson Cline about backing you, assembling a team of top-notch scientists."

"I'm not interested."

"You run into some money I'm not aware of? It sure didn't sound like it a few minutes ago."

"What's that supposed to mean?"

"I was in the waiting room when Clancy told you your check bounced."

Jed clenched his jaw in anger.

"Why don't you just talk to them?" Sandy said. "At least tell them what you're working on?"

Jed shook his head. "What do you take me for?"

"Give it up, Jed. You know I don't take you for a fool. Anything but. Our people would sign an ironclad nondisclosure with you. You have nothing to fear. Manson Cline is hardly in the business of stealing other people's research. But they are certainly in a position to help you with yours."

"What? So they can buy up the rights, just to keep it from ever hitting the market? Right now Manson Cline has a monopoly on brucellosis. Why would they want to invest a couple hundred million on a new vaccine?"

"Maybe because it's a better vaccine."

"You and I both know that wouldn't justify the expense. Not as long as they've got the current market cornered. If and when I take my research to someone, it'll be someone you never heard of. Someone I can trust to put this vaccine to its full potential. At a price that regular people can afford. What it won't be about is cornering the market, or stock value, or prestige. It'll be about preventing the disease. Period. Now I've got work to do, Sandy."

This time the hurt in Sandy's expression seemed genuine.

"Maybe you ought to get out of here once in a while, spend some time in the city."

"And what's that supposed to mean?"

"Maybe you're spending too much time around those

redneck, militia types that hide out in this part of the country. The ones who think that having a profitable business equates to abandoning ethics, or having a genuine interest in making this world a better place."

"Read any papers recently? The name Enron sound familiar?"

"You know, Jed, I was just excited about what I'd heard about your research, just trying to help an old friend. At least that's what I thought we were."

The sincerity in her voice startled Jed into silence. He watched, mute, as Sandy rose from the chair and stormed out of his office.

But about halfway down the hallway, she turned and retraced her steps.

Standing at his doorway, she eyed him coolly.

"Tell me something, Jed."

"What?"

"Do you ever get tired of living up there on that pedestal of yours?"

Jed opened his mouth to respond, but Sandy didn't give him a chance. She turned and strutted away, her attitude fully restored.

Convinced that he'd lost any aptitude he'd ever possessed to get along with women, Jed pushed back from his desk.

As he passed Clancy, kneeling next to the filing cabinet in her office, he called out, "I'll be in the barn."

Clancy called after him.

"Wait, you had a call. When Sandy was in with you. I didn't think you'd want to take it with her there."

"Oh?" said Jed, mildly curious about Clancy's decision not to disturb him—since she'd rarely shown such acuity. "From who?"

"Rebecca. She wants you to call her right back. She said it's important."

* * *

AS HE SPED to the Double Jump, Jed found himself hoping the insurance check he'd been promised would come through before they tried to repossess the truck. He'd hate to give it up. Eighty-five miles per hour and it purred like a kitten.

His conversation with Rebecca had been short.

For appearance's sake—male pride kept him from allowing Clancy to see how news of Rebecca's call affected him—Jed had maintained a calm pace as he walked back to his office, shut the door, and standing next to his desk, dialed the number.

Still, he couldn't stop his heart from skipping a beat when she answered.

"Clancy told me you called," he said, a rather ineloquent icebreaker after three weeks without communication.

"Jed. God, it's good to hear your voice."

"Yours, too."

"I miss you so goddamn much."

"I miss you, too, Becca," Jed replied. "Is everything okay? Something wrong with Peyton?"

"No, dammit. Nothing's okay. I need to see you, Jed. I need *you*. I don't even understand why we're doing this."

"Because I was driving us both crazy."

"Well, has this accomplished anything? Haven't we tried it long enough?"

"I'm not sure anything's changed."

"I'll *make* it change. Please, Jed, come see me. Now."

He'd hung up and, this time, bounded down the hall at a lope, indifferent to Clancy's curious eyes.

"I'll be at Becca's," he'd called as he passed her open door.

The twenty miles to the Double Jump took less than fifteen minutes.

Rebecca sat waiting for him on the front porch, looking incredibly sexy in jeans and a white cotton peasant blouse that

bared her sun-browned shoulders. Jed could tell that she'd
curled her hair, soft curls that hung loose and low, dancing
over her shoulders and breasts.

As Jed emerged from the truck, she rose from her spot on
the top step and, with her two loyal dogs following behind,
met him halfway to the house.

A bolt of lightning streaked the sky to the east, reverber-
ating like a dim echo through banks of black clouds as the
two embraced, silently, paying no attention to the truck
carrying several ranch hands that pulled up to the barn.

They went straight upstairs, to the bedroom.

Jed did not want to talk, or think. He knew either would
spoil the moment. Rebecca had apparently come to the same
conclusion.

After they'd made love, they lay, windows open, a cool
rain blowing in. Thunder shook the house, and sky, and what
seemed the entire world.

Jed thought it a bad sign.

They hadn't solved a thing, just proven they'd missed
each other like crazy.

"What are you thinking?" Becca said.

He could feel her staring at him. "I'm wondering how I
can stay away from you."

"You don't have to."

"Yes I do. Until I can sort things out, stop being such a
jerk."

"I've thought of a way." Her voice sounded ripe with anticipation, almost mischievous.

Jed turned, studied her. "How?"

"Marry me."

"What?" he said, rising onto an elbow to study her.

Tucked under each armpit like a bib, the white sheet contrasted starkly with her tan.

"All our problems stem from you not trusting me, right?"
Rebecca asked. "I'm telling you I want to marry you. That

you're the only man I'll want, for the rest of my life. For months now it's what you've been saying you want. I'm ready, Jed. It's what I want, too. How can you not trust me when I'm promising to spend the rest of my life with you?"

Jed's eyes searched hers, looking for, but not finding, some sign that this was some kind of joke. That she was kidding him.

"You're serious about this?" he asked.

Still cloaked tightly in the sheet, Rebecca slid closer to him.

"Yes. I want to prove to you that you can trust me. I want to start planning our future together. Will you, Jed? Will you marry me?"

Cupping her chin in his hand, Jed pulled her lips to his, his head swirling with the thought of waking to this vision every morning for the rest of his life.

Was this an insane solution to the problems they'd been having or did it make some kind of twisted sense?

He sucked the scent of her hair deep into his lungs— alfalfa, they must have cut the south pasture that day—and pulled back to eye her.

"You're sure?" he asked.

"Yes," Rebecca said. "Marry me, Jed."

A slow grin spread across his face.

"Okay," he replied. "Let's do it."

"So who was in your office with you today when I called?" Rebecca asked. They'd gone to dinner in Ennis to celebrate. Antonio's—an Italian restaurant that catered to rich out-of-state anglers and hunters. "Clancy was playing coy with me. When we're married, I'll put an end to that."

Jed looked at Rebecca from over the wine Antonio had sent to their table when he heard the news.

"Do you really want to marry me, Rebecca?"

"Yes, Jed. I do."

"When?"

She threw back her head, letting her laughter peel like a bell through the dining room, which earned Jed envious glances from the other diners, most of whom at this time of year were visiting fly fishermen, the backbone of Ennis's tourist economy.

"I haven't thought that far yet," she answered gaily. "I was just worried about convincing you that it was the right thing to do."

"Christmas," Jed said.

Rebecca pursed her lips, then shook her head. "No. I want us to get married outside, Jed. At the ranch."

"That would mean within the next couple months, unless we wait until next summer."

"There's no way I can plan a wedding for this fall. I want everything to be perfect. Next June. How does that sound?"

Jed lifted his wine and took a long sip.

"Don't pout, Jed."

"I'm not a patient man, Becca. Not once I get my sights set on something."

"You'll live," Rebecca said. She leaned forward, clearly in a playful mood. "Now, answer my question. Who was in your office today that Clancy didn't want me to know about?"

"Just a rep from one of the pharmaceutical companies."

"Sandy Beeman?"

Rebecca had run into Sandy once before, at the clinic. Jed had halfway expected fur to fly that day, especially when Sandy told Rebecca about a rodeo she'd attended with Jed.

"Yes," he answered.

"I thought you said she just dropped off samples."

"Usually she does, but she'd heard about my research and wanted to talk to me about it."

"What *about* your research?"

"She thinks Manson Cline might be interested in backing it."

This news caused Rebecca's entire posture to go rigid. "You didn't tell her you were interested," she said, "did you?"

"No, Mrs. McCane, I didn't say I was interested. In fact, I was downright rude about it. But maybe I spoke too soon."

"What do you mean?"

"Well, it got me thinking. You know, I've always worried that one day *Brucella abortus* could mutate and become more dangerous. Even deadly. It happens all the time. Manson Cline could get this vaccine out a lot faster than I can. And there's another thing I hadn't thought of when Sandy first brought the subject up."

"What?"

"Us. You. We weren't engaged when I talked to Sandy. That changes everything. I'll never get rich as a country vet. And the Double Jump, well, you never talk about finances, but I have the feeling you're under a lot of pressure." He thought back to that evening Becca spent on the phone with her banker. "There are no guarantees any more when it comes to ranching. We both know that. A deal with Manson Cline could make a big difference."

Rebecca straightened abruptly, leveling her gaze on Jed. There was no mistaking the you're-treading-on-dangerous-ground look in her eyes.

"Don't you do it, Jed. Your heart and soul are in that research. You're not in this for the money."

Jed's hand rested easily on the table, curled around the stem of his crystal wine goblet. Now Rebecca reached for it.

"Listen, Jed, you said that scientist from Rocky Mountain Labs keeps calling you. If you want a partner in your research, why don't you talk to him?"

"I don't know. I just got a bad feeling about the guy over the phone."

"How can you tell anything about a person from a phone call? What didn't you like?"

"I don't know. Just a feeling I got."

"How can it hurt to just talk to him? You said you're only considering Manson Cline because of the difference it could make to our future. Well, wouldn't it make things easier on us if you had someone helping you out—both financially and timewise? Why wouldn't you at least talk to this guy, see what he has in mind?"

"I guess it wouldn't hurt."

She smiled and brought his hand to her lips, kissing it. "Thank you."

She lifted her eyes to his. "Now promise me," she said. "Promise me you won't even *talk* to Manson Cline. Not one word."

"No wonder I love you."

"Why?"

"Because, aside from being so good-looking you stop traffic, not everything's about money to you."

Later that night, Jed had just dozed off when Rebecca nudged him.

"Jed?"

"Hmm?"

"Did you ever hear the story about Running Wolf?"

"Everyone's heard about Running Wolf. He was the guy someone killed for bringing his buffalo to graze on public lands."

"'Spose they'll ever find who did it?"

Jed lifted up on one elbow. "You are the most fascinating woman," he said, smiling groggily. "Why would you be thinking about something that happened before you were even born?"

Rebecca smiled back, but even in the dark, he sensed something off about her.

"I don't know. I guess the talk about your vaccine, and the brucellosis. It got me thinking about the whole situation with the bison. It all kind of started with Running Wolf, didn't it?"

"Yes. They say the ranchers thought that if they let people get used to the idea of bison grazing on public lands, like elk or deer, then eventually it'd squeeze the cattle out. They say that's why the ranching community protected whoever shot Running Wolf. They knew he did it for the good of the cat-tlemen."

Rebecca lay back down, staring at the ceiling.

"It's kind of a romantic idea, don't you think? That he did it for the good of ranchers everywhere?"

Jed fell back onto his pillow, then rolled over and threw an arm around her.

"Killing's not my idea of romance," he whispered in her ear.

"Want to see what is?"

SIX

*M*aybe that's why *we're meeting in Darby.*

Immediately after he'd hung up from their call, Jed wondered why Nicolas Sandburg had set their meeting outside his office; but now, as Jed cruised slowly through the sleepy streets of Hamilton, Montana, the barbed wire gave him a clue. It ran in two strands along the top of an eight-foot chain-link fence that surrounded a complex of buildings that, were it not for the blatant security precautions, might otherwise appear to be a college campus. A white entrance station, manned with two uniformed guards hosted a sign declaring: BE PREPARED TO SHOW TWO FORMS OF VALID ID BEFORE ENTERING.

Rocky Mountain Laboratories, or RML as the locals called it, served as one of the nation's only Biosafety Level 3 research facilities, and the barbed wire and several prominent signs made clear that safety topped the list of the National Institutes of Health, the federal agency that ran the facility.

The stringent security must have prompted Nicolas to suggest that he and Jed meet elsewhere. Still, thought Jed, as he eyed the massive brick buildings, there were plenty of restaurants in Hamilton. Why the neighboring town of Darby?

As Jed pulled into the parking lot of the café picked by Sandburg, a late-model blue Volvo, coming from Highway 93, pulled in simultaneously from the other end of the parking lot, which was half full, mostly with beat-up pickups and equally battered Chevys and Buicks, from a time when cars lived up to the description "full-sized."

The Volvo's license plate gave its occupant away: *"SrScntst"*

Sandburg guided the Volvo into a space at the back of the lot and climbed out. Short and stocky, with thinning blond hair worn in an overgrown crew cut, he scanned the vehicles.

The veterinary symbol on the side of Jed's truck caught his eye and he headed toward Jed. Jed thought he moved more like a former football player, or better yet, a wrestler, than a scientist.

"Dr. McCane?" the man said, stretching his hand out as Jed climbed out of the truck's cab.

"Yes. You must be Nicolas."

"I am indeed," Sandburg answered, then added, "Perfect timing."

"Yes," Jed replied. "Perfect."

They crossed a small vestibule to enter the café, a large, airy room with aged linoleum floors. Booths with red Formica-topped tables lined the wall with windows. A waitress looked up from wiping a table and called out, "Mornin,' Doc. Rest your bones wherever your heart pleases."

Sandburg nodded, gave her an empty smile, and slipped into a booth. Jed followed suit, settling opposite the scientist.

"How was the drive over?" Sandburg asked.

"Fine," Jed said, eager to dispense with small talk.

Sandburg picked up on this.

Grabbing the empty coffee cup from the place setting

before him, he lifted it in the air, catching the waitress's attention, then directed his attention to Jed.

"Well, as I said when you returned my call—and by the way, thank you for doing that—I've been hearing some very exciting news about this brucellosis research you're doing."

"It's coming along nicely. I think it has real promise."

"An aerosolized vaccine would be revolutionary, that's for sure."

"An oral or aerosolized brucellosis vaccine is the only way to wipe out *Brucella abortus* in wildlife. The last remaining wildlife reservoir for *abortus* is the elk and bison in this area. We don't have enough holding facilities to vaccinate every animal. It's logistically impossible."

"How about efficacy? How does your vaccine compare to RB51?"

"That's an unknown right now, but since its mechanism is improved I expect it to be equally effective, if not more so."

"More so?"

"Yes. The original standard vaccine for brucellosis, Strain 19, was a problem because its induction of antibodies in vaccinated animals was often interpreted as evidence of actual infection. It caused ranchers to spend enormous amounts of time and money to determine whether positive test results were caused by vaccination or infection."

"I'm aware of Strain 19's potential to confuse diagnosis of true infections. That's why it was taken off the market when RB51 was developed."

"It's definitely less of a problem with RB51, but RB51 still has the potential to show a false positive for infection. The vaccine I'm working on won't do that. At least in theory. Also, my vaccine should be safe for pregnant cows, whereas pregnancy is contraindicated with RB51 due to its potential for abortion."

Sandburg listened with rapt attention.

"That's impressive," he said when Jed finished. "And

exciting. Very exciting." He paused. "You mentioned an improved mechanism of action with your vaccine. You mean in addition to the delivery?"

Sandburg was fishing. The scientist might consider Jed no more than a country-bumpkin vet, but Jed knew better than to divulge the answer to this question.

He simply nodded, which only managed to pique Sanburg's interest further.

The waitress arrived, steaming coffeepot in hand. Both men fell silent as she poured two cups of black coffee.

"Ready to order?" she said, eyeing Jed curiously but settling on Sandburg.

"Give us a few minutes, will you?"

"No problema. Just holler."

Sandburg gave Jed a condescendingly bemused look, which he made no attempt to hide from her. Jed found it arrogant, and insensitive.

"We'll do that."

Once she was out of earshot, he turned back to the conversation.

"Let me tell you a little about myself."

He waited for Jed to respond with, "Please do," then cleared his throat.

"My background is with the CDC. I was part of the team that developed the AIDS cocktail. You're certainly aware of its success. I've also been chosen to work as part of a select team, handpicked by the NIH." He leaned forward, across the table, and lowered his voice. "This is highly confidential. We'll be responsible for the development of vaccines for all the major bioterror threats: anthrax, smallpox, ebola."

"Why is that confidential?"

"Just that we'll be dealing with those agents here, in Hamilton. The locals aren't exactly excited about the prospect of it. You know. Paranoia. Silly stuff."

"I'm impressed," Jed said. He studied Sandburg. "But

hearing your credentials makes me wonder why you'd be interested in a brucellosis vaccine."

"That's easy," Sandburg replied. "Let's be honest."

"Let's."

Sandburg's voice took on a conspiratorial tone, as if the two of them were old buddies discussing an old friend who hadn't measured up to expectations.

"The government doesn't exactly pay well. And with a team of twelve, there's no real glory, either. I've been on the lookout for opportunities to not only make some money, but make a name for myself. Your vaccine seems to have the potential to do both."

It suddenly struck Jed. The reason for meeting here, at a café in Darby. Research institutions had strict policies regarding their scientists' conducting research outside the scope of their employment. Sandburg didn't want anyone at RML to know he was talking to Jed.

"You mean you're interested in your individual capacity, *outside* of RML?" he asked.

"Of course." Sandburg laughed. "You didn't think a facility like RML would commit valuable resources to an insignificant project like yours, did you?"

Jed's dislike of the man had been vague until now, but it crystallized at this moment.

"Brucellosis may not rank up there with smallpox, or anthrax, but it's hardly a 'little' problem. It holds the potential to devastate the cattle industry. The state of Montana's economic well-being is inextricably tied to maintaining its brucellosis-free status. And while it doesn't kill anyone, you of all people should be aware of the misery brucellosis has caused, and continues to cause, in third-world countries."

He'd assumed that Jed's lowly status as a country vet would ensure his adulation of a man like himself—a bona fide, top-level research scientist. Now Sandburg realized that he should have reined in his arrogance.

But the realization came too late.

"Dr. McCane, I apologize. I certainly didn't mean to offend you. Believe me, I take brucellosis seriously. I realize the importance of your research. I'm very eager to examine what you have. Why else would I want to get involved?"

"I haven't figured that out yet," Jed said, pushing abruptly away from the table just as the waitress arrived. He stood and stared down at Sandburg. "But one thing I *can* figure is that I can carry on my research without your help."

"Dr. McCane, please sit down. Let me explain."

"You ready to order?" the waitress asked, eyeing Jed suspiciously.

"Actually," Jed said, "I'm leaving."

He tossed two dollar bills on the table, turned and strode out of the café. Exiting the first of two sets of doors, Jed noticed a poster on the wall that he hadn't caught on his way in, with Sandburg.

Now the picture of several brick buildings, set back behind a fence—a fence topped with barbed wire—caught his eye and he stopped to read it.

Notice: **Important Meeting**
Hamilton/Darby Concerned Citizens for Safety
Monday night. Q&A on Rocky Mountain Labs' proposed
conversion from BSL-3 to BSL-4.
Is our community safe?

SEVEN

LIFE WAS GOOD right now. Oh, so good.

To Jed's surprise, their engagement did just what Rebecca intended it to do. Jed's sense of distrust had disappeared.

In the days and weeks after their engagement, Jed's spirits flew high.

After his trip to Darby, Rebecca seemed disappointed at first about Jed's decision not to work with Sandburg, but after Jed described how the discussion with Sandburg went, the arrogance the scientist had displayed, and the fact that RML had nothing to do with his offer, she'd quickly come around to Jed's way of thinking.

And summer had always been Jed's favorite time of year. Hot dry days that went on forever insured maximum productivity and promoted a sense of camaraderie between Jed and the ranchers.

Life was good.

Which made the e-mail all the more hideous.

He recognized the sender right away. Bs169. No subject in the subject line.

Make copies of all your data. Protect your lab. They're
about to strike again.

Strike again? What the hell did that mean?

"What's that?"

Jed turned. Rebecca had entered the library, and now
stood looking over his shoulder at his computer screen.

"Jed?" she said, her voice indicating alarm. She bent at
the waist, eyeing the screen. "What is that?"

Jed quickly clicked delete and the screen went blank.

"Why'd you do that?" she cried.

"Becca, hold on. Calm down. I didn't see any reason to
upset you. It's just some kind of joke. I've received them
before."

"You have? Why didn't you tell me?"

"It wasn't worth mentioning. It's just a joke. One of the
guys jackin' me around a little."

"Why did it say they were striking *again?* That means
they've already done something. What? What did they do?"

"Nothing. I swear, Becca. I have no idea what they're
talking about. It's just some sick joke."

"Jed, we're engaged to be married, and sharing is what
marriage is all about. You must promise to tell me everything. Everything. Do you understand?"

Was it Jed's imagination or was Becca now giving *his* un-
reasonable behavior just prior to their engagement a run for
the money?

"I promise," he said, having no intention whatsoever of
keeping Becca informed if more of these disturbing e-mails
arrived.

"Okay," she said, issuing a short sigh of relief. "Have
some coffee and toast before you go?"

"Sure. I've gotta make a quick call to Clancy first. Be
right there."

Thinking Rebecca had left the library, he picked up the

telephone and dialed the office. He started off each morning with a call to run over his schedule with Clancy.

As he waited for her to pick up, he heard a creak of leather and turned.

Rebecca stood behind him, rummaging through her briefcase, which sat on a chair next to the door. She glanced up at him.

Jed smiled reassuringly at her, just as Clancy came on the line.

"Mornin,' " he said, turning back to his day planner laid out in front of him.

"Morning, Jed," Clancy replied.

"How're my cows looking?"

"Great. Fantastic. They just ate an entire bag of Red Delicious apples."

"Clancy, I told you. You're not supposed to be around those cattle. I told you just to look through that special glass I put in there."

"IGA was having a special on the apples, Jed. I just opened the barn door and tossed them to 'em. Hell, you know me better than to think I'd risk getting sick."

"I hope so," Jed replied.

Even though the only way brucellosis could be transmitted was by direct contact with the blood or placenta of an infected animal, he'd lectured Clancy several times about staying out of the fully enclosed barn.

Still, Clancy had a habit of disobeying him from time to time by tossing in goodies to the grateful cattle, like the apples she'd bought on her way home from work the night before. While he chastised her for it, Jed saw no real harm in it.

"Any new calls this morning?" he asked. "I'm about to head out."

"No. Nothing new. I'll beep you if anything comes up. Here's what I've got for you: eight A.M. at Andrew's, nine at Mitch's place. Ten-thirty at Elroy's—"

Jed interrupted her.

"That only gives me half an hour to drive forty-five miles, assuming I'm at Mitch's an hour."

"You can do it," Clancy said cheerfully. "Eleven-thirty at Nada Quinn's."

"Nada Quinn? I don't have her in my book here."

Nada Quinn, a widow, lived alone, down in the southwestern corner of the state. Her husband had once worked for Yellowstone National Park, in law enforcement, and after his death, despite the lonely and harsh country, Nada stayed put. Jed usually called on her once a year, when it came time to vaccinate her only companion, a horse named Sugar.

"Guess I forgot to tell you I squeezed her in. Her mare's losin' weight. She's worried. Not an emergency but since you're all the way down there, I figured you could stop and check her."

"Okay," Jed said. "Go on."

As Clancy reeled off another six calls, Jed ran his finger down the lines of his day planner.

"Yep, got 'em all," he said. "Looks like I've got a long day ahead of me. That should put me back up in the office after eight. Guess I won't be seeing you today."

"Guess not. Unless I decide to come in and balance the books after I take Lance to a sleepover he's been invited to."

"No need for you to do that, Clancy. Balance the books during the day."

"Hell, Jed, there's never time. Someone's either stoppin' for supplies, or just to visit. And the damn phone never stops ringing anymore."

"West Nile?"

"That and the normal stuff. Colics, founder. Everyone wants advice over the phone, nobody wants to pay for a visit any more."

"These are hard times for small ranchers."

"They're not exactly easy for you, either," Clancy replied.

Touched by her protective attitude toward him, Jed chuckled. "I'm getting by just fine."

He hung up and turned to see if Rebecca was still in the library, but she'd left.

He found her in the kitchen, at the sink, just rinsing out the coffeepot. A loaf of unopened wheat bread lay on the counter, in front of the toaster.

Jed glanced at his watch, then walked up behind Rebecca, lifted the hair off one side of her neck and gave her a kiss. Her skin felt warm and slightly fuzzy, like a sun-ripened peach. He wrapped both arms around her and pulled her tight against his body.

"Don't bother," he said. "I've got a big day ahead of me. I'll grab some coffee on the road."

Becca wiggled out of his hold and turned to face him. Jed thought she still looked troubled.

"Sorry about breakfast," she said. "Guess I'm in slow motion this morning."

"Don't apologize. It's not a problem."

"You're sure?"

"Yep. And listen, I've got calls till seven, then I need to get up to the clinic, so I'll just stay in town, at my place, tonight."

"Oh, Jed, do you have to? Can't your research wait a day or two?"

"Not this. I want to run some tests on the cows I exposed to virulent *Brucella abortus* last week."

"The ones you'd vaccinated with your new vaccine?"

"Yep. I vaccinated them two months ago. I'm anxious to see what the exposure did. Plus, I'm keeping a close eye on the two who are pregnant." He put his arms around her waist and pulled her to him, hip to hip. "I'm close, hon. Really close. They were the cattle I vaccinated by swabbing their nostrils. Do you know what it'll mean if the samples show they didn't get the brucellosis, that they've developed resistance? The next step would be an aerosol." Sometimes Jed found his research almost as exciting as he found the gorgeous woman pressed against him. "I could fucking spray cattle, even buffalo and elk, and wipe out brucellosis once and for all."

Rebecca's smile was wistful.

"That's wonderful, Jed. Really. But I just hate it when you don't come back here."

"Just tonight. I promise to be back tomorrow."

He packed up his new truck—the check had even come through, that's how much his luck had turned—and headed out.

The first calls of the morning were routine.

He stopped for coffee in Pony and later regretted not buying some food. The day left him no time to stop again for something to eat.

He was running late when he arrived at Nada Quinn's house.

Nada answered the door in her apron. "Have you eaten yet, Dr. McCane?"

Jed would ordinarily have said no. Ranchers were the world's most generous people. When he first started his practice he was always being offered meals, and soon found out that if he accepted the offers, he'd not only run behind for the rest of the day, but would also grow big as a barn. After a year of polite acquiescence, he'd let his new policy be known. No food for Jed McCane.

But his stomach begged him to make an exception this time.

"Actually, Nada, I'm starved."

She broke into a huge smile.

"Wonderful. I have a stew on the stove right now. Let me just throw some rolls in the oven."

"Great, though I'm afraid I'll have to eat and run. Clancy's got me booked solid today. Why don't I look at your mare now?"

"That's fine. I know she just squeezed me in 'cause I was worried about Sugar, and I'm grateful for that. If you'd like, I'll put it in some Tupperware and you can even take it with you."

As thoughtful as the offer was, Jed suspected Nada Quinn led a pretty lonely existence, and that she'd appreciate some company.

"That's okay," he said. "If you'll join me, I'll just make it quick."

"Of course. Now if you go on out, Sugar's in the barn. I'll be right there."

True to her word, Jed had barely had time to check Sugar's vitals before Nada appeared in the barn.

"How old did you say Sugar is?" he asked.

"She'll be nineteen next spring."

Jed lifted a hind leg, twisting it up behind the horse to get a close look at it. As he picked it out, he noticed several rings along the hoof wall.

"She founder recently?"

"Yes. A couple months ago. She's always been a bit of a problem that way. Luckily I don't have to bother you when she does, 'cause that young man, the farrier from West Yellowstone, well, he's been able to get her sound again every time."

"Brian Johannsen? He's good. No doubt about it. How long's she had this woolly coat?"

Despite the summer heat, Sugar sported a thick, wavy coat.

"She just doesn't shed out any more. I'd say that started a year ago."

"What I think we have here, Nada, is a case of Cushing's disease."

"Oh, my."

"The weight loss, founder, and especially the coat. It's not that unusual. A lot of horses develop it at Sugar's age."

"Can it be treated?"

"There are a couple new drugs that work wonders with some horses. But they're expensive."

"Money's not an object with Sugar. I don't have much, but I'm frugal. I have some savings. Sugar comes first."

"I'd like to take some blood today," he said. "Then come back and draw some again day after tomorrow. That way I can get you a definitive diagnosis, but I'm ninety-nine percent sure that's what we're dealing with."

"Thank God you can treat it."

"Not every horse responds, but if the tests come back positive, I'll start her on Pergolide. It'll take a month or so to see if that's going to work." Jed found himself wishing Nada had called a year earlier, when the first obvious signs—the woolly coat—had shown up, but he knew from the expression on her face that her delay in calling it to Jed's attention wasn't due to lack of concern about the mare. "I'd say we're catching this fairly early. I think Sugar's chances are good."

"Thank you, Dr. McCane."

"Please call me Jed. Everyone does."

"Jed."

After he'd drawn some blood, Nada disappeared back into the house to see to their lunch. Jed went to his truck, labeled and stored the blood, and began writing out an itemized receipt with the suspected diagnosis.

Inside the house, he heard a phone ring.

He'd just pulled out the water nozzle to wash his hands from the tank he'd had installed in the back of the truck when Nada appeared beside him. She carried a large plastic bowl with a blue lid on it and a huge wad of aluminum foil—which no doubt contained several biscuits.

"That was Clancy on the phone," Nada explained. "Dutch Marsh called. One of those prize bulls of his got caught up in barbed wire. I guess he needs to be stitched up. Clancy told Dutch you'd come right over. She said to tell you she called all your other appointments and pushed them back an hour."

She raised the offerings in her hands.

"I just packaged these up for you to take with you."

"Thanks, Nada. I appreciate it."

Nada watched Jed wash up, then followed him to the driver's side of the truck. Once he'd climbed in and buckled his seat belt, she handed him the food, which he placed carefully on the seat next to him.

When Nada continued to just stand there after he'd shut the door, Jed knew something was on her mind.

"Sugar should be fine, Nada," Jed said through his open window. "Try not to worry."

"It's not that, Dr. McCane. Jed. I . . . I probably shouldn't even be saying anything, 'cause all I've heard were rumors. You know, I'm not exactly one of the fraternity down this way, but still, I do know some of the wives, and I hear things."

"What is it, Nada?"

"Well, I was playing bridge with a group I belong to a few weeks ago and your name came up. I had the feeling you weren't that popular with a couple of these gals, so I just kept my mouth quiet, didn't say you were Sugar's vet. Anyway, from what I heard, not everyone's that happy about that vaccine you're working on. Someone even made some remark about that accident you had not being an accident."

Nada's dry skin flushed with embarrassment at making this disclosure. "You're such a nice man, Dr. McCane. I just thought I should tell you."

Partially to spare Nada, and perhaps also as a personal defense mechanism, Jed hid his true reaction to this news.

He'd never connected the accident he'd had returning from Cyrus Gibbons's that night with the e-mails. Until now. Is that what the last one meant by "they're about to strike *again?*"

"I appreciate it, Nada," he said calmly. "But there's really nothing to worry about."

He turned the ignition, and the truck hummed to life.

"Thanks again for lunch. I'll return your Tupperware when I come back to draw more blood."

JED DIDN'T LIKE Dutch Marsh, and he had no illusions about how Dutch felt about him.

Dutch had refused to pay the full amount of Jed's last bill, claiming the previous vet—who hadn't been around in more than twelve years—would've charged half Jed's fees. Clancy had explained to Dutch that the lab work for brucellosis testing for his herd had almost doubled in price over the past decade, and that (in light of Dutch's annual whining) Jed hadn't even charged him mileage, nor for his driving time, only the standard fee for a farm call.

Still, Dutch's check had arrived, two months late, with his recalculations scrawled in a wild hand across the itemization sheet Jed left him, and made out for only $340 of the $525 due.

Clancy had responded by calling Dutch and leaving a message. Jed would not come out and test again until the remainder was paid in full.

But a bull caught in barbed wire was another thing.

By the time Jed arrived, Dutch had extracted the huge Blackfaced steer from the fence. Crazy with pain and fear, and pretty much trapped by Dutch and his pickup, the animal hovered in a corner where two stretches of fencing met, pawing the ground, eyeing Jed's arrival. As he approached, climbing through two strands of the fence with his metal case in hand, Jed could see several gashes on the animal, one of which left a section of skin hanging like the flap of an envelope, and muscle exposed. The ends of a length of rusted barbed wire, still embedded in the steer's skin and thick fur, protruded from either side of one particularly nasty gash across his chest.

Dutch might well be one cheap asshole, but he was fearless,

and strong as an ox, and Jed felt grateful for his assistance, first in wrestling the two-thousand-pound wounded animal to a position where Jed could get him tranquilized, then knocked out cold, and then, in hoisting its dead weight around, several times repositioning its massive head and forelimbs, so that Jed could sew at least five deep gashes, which ran in length from seven inches to thirty-two.

They worked, side by side, the midday sun baking their backs. Neither man mentioned the billing dispute.

Dutch had stripped down to his jeans. His massive belly hung low, brushing back and forth across the steer, coating his ghostly white skin with blood. Dutch either didn't notice or did not care. In fact, his sublime expression made Jed think the rancher rather cherished this rare and close contact with the creature.

Clipping, disinfecting, then sewing was slow work, and their mutual dislike, which made idle chatter unnecessary, also gave Jed time to ponder that morning's e-mail in a new light—shed by Nada's warning.

Jed had originally scoffed at the notion that anybody could be displeased by his research, but now, after hearing what Nada had to say, he had to revisit that attitude, look at the warnings from a new angle.

Was someone actually upset enough about his research to be planning to sabotage it in some way? If so, why?

And was there any truth to the implication Nada overheard that his accident had *not* been an accident? Was that what this morning's e-mail referred to when it said someone was about to strike "again"?

Dead Man had, after all, insisted that someone loosened the lug nuts on Jed's wheel, but Jed had thought it the imagination of a man who'd long ago pickled his brain with alcohol.

And then there was the biggest mystery of all.

Who was sending Jed the warnings?

As he tied one last length of catgut onto his needle and plunged it back into the steer's hide, Jed made up his mind that that night, when he got back to the office, he would send a more strongly worded reply.

"Good work," Dutch muttered grudgingly, breaking Jed's deep reflection.

"Thanks," Jed replied.

He fell silent, then, impulsively, figuring he had nothing to lose, said, "Tell me, Dutch, what would you think of a brucellosis vaccine that could be sprayed on?"

"Wouldn't need *you* if all I had to do was spray," Dutch shot back defiantly.

"Exactly. That'd be just one of the benefits."

This response—Jed's obvious willingness to lose a key piece of his business for such a breakthrough vaccine— seemed to earn Jed some respect from Dutch.

Jed sensed that Dutch understood what Jed was doing, probing for "inside information" from the cattlemen's informal yet exclusive club, of which Dutch was a key member. He felt Dutch eye him, a quick glance out of the corner of his eye, debating whether to offer any insight.

"You got bigger issues than vet bills to deal with 'fore you get everybody down this way to support that work you're doing."

Jed kept his eyes fixed on the needle he'd just punched through the steer's tough hide. The last stitch.

"Such as?"

Each man continued to stare down at the steer, refusing to validate the conversation with eye contact.

Jed's peripheral vision picked up Dutch's exaggerated jaw and lip movement as he chawed deliberately on his mouth full of tobacco. Still silent, he lifted his chin and spit, expertly missing the steer.

Jed finished the last stitch. Adeptly brandishing the pliers that held the curved needle, he threaded it around, under, and through the cat gut, pulling tight to form a knot. Then he repeated the motion four more times and cut the line.

He pushed back from the animal, which had started stirring, and stood, still waiting for Dutch to answer.

He'd been hunched over the steer for the better part of ninety minutes and his back had decided not to let him stand straight now.

Dutch didn't seem to have the same problem. He got up and reached for his shirt, which lay on the ground behind them.

"Just send me the bill," he said over his shoulder.

Then he strode to his pickup, climbed in, and with Jed watching and the steer stumbling back onto its feet, roared away across the bumpy pasture.

EIGHT

THE BOARDS CREAKED beneath her slight frame as she crossed the porch to knock softly on the screen door.

"Coming," a voice called out.

Colleen Talks to Sky waited, the breeze at her back cooling her neck. On the drive out, she'd twisted her long black hair in a knot and clipped it on top of her head, to keep from being blinded by it blowing in her face. As usual, she drove with both front windows wide open, relishing what could be the last hot stretch of the year. Her car had air-conditioning but Colleen had only used it once, when she drove old Leslie Wise Hawk to the hospital that time.

Standing there, she heard the padding of feet on stairs, and in a moment, Dusty Harrison appeared on the other side of the screen door.

She'd only met him once, at Torry's funeral, and Colleen could tell that Torry's father did not remember her now. He looked at her warily through the screen, as any Montana rancher might upon seeing an Indian woman, uninvited, at his door.

"Can I help you?"

"Hello, Mr. Harrison," she said. "My name is Colleen Talks to Sky. We met at Torry's funeral. I was a friend of his."

For a moment, it appeared Dusty Harrison—a large and, until that moment, hard-looking man—would cry.

"He talked about you," he replied in a soft voice that bore no resemblance to the earlier one.

Torry had told Colleen about the arguments—"all-out battles," he'd called them—he'd had with his father. She wondered now if those battles had occurred when Torry had spoken of her to his father. If so, this visit may not have been a good idea.

But in the next instant, Dusty pushed the squeaky screen door open.

"Please," he said. "Come in."

Colleen stepped inside.

Any Indian who lived on a reservation—or even the urban ones who kept close enough bonds to visit—had experienced death more times than he or she could count. For death was an integral part of reservation life. Death of the old, death of the young. Death by illness, by violence, at the hands of a drunken driver, or at the victim's own hand.

Death of those who should not die. Like Torry Harrison.

Half Cheyenne and half Lakota, like most her native brothers and sisters, Colleen was intimately familiar with death, and its aftermath. And the moment she stepped inside the old Harrison ranch house, she recognized—could literally feel—the grief that now inhabited it. Could smell it, really.

Without asking her the reason for her visit, Dusty Harrison led Colleen to the living room.

"Please sit down," he said, motioning toward a burgundy couch, its velvet worn and faded. A large ivory doily adorned its back, and gave the only hint of a mother Torry had told Colleen about. She had died when Torry was still a little boy.

Colleen sank into the couch, feeling several distinct springs beneath her, and watched as Dusty pulled a hard-backed chair from a corner. He positioned it about three feet away, at an angle, and lowered his frame—she could see he'd lost weight since the funeral—into it.

"Mr. Harrison," Colleen began. "One of my reasons for wanting to see you is to tell you what a great man your son was, and how much he meant to me. To all of us. But there's another—"

She stopped.

Tears had begun sliding down the leathery face in front of her.

Colleen had watched Dusty Harrison closely at the funeral, trying to judge this man who had been the source of such great anguish, and great love, in her friend's life. He had not cried that day.

Something told her that this was the first time.

She leaned forward and placed a hand on his forearm, but did not say a word.

At her touch, Dusty dropped his face into his hands, and huge, strangely silent sobs—the sobs of a man to whom this act was as foreign as the death of a healthy young man— racked his shoulders.

"What did I do?" he finally gasped between sobs. "How could I have pushed him away?"

"Torry understood. He loved you and respected you. He told me when he was a little boy, you were his hero."

She talked in a soothing, songlike rhythm, her voice rising at the end of each phrase.

"Not any more."

"You and he may have had your differences, but his love for you—and his respect—did not waver. I know that. He told me."

Dusty let his hands fall to his knees and, still hunched over, lifted his eyes to Colleen's.

"Were you and he . . .?"

What would he say, wondered Colleen, if the answer were yes? After all, she was not only Indian, but also fourteen years older than Torry.

"No, we were just friends. We met two years ago, when he became involved with our campaign."

"The buffalo group."

He said it without anger, or resentment.

"Yes."

"That's when our relationship really went bad. But it had already been falling apart."

He looked slowly around the room, then, as if what he saw—pictures on the mantel, a TV with metal rabbit ears, a book shelf filled with dusty volumes—took him back in time, he continued.

"We'd always been so close. Ever since his mom died. We worked side by side. He loved it, he loved this ranch and the life we had. Sometimes his mother would want him to sleep in, she'd scold me to be extra quiet, so I'd go out there in the barn, keep the dogs locked in the house so they wouldn't make a ruckus outside his window, and start to saddle up my old mare, and every time—I mean it, every single time—Torry would show up before I had a chance to ride out of here. He just couldn't stand the thought of missing out on a morning checking on the cattle, or riding the fence line. Even after his mom was gone, I never saw a boy with such a love of the outdoors, so much enthusiasm for every single day on this place. And then it all began to change."

Colleen remained silent. Dusty Harrison's eyes traveled everywhere but to Colleen as he spoke.

"It was when he went off to Missoula, when he met that girl—her father was a Democrat, I remember that—and changed majors, to environmental studies. That's when he started coming home from college and telling me how wrong it all is. How public lands shouldn't be used for grazing. That ranching was ruining our environment."

He turned now and locked eyes with Colleen.

"How would you feel if you devoted your entire life to a tradition that you considered honest, hard work, never complaining about the poor pay or the long days, or the cattle you raised from this big"—he lifted his hands in the air in front of him, palms two feet apart—"coming down with hoof-'n-mouth and dying on you; because no matter what the hardships, no matter how miserable some of those times might've been, there was nothing in this world that gave you a better feeling, nothing, *nothing* that gave you more pride, than riding out into those hills on a beautiful spring morning to look for new babies. Nothing that compared to the sight of what you had built and cared for with your own two hands.

"And then one day, the child you adored, your best friend in the whole world, your only family, turns on you, and on the life you've worked so hard to build. How would that make you feel?"

Colleen did not attempt an answer; nor did Dusty expect one.

"I'll tell you how it made me feel. It made me angry. It made me plenty sad, too, but most of all, at first anyway, it made me angry.

"But he wouldn't back down. Not my Torry. He's always been headstrong. He just kept lecturing me. Is that what I sent him off to school to come home and do? He'd lecture me about how the cattle industry is ruining the soil, and the water. About those damn wolves, and the buffalo. He blamed ranchin' with endangering them, too. Said we're the reason all the fish—the cutthroat and grayling and bulltrout—are in danger." He locked eyes again with Colleen. "How can that be true? You tell me. How can what I do cause that many problems?"

"Do you really want me to answer that?"

"Yes, I do."

Colleen took a deep breath, preparing herself for the battle that she expected to ensue.

"Torry was right," she said, "but it's not just you, Mr. Harrison. It's the whole industry. Ranching is the number one cause of damage to our waterways and our public lands. It causes erosion, habitat destruction, flash flooding, exotic weeds. Our government kills hundreds of thousands of wild creatures each year to protect ranchers' cows against predators."

"You sound just like him. All your uppity scientific talk—"

"You asked me why Torry felt like he did."

Simply hearing his son's name again silenced Dusty momentarily.

He shook his head slowly from side to side.

"You're right. I did. And then I didn't show you any respect when you gave me an answer." He paused. "I didn't show Torry any respect, either.

"I *knew* that boy, I knew he had the damn purest heart God ever gave a human being. And I knew he had a good mind. Hell, when he was a kid, he could rattle off sports statistics like nobody's business, he taught me all there was to know about astronomy. He could name every goddamn star in the sky. Deep down, I knew that if Torry felt that strong about something, there had to be some truth to it. But I never once told him that. 'Cause I was scared. I was scared of what he knew and I didn't. I was too scared to open my mind to what he was saying, cause this—this life, this ranch—it was all I had. Or at least that's what I thought. Now I realize that none of it means a tinker's damn to me without my boy."

He swiped at his eyes with the back of his hand.

"He told me once . . . we'd been arguing. He'd come up from Yellowstone, from his ranger job down there at Mammoth. And here I'd been telling him what an ungrateful, naïve bleeding heart he'd turned into, and how disappointed in him I was, and he'd just started walking out on me, said he hadn't come up to fight, said he was goin' back to Yellowstone, where he belonged.

"But he stopped. Right there, at that door. I was sittin' right here, in this chair, and he stopped and he turned to me and he told me, 'Dad, you're the reason I'm who I am. It was you who taught me to love this earth, to love all the animals, and the water, and the trees. It was the greatest gift you could ever give me'."

The tears flowed freely again, and this time, Dusty did nothing to stop them.

"And then he turned and he walked out of this house. And that was the last time I saw him. Two weeks later, they called to tell me he was dead. That he died trying to save those back-country campers from that wildfire."

"He was a hero," Colleen said softly. "He saved those two couples. If only he'd turned back with them. But he died like he lived, Mr. Harrison, fighting for what he believed in, what he loved most. And he loved Yellowstone. He loved his job. A lot of people never, in their entire lives, experience that kind of passion that Torry felt."

"I know that, young lady. And it gives me great peace. I truly mean that. I have a lot of regrets, but one of them isn't that I forced Torry to follow in my footsteps. At least he got to live the life he wanted to live. I may have argued with him, I may not have understood, but at least I didn't stand in his way."

Now Colleen's eyes filled with tears.

"He appreciated that, Mr. Harrison. The last time I saw Torry he told me the only thing that kept his life from being perfect was that you two weren't as close as you used to be. But do you know what he said to me?"

Dusty looked at her eagerly, like a child. "No, what?"

"He told me he thought that eventually, you'd come around."

The loud, raucous laugh startled Colleen.

"That son of a gun said that, did he?"

"Yes. He did."

"I'm glad. I'm glad he was feeling that way. And I appreciate your coming here to tell me that, Miss Talks to Sky. It will give me some measure of peace to know it still mattered to Torry."

The moment had finally come. Colleen Talks to Sky took in a deep breath, cleared her voice and plunged ahead.

"Actually, Mr. Harrison, that's not the only reason I've come . . ."

NINE

THE DAY NEVER got any better. The unplanned call at Dutch Marsh's cost Jed a client and, quite possibly, a patient.

After making the other three calls scheduled after Nada Quinn, he arrived at his four P.M. appointment at Frank Thompson's small outfit, just outside Big Sky, at five forty-five.

The call sheet said that Jed was there to test and vaccinate Frank's horse herd—about twenty head—for West Nile but when Jed stuck his head in the barn, looking for Frank, he found an agitated Frank and a horse in dire distress.

"What happened?" Jed said as he trotted toward the two, who stood in the center aisle, between two rows of stalls.

"Colic," Frank answered. "He's been colicky all day. I been walking him around, waiting for you to get here, but when you didn't, I left him to go call you—hell, I wasn't gone more than fifteen minutes—and when I got back, he was rollin' around on his back. I think he went and twisted his damn gut."

Jed could see immediately that's exactly what had happened.

A horse that colics will usually either make it through the

painful gastrointestinal episode on its own, or aided by fluids that Jed could give, either intravenously or through a tube into the stomach.

Old-school ranchers, like Frank, believed you could walk the colic away. The walking itself didn't do a damn thing, but it did have value (which explained why most ranchers rarely called for help): keeping the horse moving meant keeping it on its feet. A colicky animal often had an inclination to drop to the ground and, in an effort to relieve the pain, twist. If it rolled and twisted just the right way, the intestines could actually form a knot. The only way to save a horse once that happened was emergency surgery.

Jed wasn't equipped to do that type of surgery on-site. The only chance of saving Frank's gelding would be to transport it to Ennis.

Jed warned Frank the horse might not make it.

Faced with that prospect, and an expense few small ranchers can afford, Frank Thompson made the only choice he could. He told Jed to put the animal down.

Sick at heart, for both the animal and Frank, Jed humanely put the horse out of its misery.

"If you'd gotten here on time, none of this would've happened," Frank informed Jed after he'd vaccinated and tested the herd.

JED HAD DRIVEN the road back to Ennis enough to know that there were just one or two little windows along the highway where he could get cellular coverage. As soon as he entered the first, he called Clancy. It was already six-thirty so he tried her at home.

"I thought you told Nada you'd called all my afternoon appointments to tell them I'd be an hour late."

"I called everyone. The only one I couldn't get a hold of was Frank Thompson."

"Didn't you leave him a message?"

"He doesn't have voice mail. Or an answering machine. It just rang and rang . . ."

"How many times did you try him?"

The line went silent.

"Clancy?"

"I . . . I don't know, Jed. I guess just the one time. I called everyone on your schedule, including Frank, then things got crazy and I just forgot about it."

"Frank said he went into his house to call us. Didn't you get his call?"

"I must've been in back. Several people came in this afternoon for supplies."

"I don't get it. Why wouldn't he call back?"

"Uh, Jed . . ." Clancy's voice sounded heavy with dread. "There was a message from Frank. But he just said it was Frank Thompson. He didn't say what he wanted."

"And you didn't call him back?"

"I didn't even know he'd left it till just before I left the office, when I checked voice mail. By then I figured you'd already have gotten there."

Jed's unreleased frustration and anger seethed into his veins and arteries, raising his blood pressure.

"Well, guess what?" he said. "Frank's gelding colicked. I had to put him down. Frank blames me for being late."

Jed heard Clancy gasp, but lost in his own agitation, he did not try to comfort her.

It was Clancy's responsibility to prioritize his calls. He—and all his clients—relied on Clancy to make sure things like this did not happen.

"Jed?"

After ten years together, Jed knew Clancy well enough to recognize that she was crying. "Yes?"

"I'm sorry."

He did not respond. The line suddenly filled with fuzz,

and he welcomed the fact that he was about to lose coverage.

"Why don't you let me muck out the stalls tonight?" Clancy said, her voice so broken by static—or so shaken by guilt—that Jed found it hard to discern her words. "I promise I'll wear a mask and gloves. You should go have a drink somewhere."

"No," Jed replied. "I've got lab work to do. I have one more call then I'll head to the office. I'll take care of my cows, Clancy. You just stay home."

The way he said it sounded more like he didn't want to see her, which he realized later was probably how he intended it, rather than that he wanted to spare her the trouble.

The line went dead.

He could have tried to call her back later, when he entered another short stretch of road where he knew he got coverage. He could have told Clancy it wasn't her fault, that Frank should have called the office earlier in the day, when he saw his gelding was colicky, which Clancy could then have conveyed to Nada, along with the news about Dutch Marsh's steer. He could have said that Frank should have kept calling, or at the very least, left a detailed message when he did.

Jed could easily have called her back and told Clancy that.

But he didn't.

As Jed drove west, the sky went through its usual magnificent panoply of colors—from a robin's egg blue, to pink, to an orange that led one to believe the forests on the other side of the mountains were raging with fire—before gracefully dropping its black curtain.

Jed pulled into Ennis around nine P.M. He stopped at the twenty-four-hour market for a cup of black coffee and a submarine sandwich.

As he approached the clinic, a quarter mile north of town, the lighted office building surprised him. Then he saw Clancy's Pathfinder.

He shook his head. He didn't really feel like seeing Clancy, apologizing to her, or comforting her. Right now, Jed felt *he* was the one who could use some comfort.

The barn, some fifteen yards behind the office building, was black, its exterior lit only by the flood light in the driveway. As Jed pulled into the long drive that led to the clinic, a new patch of light fell across the parking lot, signaling that the side door of the office building had opened.

Clancy emerged. She did not see Jed's truck approaching.

Steering with one hand while eating the sandwich with the other, Jed watched as she strode across the lot to the barn. She appeared to have a bag dangling from her hand. More apples.

Jed stuffed the last bite of his sandwich into his mouth, debating whether to honk to catch her attention. Despite the fact that he wasn't exactly eager to see her, he could not suppress a sense of warm affection at the sight of her there, late at night, going out of her way to give some penned-up cattle a treat.

As Clancy reached for the door, he punched the truck's horn.

Her free hand already on the door's latch, Clancy turned. Even from that distance—about thirty yards—Jed could make out the smile, the look of relief. They knew each other so well. Clancy would know that Jed's honk signaled he'd forgiven her. She lifted the latch.

The blast seemed to occur in stages.

First, the door blew off its hinges, carrying Clancy with it, pushing her with brutal force ten feet into the air.

Almost as if in slow motion, with a deafening roar unlike anything Jed had ever heard, the rest of the barn followed suit, erupting skyward in a giant ball of fire.

"Clancy," Jed screamed.

He jumped out of the truck with it still rolling.

Running through a virtual storm of debris raining down from the sky, Jed found Clancy twenty feet from where he'd last seen her. The lower half of her body was covered by the door—a solid, heavy panel, built to prevent mischievous children from entering the barn and coming near the lab animals. Jed threw it off and fell to his knees beside her.

Clancy's eyes were closed, but apparently protected by the door, her face, unscathed, still held a trace of her smile.

Jed cupped it with both hands.

"Clancy," he wailed.

He knew she was already gone. Knew the entire thirteen minutes he administered CPR, waiting for the EMTs, Randy Spencer and Eileen King, to arrive.

Jed had known Randy since high school, which was a good thing because when Randy tried to pull Jed away from Clancy, Jed rose from the ground in an irrational rage, swinging at him, screaming, "Don't touch her, don't touch her."

"I have to try to help her, Jed," Randy said. "Calm down. And it looks like you need treatment, too."

Jed hadn't even noticed the burns on his hands, and the back of his head and neck. Burning embers and debris had coated him as he knelt, trying to bring Clancy back to life.

"She's gone," he sobbed, dropping back to his knees beside Clancy.

"No one can help her."

JED FELT THE stares at the funeral.

He and Clancy had worked together over ten years. Everyone knew that their relationship could be cantankerous, but that, when it came down to it, each felt a loyalty and protectiveness for the other that rivaled that found in most marriages.

Many of those in attendance, which included pretty much the entire town of Ennis and the majority of the ranchers they'd served, some of whom had driven over a hundred miles for the service, offered Jed kind and sincere words of condolence. Yet he distinctly felt others holding back when they approached him—if they approached him at all. Was he going crazy, or did they blame him for Clancy's death?

In fact, aside from Becca, it seemed to him that the only one who didn't look at him with at least some hint of question in his eyes was Lance. After the church service, during which he sat with his grandmother, with whom he would now live, Clancy's son's first priority had been to find Jed. Throughout the potluck that followed, which took place at one of Clancy's neighbor's house, Lance clung to Jed's hand for dear life, as if the physical connection with Jed somehow brought his mother closer.

"I'm here any time you need me, buddy," Jed told the little boy. "I'll stop by your grandma's and take you to the park. How's that sound?"

Lance nodded his head, and tried to smile, but then his eyes traveled over Jed's left shoulder.

Jed turned to see Lance's grandmother, Clancy's mother, glaring at him.

"That's not a good idea," she said, reaching for the boy's hand.

As they turned and walked away, Rebecca grabbed Jed's hand. She clung to it, practically daring anyone else to shoot a harsh glance Jed's way.

But even Rebecca and her fierce love couldn't prevent Jed from noticing the white sheet of paper stuck under the windshield wiper of his battered truck—which had rolled into the burning barn but, amazingly, had not been destroyed in the blaze—as the two walked slowly back up the long drive in the cool misty morning.

Jed honed in on it from fifteen yards away, picked it up like a bird of prey spotting a field mouse, and made a beeline for it.

"Don't," Rebecca cried, running to beat him to it.

But Jed wouldn't allow that to happen.

Holding her at bay with one arm, he reached for the paper,

then, slowly, almost as if he knew what it would say, he turned it over.

The ink had run in the morning's dampness, but the writing was still easy to read.

It consisted of only one word.

Murderer.

TEN

MORNIN', JED."

Old Agnes Shiffer barely glanced up from her desk, upon which was spread last week's *National Enquirer,* as Jed entered the office.

"Morning, Agnes."

Jed strode right past Agnes, down the short hall to Henry Carroll's office. He did not need directions. His visits to the sheriff had become a daily thing.

Henry Carroll looked up when Jed appeared in his doorway and frowned. The hair on Jed's arms stood straight up.

"What?" Jed said. "You get that report back yet?"

Henry pushed back from his desk, rocking back in his spring-loaded chair. He removed his bifocals, dropping them on top of the report he'd just been reading.

Henry was a man of average height and build, but, coming from a long line of old West lawmen, many of whose photographs adorned his office walls, he wore the uniform and badge with such pride that he seemed much more imposing than his size warranted.

"This is it, right here," he said. "Come on in, Jed. Have a seat."

Jed lowered himself into the empty chair on the other side of Henry's desk.

"What'd they say? What did the Butte inspectors find?"

Henry shook his head.

"You're not gonna like it, Jed. They say it was that tank of liquid nitrogen you had inside the barn, for that high-tech refrigerator of yours. The one you said you stored your samples in. Something caused it to explode. It was an accident, son. Just like I've been telling you."

Jed leaned forward, his fist clenched on the edge of Henry's desk.

"It was no accident, Henry. You know it. *I* know it. Someone murdered Clancy. They meant it for me, but they got Clancy instead."

"That's not what the experts are sayin', Jed."

The sheriff grabbed the report and extended his hand across the desk. His bifocals tumbled to the floor, but he kept his eyes on Jed.

"Here. Read for yourself. I'll even have Agnes make you a copy."

Jed swiped at the paper, knocking it away.

"What the hell set the tank off? I saw it, Henry. She just started opening the door. That's what triggered it. Her opening the door."

"Jed, this isn't the big city, where people rig doors with bombs. Who do you think's gonna do something like that down here in Ennis? Hell, nobody'd even know how."

"I told you, Henry, I'd been getting warnings. Someone tried to tell me something bad was gonna happen."

"I'm still checking on those," Henry replied. "I got someone from Billings, an Internet expert up there, tryin' to trace 'em. But you know the Internet, Jed. It's ripe for hoaxes.

Those probably came from some bored kid who lives around here. Or more likely, someone from New York. Or California. Hell, Jed, you're a well-liked man around here. Our only vet within a hundred miles. Nobody'd want anything to happen to you."

Frustration and anger boiled over in Jed. His fist came down hard on the desk.

"It's not *me*. At least, that's not what started it. It's my research."

"Jed, I told you. My heart's hurtin' as much as yours about Clancy. Everyone here in town is just sick with grief over it. And I'm sorry about your cattle. And your research. Don't you know that if someone did this deliberately, I'd exhaust my last breath trackin' the son of a bitch down? But that's not how it's looking. What more can I do, Jed?" Henry's eyes pleaded with Jed for understanding. "Tell me that. What more can I do?"

Jed stood abruptly. Staring down at Henry, he said, "Find whoever did it, Henry. 'Cause if you don't, I will."

For the first time in the week that Jed had been visiting him, Henry Carroll's eyes lit with the infamous temper Jed had heard stories of.

He stood, and though nearly a head shorter, met Jed's glare with his own.

"Jed, I've been trying to be real patient with you. I've let you come in here nearly every day now and accuse me of everything from being an idiot to purposely sitting by while the murderer of one of the nicest little ladies you're ever gonna meet goes scot-free.

"And I've taken it, 'cause I know you, Jed. I know you're a good man, and I know you're upset. I sympathize with you. But when one of my citizens starts talkin' like they're gonna take the law into their own hands . . . well, Jed, I just gotta draw the line there."

Henry's eyes narrowed into slits, lines flaring fanlike from their corners. His voice dropped low, and he raised a threatening finger at Jed.

"I suggest you take a vacation, Jed. Get away. You and Rebecca."

Jed stared back at him in silence, unapologetic, unbending.

"You leave law enforcement to me, Jed. You hear? 'Cause if I hear otherwise, I won't tolerate it. You got that clear?"

IF JED WANTED to test his belief that the locals' attitude toward him had changed, he'd picked the right place. At some point in the day, nearly half the county stopped in at Rini's Drug Store, either to pick up mail or a prescription, or to eat in the small café that occupied the back of the store.

Although if was not yet eight A.M., when Jed pulled his truck up in front of Rini's, the sun already shone bright and hot.

As he stepped inside the store, Jed instinctively removed his battered straw hat. It didn't hold much resemblance to the meticulously shaped hat it had once been. When its brim had begun unraveling—a result of having been stepped on by one too many cows or horses—Jed had simply cut the loose strand off, which only hastened the unraveling process. But cowboys like Jed developed deep attachments to their hats, and he was none too anxious to break in a new one.

The subdued hum of voices and a quick glance around showed him half the booths were already occupied, but as he strode slowly to the counter, not one person seated in them called out a greeting to him.

These days Becca sounded just like Henry Carroll. She kept telling Jed he'd become paranoid, that his belief that people had turned on him existed only in his mind, and not in reality. But Jed knew better. He'd received the same reception yesterday. And the day before.

What Becca didn't understand was that he really didn't care right now what anyone thought of him. Finding Clancy's killer was about all that mattered to Jed.

Henry Carroll claimed to be working every angle, but Jed didn't get a good feeling about Henry's chances of actually finding the culprit—whether that was because he didn't trust Henry's abilities, or his sincerity, Jed did not know—so Jed had devised his own plan.

Despite Henry and the Butte Fire Department findings, that the explosion that killed Clancy had been an accident, Jed knew better. Clancy had been killed by someone out to get Jed. Or—if the e-mails could be believed, and right now, they were about as credible as anything else; hell, right now they were about all Jed had—at the very least, out to stop his research.

So far as Jed could see, if Henry wasn't getting anywhere with his investigation, there was only one way to find Clancy's killer.

He'd started spending nights back at his house. He couldn't bring himself to hire someone to replace Clancy, not when he believed that she'd been murdered because of his research; which meant that he needed to stop by the office every morning to check for calls. He told Becca her place was too far out of town to make that practical if he slept there. He didn't mention to her his fear that Rebecca might not be safe in his presence.

Besides, he'd begun building another barn, which Jed needed to oversee. He'd also arranged to purchase more cattle, to replace the experimental herd that had died in the explosion.

He'd made sure everyone knew about his plans to continue his research. He approached nearly every cattle rancher he called on, asking if he could buy a head or two from them for his "study, which was going well," but to a man, they refused. In the end, he'd had to go outside of the region, to Wyoming, to purchase a dozen head.

He still had no idea who was behind this, why anyone would find research that stood to save the very ranchers he served huge amounts of money so threatening—but he did know one thing for sure.

In addition to the fact that Jed saw continuing his research as a way to draw its saboteurs out, Jed also refused to allow them—even if he didn't know who "they" were—to stop his work on a new brucellosis vaccine.

To do so would make Clancy's death all the more senseless.

Becca, on the other hand, kept insisting that he give up the research. She did not believe that the explosion that killed Clancy had been intended to get Jed, or at the very least, his lab animals. Still, she'd argued, if there was any chance Jed was right about it, why would he proceed? Every time they'd been together they ended up fighting about it, so it was just as well that Jed was sleeping in town now.

But the fact that Jed could walk past half a dozen tables, all filled with ranchers or their hands, without a single greeting being called out to him pretty much blew into smithereens Becca's theory about him still being so popular.

"Coffee, Jed?"

Jed nodded as the lone waitress behind the counter paused on its other side, one hand balancing a tray of plates overflowing with rancher-sized breakfasts, the other holding a steaming pot of coffee as black as a crow.

"Thanks, Ruthie." He pushed his cup forward and watched as she filled it. "And I'll have the special."

"You got it."

He turned to his newspaper, the *Bozeman Gazette*. An article about the Cattlemen's Association mounting a PR campaign against Yellowstone's wolves. The ranchers were hell-bent on reversing the 1995 decision to reintroduce wolves to the park.

"Morning, Jed," a deep voice said from over his shoulder.

Jed turned.

An unshaven and disheveled Tom Barton squeezed into the space beside him and seated himself on the next stool.

"Hi, Tom."

"You doin' okay?" Tom asked.

"Yeah. I'm okay. What brings you to town?"

"I took a room over the fly shop," Tom said. "Emma kicked me out."

"Sorry to hear that, Tom."

"Probably just as well. Neither of us was doin' the other any good." He nodded as Ruthie poured him a cup of coffee. "How 'bout you and Rebecca? You two still engaged?"

"I think so," Jed answered, staring into his coffee. "I've been staying in town since what happened. She's not too happy with me, but so far she hasn't called off the engagement."

"That's good, I guess."

"I guess."

They fell into the state both men were most comfortable with. Silence.

A barrage of loud laughter that erupted from the table nearest them caused Jed to turn and look over his shoulder. He recognized several workers from local ranches, though he knew none by name. One, who hadn't bothered to remove his Stetson when he entered the café, stood out, not only as the loudest, but also the crudest.

When he caught Jed looking at him, he cranked the volume up on his story another notch.

"So I see these two long-haired types," he said, his words garbled by the eggs and bacon he shoved into his mouth as he spoke, "couple of fuckin' hippies. And they're loading that dead deer into the back of a car. I mean, like *inside* the fuckin' car, through its hatchback."

Another roar of laughter erupted from the table.

"What they want a dead deer for?" one of the others at the table asked.

"They eat it," the big mouth replied.

"You shittin' me?"

"No, I'm not shittin' you. Those fuckin' buffalo huggers eat roadkill. This ain't the first time I seen it. That's what they live off out there at that compound of theirs."

"Anyone ever actually seen the inside of that place?" another of the hands asked.

"How do you suppose they afford it?"

A cowboy dressed in dirty Carhartts and mud-crusted boots lifted a forkful of ham into the air. Ketchup dripped off it onto the handle of his coffee cup as he shook it for emphasis.

"My brother works for the phone company," he said. "He put a line in out there. He says it's true. He saw it, in the kitchen. They got this big aluminum pot with 'roadkill' written across it."

This news brought the loudest laughter of all, which clearly made the speaker heady.

"My brother says the place is like a fuckin' hippie commune or something. Beds and dogs everywhere. All this propaganda shit coverin' the walls."

At that precise moment, Ruthie arrived with the special, and also to take Tom's order. Jed leaned back, trying to pick up the rest of the conversation but he could not hear over Ruthie and Tom's discussion of how thick the bacon had been sliced.

Jed did learn that Tom liked it thick.

Something about the cowboys' conversation struck a chord in Jed. He didn't understand what, or why. He'd never paid much attention to the Buffalo Field Campaign before. Why he would care now didn't even register as he sat there. Still, he strained to hear the rest of the conversation. The group, however, had now lowered its volume and Jed could no longer make out what they said.

By the time Ruthie finished taking Tom's order, the big mouth who refused to take off the hat and one of the other cowboys got up, tossed a handful of dollar bills on the table, and sauntered out the door with comically identical, bow-legged swaggers.

The conversation about the Buffalo Field Campaign ended with their departure. The three hands remaining at the table fell into talking about an upcoming rodeo in Missoula.

Jed felt agitated by what he'd heard, but he couldn't, for the life of him, understand why.

When Tom tried to start a conversation, he bolted his food down, suddenly eager to leave. But Tom had grown chatty.

"See you're buildin' another barn," he said.

"Yep. Got cattle coming from Thermopolis a week from Tuesday. Gotta at least get it halfway ready by the time they come."

"You're buyin' Wyoming cattle, huh?"

"I didn't have much choice," Jed answered without elaborating.

"Well," Tom said, "you need some help with that barn, you let me know."

Jed glanced sideways at him.

"You lookin' for work?"

"Not exactly lookin'. Me and Emma put the ranch up for sale. One of those big out-of-state corporations just made an offer. It wasn't for half what it's worth, but we're not in a strong position to bargain. Still, if the sale goes through, I'll be able to take a little time figuring out what to do. I'd be happy to help, with the barn or anything else, for that matter. If you need it, that is."

It dawned on Jed that this was Tom's way of telling him that Tom, for one, hadn't turned on him.

Jed twisted sideways on his stool to meet Tom's gaze.

"Thanks, Tom. I appreciate that. But if you really want to help me, what you can do is let me know if you hear any rumors that might help me find out who caused that explosion."

One of Tom's bushy eyebrows sprang up in shock at Jed's suggestion that Clancy's death had been anything but accidental.

"I heard the sheriff's callin' it an accident," Tom replied.

"It was no accident, Tom. The only thing about it that wasn't planned was Clancy being there, and not me."

Tom stared at Jed. Jed knew Tom to be a simple, decent man. A man of his word. Someone not quick to judge, or abandon old friends.

He could see Tom wrestling with Jed's implication.

"What makes you think I'd hear anything like that?" Tom asked. "You think someone we know could be behind what happened to Clancy?"

Jed knew he risked alienating this man, an old friend who'd just declared his continued loyalty to Jed. Still, honesty was as essential to Jed as clean air to breathe.

"I don't know what to think any more, Tom. My assistant got killed, and I'm suddenly a very unpopular man in these parts. I don't think that's a coincidence."

Tom Barton quickly turned his attention to his plate. Jed could not read how his words had affected him, but he noticed that Tom merely pushed his biscuit around in its gravy and did not eat.

"Listen," Jed said. "I'd better get to work. Good to see you, Tom. And good luck with that offer on your ranch."

Without looking up, Tom nodded.

"You too, Jed."

With exaggerated motions, he stuffed half a biscuit into his mouth, making further conversation impossible.

Back in his truck weighted by the fear he'd lost another friend, Jed's thoughts kept returning to the conversation he'd overheard.

Why had the cowhands' conversation left him with this unsettled feeling? He'd heard locals complaining about the Buffalo Field Campaign activists for years now, ever since the movement was founded in 1997. Jed wasn't a particularly political person, nor someone to whom criticism came easily, but he'd tended to agree with the locals who considered the activists little more than bored troublemakers, too lazy to get a real job.

And then there was the fact that they were always butting heads with the Cattlemen's Association, an association founded to protect the rights of Jed's clients. Another good reason not to like the hippie types who drifted in and out of the Buffalo Field Campaign compound with each new winter season.

Yet the comments he'd overheard did not sit right with Jed.

An image suddenly popped into his mind. The pamphlet he'd retrieved from the wastebasket in Rebecca's laundry room.

That was it—the reason the conversation he'd just overheard provoked such a strange and strong reaction in Jed.

He'd picked the paper up on the road the night of his accident.

Suddenly he realized where it must have come from. The two young people who'd stopped to help him—who no doubt saved his life. Hippie types. With a dog, and a car plastered with bumper stickers.

That night, he'd been sitting in the cab of his wrecked pickup, in daze, when he heard them pull up.

And what had they done? Jed had heard them stop, and he'd naturally assumed they were coming to his rescue. But instead, he'd listened, confused—shocked, really—to hear the girl calling out that the steer had already started to decay.

The cowboys had laughed about it in the café.

Those two young people had stopped to see if the dead steer—roadkill—was fresh enough to eat!

My rescuers that night must have been from the Buffalo Field Campaign.

The pamphlet must have fallen out of their car. The wind had picked it up, blown it across the road to the smoldering scrub grass, and when it caught fire, Jed had extinguished it and stuffed it into his pocket.

He pictured the car now, disappearing into the night. The type of vehicle he'd expect an environmentalist to drive, a rarity in pickup country.

Equally vivid, the quiet, determined courage of the girl came back to Jed.

Megan.

Yes, Megan was her name.

But what was the guy's?

Jed could picture himself bending low, sticking his hand inside the car and introducing himself.

They'd both given him their names, but now he could only recall the girl's.

He remembered something else about her, as well. Those hauntingly beautiful, penetrating eyes. He could still see them, even now, weeks later.

How did someone like her, Jed wondered, someone that pretty, courageous, and competent, get involved with people—a cause—like that?

Satisfied that the encounter—and the feelings of gratitude, perhaps even a need to defend his rescuers, it gave rise to—explained his strange reaction to the conversation he'd overheard at Rini's, Jed heaved a sigh of relief.

Had he made the connection while he was back in the

café, he'd probably have jumped to their defense, but the way things stood right now, it was probably better he hadn't. He had enough problems on his hands already.

As he pressed down on the accelerator and headed toward his first call of the day, he tried to picture the girl, Megan, living in the hippie-type compound he'd heard the one cowboy describe. Or protesting.

He'd heard those Buffalo Field Campaign people did some pretty crazy stuff.

ELEVEN

THE SIGHT OF the big mutt's back foot swatting spastically into the air, trying to reach an imaginary itch as Megan scratched behind its left ear—the one missing a good portion of its outer edge—made her giggle.

"I ought to give you a spanking," she said. "That's what I ought to do."

Pie paused mid-scratch to stare up at Megan with big, loving eyes.

The two sat in the sun, on makeshift wooden steps—rotting beams salvaged from a turn-of-the-century barn up by Pony that had collapsed under the previous winter's five feet of snow.

Hours earlier, Pie had returned from six days' absence, and despite the tearful scolding Megan had given him upon seeing him come loping across the west meadow like a wolf (which everyone at the compound speculated he was, at least in part), he was now eager to win his way back into her good graces.

Aside from her joy at Pie's return, summer also happened to be Megan's favorite time of year. Time to regroup, rest up, organize for the coming months. The calm before the storm.

Soon, Megan thought as she studied the sky to the north, the weather would change and when it did all hell would break loose.

Almost as if a sign of that premonition, the rickety screen door at the back of the massive log house at the bottom of the hill creaked open. A shaggy-haired man in his early twenties, dressed in a rumpled T-shirt and shorts two sizes too large, stuck his head out, clearly none too happy at having been awakened at this hour.

"Megan," he called. "Phone."

"Thanks, Brownie," Megan called back. "I'll take it in the office."

The steps upon which Megan sat were part of a well-worn path linking the big house to two much smaller, crudely constructed structures that sat uphill, one twenty, the other thirty or thirty-five yards away.

The one farthest uphill, strategically placed in a draft that almost amounted to a wind tunnel that had been formed a decade earlier when Montana Power cleared a path for electric lines, was simply known in the campaign as the shitter. The plumbing inside the main house had never been up to snuff. The one double standard observed by the Buffalo Field Campaign had, at Megan's insistence, been the passage of a rule that allowed the women to use the inside toilet, but relegated the men to the outside.

Megan had nearly been voted off the board of directors over that one, but she'd stood firm. An unusually high number of female volunteers that year had passed the proposal, and also kept her in office. And aside from the noticeable drop in bathroom floods, after getting used to it, most of the men seemed to take a kind of pride in trudging up the hill once or twice a day, sometimes in waist-deep snow, newspaper, book, or campaign literature in hand; and so, by the time elections came around again, no one made a serious effort to oust Megan, though at the most recent election, there had been a proposal that for one year the roles be reversed—that men use the indoor toilet, while the women would be allowed to enjoy the more "natural and pure" experience.

No one had seconded it.

Megan had helped in the construction of the closer of the two back buildings. A small A-framed structure that served as the campaign's office.

With Pie tagging along behind, Megan stood, stretched leisurely, face to the sun, then bounded energetically up a dozen steps to the A-frame.

Inside, she dropped onto a tree stump that served as a chair and picked up the phone.

The warm laughter that greeted her immediately gave away her caller's identity.

Colleen Talks to Sky.

"Hau kola," Talks to Sky said.

"Hau kola to *you*," Megan replied, the pure pleasure of the morning ringing in her voice. "Guess who's back?"

"That mutt Pie, I 'spose."

Megan laughed now. "None other."

"He probably got tired of runnin' with the wolves. After a while he always figures out they don't eat near as well as he does there at the compound."

"I thought maybe I'd lost him for good this time," Megan said. "You're probably right, he's definitely skinnier. Hey, I thought you were leaving for those hearings in D.C. today. You're too busy to be calling to check on Pie."

"I'm at the airport in Helena now. But I had good news I wanted to share right away. No, good isn't good enough. This ranks as great news."

"Tell me."

"We got it."

Megan jumped up from the stool. "You don't mean the grazing allotment?"

"Yes."

Megan's war-cry-like whoop echoed out the door and along the draw.

When it stopped, she could still hear Colleen's laughter on the other end.

"I always thought you might be part Lakota," Colleen said.

"You mean no one figured it out?" Megan asked.

"No. Jim Pritchard's known Dusty for so long, it never even occurred to him that Dusty could be on our side on this. Dusty's done a great job of hiding it. And now it's paid off."

"Is it a done deal?"

"So long as Dusty doesn't get cold feet. And he won't. Dusty's never gone back on his word in his life. Two thousand four hundred acres, right at the park's border. Just think, Megan."

"The bison will be able to graze Horse Butte safely."

"Exactly. Dusty's gotta run some cattle on it. The rule says that if there aren't cattle run there, the Forest Service can take the allotment back, but Dusty's not worried about it. He knows his cattle aren't gonna pick up brucella from the bison that were there earlier in the year. He's going to tell the papers and write letters, saying there's no reason to kill more bison. He says he'll make sure they don't use his cattle as an excuse for the slaughter. It's what we've been praying for."

"Oh, my God, Colleen. This is unbelievable."

"The Creator's looking out for the buffalo."

"You're not kidding."

"But don't forget, no one must know. If the Cattlemen's Association gets wind of this before the papers are actually signed, they'll find a way to undo it. You can bet your life on that."

"I can tell K.C.?"

"Of course. But no one else. At least for now. Got it?"

"Got it."

*   *   *

CLAY KITTRICK'S MESSAGE had been the last one left on the machine that morning, but when Jed finished listening to it, the DOL agent's call was the first one Jed returned.

"Morning, Clay. This is Jed McCane."

"Morning, Jed. Thanks for returning my call so promptly. You guys got the same nasty front down there?"

"Not yet. But I can see it coming. So what's up, Clay? You said you needed to talk to me about something important."

"You bet. I do. Rumors are you've got some Wyoming cattle coming up."

"That's right."

"These cattle for that research you're doing?"

Remembering Clay's lack of cooperation when Jed tried to get his approval to draw blood from the park bison that were captured at Horse Butte, Jed hesitated briefly.

"Yes, they are."

"How's that looking, your research?"

Clay's tone took Jed aback.

"It's had some setbacks," he said cautiously. "I'm sure you've heard."

"Damn shame," Clay replied. "I'm sorry about your assistant, Jed. Never met her but I hear she was a nice gal. I hope it doesn't slow down your research too much. That vaccine would be a godsend to these parts."

"That's how I see it."

"So tell me, Jed, why is it you're buying Wyoming cattle instead of staying in the valley? Or coming up this way?"

"Guess you haven't heard *all* of the story. The reason I'm buying from a rancher outside Thermopolis is that nobody here in the valley would sell to me."

"You're kidding."

"No, I'm not, Clay."

There was a pause.

"Now what the hell do you make of that?"

Jed did not know what to think about Clay's sudden friend-liness.

"I don't know who's behind it, but for some reason, this vaccine I'm working on has a lot of opposition."

"That makes no sense," Clay said. He paused. "Want me to do some digging? See what I can find out?"

"That'd be great, Clay," Jed replied, still wary. "I could use all the help I can get."

Jed heard Kittrick sigh.

"Well, Jed, you know, I'll have to send someone out there to test the cattle when they get there. No offense to you, of course, but it could be construed as a conflict of interest to have you test your own herd."

"I understand. I'll be sure to let you know when they arrive."

"Thanks for understanding, Jed. You know, I might just pay a visit down that way when they do get there. The DOL's got a huge interest in seeing that someone develops a more effective vaccine. Sounds like maybe I should get myself a little more involved in what's happening down that way."

"That'd be great, Clay. Thanks. I'm expecting the cattle next Tuesday. 'Course, you know how that goes. But I'll be sure to contact you as soon as they arrive."

"Okay, Jed, then I'll be talking with you soon."

"You bet," Jed said. He hung up the phone, relieved that, for once, Clay Kittrick hadn't been difficult to deal with.

Truth was that Kittrick had been downright supportive, even encouraging, about Jed's research.

Somehow that fact bothered Jed almost as much as Kittrick's earlier attitude.

TWELVE

WHO THE HELL is sending you those e-mails?"

Jed pushed his hat back off his forehead and squinted at Rebecca, who stood at his truck's open window, her face impossible to see in the glare of the sun, setting high over her shoulder. Her hair, wild and frizzy from a day spent rounding up cattle on horseback, formed a diaphanous halo around her head.

He'd been driving down Highway 2, on his way home from work, when he heard honking behind him. A thrill ran through him when he recognized Rebecca's blue Explorer in the rearview mirror. They hadn't seen each other in three days and he'd been missing her like mad. He'd pulled right over, onto the road's shoulder.

It had only taken a few minutes to start arguing.

Still, watching her stand there, her bare, brown arms braced against his truck's door, Jed wanted to pull her toward him and kiss her bare neck, which he knew would taste salty, from sweat and sun.

But annoyed by her tone, instead he replied, "Why would you say it like that?"

Rebecca shifted toward the left, blocking the sun, and he could see in her eyes how upset she was about the recent turn of events.

"Because whoever it is has you believing this nonsense," she answered. "And because you do believe it, you're staying in town, away from me. That's why."

"What makes you so sure it's nonsense? When was the last time you heard of a barn—one that just happened to be full of animals being used in research—blow sky high at the very moment someone laid a hand on its door? When, Becca? Tell me that."

He was wound so tight, even the slightest provocation might have sent Jed driving off in anger. But instead, Rebecca reached inside and surprised him by laying her hand softly on his left cheek.

"Look what this is doing to us, Jed. We're hardly talking to each other. I haven't seen you in three days."

Melting, Jed placed his own big hand on top of Becca's, to ensure she did not pull it away. God how he'd missed her touch.

"I can't just go on with my life," he said, "pretend none of this ever happened."

"I don't know why not, Jed. What is this accomplishing? It's only making both of us miserable. Come home with me tonight. Please. I have something I want to tell you."

"What?"

"Only if you come back with me."

Jed stared at her. She could feel how badly he needed her right now and was working that, leveraging it.

"I was gonna work on the barn tonight. Livestock Transport left a message today. They're delivering my cattle next Tuesday. I've still got some doors and the loft to finish before they get here."

"Jed, you know as well as I do that once those cattle are

there, you'll be afraid to leave them overnight. This could be one of our last chances to be together in a long time."

Jed removed his hand from hers, reached for the ignition and turned the key.

"Let's go," he said. "I'll follow you."

Back at the Double Jump, Becca insisted on cooking dinner for him. All Jed wanted was to go to bed with her, make up for lost time, but he could see that Becca had decided she would be the one to set tonight's rules. She needed to reestablish at least some degree of power over this relationship over which she'd recently lost so much control.

She also wanted to talk.

"Guess what?" she asked him over the cookies she had baked for dessert. "I'm going to run for president of the association."

Jed drew back, a cookie halfway to his mouth.

"You're kidding," he said. But seeing the expression on her face, he quickly added, "Aren't you?"

"No. Of course not. I've always told you how proud it would make Daddy if I could follow in his footsteps."

"Yeah, and you've also always told me that you knew that'd be impossible. That there'd be no way in hell a woman could ever be elected head of the Cattlemen's Association."

"Well, I was wrong. I think I can win. I'm doing it, Jed. I'm running. I just threw my hat in the ring today."

"Without even talking to me first?"

Rebecca visibly bristled.

"Just how was I supposed do that? Talk to you? You're out of cell phone range from sunup to sundown, and nowhere to be seen at night. Today was the final day to announce my candidacy. That's why I was looking for you. I wanted to tell you in person, not have you hear it from one of your clients tomorrow."

"Rebecca, you know all I care about is that you not get

hurt. Which is why I think this is a terrible idea. You don't stand a chance of getting the votes you need. You're just setting yourself up to be disappointed."

Rebecca's posture had gone from relaxed to steel-rod-in-her-spine straight. Jed could see he'd crossed onto shaky ground.

"That's where you're wrong," she said, her voice rising defensively. "I've got some influential backers. Ranchers with pull. They've encouraged me to run. They think I can win."

What sounded very much like a snort of disbelief (perhaps because it was just that) escaped Jed's mouth.

"Such as who?"

"Such as Cyrus Gibbons, that's who."

Jed's eyes widened. Not finger-in-the-electric-socket wide, but wide enough for Rebecca to notice.

"Cyrus Gibbons is encouraging you to run for president of the Cattlemen's Association?"

"I see it surprises you to learn that not everybody in this valley thinks I'm some kind of joke," Rebecca replied, her jaw set.

Abruptly she pushed back from the table.

She stood and walked to the sink, turning her back on Jed.

He jumped up and followed her, placing a hand on her shoulder. But Rebecca refused to face him, focusing instead on washing the pots and pans from dinner.

So much for making love, thought Jed.

"That's not fair, Rebecca," he said. "Nobody believes in you more than I do. You know that. But am I surprised to hear Cyrus Gibbons is backing you? Hell, yes. He's the last person I'd expect to vote for a woman as head of the Cattleman's Assocation. And I can't believe my reaction would shock you."

Suddenly Rebecca pivoted to face him.

"I can help you, Jed. If what you say is true, and I still don't believe it, as president of the association, I'd be in a position to win everyone over. I could convince all the ranchers that your brucellosis vaccine would be fantastic news."

"That's what I don't understand, Becca. Why would they not think that already? It makes no sense."

"Oh, you know these old cattlemen, Jed. They hate change. The idea of a vaccine that's sprayed on is just too radical for them. That's all it is. But I can help them get behind it. I'll invite you to speak to the whole group. Make sure they understand."

"I'm not sure I even care what they think right now."

"What about your business? You said it's dropping. You can't afford to lose your practice, Jed. You've worked too hard. What would you do?"

Jed had been wondering the same thing.

"I could always cut a deal with Manson Cline. Devote myself to research."

"Over my dead body. And yours. You know you're not cut out to work for some big corporation. You'd be miserable, Jed, and you know it. And I'm not about to let you work for the same company as that bitch."

"Her name's Sandy," Jed said, knowing it was childish to taunt Rebecca, but unable to resist.

" 'Bitch' works for me," Rebecca replied. "You need the ranchers' support, Jed, and as president of the association, I can help you regain it."

"I don't suppose I have any say in your running or not anyway, do I?"

"No, not really."

"Then can we just cut this conversation short and go upstairs?"

* * *

MAKING LOVE WAS better than ever, though Jed couldn't completely dismiss the thought of the misery that lay ahead. Rebecca had no chance, none whatsoever, of being elected president of the Cattlemen's Association. Still, he did his best to remain in the moment and enjoy himself.

After they'd exhausted themselves, Jed started dozing; but Rebecca apparently wasn't sleepy.

"Jed?"

"Hmmm?" he answered groggily.

"Dusty Harrison's a client of yours, isn't he?"

"Yes, why?"

"Just wondered. Cyrus was asking about him yesterday."

She grew silent. Jed had just begun dozing again when she said, "How many head does he have?"

Jed sighed. Exhaustion had set in.

"Who?"

"Dusty."

"I don't know," Jed mumbled. "Maybe a hundred."

"He planning to buy more?"

Jed's eyes fluttered open. "No," he said. "He told me his heart's not in it any more. Ever since his boy died."

"He said that?"

"Yeah. I don't mean he's getting out or anything." Jed yawned. "Just that he didn't sound like a man who'd be buying more cattle."

Rebecca grew quiet.

"So he has about a hundred head?" she said.

"That's how many vaccines he ordered. A hundred. Should be in any day now." He squinted, trying to make her face out in the dark. "Why're you so interested in Dusty?"

"I'm not. It's just that Cyrus asked if I could find out what you knew."

"Why would Cyrus ask you to do that?"

"I don't know," Rebecca replied. Now she yawned, and

turned her back to him, burrowing in under the comforter.

Jed couldn't fall back to sleep after that.

But several minutes later, when he reached for Becca, her soft snoring stopped him cold.

THIRTEEN

JED RARELY READ the local *Gazette*. When he bought a newspaper, it was usually the one out of Billings or Butte. Still, the picture on today's *Gazette* caught his eye and he bent for a closer look.

A mash of crumpled metal, leaning up against a tree like a flattened pop can stood on end.

Jed's gaze lingered on it.

Photos like these on the front page of the local paper weren't anything new. Small-town publishers seemed to have an affinity for automobile accidents that took place in their quiet communities. A fatality almost always took front and center on the next morning's edition.

But for some reason, the sight of the crushed truck caused a shiver to run down Jed's spine. Even in its mangled state, it looked familiar.

He bent to read through the door of the newspaper box outside Rini's. The thick plastic window, scratched and clouded over by time and weather, made the small print beneath the photograph even more difficult to read.

"Harrison's truck crashed into this tree."

Heart pounding, Jed reached into his pocket for two quarters.

Eyes still glued to the picture, he dropped them in the slot, lifted the door and grabbed the only remaining paper.

Stepping aside for two customers leaving Rini's, he began to read.

TRAGIC ACCIDENT CLAIMS LOCAL LIFE

Longtime Madison Valley resident and well-known rancher Dusty Harrison died yesterday in a one-vehicle rollover accident on Highway 2. Sheriff Henry Carroll says it appears Harrison lost control of his vehicle when his left rear tire blew out. After rolling once, the Ford truck smashed into a tree, instantly killing Mr. Harrison.

Harrison served as president of the Madison County Livestock Association from 1986 to 1990 and was a member of the Madison County Republican Central Committee. He had recently purchased Reed Jones's long-held grazing allotment for the Horse Butte district, which led some to speculate that he was planning to expand the ranching operation he's run south of Ennis for the past thirty years. The allotment has reverted back to the Forest Service. Jim Pritchard, Forest Supervisor for the Gallatin National Forest, had no comment about plans for the allotment in the immediate future. Dusty Harrison was preceded in death by his son, Torry. Torry worked as a ranger in Yellowstone National Park and died evacuating backcountry campers during the recent wildfires. Should friends desire, the family suggests that memorial contributions be made to the Shriners' Hospital in Butte, or the Western Heritage Museum in Ennis.

Stunned, Jed stood staring at a small photograph of Dusty, wearing his trademark hat and overalls. Also the toothy smile Jed knew him for.

"Coming in?"

Jed looked up. A fisherman dressed to the nines in pricey new garb smiled at him as he held the door open. Some other time Jed might have appreciated the obvious fact that Fish and Fly, the local river outfitter, had made a small fortune on this one. But right now he barely noticed.

"No," he answered.

Abruptly, he turned and headed for his truck.

JED ROARED UP the long driveway, eyes fixed on the sight of Rebecca holding the leads to two horses. She appeared to be chatting animatedly with the rear end of a skinny cowboy— the horse-shoer, who was bent double over the hind feet of her prized paint, pounding nails into its new shoe.

"I need to talk to you," Jed said as he slid out of the truck and strode up to her.

Excusing herself, Rebecca tied both lead ropes to the three-rail fence, then followed Jed several yards away. The shoer, several small tacks sticking out from between his tobacco-stained lips, eyed Jed warily, then went back to work on the paint.

As soon as they were out of earshot, Jed turned on Rebecca.

"Why did you ask me about Dusty Harrison the other night?"

"I told you. Cyrus was curious."

"Why?"

"I don't know."

"You mean someone you hardly know asks you to get information from me about someone else you don't know all that well, and you don't even bother to ask what it's all about?"

"Jed, what's the big deal? This is ranching country. Everyone always wants to know everyone else's business. It's been like that forever. We're all competing for the same sellers. It's not like Cyrus wanted top-secret information. He just wanted to know if Dusty was planning an expansion. There are lots of other ways he could've found out. I suppose asking me to ask you just seemed the easiest."

Jed thrust the folded paper at Rebecca.

"*Here's* the big deal," he said. "Dusty's dead."

Rebecca's gasp at the sight of the picture he shoved in her face gave Jed a twisted sense of satisfaction. Numbly, she took the paper from him.

"Oh, my God. When did this happen?"

"Yesterday. Two days after you were asking me about him."

"Jed. What are you getting at? What does this have to do with me asking you about Dusty's ranching plans?"

"I was hoping you could tell me."

"Are you serious?"

"Dead serious. Pardon the pun."

"Jed, what's gotten into you? It says right here this was an accident. You're not thinking clearly."

Jed ripped the newspaper from her hand.

"Look at this," he said, stabbing the second paragraph of the story with his index finger. "It says here that Dusty lost a wheel. That's what caused him to lose control of his truck."

"So what?"

"So, that's exactly what happened to me. *On my way back from Cyrus Gibbons's place.*"

Holding both hands up in the air, Rebecca actually took an uneasy step backward, away from Jed. "You can't mean you think the two are connected. Tell me, Jed. Tell me that's not what you're trying to say."

Jed grabbed both her wrists. "Of *course* they're connected."

He didn't realize he'd started shouting, nor that his grip would leave deep imprints on Rebecca's wrists, until she shook loose of his grasp.

"What's happened to you, Jed?"

"Well, let's see," he answered. "I almost got killed when my truck lost a wheel and rolled off the highway. My assistant was blown to pieces when my barn exploded. Oh, yeah, and my entire herd of experimental animals. Now one of my clients, a man who dedicated himself to the ranchers in this county, is dead—coincidentally, just days after Cyrus Gibbons asked you to find out what he's up to." His voice rose in volume with each sentence. *"Do you really need to ask what's happened to me?"*

"How are they connected?" Now Rebecca was shouting, too. "How, Jed? Tell me."

There. Rebecca had voiced it. The flaw in his theory.

It was based on nothing but gut instinct, and what Sheriff Carroll called coincidence.

"I don't know," Jed answered, dropping his voice. He'd noticed the shoer staring at them. "I don't know yet. But they are."

The farrier had straightened and now studied them, clearly trying to assess the situation and decide whether Rebecca needed help. Apparently deciding Rebecca might be in danger, he started toward Jed and Rebecca, reaching behind him as he walked, into the back pocket of his overalls.

"You need help, Jed," Rebecca said, as the man stepped up to her, the heavy metal rasp he'd been using to trim hooves clutched in a half-raised hand.

Contrary to what the shoer probably thought, it wasn't the threat implied in the way he held the file that stopped Jed, that caused him to turn away and return to his truck.

It was the look in Rebecca's eyes. And her final words to him.

"Don't come back until you get it."

THAT NIGHT, HE couldn't sleep.

He'd already felt as though he were going mad, but the fear

in Rebecca's eyes, the way she stepped close to the horse-shoer for protection . . . and her words.

You need help. Don't come back until you get it.

Was Rebecca right? Was Jed overreacting? Tying invisible strings together into a web that did not exist in the real world?

Sleep was hopeless. Jed threw his legs over the side of the bed, stood, then lumbered over to his desk. He would review his research. Maybe the answer lay there, in the data. Something, somewhere, had to explain what was happening. A review of his research might be a good place to start.

He logged on.

"Good evening, Jed. You've got mail," an absurb voice announced.

Jed clicked on his mailbox, then let out a string of obscenities when he saw it.

An e-mail from BS169.

He'd blamed everything on the e-mails. All this hell began when they started coming.

Still, his heart raced as he clicked on the envelope.

They're planning to intercept your shipment of cattle.

That was it. Nothing more. No explanation of who, how, or why. Just another cryptic warning.

Shaking with rage, Jed couldn't type his reply fast enough, the click-click-clicking the only sound in the black void of his bedroom.

Who the hell are you? Why should I believe you? How are you getting your information?

He poised the mouse over the send icon, then froze. Unable to stop himself, he slid the mouse back over the text of the message and added:

Do you know anything about Dusty Harrison?

He clicked on send.

Too agitated now for the clear mind necessary to review his research, he threw a pair of gray sweats on and headed out the door.

He ran.

Down the long drive to Highway 287, then toward town. He glanced back at the clinic. In the darkness, the shadow cast by the barn practically filled the parking lot, making the new structure appear larger than it really was.

Even from the highway, he thought he smelled its fresh lumber, a scent that normally pleased Jed but now only served as a reminder of why it had become necessary.

He hadn't run in years, but as crappy as his legs and lungs felt, the longer he ran, the better his mind felt, and so he continued. Through town, which stretched the length of four blocks.

Past Clancy's house, a small gray frame structure, its neatly kept yard now overgrown. Lance had moved in with his grandma.

Jed lumbered on, south, over the bridge across the Madison River. Ever since moving to Ennis, winter or summer, he'd rolled his truck's windows down and slowed whenever he crossed it, so in love was he with the sound of its rushing water. He'd bragged once at Del's that he knew that stretch of the river so well he could tell the time of year, down to the month and week, simply by listening to it. No one ever thought to challenge him on it.

He sprinted along the highway, suddenly feeling light on his feet, and fast, past the Rainbow Valley Inn and the El Western, log-style motels popular with tourists, especially the fishermen and hunters that each fall brought.

Finally, just over six miles from his house, at no particular benchmark, Jed's body mutinied. He stopped, doubling over.

His heart hammered in his chest. Each painful breath seared his lungs.

He fell to the dewy grass along the side of the road, lay there, gasping for air, first on his side, holding his gut. Then, when breathing became easier, he turned onto his back and stared at the stars.

He dozed then, but only for a few minutes, until a semi roared by on its way to Butte.

Jed rolled to his knees, then slowly, achingly stood. His throat and muscles burned for water. As he straightened, his left foot cramped, contorting it within the confines of his shoe. Jed relished the pain. He bit down, wanting with all his heart to scream, but not from physical pain. He wanted to shout and curse over the hell his life had become.

The spasm passed.

He harbored no thoughts of running home.

He began walking. A blister burned his left heel. Each step rubbed another layer of skin away. The back of his sock grew wet.

He'd accomplished what he'd hoped.

Numbed his mind, if not his body. Saved his sanity.

At least for tonight.

As he passed the Rainbow again, a truck with a Fish and Fly logo, trailing a MacKenzie River boat, pulled into the parking lot, its tires crunching the gravel like corn popping in a microwave. Guides, there to pick up clients. The fact that daybreak was still an hour away told Jed that the outfitters must be taking their clients an hour or so away, probably to float the Jefferson or Yellowstone.

A few lights now glowed when he passed back through town. The bakery, and Rini's café, which opened at five.

Three hours after leaving, Jed finally limped down his driveway.

As soon as he hobbled into his office, he dropped into the chair at his desk and went online.

His e-mailer must also be an insomniac.

A reply, from BS169.

Jed clicked to open it.

They killed Dusty.

That was all it said.

HE MADE THE call from a phone booth later that day.

"An empty truck?" the voice on the other end repeated in disbelief. "You're comin' all the way down here and driving back an empty truck?"

"Yes," Jed replied.

"And you mean to tell me you don't intend to pick the cattle up on your way through Thermopolis?"

"No. I'll want you to pick them up and deliver them to me later, after I return the truck. For now, just have the truck ready."

"I gotta tell you, Doc, ain't none of my business, but you don't hafta come all the way down to Casper to rent a fuckin' truck."

"Will you rent it to me or not?"

"'Course I will. If I don't I'm gonna end up with dead time. Dead time costs me money. I already had those two days blocked off for you."

"Good," Jed said. "And make sure it's the same truck you always use for hauling cattle."

"What difference it make if you ain't haulin nothin'?"

"It makes a difference," Jed said, finally losing patience. "Like I said, I'll pay you the same rate you quoted for hauling the cattle up to me from Thermopolis. And you won't even have to provide a driver."

The line went temporarily silent and when he spoke again,

Jed could hear suspicion creeping into the mind of the Live-stock Transfer, Inc., owner.

"What kind of experience you got with a big rig?"

"Plenty," Jed lied.

"What if you get in an accident and my insurance company refuses to pay 'cause you're not my reg'lar driver?"

"I told you. I'm insured. It'll be covered. I'll give you my insurance agent's number to verify that."

"Strangest damn request I ever got."

"I'll be there day after tomorrow," Jed replied.

FOURTEEN

JED WAITED UNTIL he'd climbed inside the cab of the huge transporter and pulled out onto the highway. He took a long look in the rearview mirror, and both side-mounted mirrors. Nothing. Of course, he hadn't expected to be followed.

What he did expect would take place down the road, somewhere after Thermopolis, he figured, but well before Interstate 90. A two-hundred-mile stretch of road that undulated and twisted along rivers, across plains, up foothills, and finally, over several mountain passes.

Of course, maybe he'd gone mad, expecting anything at all to happen. Giving that much credence to the e-mails. Going to these lengths to test his theory.

Assured by the sight in the mirrors—an empty ribbon of highway snaking its way over row after row of gentle hills behind him—he removed his cowboy hat, unzipped his coat (an old letterman's jacket he hadn't worn in two decades), and removed the bright orange hat he'd lifted from a peg on the wall inside the offices at Livestock Transfer, Inc. The hat was streaked with dirt, its bill crusted with fresh mud. Above the bill, it said: *LTI*. He pushed it down on his head and looked in the mirror. Perfect. Much better than the new one he'd bought on his way to the airport, at the truck stop outside Butte, which said *TRUCKERS HAUL* in the front, and *ASS* across the back.

Next, he reached inside the bag for sunglasses. At the truck stop, he'd noticed most of the long-haul drivers were wearing a mirrored style. He'd bought himself a pair.

His cell phone suddenly rang.

He looked at the caller ID, but all it said was *OUT OF AREA*. No phone number.

He'd left a message on the machine at the clinic, instructing callers to contact the Butte vet he'd arranged to cover for him in the event of emergencies. But many of his clients knew his cell phone number. It was simply not in Jed's nature to leave them high and dry.

"Hello?"

"Where are you?"

Rebecca.

Jed's pulse quickened.

He'd hoped to make this entire trip without having to tell Rebecca about it. He knew what she would say. The last time they'd talked she'd told him to "get help."

Jed didn't think this trip was what she had in mind.

Still, he'd never lied to her. Not once. Starting now could doom whatever future they might still have.

"Way out of town," he said, wincing as the words left his mouth.

"Ranch call?"

She didn't usually ask.

"Um-hmm."

"Will you be gone all day?"

"Most likely."

Rebecca paused, and at that moment Jed felt certain she knew. Was she laying a trap, trying to see if he'd tell her the truth about where he was and what he was doing?

He opened his mouth to come clean.

"I called to say I'm sorry, Jed."

Taking in a deep breath, Jed answered, "That's okay, Becca. I can understand. I know I haven't been myself."

"It's just that all this . . . all this *stuff,* it's changed everything. And I just want it to go away. What happened to Clancy, what happened to Dusty. What's happening to us. I guess I think that if we ignore it, if we refuse to believe any of it's connected, we can get back to normal. And I know you're not able to do that, Jed. I know you feel responsible in some way."

"I do feel responsible," Jed said. "There's a thread tying it all together, Becca. I feel it. I just can't prove it. Not yet."

"Can you come see me tonight? I can't do it, Jed. I can't be without you."

Jed's heart, which had calmed down some, now twisted in anguish.

"I'd give anything to see you tonight, honey. But . . ."

"But what?"

But an anonymous e-mail told me the cattle will be intercepted, and I can't in good faith put an innocent truck driver in danger; plus I want to find out once and for all if my e-mailer's right. So I'll be driving an empty truck across two states tonight.

Realizing how insane it all would sound, and not willing to risk another argument with Rebecca, Jed replied, "But the cattle arrive tonight. And I need to be there to accept delivery."

FIFTEEN

TEN MILES SOUTH of Cody, Wyoming, Jed first spotted it in his rearview mirror.

A yellow pickup. Eyes fixed to his side mirror, Jed slowed, deliberately narrowing the distance separating them. In less than a minute, he could make out the shape of two cowboy hats inside the cab, and the familiar pattern and coloring of a Montana license plate. The truck even looked vaguely familiar.

Earlier, there'd been a car—a newer Lincoln Continental—that had roused Jed's suspicions, but it had since turned off the highway.

The cattle Jed had arranged to purchase came from a ranch south of Thermopolis. He had no idea how much knowledge his enemies possessed about his arrangements for the cattle, but to cover all the bases, he'd pulled off at the Thermopolis exit and had actually located the ranch he'd arranged to buy from. Instead of pulling in to its long drive, however, he went on, to the next driveway. A bone-thin, pale woman appeared at the front door and stood on a porch that looked ready to either cave in or topple sideways. Jed made up an address he was looking for and she waved him north. Jed asked for permission to turn the big rig around in her field, but disinterested, she'd already disappeared back inside.

After turning around, before pulling back out on the two-lane road that spread across flat and barren country, Jed eyed both directions. There had been no sign of another vehicle. But once he got back on Highway 120, headed for Cody, he'd noticed the Lincoln.

Wyoming and Montana drivers had no patience for slow, weighted-down semis on their narrow, two-lane highways. Any vehicle that let slip an opportunity to pass the semi raised a red flag in Jed's mind, which was why the Lincoln had caught his attention. For over three miles, it hung behind, despite numerous opportunities to speed ahead.

When it turned off at Dry Creek, Jed briefly entertained the possibility that he'd been crazy to believe the e-mail.

Then the yellow truck appeared in both side mirrors, so suddenly that Jed felt certain it had been sitting, hidden along the highway, waiting for the LTI truck to pass. It sped to within four or five car lengths of Jed, then slowed to match his speed for the remaining miles into Cody.

Once they entered Cody, Jed suddenly realized that he'd made one potentially disastrous mistake. Both sides of the LTI truck consisted of horizontal slats separated to allow venting. Each slat angled slightly down and out, creating a slight hood over the next, and making seeing inside the trailer difficult, but if a person were close enough, not impossible. The rank odor of the transporter would never give Jed away. Even empty, he smelled it whenever he opened his window. But if the yellow truck happened to pull even with him for any length of time, its occupants might be able to see that the trailer was empty.

The pickup, however, never took advantage of the four lanes through most of Cody to attempt passing the tractor-trailer. Instead, it hung back, always two or three cars behind, confirming Jed's suspicions. Had he drawn out Clancy's murderers?

Perhaps Dusty's also?

Come and get me.

Jed glued his eyes to his mirrors; his hands clamped down on the steering wheel like steel vises.

Come and get me.

Pure, powerful volcanic rage raced through him, along with an anticipation so keen and sharp that it took every ounce of his willpower to resist stopping the truck in the middle of the street. There was nothing Jed wanted more than to climb out, storm back to the yellow truck, pull its occupants out onto the street and beat a confession out of them.

He would do so, he promised himself that. But not now. For now, he had to stick to his plan.

He had to find out, once and for all, if his—and his anonymous e-mailer's—suspicions were true.

As it had a dozen times since he'd received the last cryptic e-mail, the question it gave rise to came back to Jed.

The message had used the word "intercept."

Did that mean kidnapping the cattle, taking them to some other location? If so, why? Maybe they planned to do something to them to sabotage Jed's research. It was possible. If Jed's enemies had enough know-how, they could infect the cattle with any number of diseases that held the potential to sabotage Jed's research by wreaking havoc with his data. Such a plan, if it had gone undetected by Jed, could make his data useless, delay legitimate research months, even years. Bad data could destroy Jed's credibility—a key ingredient to taking research to the next step, developing a marketable product.

Did Jed's enemies have that know-how?

There was one other possibility, one Jed was more inclined to believe. That "intercept" meant destroy. Destroying the cattle Jed intended to use for research (along with

another innocent life) might be another way to wear Jed
down, frighten him into submission.

Either way, Jed saw this trip as his way to confirm the validity of the anonymous e-mails.

On the edge of town, past the Buffalo Bill Historical Center, traffic thinned. Ahead, the last traffic light in Cody turned
from green to yellow.

Jed glanced in the side mirror, then gunned the truck right
through a red light.

The pickup followed.

ONCE OUTSIDE OF Cody, his pursuers apparently decided they
were in no hurry.

As Jed continued north on 120, they fell back. At one point,
Jed even thought he'd lost them. Then the yellow speck reappeared in his side mirror.

Fifteen miles outside Cody, an electric highway sign
flashed *SLOW*.

Another, yards ahead, warned: *RIGHT LANE CLOSED AHEAD*.

A single line of cars had formed ahead. A flagger stood,
two-way radio in hand, chatting amiably with the driver of
the first car.

The rig's jake brakes squealed under Jed's inexperienced
touch as he brought the truck to a noisy stop. The flagger
glanced up.

Directly behind Jed, the yellow truck slowed. At first it
hung back, its driver no doubt reluctant to give the LTI trucker
a glimpse of its two occupants; but as cars and trucks began
lining up behind it, it had little choice but to inch slowly forward, until it almost filled the side mirror on Jed's door.

Still, the cowboy hats hid the men's faces from Jed's
probing eyes, which were themselves hidden by his mirrored
sunglasses.

Jed did feel almost certain, however, that he recognized

the truck. Jed watched as the flagger started moving slowly down the line of cars, chatting with each driver, occasionally holding the two-way to his mouth and speaking into it, then waiting for a reply, which he promptly passed on to an eager audience.

The door to the car ahead of Jed opened and the driver got out.

He walked toward the flagger, then stood listening to what he was telling a helmeted motorcyclist.

After the flagger passed them, two cars had pulled onto the left shoulder of the divided highway and now slowly made their way forward past the line standing still.

Jed broke into a sweat.

The yellow truck had now pulled so close that Jed could only see the corner of its rear tailgate in his right-side mirror.

Jed's eyes jumped from side mirror to side mirror, watching for someone to appear. If either of the yellow truck's occupants decided to walk up ahead and see what the problem was, they'd see the empty trailer. His ruse would be up.

His pursuers would vanish, leaving Jed with nothing more conclusive than what many, including Rebecca, would call coincidence. A yellow truck with Montana plates, perhaps from Ennis, following Jed down the highway. He could just hear Rebecca now. Or Sheriff Henry Carroll.

When the flagger approached his window, Jed kept his eyes on the side mirrors.

"What's up?" he asked nonchalantly.

"Road construction up ahead," the flagger said. "There's been a little accident with the equipment. Road'll be closed for a while."

"How long's a while?"

"They're saying at least an hour. But you know how it is. Could be shorter. Most likely longer."

"Damn."

"You carrying livestock?" the flagger asked sympatheti-
cally.

Jed did not respond. Instead, he pointed at the cars—
another had joined the procession—moving along the road's
shoulder. "Where're they going?"

"Didn't wanna wait. They're turning off up ahead. Chief
Joe Highway's only half a mile up, over that next rise."

Jed's gloom lifted with his words.

"That's what I'll do, too. Can't keep my load sitting here
in the hot sun."

"You sure that's a good idea? Two passes that way. Dead
Indian, and then Beartooth. I wouldn't want to drive a rig
this size over either."

"Dead Indian's not that bad. Maybe I'll cut through the
park after that."

The flagger looked startled.

"You new to truckin'?"

"No," Jed replied, sensing he'd given his charade away.
"Why?"

"Park doesn't allow semis through it, that's why."

Damn.

"If you take the Chief Joe byway, you're stuck going up
Beartooth, and then into Red Lodge. You sure you're ready
for Beartooth?" the flagger said, not trying to hide his skep-
ticism. "Hell, that's eleven thousand feet."

The car in front of Jed suddenly swung over onto the
shoulder. Almost at the same time, Jed noticed the outside
edge of a yellow door appear in his side mirror. The driver's
door.

"Won't be a problem," Jed said, eyeing the space left by
the car in front. He shifted into gear as he spoke. "Looks like
the people behind me are getting impatient. I'll let you keep
moving."

"Okay, then," the flagger said.

As he headed toward the yellow truck, Jed saw him bend to look inside Jed's trailer.

"Shit," Jed muttered to himself. Would the yellow truck's occupants question the flagger about Jed's load?

But as he pulled out, Jed saw the truck's door close. With the flagger approaching, the yellow truck, pulled onto the shoulder, behind Jed.

Jed inched his truck forward, almost clipping the vehicle ahead of him. Its driver honked and stuck an arm out the window, middle finger in the air.

Breathing easier now with the yellow truck at his tail, Jed picked up speed on the highway.

As the flagger predicted, just over the first rise, Jed saw the turnoff. He swung the truck west, onto the famously scenic road that headed toward Yellowstone. When it began to climb, he dropped into low gear. He'd taken this drive many times before and knew to expect the sharp, winding turns, switchbacking their way up to Dead Indian Overlook.

He thought back on the family vacation they'd taken when Jed was seven. His mother had explained the meaning of the highway's name to Jed and his sister, Laurel. The image of Chief Joseph and his band of Nez Perces' legendary flight in 1877—along the very route that now, even paved, seemed to defy the possibility of travel—had stayed with Jed throughout his childhood. Even then, he'd hated the name. Dead Indian Pass. Had anyone ever named a highway Dead White Man Pass?

After the overlook, the road began dropping, crossing first Dead Indian Creek, then Sunlight, then, before reaching Beartooth Highway, Crandall Creek. For the time being, Jed breathed easy.

His pursuers could not have anticipated this change in route. They had to be regrouping, making contingency plans. And Yellowstone visitors meant enough traffic between Cody and Cooke City to ensure that nothing much could happen along the Chief Joe Highway.

Beartooth Highway and Pass, however, would be another story.

JED HAD LITTLE difficulty piloting the semi down the other side of Dead Indian Pass, past Swamp Lake to where it met 212—the infamous Beartooth Highway.

As the rest of the traffic turned left, toward Cooke City and Yellowstone's northeast entrance, Jed swung the big truck due east.

The yellow truck followed him.

The first road sign Jed passed declared, BEARTOOTH HIGHWAY PERMANENTLY CLOSED OCTOBER 15 THROUGH MAY 31. BE AWARE THAT OFF-SEASON SNOWS MAY ALSO FORCE CLOSURES.

Jed thought it an ominous sign.

Under the best of circumstances, Jed knew it would take no less than three hours to travel the sixty-plus treacherous miles up and over Beartooth Pass and into the small town of Red Lodge, Montana. Even without a load, the LTI semi groaned its way up as the road began to climb and wind.

As he climbed, Jed started seeing patches of snow on either side of the road, snow that had never melted from the previous winter. The north flanks of the twenty-some peaks in the Beartooth Range that reached twelve thousand feet in elevation sported year-round glaciers.

In the space of just a few miles, the lush forest ecosystem transformed to hardy alpine tundra, vegetation suited to another world entirely than the one Jed had just driven through. Two-thirds of the way up, Jed spied mountain goats grazing. He suspected the black dots zigzagging their way down distant planes of white to be backcountry skiers.

Even the yellow truck seemed incapable of speed as, behind

the semi, it labored its way up the relentless switchbacks that extended as far up the mountains as the eye could see.

When Jed first turned onto Beartooth Highway, the sky had been a brilliant blue, but at the lowest elevations, he'd spotted clouds ahead. Now rain pelted the windshield. A squall, dark and angry, had moved in, clinging stubbornly to the highest peaks, completely obscuring Montana's highest, Granite Peak.

Having grown up in Montana, Jed knew that on passes as high as Beartooth—nearly eleven thousand feet—sudden snowstorms could be expected any month of the year.

He knew one other thing as well: empty or not, his experience driving pickup trucks hauling horse trailers had not adequately prepared him for driving a vehicle this size on a pass like Beartooth, especially if the weather turned ugly. He'd made it this far, but ascending one of the highest and most rugged mountain ranges in the lower forty-eight states would be a piece of cake compared to the descent.

Maybe he should have risked sitting back there on the highway.

The rain picked up, whole sheets of water the wipers could not keep up with. Traffic—what there was of it—had slowed to a crawl with the decreasing visibility.

And then snow began to fall.

All the vehicles on the pass, including the yellow truck, had turned on headlights and slowed to a crawl. Soon Jed could not distinguish the pickup from several other vehicles that moved in and out of sight as they rounded one bend after another behind him.

Wind whistled through the LTI cab from the gap where an insulation strip had once lined the windows. The wind picked up the higher Jed climbed. Suddenly, as the truck crested one of the last rises, a powerful gust pushed it sideways.

At 10,947 feet up, Jed crested the pass.

He knew from other trips along this road that the view at Vista Point was nothing short of spectacular, extending for hundreds of miles, well into the Absarokas to the west and across plains, state lines, snowfields, and lakes in every other direction. But this day, the top of the world was an eerie place to be, socked in by a storm, and Jed had his hands full keeping the big vehicle on a straight course on slick roads, with gusts of wind reaching sixty miles per hour.

Jed hadn't seen the yellow truck's headlights in his rearview mirror for several switchbacks. He focused on the road, determined to keep the truck moving at a speed he could control.

At first Jed had trouble distinguishing it in the windblown snow, but when Jed thought he saw smoke through his side window, he rolled it down. The awful odor of rubber burning confirmed his worst fear. He'd been riding his brakes too hard. They'd started burning out.

With thirty miles of steep downhill driving ahead of him, he had no choice but to let up on them, allow the big transport to pick up speed.

Tensely clinging to the wheel, face pressed closer to the glass, Jed let the truck go from thirty to thirty-five miles an hour, budgeting his use of the brakes. When the smell got worse, he let up more. Forty miles per hour. Terror pulsing in his temples, Jed squinted through the falling snow.

He began passing cars, even four-wheel-drive pickups. Should he stop? To do so with the yellow truck still somewhere behind him meant losing his chance to confirm the authenticity of the e-mails. But continuing down the mountain with faulty brakes amounted to suicide.

He hadn't seen his pursuers for a while now. Perhaps, they too had pulled over.

Realizing he had no choice, Jed began looking for a safe place to pull off the road.

Almost miraculously, a sign appeared up ahead. He

remembered it, knew what it said, even before its letters became readable:

RUNAWAY RAMP, 1 MILE.

Thank God. All he had to do was make it to the ramp.

Jed pushed down on the brakes, beginning his preparation to stop. The truck had entered a particularly steep decline. But with a start, Jed saw the needle on the speedometer climb.

Instead of slowing, the truck accelerated.

Jed pumped the brake pedal, stomping on it as the horrifying realization hit him.

He'd lost his brakes.

As the truck continued to accelerate, Jed struggled to downshift, but even that barely slowed the massive truck.

Hurtling down the pass now, Jed headed into a series of sharp switchbacks.

His plan to bring the truck to a controlled stop at the runaway ramp had, just seconds earlier, been a prudent decision. Now he had no choice.

Another sign sped by in a blur:

RUNAWAY TRUCK RAMP: 1/4 MILE

Jed had become so focused on the road ahead that at first he didn't notice the headlights approaching at a rapid pace from behind. They disappeared into his blind spot on the right side of the truck. When they reemerged at his side, Jed recognized the yellow truck.

It pulled alongside him, on his right.

The truck is driving on the shoulder.

Jed needed to cross that shoulder to enter the runaway ramp.

He punched down on the horn with the palm of his hand. The smaller truck ignored it, continuing to match the transport's pace, taking the turns with much more ease than Jed, who now also had the presence of the yellow truck to complicate his driving.

With the runaway ramp finally coming into view, Jed

realized the plan. The driver of the yellow truck knew he'd
lost his brakes.

He's going to block the transport from entering the ramp.

Sweat pouring off his chin, Jed tried the only thing he
could think of doing. He accelerated. But again, the yellow
truck easily matched his speed.

The ramp's entrance raced toward him.

Jed blasted his horn again, once, twice, then kept his fist
on it, spewing a string of obscenities.

"Son of a bitch," he yelled. "If that's how you want it . . ."

He jerked the steering wheel right, hitting the truck, then
back again.

"Out of my fucking way."

The yellow truck began swerving erratically, brushing the
side of the semi, then ricocheting away, its driver now clearly
fighting for control.

With the ramp rushing at him, Jed eyed his last, split-
second chance and cut hard to the right, just clearing the rear
of the smaller truck.

The LTI truck exploded onto the ramp, hitting it left of
center. Jed lurched forward as it sank into inches of gravel,
slowing immediately.

"Yes," Jed yelled.

But relief gave way to the realization that, with no load to
weigh it down and the excessive speed at which he'd entered
it, the ramp might be too short to allow him to stop completely. Less than three-fourths the length of a football field
remained ahead, and the semi still barreled up its incline at
over fifty miles an hour.

Would the ramp be long enough? And if not, what lay beyond its crest?

Desperate, Jed began zigzagging up the remaining length
of ramp, trying to buy more stopping distance.

The tactic worked. Enough that Jed even dared a glance

out the side window. The yellow truck had stopped up ahead, pulled over on the side of the road.

Fighting an impulse to reach for his door handle right that moment and go after its occupants, as he approached the end of the ramp, more confident now, Jed prepared for one final turn to the right, away from the highway below.

That's when it happened.

He swung the truck gently toward the left edge of the ramp. Then, with the needle on the truck's speedometer plummeting, Jed jerked the wheel right.

He realized instantly that he'd cut too sharply. The cab listed left. In the next second, the right front wheels lifted off the ground and Jed felt the truck going into a roll. Slowly at first—so slowly that he felt certain gravity would plop it right back down.

But then the gravel at the left edge of the ramp gave way under the weight of the truck's left wheels. Rocks clattered down the rocky cleft between the man-made hill and the highway. And with the "vee" between the truck's cab and trailer leading the way, the big rig began to topple sideways.

With lightning quickness, Jed opened the door to jump clear, but earth—hard, cold earth—rushed at him, slamming it shut. He pulled his left foot clear just in time, then struggled to free it from the space between the door and seat, where it had been lodged, all the while fighting images of its amputation had he not acted quickly enough.

Skidding on its left side, dust and snow flying, the air filled with the ear-punishing scraping of metal against rock, the transport slid a dozen yards, then crashed down off the ramp, onto the highway.

Sparks flying like a giant Fourth of July sparkler, it continued its slide across the four lanes.

Jed knew the truck had enough momentum to carry it across the entire road. Freeing his stuck foot just in time to fold into a ball, head cradled in his arms, he prepared himself to go over the other side, into the abyss.

Suddenly, a violent jolt threw him forward, into the corner between the door and the windshield. He imagined he'd started into a free fall.

Instead, he realized in the next instant, the cab had come to a dead stop.

Slowly, he pushed away from the corner and peered out the driver's window.

The metal railing had been peeled away like the top of a sardine can, but the bumper of the cab had wrapped itself around a single post, which stopped the entire truck dead in its slide.

Just enough distance separated the posts, however, to allow the trailer to continue its momentum, crashing through the metal rail, into a black void of empty space, where Jed could now see it dangling, swaying like a writhing snake preparing to strike.

The cab shuddered and trembled as Jed felt the guardrail's hold on the cab being strained to its limit by the weight of the trailer. Then, with a deafening roar, the connection between cab and trailer snapped, and, now in silence, the trailer became airborne.

It flew—for what seemed to Jed an eternity—and then he heard it crash, like a meteor, back to earth to begin its descent down the steep mountainside, in a steady, low thunder.

Stunned, Jed stared into the void he'd narrowly escaped. Commotion outside—people running to come to his rescue—suddenly drew his attention back to the road.

Ahead, on the side of the road, sat the yellow truck. One of its occupants, face pressed to the window, strained for sight of the trailer, still rolling, flattening everything in its path.

Even a thousand yards above where it came to rest, Jed felt the rumble of its final impact, saw the cloud of earth mushrooming from below, like an atomic bomb.

Several people had pulled over to come to Jed's aid, and now stood discussing whether it was safe to enter the cab to free Jed. The cab was perched precariously above the drop-off and clung to the post by a bumper dangerously ready to break free of the truck's body. A man in tan overalls jogged back to the supersized pickup he'd left in the middle of the northbound lanes. Opening the shell on the back of the truck, he lifted a heavy length of metal chain and huffed his way back to the gathering crowd, where several other men joined him and headed cautiously toward the cab.

Jed could not take his eyes off the yellow truck.

An anger like nothing else he'd ever experienced took hold of him, as he sat, helpless, unable to go after it.

As the group of men huddled around the post, discussing how best to secure the front axle to it with the chain, the yellow truck suddenly lurched forward.

Jed watched it disappear into the mist.

SIXTEEN

NO IFS, ANDS or buts. You're staying," the doctor declared as she stood over Jed.

He lay on a hospital bed in a room no bigger than Rebecca's walk-in closet.

"We're keeping you overnight for observation. You're in no condition to travel."

"This is ridiculous," Jed replied. "I can't waste a day in bed. I've got a full schedule tomorrow. I've got patients, too, you know. Besides, I'm fine."

He'd liked her, the doctor, at first, but right now, Jed despised her cautious nature.

"Your unequal pupils and that knot on your head say you're *not* so fine," she replied. "I'm keeping you overnight for observation. I'll be in at six A.M. tomorrow. If you do well tonight, I'll get you out of here before seven. You could be back in Ennis by ten."

"My first appointment's at eight," Jed replied childishly.

Red Lodge's only ER doctor did not appear moved.

"Well, that's the best I can do."

She nodded toward Jed's laptop, which sat on a chair next to the bed.

"I see your laptop made it out of that tangled mess the EMTs described to me. Why don't you write a book while you're here? You can make me the star."

"Very funny."

She scribbled several lines in Jed's chart, looped the chain of its clipboard over the end of the bed, and turned to leave.

As she paused at the door, the professional veil over her dark eyes suddenly lifted, transforming her face into that of a much younger woman.

"You know, I've been trying to resist," she said, " 'cause it's obviously none of my business, but I just don't think I can." She paused. "What's a vet doing driving a semi over Beartooth?"

"That's a long story," Jed replied.

She studied him, clearly intrigued.

"Put it in the book," she said, then she disappeared down the hallway.

Jed stewed as he watched her go.

Once she was out of sight, he got up, crossed the room, which took three steps, and grabbed his laptop off the windowsill, where the nurse's aide had propped it, next to the telephone.

His head screamed in protest as Jed bent down, running his hand loosely along the phone cord, which ended at a jack on the wall next to his bed. He pulled the retractable modem line out of his laptop, plugged it into the jack and fired up his computer.

It seemed to take forever for the MSN icon to pop up on the screen. Jed clicked on it, then entered his password.

The static that signaled the modem dialing brought him a strange sense of comfort.

He went directly to e-mail, clicked on the last reply he'd received from BS169 and typed:

> You were right about them intercepting the shipment of cattle. It's time to stop playing games. We have to meet. If you refuse to identify yourself and help me get to the bottom of this, the next blood will be on your hands.

Angrily, he clicked on send.

Jed knew that if he went to Sheriff Carroll about this latest incident, in short order, he'd hear back that his "accident" had been just that. In addition, Jed would be labeled a paranoid nut for having rented an empty truck in an effort to prove the legitimacy of his claims that someone was out to stop his research.

Even if he were to return to Ennis and be lucky enough to find the yellow truck, he'd have no proof of anything.

There was only one person who could help him identify his enemies—and stop them.

His anonymous e-mailer.

Every one of his e-mailer's predictions had come to pass. Someone out there knew who was behind the string of recent events. Jed should have focused on that person from the start, instead of trying to conduct his own investigation.

Jed would find his e-mailer and force the truth out of him. Suddenly, the sound of a door opening turned his attention to the bottom right corner of his screen. A message popped up.

"You've just received an e-mail from POSTMAN.

Scowling, Jed clicked on his mailbox. Sure enough, a new email had just arrived.

The subject line sent a chill through him.

RETURNED MAIL. MESSAGE UNDELIVERABLE.

With a sense of dread, Jed clicked on the envelope.

Your email was undeliverable for the following reason: invalid address or address no longer in existence.

It was the email he'd just sent to BS169.

"No," Jed shouted impulsively.

A male nurse passing in the hallway came running in.

"You okay?" he asked, eyes carefully scrutinizing Jed.

Jed waved him off.

"I'm fine. Just some bad news in an email. Sorry."

"No apology necessary," the good natured nurse said. "Your buzzer's right there if you need me."

"Thanks."

When he'd gone, Jed got back up, unplugged his laptop and reconnected the telephone.

His sister in Seattle picked up on the third ring.

"Where are you calling from?" she asked.

"A friend's," Jed lied. "Why?"

"Because caller ID says you're at Red Lodge Hospital, that's why. What's up, Jed? What's happened?"

"Nothing Laurel, I promise. I'm fine. I just had a little accident and they're keeping me overnight for observation."

Her gasp weighted him with guilt.

"Jed, no. Should I come?"

"No, you definitely should not come."

"Was Rebecca with you? Is she all right?"

Rebecca. What if Rebecca dropped by the clinic tonight? Did he dare call her from the hospital?

"No," Jed replied. "I was alone."

"Thank God. What happened? You don't have clients all the way over to Red Lodge, do you?"

Even though she'd moved away right after high school, Laurel still knew every corner, every nook and cranny, of Montana. Enough to know Red Lodge was not on any of Jed's routes.

"Listen, sis, I don't mean to be rude, but I really called to talk to Ian. It's important. It's a computer thing."

Laurel's husband, Ian, held a Ph.D. in computer science and worked at Microsoft.

"This is a little weird, Jed," Laurel said. "A computer problem that important when you're in the hospital? You're gonna have to explain it to me, you know."

"I will. I promise. But later. Just put Ian on."

Jed could hear Laurel holding her hand over the phone's mouthpiece as she no doubt told Ian that her baby brother was acting very strangely.

"Hey, Jed, wazzup?" Ian said, in keeping with his habit of compensating for being a geek with the use of the latest vernacular.

"Ian, listen, I need your help."

"You got it, man."

"I've been getting anonymous e-mails. I've replied to a couple of them and they—my replies—have always gotten through. But I just sent one a little while ago and now I get this message saying it's undeliverable."

"Did you use the reply button to respond?"

"Yes."

"Did the error message say the address wasn't valid?"

"Yes," Jed replied impatiently.

"How long's it been since you last got an e-mail from them?"

"I don't know. Let's see. Two days. No, more like a day and a half."

"Sounds to me like they just closed that account. What'd you do, bro? Send them a picture of yourself?"

"Damn," Jed muttered. "You sure?"

"Your earlier replies got through okay?"

"Yes."

"Then that's about the only explanation for the error message."

"Well," Jed said anxiously, "can I trace who wrote the e-mails I've received? I mean, if you have an e-mail address, can't you trace it back to the sender?"

"Can *I* trace it? Or *you* trace it? Is that what you mean?"

"Yeah, I guess so."

"Listen, bro, if the person knew what he was doing, could be the only one who can trace it is the feds."

"The FBI?"

"You got it."

"I can't just call up the FBI and ask them to trace an e-mail for me."

"No, it's not quite that simple." Ian paused, clearly enjoying this opportunity to impress the brother-in-law, who, until now, he'd had little success in developing a rapport with. "Let me give you an example. Let's say I go to a local cybercafé and use their machine to sign up for a free Hotmail account, then I start sending you e-mails with kinky subject lines like 'Bad Boys like watching farm girls with their animals.' You, of course, delete them religiously without opening them, for you know that once you open them, you're in a shitload of trouble. But then one day you accidentally click the open button instead of delete, and the picture that comes up traumatizes you so irreparably that you contact the FBI and lodge a formal complaint.

"The feds, after eagerly viewing the offending photo and retrieving the deleted e-mails, then contact a hotmail.com systems administrator and request any logs, which leads them to the IP numbers currently used by that cybercafé."

By this time, Ian was totally immersed in the fantasy he'd concocted and Jed had no choice but to hear it out.

"Now the FBI goes to the café, where a luscious barrista named Portia tries to recollect her memories of various routine computer users at the café. Since I've e-mailed you a dozen times by now, all the while undressing Portia with my eyes, she tells the feds she thinks she may know the culprit. A list of the dates you received the offending e-mails allows Portia to match it with one particularly memorable exchange we had one day about sheep while she served me a double tall, wet cappuccino with extra foam. Lucky for the feds, there's a videocam above the door and Portia quickly picks me out.

"Armed with my picture, the FBI canvasses the east side and eventually they find me," Ian finally concludes, "in the midst of masterminding the next sasser worm."

Her concerns about Jed apparently having given way to her appreciation of her husband's quick wit, Jed heard Laurel's giggles in the background. Jed had never understood Laurel's attraction to Ian, but so far, it had withstood the test of time.

"So your answer is no," Jed said simply.

"That's right. Without the feds, that is."

"Well, then I guess I'm out of luck," Jed said, the disappointment thick in his voice.

"Wait a minute, bro. You asked if an anonymous e-mail can be *traced* and that's my answer; but that doesn't mean you have to give up finding out who sent it."

"What do you mean?" Jed asked.

"What name did she use to send it?"

"It was anonymous. I told you. I don't even know if it's from a man or woman."

"No, I mean the nickname. What's his or her cybername? You know, from the e-mail address."

"BS169. Why?"

"What's your e-mail address?"

"Mine?" Jed parroted. His patience with this game Ian was playing had grown thin.

"Yeah, what is it?"

"Montanavet@msn.com."

"There you go. Mine's cybergeek1024@msn. For reasons you and I both know, the cybergeek part doesn't need explanation. The 1024's my extension number at Microsoft. Get my drift? That name may be innocuous, but it has to mean something. Especially taken together with the context of the messages—which by the way I've noticed you're not inclined to share with me."

"You actually think I haven't thought about what BS169 means?"

"Well, since it's about all you've got—especially now, in light of the fact it appears your e-mailer just changed addresses—I'd think harder."

Jed offered an abrupt thanks to his brother-in-law and hung up, dejected.

Lot of help Ian had been. If the moniker BS169 meant anything to Jed, he would've thought of it by now.

Dejectedly, he pushed the cubed steak, mashed potatoes with yellowish-gray gravy, and green beans they served him for dinner around on the plate. A small cup held a slice of angel food cake with defrosted, previously frozen, blueberries on top. Jed couldn't tell whether the watery blue stains dripping over the cake was meant to be syrup, or simply liquid from defrosting the berries.

Deciding to forgo dinner, he pushed the tray aside, debating whether to bolt the place. But the reality was he felt like shit, and he hadn't arranged for a rental car to get back to Ennis. With the exception of several restaurants and half a dozen bars, the town of Red Lodge had shut down for the day. He could either check out of the hospital and into a motel, or stay put.

Staying put seemed the easier, and more logical, of the two.

The orderly who'd brought dinner to him reappeared. In his hands were several thin, well-worn magazines.

"Not much reading material to offer," the good man said with an apologetic grin. "But since this room doesn't have a TV, I raided the waiting room for you."

Jed reached for his offerings.

"Thanks," he said, managing a false smile.

When the orderly had gone, Jed tossed the periodicals on his bedside tray.

As he did so, he noticed a corner of something—a piece

of literature—sticking out from the top of one of the magazines, stuck between its pages. The graphics—what he could
see of them—looked familiar. Jed reached for the magazine,
and slid the folded paper out.

He recognized it immediately. The same newsletter he'd
picked up off the road that night his truck lost a wheel.

Published by the Buffalo Field Campaign.

He'd thrown the last copy away that morning at Rebecca's
house; but now that Jed believed his mysterious rescuers that
night had come from the Buffalo Field Campaign, his curios-
ity, and boredom, drove him to unfold the newsletter and read.

The moment he did, something about the headline of the
first story caused Jed's pulse to quicken.

*ONE HUNDRED SIXTY NINE PARK BISON SLAUGH-
TERED BY THE DOL. BUFFALO SOLDIERS VOW NOT TO
ALLOW MORE DEATHS.*

He started reading about the activist group, who had named
themselves "buffalo soldiers"; about their willingness to put
themselves in harm's way to end the slaughter of bison that
roamed outside of Yellowstone's boundaries.

After the first paragraph, Jed's eyes darted back to the
headline.

One hundred sixty-nine.

In numerals, 169.

Buffalo Soldiers vow not to allow more deaths.

Buffalo Soldiers—BS.

Jed bolted upright, groaning from the sudden movement.

Throwing his legs over the side of the bed, he reached for
the pile of neatly folded clothes on the chair, then stood and
dressed himself.

Grabbing the newsletter, he eyed the Cameron, Montana,
address running under the group's logo.

At the sound of a cart rattling down the hallway in the direction of his room, Jed quickly retreated to the shadows, flattening himself against the wall behind the door. Eyeing the open window across the room, he waited for the cart to pass, then headed for it.

The clock on the wall above the bed read just after 1 A.M.

Jed slipped out the window's opening.

For the first time, his heart toyed with the hope that he might finally get some answers.

BS169.

His anonymous e-mailer.

The e-mails had come from the Buffalo Field Campaign.

SEVENTEEN

IN HER DREAM, it had become the sound of a gun firing. *Pop, pop,* then *pop-pop-pop-pop,* in rapid succession.

Megan screamed.

Houdini! Run. Run, Houdini.

Finally outsmarted, the big beast turned and headed at a lope for the nearest stand of trees. However, just before he reached it, another helicopter appeared out of nowhere, directly overhead, and again, shots rang out from above.

No, screamed Megan. *No,* as she ran toward the giant form, where it crashed to the earth.

No.

A wet nose on her palm roused Megan; but in that momentary twilight between sleep and consciousness, she still stood in the knee-deep snow, watching the nightmare unfold. So real was that sense that she now feared looking down at her hand; so sure was she that she would find it coated with the blood of her beloved Houdini.

But then Pie's whimper, and another thrust of his wet nose, drew Megan all the way back to realty.

It was only a dream, she thought with profound relief.

But wait. The shots hadn't stopped.

Finally Megan realized they weren't gunshots after all.

Someone was pounding on the back door.

"K.C.," Megan whispered, rising onto one elbow and straining to see the form on the floor next to her bed. "K.C."

K.C. simply responded with a foggy, "Not now."

With Pie at her side, Megan rose, stepping over K.C. on her way to the kitchen.

A single bulb on a post outside the back door threw light across the kitchen floor as Megan padded barefoot across it, wearing a long-sleeved thermal T-shirt and gray sweats against the Montana chill.

The pounding increased in intensity, which puzzled Megan. No one at the compound ever locked the back door. The front door, yes, but never the back. The latch must have stuck again, must have locked one of the guys out after a trip to the outhouse.

It had to be someone from the campaign. Otherwise Pie would be growling.

"Hold on, hold on," Megan mumbled.

Annoyed, she reached for the knob, which turned easily, and pulled the door open, already turning away, as she did so, to head back to bed.

But in that split second, out of the corner of her eye, she caught enough of the vision filling the doorway to make her gasp.

It was enough of a glance to know this person did not belong to the camp.

Megan pivoted to face this stranger: a large man, the light at his back making him appear even bigger than his true size.

Megan could not make out his face, but she literally felt his agitation. An agitation so keen it sent fear—pure, unadulterated terror—racing through her like an electric current.

Pie, however, responded to this unwanted presence with a wagging tail.

Instinctively, she tried to slam the door shut, but a big booted foot blocked her attempt.

She opened her mouth to call for K.C. but then the stranger said, *"It's you."*

The voice stopped her.

She froze, eyes fixed on the face, still unrecognizable in the dark.

"You're the one who's been sending me those e-mails," he said, stepping forward.

At last, the light from outside fell across his face.

Megan gasped. "You! How did you . . . ?"

Behind her, she felt K.C.'s presence.

Pie had begun whimpering, pressing his nose into the man's hand.

"Dr. McCane," K.C. said soberly. "We wondered when you'd finally find us."

"How?" Jed asked, the words coming in a rush. "How could you know that my wheel coming off wasn't an accident? And that they planned to intercept my cattle?"

They'd taken him outside the main house. A crescent moon illuminated several crude steps that had been cut into the hillside, then defined with sections of logs, as they climbed to a small A-framed structure. Stepping inside, the girl, Megan, flipped on the light—a single bulb dangling overhead—and Jed saw that the building functioned as an office.

Every inch of wall space was covered with something—mostly posters from the Buffalo Field Campaign and other environmental groups, but also political cartoons, articles from newspapers (including a recent New York Times piece featuring a picture of Megan on cross country skiis, half a dozen bison behind her in the snow), and several prominently posted warnings ("Be on the lookout for an undercover DOL agent going by the following names . . .").

Jed watched as the man—he still could not remember his name—and Megan exchanged glances. It seemed they were assessing how much it was safe to reveal.

"Damn it!" Jed said. "I just checked myself out of a hospital in Red Lodge. Someone tried to run the cattle truck I was driving off Beartooth Pass. So don't play games with me. I want answers and I want them now."

"*You* were driving the cattle back to Ennis?" K.C. asked.

"The cattle weren't in it."

"You drove an empty truck?" Megan asked.

"I got your warning," Jed replied. "I decided to see if it was real. It was. And now I want answers. Like, how did you get this information? And why wouldn't you identify yourselves to me?"

Megan nodded at the man.

"Tell him, K.C."

K.C. glanced at the clock on the wall. Megan did the same. "It's safe," she said. "He'll be sleeping."

Scowling in confusion, Jed glanced from one to the other. Who the hell they were talking about?

As Jed watched, K.C. went to the desk, reached under it to turn on the computer, then lowered himself to a stool.

The hum of the hard drive penetrated the uncomfortably thick silence. When K.C. flipped the monitor switch, a close-up of a massive buffalo, its eyelashes, nose, and mane frosted with snow, filled the screen.

Soon icons began popping up, one at a time, along its outer rim. K.C. clicked on the Skynet logo.

A sign-on box popped up. K.C. typed: "CGibbons"

He pressed tab, then in the box marked "password" entered a series of letters and numbers, all of which showed up as asterisks.

Jed moved closer, drawn to the screen, staring over K.C.'s shoulder, with Megan at his side.

The home page that appeared surprised Jed. It displayed stock market quotations, business news, and agricultural indexes. K.C. moved the mouse to the menu and clicked on the mailbox. At least a dozen new e-mails appeared.

"Look," Megan said, pointing at the screen. "A new one from Red Dawn."

"Red Dawn?" Jed echoed.

K.C. twisted to look at Jed, a gleam in his eye as he explained.

"Some of what we've learned—what we've sent warnings to you about—came from e-mails exchanged between Cyrus and someone who goes by the screen name of Red Dawn."

He turned back to the monitor and pointed to the e-mail that had caught Megan's attention. The subject line was blank. The sender name read "Red Dawn."

"But we can't read this one until Cyrus opens it. Otherwise he'd know we've been in there."

The name he'd just seen K.C. enter in the sign-in box suddenly popped back into Jed's mind.

"CGibbons."

Jed fell back half a step.

"*Cyrus Gibbons?* You mean to tell me you've been hacking into Cyrus Gibbons's e-mail?"

Jed's indignation caused a look of exasperation to pass from K.C. to Megan.

"Cyrus Gibbons happens to be a client of mine," Jed said. "And a close friend of my fiancée's. You think I'm going to stand by while you invade his privacy like this?"

When neither answered, he continued.

"You people don't believe in laws, do you? You think your off-the-wall ideologies justify any kind of behavior. Even this." He pointed at the screen. Then, glaring at both of them, he said, "I'm out of here."

He pivoted and headed for the door.

Megan's voice stopped him.

"Cyrus Gibbons knew you'd lose a wheel. Two days *before* it happened."

Her words stopped Jed dead in his tracks.

Slowly, he turned.

Beckoning Jed with a nod in the direction of the monitor, K.C. said, "C'mon, man. Just take a look. What's that gonna hurt? Hear us out. That's all we're asking."

Megan, silent, just stood looking at him with those eyes. He'd never forgotten them.

These were the same two people who had risked their own lives to save his, to pull him out of his truck.

The night he was returning from Cyrus Gibbons's.

Could the Cyrus connection back then, and again now, simply be a coincidence?

Reluctantly, unable to stop himself, Jed stepped forward to stand behind K.C. again.

Jed watched as K.C. scrolled down, toward the bottom of the e-mails.

It came to rest on one sent to Red Dawn six weeks earlier.

A double click and it opened.

"Accident" to take place on way home from late-night "emergency" call.

Refusing to believe that these cryptic words referred to the night his pickup lost a wheel, Jed said, "That doesn't prove anything."

"Look at the date," K.C. replied. "That was two days before we met you on the road that night. Two days after Cyrus wrote this e-mail, you were on your way home from his place and you almost got killed." Brown, intense eyes drilled into Jed. "Don't you see? *The plans for your accident were already in place.*"

Jed felt Megan's hand on his elbow. He turned and looked down at her.

"Was it an emergency call that night at Cyrus Gibbons's?"

Jed thought back to the night. He had stitched Cyrus's mare up. She'd run into some machinery that Cyrus said had been left by a careless hand in the middle of the pasture, puncturing her chest, ripping it clean away from the sternum.

It couldn't possibly have been planned; for if it were, that meant . . .

Jed closed his eyes, trying to shut out the images those thoughts gave rise to.

"Show him some of the others," Megan said. Despite her gentle demeanor, and soulful eyes, Jed sensed a steely determination emanating from her, aimed squarely at Jed.

K.C. nodded.

The name Red Dawn appeared frequently as K.C. scrolled down the column, scrutinizing the dates. The blank subject lines gave away nothing. Finally, he stopped and clicked on one dated just days earlier.

Intercept of cattle a go.

There it was, in plain print. Nothing vague about it.

Cyrus Gibbons had planned the intercept of Jed's cattle. He was informing someone—this Red Dawn—of that fact.

Even Jed could not deny it.

K.C. and Megan had been studying Jed for his reaction.

"Still worried about invading this guy's privacy?" K.C. asked, a cocky note of triumph in his voice.

It was difficult for Jed to pry his eyes off the computer screen, but an urgency surged through him.

"I have to warn Rebecca," he said. "She thinks Cyrus is a friend. He's backing her bid to become president of the Cattlemen's Association. She could be in danger."

K.C. looked over his shoulder at Megan.

"Now?"

Megan nodded.

"Yes."

"What?" Jed said, his voice filling with anger. He'd had enough and didn't want to hear more.

K.C. changed screens, clicking from "mail sent," to "mail received."

When the screen again filled with messages received by Cyrus Gibbons, he scrolled to one *from* Red Dawn.

Shooting one last glance Jed's way, he clicked.

Jed says there's no way that Dusty Harrison is expanding his cattle operation. He only ordered his standard # of vaccines: 100.
P.S. Why would he need Horse Butte?

Jed felt the hair on his neck bristle against his flannel shirt as he leaned forward to read the time and date of the message.

"This one was sent two days before Dusty Harrison died," Megan said solemnly.

Jed had stayed at Rebecca's two nights before his death. He remembered telling her that, accusing her. That had been the night she'd quizzed him about Dusty.

It all came rushing back to him now.

After seeing the *Gazette* with news of Dusty's death, he'd gone to Rebecca's house and confronted her.

He remembered forcing her to look at the paper and telling her that Dusty was dead.

Rebecca had gasped, and asked when it happened.

"Yesterday," he'd answered. "Two days after you were asking me about him."

Now, with Megan and K.C. studying him, and Pie whimpering at his side, Jed's world began to spin.

He'd spent that night with Rebecca. She must have waited

for him to fall asleep, then sneaked downstairs to e-mail Cyrus about what she'd learned from Jed.

Red Dawn was Rebecca.

"THIS CAN'T BE," Jed said angrily. "That can't be from Rebecca."

"You asked why we didn't identify ourselves," K.C. said. "The way you're reacting right now is why. We didn't think you'd believe what we'd discovered about your fiancée. We thought any hint of her involvement would turn you away. We thought the best approach would be to send you the warnings, hoping you'd listen."

Megan joined in.

"From the start, we suspected your girlfriend was Red Dawn because of the information she had about you, but we still weren't certain until she sent this e-mail. We knew if we tried to implicate her, you'd probably discount *everything* we told you."

Stepping back, distancing himself from these two messengers of evil, Jed said, "Rebecca wouldn't betray me like this. If she wrote that, she can't understand what she's gotten herself involved in."

"She does understand," K.C. said. "Look, look at this last e-mail Cyrus sent her."

He clicked on the back arrow to return to the "sent" messages, then clicked on an e-mail Gibbons sent the day before to Red Dawn.

You were right about Dusty. Colleen Talks to Sky was behind his application for HB.

"I don't see what this proves," Jed said. "I don't even understand what it means."

Megan took over.

"Dusty Harrison leased the Horse Butte grazing allotment to help us out. The Buffalo Field Campaign's founder, Colleen Talks to Sky, was a friend of his son's. She talked Dusty into applying for the allotment. He was only going to run a token number of cattle on it. He was going to let the buffalo use it instead. Cyrus figured that out, partly from what your fiancée told him about Dusty not having plans to expand his operation. He had enough good pasture for a hundred cattle. He didn't need Horse Butte. We believe that's why Dusty was killed."

"You think Dusty was murdered?"

"Yes."

"Now you're trying to tell me Rebecca's involved with murder?"

As angry as he wanted to be at these two for the insinuations about Rebecca, a nagging memory of his own reaction the day he'd read about Dusty's death made him think twice.

He'd never forget her response when he'd confronted her.

She'd told him he'd gone over the deep edge. That he needed help.

Jed had believed her denial that day.

He had to continue to believe it now. To do otherwise was unthinkable, not even an option.

Megan appeared to sense the struggle taking place in his mind.

"Why would Cyrus send her that kind of e-mail if she wasn't involved?" she asked calmly.

"I don't know, but there has to be an explanation. I'll talk to her. Clear this up."

"No," K.C. said sharply. "You can't tell her you know."

"What do you mean?"

"If you tell her what you've learned," Megan replied, "and how you learned it, we'll lose our only way to keep track of what's going on."

"How the hell have you managed to get into Cyrus's e-mails in the first place?"

Megan looked K.C.'s way.

"I used to work with Cyrus," K.C. said.

"You worked on Cyrus's ranch?"

"Hard to believe, eh?" K.C. replied, finally grinning. "I wasn't always a hippie activist. I worked on half a dozen cattle ranches during high school and college. In college I majored in wildlife biology. I even went to grad school in range science. I wanted to work with the government, as a range conservationist. In other words, I wasn't born hostile to ranching. That came about gradually. I met Cyrus during school, when I did an internship with the Montana Cattlemen's Association. Cyrus was president then. It was during that time that I began changing. I was taking some environmental study courses at the U and for the first time, I was seeing the damage the livestock industry does to our environment. I realized I was working on the wrong side of the fence. Before I quit the association, I managed to get a hold of Cyrus's password. I had the feeling it would come in handy." He chuckled. "Cyrus is one of those old farts who can barely peck out an e-mail. It's never occurred to him to change his password. He figured once he sent an e-mail out into cyberspace, all trace of it vanishes.

"If you tell Rebecca we're reading Cyrus's e-mails, he'll finally wise up. We won't stand a chance of finding out what they're up to."

"You're suggesting that I pretend none of this ever happened?" Jed replied, incredulous.

"Exactly. It's the only way, Dr. McCane. Can't you see? As much as we've learned from monitoring Cyrus's e-mails, we still don't know enough or have enough evidence to stop them. We still don't have the big picture. If you disclose what we've shared with you tonight to your fiancée, our information pipeline will close and we'll have no way to stop them."

"Stop them from *what*?"

"From sacrificing this country's last truly wild, free-roaming bison for a hopeless cause."

"A hopeless cause?" Jed parroted in disbelief. "That's what you think ranching is?"

Making no attempt to hide his disgust, K.C. shook his head in amusement.

"You people just can't face fucking reality, can you? Ranching isn't sustainable. It's not only destroying the ecosystem in the West, but ranching as you and your clients know it just isn't commercially viable any more. It's a lose-lose proposition for everyone and everything—the ranchers, the animals, the land, and the rest of the people in this country. Cyrus knows that. He saw it up close as president of the Cattlemen's Association. And like all the other cattle-industry lobbyists, in his desperation, he's striking out at the one thing he can strike out at. Bison. They symbolize everything these people fear most: environmentalists, losing the dispro-portionate influence they've always held on the West and its resources—resources they've squandered. The sense of enti-tlement people like Cyrus feel makes me sick. Ranchers have such a romanticized image of themselves that they think we should all fucking bow down and roll over while they rape this land.

"For what? A fucking slab of meat? Hell, if we have to have meat, raise the cattle back East, or in the Midwest. Did you know it takes seventy-three times as much land to raise a cow in Montana than it does in Iowa? Or that private lands in Maryland alone produce as much beef as Montana's BLM and Forest Service lands combined? Ranching in the West makes no sense. And the fear that the rest of the country's going to get wise to that fact has ranchers scared shitless, and striking out at the easiest targets. The buffalo. Well, we don't have the big money or the power that the cattle indus-try does. We don't have powerful lobbyists to look out for the bison's interests. And that's why from time to time we have to play a little dirty. That's why we're asking you not to betray the confidence we've placed in you by showing you these e-mails."

"Breaking the law isn't just playing a little dirty," Jed replied.

This infuriated Megan even more than K.C., who simply grinned and shook his head.

"How can you even compare what we've done—hack into Cyrus's e-mails—with the loss of your assistant's life?" she said. "And Dusty's? With sabotaging honest, valuable research that could benefit the entire world, and not just cattle country?

"You say you don't understand us, well, I don't understand you. I don't understand a loyalty to a fiancée, or clients, or a way of life whose means of dealing with anything that gets in its way is to destroy it. If you condone that, then go ahead and leave, Dr. McCane. You're not the man we hoped you'd turn out to be."

Every instinct Jed had ever had, every loyalty he'd forged, was now being turned upside down.

"I intend to find who's behind Clancy's death. And if Dusty was actually murdered, I'll do everything in my power to see that his murderer is punished. But I refuse to believe that Cyrus Gibbons is a murderer. And I know—with absolute, hundred-percent certainty—that Rebecca isn't capable of having anything to do with what happened to Clancy or to Dusty."

"Make no mistake about it," K.C. shot back angrily, "Cyrus Gibbons is capable of killing. And he's not acting alone."

Jed reached out and grabbed him by the collar, choking off his breath.

"I told you, Rebecca has nothing to do with this. Nothing. Do you hear?"

Megan squeezed in between the two, pushing Jed away, fire in her eyes.

"Like it or not, Rebecca's involved. You can choose to remain in denial about her, or open your eyes before everything you work for, everything you stand for, is destroyed. Before more innocent people die.

"But it's not just your girlfriend. We know there's someone else involved. His e-mail name is Bronco. And we think he may be the mastermind of this whole thing."

Jed instantly released his grip on K.C.'s shirt upon hearing the possibility someone else, someone besides his Rebecca, could be behind all this evidence these two had piled up. He stepped back, his chest heaving emotionally with each breath.

"Bronco?"

"Yes."

"He's a rancher?"

"We don't know. He's very clever. He e-mails Cyrus too. It seems all communication goes through Cyrus. Bronco's extremely cautious about what he says. We think he's in a position of power, but we don't know what that position is, or who he is. That's what we have to find out. What we have now would get us nowhere, accomplish nothing, prove nothing, other than making us look like a bunch of lawless radicals who hack into private e-mails. We need time. We have to let them continue to feel they've not been discovered."

Jed contemplated this new information.

He wanted to believe these two—both Megan and K.C.—had smoked a little too much weed. That they were nothing more than conspiracy paranoid fanatics.

But two people had died. And the yellow truck—that had been no accident.

And despite his disbelief that any of this could have to do with Cyrus Gibbons, deep in his heart, Jed could not completely disregard what Megan and K.C. had just told him.

Jed had argued with Cyrus and other ranchers many a time about brucellosis. He'd explained to them the fact that the elk that migrated out of the park, most of whom carried brucellosis, presented more of a threat of transmission than the buffalo. It had been one of his primary reasons for coming up with the idea for his vaccine—not because of the buffalo, but because of the elk. He'd always felt that if there were any legitimate threat to the cattle from brucellosis, it rested with the elk. Not the bison.

Elk moved freely, traveling through the same pasture the cattle grazed. Giving birth there.

Of course, elk would never be subject to slaughter. Next to the ranching lobbyists, the hunting and guiding lobbyists ruled, exerting too much power in the legislature to allow any serious consideration of dealing with elk the way bison had been dealt with.

As a veterinarian, Jed's interest was in protecting the cattle. An aerosolized vaccine, one that could be used for masses of elk, cattle, and wild bison, would offer just that protection.

Throughout the recent series of warnings followed by tragic events, Jed had never understood how anyone could feel threatened by such a vaccine.

K.C. and Megan had now given him an explanation.

But Jed refused to believe it. For, just as believing that Rebecca could be involved would destroy him, to believe this theory about the ranchers, whom Jed served and considered "his" people, would shake the foundation upon which his world had been built.

It might just drive him over the edge.

Still, he had to make some sense of what these two had shown him. The e-mails, the warnings that had proven all too prophetic. If Megan was right, he had to do everything in his power to help stop the forces at work, before someone else died.

K.C. had lowered himself to the stool, and now sat staring

at the floor. He'd clearly decided that Jed had turned out to be another dead end. One big disappointment.

But Megan's warm, dark eyes told another story. Without saying a word, Jed could feel her pleading with him. He could see she still held out hope that he'd come around. That he might be able to make a difference.

Unable to withstand her gaze, Jed turned toward the door.

"I'm going to Rebecca's right now. I'm going to get some answers."

THE SOUND OF Rebecca's voice led him to the library. The door stood open, and Jed found himself walking softly, staying on the colorful Navajo rug that ran the length of the hardwood-floored hallway.

As he approached the open door, he heard her say, "I know. We have to make certain none of this backfires . . ."

Rebecca looked up. She drew back at the sight of Jed standing there, in the doorway.

"Jed."

"We need to talk," he said. "Now."

She placed her hand over the phone's mouthpiece, clearly annoyed.

"I'm on an important call."

"Is it Cyrus?" Jed asked. It was more an accusation than a question.

"No," Rebecca replied quickly. "It's Virginia. It's about Chelsea. There's a problem. It's important, Jed." The expression in her eyes suddenly shifted from angry to concerned. Perhaps, Jed sensed, even frightened. "What is it, Jed? What's wrong?"

"I'll be waiting outside," he answered. "On the porch."

He turned and strolled stiffly out of the room. As he opened the front door, he heard the library door close softly behind him.

Outside, he settled on the wooden stairs leading to the porch, rehearsing what he'd say. He couldn't attack right off the bat. He knew Rebecca too well for that. She'd clam up like a pit bull seized with lockjaw. No, he'd just ask her calmly what her relationship with Cyrus Gibbons was about. Jed knew—hell, he felt a hundred percent certain—that she'd be able to give some reasonable explanation for the e-mails. Those people from the Buffalo Field Campaign would just have to find another way to do their spying. Cyrus was using Rebecca. She had no idea how the information she'd been supplying him was being utilized. Jed had to warn her, even at the risk that she would tell Cyrus and he'd change passwords and cut off the flow of information to Megan and K.C.

Jed felt incredibly troubled by the e-mails he'd read. He didn't want to believe Megan and K.C.'s interpretation, but as he'd driven to Rebecca's, he'd been hard-pressed to come up with any other. Cyrus was up to something. Slowly, reluctantly, he'd come to accept the possibility that Cyrus had, indeed, staged Jed's "accident." It even appeared Cyrus might be involved in Dusty Harrison's death, and Jed's accident on Beartooth Pass. But Rebecca couldn't possibly know any of that. She could not know that Cyrus was that desperate, that twisted in his dedication to a way of life.

Rebecca would tell Jed the truth—she had never lied to him—and together, they'd work through this awful situation.

If only that damn phone call would end. Typical of Rebecca, being such a good friend to her old college roommate.

Calmer now, certain he and Rebecca would get to the bottom of this, Jed decided to go into the kitchen and see if there was any coffee brewing. Rebecca kept a pot going most the day. He felt exhausted, physically and emotionally. He hadn't slept since the night before last, before he'd flown to Casper. He needed caffeine.

Heading down the hall, he glanced at the library door. Still closed.

In the kitchen, a red light glowed on the coffeemaker. An inch or two of coffee remained in the pot. He poured it, then turned to head back outside.

The phone on the counter caught his eye. He paused, then walked over to it.

He looked at the darkened caller ID screen. Beneath the screen, he saw two arrows. One pointing up, one down.

Jed pressed the arrow pointing down. The screen immediately lit up.

406–683–4432

The call had come in at 8:15 A.M. He glanced at his watch. Just five minutes earlier.

The 406 area code. Local. Not Seattle, where Virginia lived.

Beneath the number, a name.

CYRUS GIBBONS.

REBECCA LOWERED HERSELF next to Jed on the front step.

"Good," she said, looking much more friendly than she had minutes earlier, when he'd shown up at her library door. "You found the coffee."

As he sat waiting for her, debating how to approach this confrontation, Jed had decided to play it cool, but now, instead, he turned to her and blurted out, "Did you call Virginia? Or she call you?"

Rebecca's laugh infuriated him.

"What an odd question. She called *me,* silly. I told you, she's having a terrible time with Chelsea."

After the shock of seeing Cyrus's name on caller ID, Jed had scrolled down, to the next calls. All had been local numbers. He'd counted six from Cyrus, all within the past three days. No calls that morning, or the day before, from the Seattle area.

But now, studying his fiancée's face, Jed couldn't help

grasping at straws. Rebecca had call waiting. Maybe Cyrus had called first, and she'd been on the phone with him when Virginia called. The Seattle number wouldn't necessarily show up on her caller ID.

Yes, that was it. All Rebecca had to do was tell Jed that Cyrus had, indeed, called, and he would have an explanation that worked for him. He'd *make* it work. He'd leave it at that.

He drew in a sharp, short breath.

"Have you talked to Cyrus Gibbons lately?"

The laughter again, weaker, and this time, a nervousness to it.

"No," she said. "What is this third degree you're giving me?"

Jed stared at her. She was a vision, hair cascading wildly down her back—she wore a long-sleeved denim shirt and lots of turquoise that contrasted strikingly with her blond locks—and framing a face so angelic it broke his heart.

Her eyes locked with his, questioning him. Assuring him?

How many times had he looked into those eyes? He'd seen that very same look in them, a look he'd always associated with love, excitement. Mutual trust.

Had he been that wrong? That big a fool?

He had to give her one last chance.

"You're telling me that you haven't even talked to Cyrus recently?"

He literally tried to will her to tell him that Cyrus had called, then follow up with a confession that Cyrus had been pumping her for information, but that she had no idea—none whatsoever—what he had used that information for.

Come clean with me, Rebecca. Don't let them be right.

A flash of something like fear flickered in Rebecca's eyes. An almost imperceptible rigidity entered her slender frame.

Still, the fact that she did not avert her eyes from his gave Jed hope.

His entire future—and also his heart—rode on her answer.

"I haven't talked to Cyrus in a week or two," she said.

As if she sensed she'd flunked some essential test, Rebecca's voice rose as she asked, "Why?"

Everything—any chance the two of them had to salvage a future together—hinged on how Jed answered. On whether he trusted her with the truth—that he'd read the e-mails she'd sent Cyrus, and seen Cyrus's number on her caller ID.

Only by trusting Rebecca enough to give her the chance to explain would it be possible for them to move past this moment.

Jed forced himself to smile and reached for her hand. He lifted it to his lips and kissed it, hoping the gesture appeared light, and affectionate.

"Because I've been thinking a lot about your running for president of the Cattlemen's Association," he said. "And I want you to know I support you. I think you'd make a fantastic president. That's why."

He could almost see a river of relief wash through her, and he suddenly found himself admiring her on an entirely new level. He'd never known what an accomplished actress she was.

She laughed again, this time gaily.

"That's what you wanted to talk to me about?"

"Yes," he said. "It is."

He flashed involuntarily on the last time they'd made love. On how she'd told him he was fantastic in bed.

Was that an act, as well?

Radiating a sense of relief that rose to the level of exhilaration, Rebecca threw her arms around him.

"You are such a dear, dear man," she said gaily. She kissed his neck, then nuzzled him. He could feel her hot breath on the skin below his ear, and then, just the faintest moisture, from the tip of her tongue, teasing him.

He had to fight to keep from drawing back in revulsion.

"And such an amazing lover," she whispered in his ear.

EIGHTEEN

"HELLO, HOUDINI," MEGAN said softly, though she knew no one—and certainly not her beloved Houdini—heard.

The snow had just started, earlier that day. A late-summer snow, nothing that would stay for long. It dropped—floated, really—in large, bushy flakes, taking its time and meandering in whimsical, unpredictable patterns before settling lightly on the grass. A layer of green and parched brown still peeked through, and it was this that the bison—hundreds of them—rooted for. Clustered in groups of five or six, their noses to the ground, they grazed determinedly, knowing what lay ahead.

She knew many of them by name.

Houdini was easy. His size alone set him apart, his coat—darker and more ragged than the others'—and the massive hump over his neck and shoulders, which told of harsh winters spent digging through chest-high snow for food to survive. A thick coat of mud covered his hind end, protection against biting insects.

As she stood perched high on a flat rock at the top of the rocky knoll, a sudden wind caused Megan's body to tense in a shiver. She placed the binoculars on the rock beside her and pulled the zipper of her Polarfleece jacket all the way up to her chin. As she did so, movement in her peripheral vision turned her attention to the west.

A lone man strode across the lower meadow, headed in her direction. Megan picked the glasses back up and watched him cross the open expanse. He displayed no concern, no fear of the bison grazing less than a hundred yards away.

His size, and strong, purposeful stride, gave his identity away before she could zoom in on his face.

Megan hadn't expected to see him again this soon. In fact, after he'd left during the night, she and K.C. speculated that they'd never see him again.

"Dr. McCane," she called out when he'd come within earshot of her perch.

He waved and began picking his way, nimbly climbing the rocky base of the knoll.

Megan watched him. Why was he here? Had he confronted his fiancée, and now come to tell her that she and K.C. had been wrong? Megan had seen her, Rebecca Nichols, in town on several occasions. She could understand how a woman like that could wrap a man around her finger, make him believe just about anything she wanted. She'd also seen enough of the e-mails to know that Rebecca Nichols had no conscience, no soul. Only ambition and greed.

How had she responded to Jed McCane's confrontation? Had she managed to come up with an explanation that got her off the hook? If so, Dr. McCane had probably come to chew Megan out, set her straight.

When his head suddenly appeared over the crest, Megan rose to her feet. A cold breeze—or perhaps her nerves—set her to shivering again as she stood waiting for him to reach her.

Like Megan, he was dressed in fleece—a vest, with a veterinary symbol embroidered on its left chest. He towered over her.

"Hello," he said.

"How did you find me?"

"I went back to your office. K.C. told me he thought you'd be here. He told me where to look for your car, by the trail-head."

An awkward silence between them followed.

McCane's eyes swept the expanse below and around them. She could see by his expression that the spectacular view was not lost on him.

He spotted the binoculars, which Megan had left behind her on the rock.

"Mind if I take a look?"

"Of course not."

He dropped to a half-kneeling position, right knee up, with his elbow steadied on it.

She watched as he adjusted the focus. She saw him sweep the field of vision over the herd and then stop. He refo-cused. She could see he'd picked up the huge, black form— at least a third larger than all the others—at the center of the herd.

"That's Houdini," she said.

He lifted his eyes and studied her over the binoculars. "You know them by name?"

She smiled. "Not all of them. But a lot of them. Houdini's easy. I knew you'd look for him first. Everyone does."

She pointed over the left shoulder of the majestic beast.

"See that female next to him? That's Angel. She's got a dark patch across her left rump. And she's always by Hou-dini's side."

Jed swept the binoculars to the female.

After several seconds watching her, he said, "She's weak."

"What?"

Megan's voice caught. She reached for the binoculars, then trained them on the female bison grazing peacefully at Houdini's side.

"See the way she's moving," Jed said. "It's subtle, but it's there. She's weak in her hind end."

"I've seen it," Megan said. "What is it?"

Jed shook his head. "Could be anything. Parasites. An injury."

"Will she be okay?"

"I couldn't tell you that. I'd have to examine her. Up close. How old is she?"

"She had a calf last year. I doubt she's older than five or six."

"I think your pal Houdini's looking out for her."

"I wouldn't be surprised. Houdini saved her life last year."

Jed turned to look at her. "What happened?"

"It was late spring and she'd taken her baby out of the park to find food. They were grazing at Horse Butte. Houdini sensed the DOL was nearby. He always knows. He tried to block her from leaving the park, but her maternal instinct was to feed her baby.

"DOL agents were just waiting inside the treeline, sitting there on their motorcycles and all-terrain vehicles. They idle there quietly, hidden, then when the bison step out of the park, they charge them. The ATVs are so loud and fast, just seeing or hearing them terrifies the animals. The agents got Angel and her baby separated from the other bison and began hazing them, running them one way, then the other, just to wear them out. They can actually kill a buffalo that way, did you know that? Just run him or her until they drop, fall down and die. Sometimes, before they can die, the agents will get off their ATVs and just surround them, kicking them, or using sticks to beat them. That's what they do. Did you know that?"

Megan looked over at Jed McCane, but she could not read his expression.

"No," he said. "I didn't know."

"If people like you don't know, don't care enough to make it their business, why would anyone?"

Jed sighed. "Can we call a truce? I didn't come out here to fight with you."

This response disarmed her.

One of her duties with the Buffalo Field Campaign was to spend hours each week "tabling" at Tower Falls, inside the park, where people tended to heap abuse on her with amazing regularity. She'd learned not to respond, not to shoot back. It only set back their cause. Yet here she was, blowing up at Jed McCane. There was something about the man . . . or perhaps it was the sudden worry he'd instilled in her for Angel.

"I'm sorry," she said.

He eyed her. "I'm not the enemy, you know."

She studied him, wondering. Feeling just the tiniest bit sorry for him.

"I know we've dropped a lot of heavy stuff on you," she said. She suddenly found herself wondering how his confrontation with his fiancée had gone. "I'm sure you wish you'd never laid eyes on us."

"Hardly." Jed's laughter had a bittersweet quality to it. "You saved my life."

"Wait and see," Megan said softly, turning back to look at the bison.

Jed's eyes followed hers. To Houdini. The big animal took several steps forward. True to Megan's prediction, Angel followed alongside.

"You were telling me that Houdini saved Angel."

Megan nodded her head.

"That's right. He was watching from inside the trees. Several of us from the campaign were out here, trying to stop the agents—what they were doing wasn't even remotely related to the only thing they were legally entitled to do, which was capture the animals for testing. But we were on foot, and they just laughed at us, yelled dirty things at us, like they always do. We could see Angel's baby was about to drop, and Angel wasn't far behind.

"Well, Houdini charged out of the treeline. The agents all want him so bad 'cause he's never once been captured, and he's led the others back into the treeline many times, to save them. He knows that they want him. He knew that they'd give up on Angel if they thought they could trap him."

She shook her head, images of that day replaying themselves in her mind.

"He ran straight across the middle of the open field. The agents went after him right away, and that gave Angel and her baby a chance to make it to the trees."

"What happened to Houdini?"

Megan laughed.

"He ran straight for us. When they started hazing Angel, we radioed for backup and by now there were maybe thirty of us—several teams had been nearby, doing inventory on the herd. Houdini knows us. He knew we'd try to protect him.

"He walked right up to us, then stopped, and we all formed a circle around him. We just kept moving that circle toward the treeline. The ATVs can't go more than a few feet into the woods, it's too thick. We formed this human shield around him, and moved him about three hundred yards."

"You mean to tell me the DOL agents didn't try to stop you? They can arrest you, can't they?"

Megan smiled broadly. "Oh, they could've arrested us all right, if they wanted to."

"They didn't want to?"

"They wanted to, they wanted to so badly it made them crazy. But none of them was willing to touch us."

"They won't touch you? Not even to arrest you?"

"We'd all covered ourselves with blood. We were drenched in it. It's an idea we'd just come up with, and it worked beautifully. Our roving team had just started carrying buckets of blood with it. We tell the agents it's elk blood. Well, you know the incidence of brucellosis in elk. They won't go near us if they think they'll get exposed."

Megan saw the same look in McCane's eyes that she'd seen in hundreds of others. That she—all the Buffalo Field Campaign activists—were crazy. In this case, however, she had to admit it was understandable. After all, an alarming percentage of the elk tested in the area had turned out to be positive for brucellosis.

"You doused yourself with elk blood? That's pretty extreme, isn't it?"

"When your opponents aren't rational, when they play dirty, that's what you have to do."

"In what way does the DOL play dirty?"

"You means besides what I just described?"

"Yes, besides that."

"Well, let's see," Megan replied. "The brucellosis thing. It's all bogus."

"If Montana were to lose its brucellosis-free status, the consequences economically to the cattle industry would be catastrophic."

"But you know as well as I that that's not going to happen. At least not because of the Yellowstone bison. There hasn't been one known case of brucellosis transmission from a wild buffalo to cattle. To start with, for it to happen it would take cattle ingesting the placenta of an infected bison cow, within hours of its calf's birth. The bison are outside the park in late winter and the cattle don't get moved there until summer. It's just not going to happen. And bison are meticulous about cleaning up the afterbirth."

At first she thought this indisputable fact had hit home with Jed, but then he responded, "But it could happen. Theoretically. And you can't blame the DOL for doing everything in its power to protect against it, even if the threat is only theoretical."

"If that's really the DOL's agenda—to protect against brucellosis transmission to cattle—why continue to grant grazing
allotments at Horse Butte, where they know bison graze every
spring? Did you see how quickly they moved Jack Hamlin's
herd on there after Dusty died? Why do you think they did
that? It was hardly worth moving them there this late in the
year. And how did Hamlin win that allotment in the first place?
There were other applicants, better qualified applicants."

"Like the Cheyenne?"

"Yes. The Cheyenne have run cattle for years. Jack Hamlin moved here from California three years ago. He owned a
chain of restaurants there. You tell me how someone like
him gets chosen over the tribe."

Jed shook his head, and mumbled, "I don't have any answers. I don't know why that Horse Butte allotment's so
damn important to everybody. Other than the fact that everybody's worried about brucellosis."

Megan let out a half-laugh, half-sigh of exasperation.

"This isn't about minimizing the risk of transmission
from bison to cattle. If it were, they'd find a better way to do
it than the senseless slaughter of animals who test positive
on a test that's known for false positives."

She sensed a surprise in McCane at her knowledge about
brucellosis.

"Such as?"

"Okay," she said, "aside from keeping Horse Butte empty,
how about the InterTribal Council's offer to move any animals that test positive to the reservation? Why is it that
everyone refuses to consider that as an option?"

"If those bison are truly carriers, they're a threat. Regardless of where they are."

"A threat to what? Or to be more accurate, to *whom*? The
council has promised to isolate any animals that test positive
through two full breeding cycles. There's no commingling
of cattle and bison. How can there be any threat? The only

threat we're talking about here is to the DOL's slaughter program, or to the cattlemen's plan to diminish protection for the wild bison to the point they'll no longer survive."

"You really believe that? That that's the goal—exterminating all the buffalo in the park?"

"If that's what it takes to ensure that the bison represent no threat, real or perceived, to the sovereignty of the cattlemen, to the protection of public-lands ranching—yes, I believe it. After all that's happened, how can you not?"

It was a rhetorical question, one she did not expect him to answer.

Dr. McCane was no different than the rest. Someone so part of the system that he could not see the forest for the trees.

She'd dared to hope that with all that had happened—the e-mails they'd shown him, the "accidents" that were no accidents—Dr. McCane might become an ally. She'd sensed something in him that first night they met. A strength of character, a sense of integrity. They desperately needed someone like him, someone on the inside. Someone with know-how, and connections, and credibility, all of which Jed McCane possessed.

But Jed McCane was apparently no different than the others. When he'd left the compound to go and confront his fiancée about what they'd shown him, Rebecca Nichols must have worked her magic on him.

Sometimes it was hard not to lose faith, hard to continue this difficult, uphill battle.

Jed had gone back to studying Houdini.

"You don't really think Houdini did that on purpose," he said finally, "to distract the DOL, do you?"

Megan fixed her gaze on the majestic animal and said, without emotion, "I don't think. I know."

After they'd watched the herd in silence for several minutes, during which the snow stopped and a patch of blue sky appeared overhead, exposing brilliant sun that immediately went to work melting what had been deposited, Jed cleared his throat.

"I was wondering," he said.

Megan simply stared straight ahead. "What?"

"I noticed a barn out there, at your place. You know, the Buffalo People compound."

Brow creased in puzzlement, she turned to study him. "Buffalo Field Campaign," she corrected.

"Sorry, Buffalo Field Campaign."

"Yes, there's an old barn out there. Why?"

Jed finally turned and met her curious eyes. "Because I was wondering what you'd think of me keeping my experimental cattle there," he said.

"I'm not sure I understand."

"Well, it's just that if what you say is true, I can't afford to risk my research being sabotaged again. Someone thinks they just ran my experimental cattle over a cliff on Beartooth Pass. No reason to think they'll stop there."

"You want to do your research from the compound?"

"If it's all right with you."

"You'll tell everyone you gave it up?"

He picked up a small rock, turned it between his fingers, then tossed it like a dart into the open expanse. Megan lost sight of it, but heard it hit below.

"I thought about that the whole ride over here. I don't think she . . . er, *people* . . . will buy that I just gave it up. I think I'll have to make it look like I'm still doing research out of the clinic. I'll have some cattle delivered there, too."

The underlying message was clear. He'd confronted his fiancée and come away convinced of her guilt. He was now, in his own way, offering to join forces with the Buffalo Field Campaign. Even to mislead Rebecca Nichols.

"Well, yes," Megan said, a surge of excitement lifting the cloud of constant worry. "I'm sure that'd be okay,

Dr. McCane. I'll just have to talk to our board, but I can almost promise you what they'll say."

Jed stood, reached out his big hand, and grasped Megan's in it.

"Well, good then," he said. "It's a deal. But please stop calling me Dr. McCane. My name's Jed. And I imagine you'll be seeing plenty of me from now on."

Long ago, as a child, her mother had taught her to listen to her inner truth. To trust her instincts, about people, about situations.

Megan hadn't been wrong about this man after all.

As they trudged back across the meadow side by side and in silence, Megan felt a renewed sense of anticipation, of hope. She glanced back over her shoulder at the majestic animals grazing peacefully behind them. Houdini had managed to get behind Angel, and was now using her rump as a rubbing post for his massive head.

"By the way," she said, "that wasn't real elk blood we doused ourselves with that day."

She glanced sideways. Jed's face registered his surprise.

"It wasn't?"

"No. It was a mixture that one of our people came up with. He works in Hollywood, special effects. It looks just like blood, even has that sticky quality to it. You won't tell anyone, will you?"

The wind had picked up again, along with some light snow, but Megan felt almost certain she heard Jed heave a sigh of relief.

"No," he said. "I won't."

REBECCA LAY THERE, staring at the idle ceiling fan, unable to sleep. Jed had left early in the afternoon, after they'd made love.

For the first time she could recall, their lovemaking had felt forced. She'd even wondered briefly whether Jed had faked his orgasm, but she knew Jed better than that.

Still, something didn't feel quite right. Of course, she could be imagining it. After all, Jed had said all the right things. All the things he always said.

He loved her madly, she knew that.

Still, she also knew that *that*—his love for her—would not be enough. Jed's principles, his squeaky-clean ethics and idealism, along with the purity of his devotion to his job, meant he'd never knowingly agree to the plan she and Cyrus had worked out.

She loved him, too. It wasn't the same way Jed loved her, but she did love him. He'd asked her a million times why; why a woman like Rebecca, coveted by nearly every man within a two-hundred-mile radius, had fallen for such an average guy—someone unremarkable in appearance, who stood no chance to ever have any real power or wealth.

She'd always responded by telling Jed that his modesty prevented him from realizing just how special he was.

She'd known better than to tell him that it was his resemblance to her father that had first drawn her to him, and then bonded them on a path over which neither would have complete control.

The physical resemblance had struck her first.

Jed and Buck Nichols were both big, strong men; men who as far as humanly possible reflected the country they both called home and cherished—majestic, powerful, basic.

And then, each day into their friendship, Rebecca had discovered more than the outward similarities. Like Jed's idealism, his refusal to compromise even the slightest bit when it came to what he believed in. Her father had been that same way. So stubbornly principled that others, invariably less principled, sometimes considered him a pain in the ass. Rebecca saw that Jed stirred the same reactions in people—most adored him but some felt threatened by the impossibly high standards he set.

Ironically, those standards—those same principles which now hovered like a dark storm over their future—had made Rebecca fall in love with Jed.

And then, after they'd become a couple, after over a year of Rebecca's feeling the closest thing to joy she'd felt since her father's death, Jed had come up with the vaccine idea.

She'd known right away—intuitively sensed it the minute he'd come home excitedly talking about his discovery—that it meant trouble. That it would eventually spell the end of their relationship. At least, the relationship that had been real and genuine and passionate. In another sense, it had now made their relationship—at least maintaining it—more important than ever.

All those times that Jed had asked her why she'd fallen in love with him, she'd never once told him the truth.

About her father.

About why she was willing to sacrifice anything, even her genuine love for Jed, to live up to Buck Nichols's dying request.

NINETEEN

HIS KIDNEYS ARE failing. There's really no hope."

The doctor was short, bald, and like too many of his colleagues, disgustingly sure of himself. Rebecca could not place his age. He might have been an old thirty or a young fifty. She did not care which. All she wanted was information, and to have her father sedated, so that he would not try to remove the oxygen mask that was keeping him alive.

It had happened four years ago, almost to the day. The night she'd met this doctor who coolly, correctly, predicted the end of the world as Rebecca knew it.

Over the phone, the doctor—a Dr. Prigo, or Pringle, or, as she later came to think of him, *Dr. Prick*—had been abrupt, irritated at being called into the hospital on a weekend. So irritated he'd taken three hours to show up. But then, once he saw Rebecca, he'd transformed instantly. As soon as he'd walked into the room and spotted her, sitting by her father's bedside, she'd seen a change in his demeanor. It was an all too familiar reaction to her physical appearance, and Rebecca sized him up—despised him—almost immediately.

He'd suggested they go into the critical care lounge for

family members of patients. Once there, he'd even offered her tea, which she declined, and then he'd fixed himself a cup, saying—with an odd and inappropriate smirk—"You don't mind if I have some myself, do you? This may take a while."

And then he'd explained to Rebecca that her father would soon die.

"But I talked to Dr. Simms just yesterday, and he'd said he was still hopeful. That Dad was stable," Rebecca had said, pleading really for validation. "Dr. Simms said Dad's elevated BUN was probably the result of dehydration, plus the blood he'd swallowed the other night, when he got that nosebleed."

How could this cocky son of a bitch, a man who'd never even laid eyes on her father before tonight, be so certain that Buck Nichols was about to die? His regular doctor, an internist named Dr. Simms, had visited him in the hospital every day for the past three weeks. Just the day before, Rebecca had had a talk with Simms that left her feeling hopeful, almost giddy with the thought that her father might soon be discharged—even if only to a rehab facility.

Anything to get him out of this place he'd been so determined to avoid. She knew now why. She knew now that Buck had known that once he went into that hospital, he would not return. He hadn't said it to her, but the vehemence with which he'd protested going there in the first place now made sense to her. Like an old dying moose, Buck had known what lay ahead. And all he wanted was to die at home, at peace. Rebecca, in her insistence, had robbed him of that.

It haunted her, sometimes, in the middle of the night, when she'd awaken in a cold sweat; it made her wonder if she'd go mad over it.

Over the summer, Buck's strength had gradually given out on him, made him so weak that finally, by Labor Day, he couldn't stand. One September morning she'd found him sitting in a chair—the big wing chair in the living room he'd always favored, unable to get out of it.

He admitted to her he'd been sitting there all night, unable to even get up to go to the bathroom.

After a frantic phone call to Dr. Simms, Becca had promised Buck that his visit to the hospital would be short. Dr. Simms just needed to run some tests on him, find out what was sapping his strength. Once he completed the tests, he'd discharge Buck to a rehab facility, where physical therapists would get him back on his feet.

Buck seemed to sense he really had no choice in the matter. He hadn't ever agreed to go to Butte General, but when the ambulance arrived to take him there, he hadn't put up a terrible fight, to Rebecca's great relief.

Nothing had gone as planned.

Less than a week after being hospitalized, Buck contracted pneumonia. Rebecca blamed the hospital for not getting him up often enough. She'd hounded the nurses, telling them that her father needed to be sat up, moved each day. One of them had replied that her father was "a big man," as if size determined the preventive care given the hospital's patients. Rebecca had hired a private nurse to get Buck up each day, but the pneumonia had already set in.

They put Buck on a ventilator. Heavily sedated and now in the critical care unit, he could not speak to Becca, though she talked to him constantly, and several times, his eyes fluttered open.

Two days later, Dr. Simms had sheepishly informed Becca that the tip of the PIC catheter in Buck's arm had become infected. Buck came down with septicemia. System-wide poison coursed through his veins.

Still, with Rebecca by his side night and day, Buck battled for his life, like the warrior he'd always been.

He seemed to be winning—they'd actually removed him from the ventilator and removed him from critical care— when the next blow struck.

Buck's kidneys started shutting down.

For days, Becca hovered over the shoulders of nurses and doctors—by now, Buck had four of them: the respiratory guy, the blood man, the neurologist, and Dr. Simms—monitoring their every move, checking on every piece of data entered in Buck's chart. Trusting no one.

Just the day before, it appeared that Buck had turned the corner. His kidney readings hadn't improved, but at least they'd held steady. But his lungs had cleared, and his blood pressure and heart rate had stabilized.

And then, early that afternoon, Buck's always sharp mind grew foggy, confused. Becca became disturbed when he made some comments that didn't make sense. Refusing to lose hope, she attributed it to his being tired. Ever since being admitted, he'd complained constantly that with all the poking and prodding, turning and cleaning, he never got to sleep.

But late that day, Becca had looked up from a book she was reading—just in time to see Buck remove his oxygen mask.

"Dad, no," she'd cried, jumping to her feet and replacing the mask over his mouth and nose. "You need that. You have to leave it be."

Buck pushed it away, shaking his head.

"No more," he said. It came out as a croak—the result of having the endotracheal tube down his throat while he'd been on the ventilator. "No more."

"No, Dad," Rebecca said, tears filling her eyes, "you don't mean that. Go to sleep. Get some rest. You're getting better, Dad. I'll take you home soon."

He'd closed his eyes, and given in to the mask again.

And then, just as Rebecca's heart began to calm down, just as she reminded herself that her father was simply tired, simply weary of all the pain and stress, his eyes fluttered open again, and he said, "I'm never going home."

After he'd fallen into a deep sleep, a frantic Rebecca had gone searching for the nurse.

"I want to see Dr. Simms. *Now*."

But within minutes, the nurse reported to Rebecca that Dr. Simms was out of town. An associate had been called instead. Dr. Prigo.

Now Prigo tapped on the thick file lying in front of him on the table.

"The BUN doesn't tell the whole story. Your father's creatinine readings show his kidneys are operating at about one-quarter of their normal capacity. If they continue to fail at this rate, you've got a big decision to make. Whether or not to put him on dialysis, which, of course, has its own problems."

Dialysis.

Rebecca's head spun. Every day in the hospital had brought a new nightmare. Every decision she'd made—from insisting her father go to the hospital in the first place, to her choice of Butte instead of Billings—now haunted her, made her feel as if she, in some indirect way, had been the instrument of his decline.

"What problems?" she said, willing herself to remain calm.

"Your father's blood pressure is down to eighty over fifty. If it stays that low, he won't be able to handle dialysis."

"What can we do then?"

"Let him die in peace," he replied. His mistake was adding, "Which is obviously what he wants."

It felt to Rebecca as if the blood in her body had suddenly doubled in volume, all of it rushing to her head at once. She glared at Prigo.

"How dare you act like you know what my father wants?"

The doctor pulled back, clearly startled at the viciousness in the voice of such a beautiful creature.

"He's been pulling his oxygen mask off all day, hasn't he? Isn't that why you had the nurses call me in?"

"He doesn't know what he's doing."

"The nurse tells me he's been saying he wants to die for several days now."

"He's in too much pain to understand what he's saying."

The look this remark spawned on the doctor's face was so condescending and smug that Rebecca wanted to backhand it off.

"My experience has been," Dr. Prigo said, "that when someone in your father's condition, and his age, says he wants to die, he means it. It usually means they know—even before their vitals or blood work tell us—that the end is near."

Rebecca grabbed the edge of the Formica table. Held on for dear life.

Something began happening to her. A heart attack? Her chest hammered erratically under her light sweater. She felt on the verge of passing out.

Maybe she would die along with her father.

As the doctor continued his cavalier discussion of the fate of the only person in the world who meant a goddamn thing to her, Rebecca frantically assessed her options. Try to stand up and excuse herself—walk away—before she fainted? Or sit there and hope the feeling would pass?

She had an animalistic need to escape the situation, to run from this grim prognosis, for she felt—acutely, instinctively—that it threatened her very survival.

Only her anger saved her. Allowed her to overcome what she would later recognize as a panic attack. The first of many to come, which to this day, four years later, still haunted her.

"My father came in here just needing some help to walk," she said, her voice shaking with a primordial fear. "In three weeks, look what you've reduced him to."

She began shaking her finger at him, like the Catholic nuns did to her in grade school when they found the dirty words she carved into her desk.

"Don't you sit there and tell me that he's going to die now.

You're the ones who put him in critical condition. *You save him.* Do you hear?"

She hadn't realized she was standing, or shouting, until the look on the doctor's face registered.

Prigo's show had backfired, and now that he realized that, he looked literally scared to death, just waiting to bolt.

"Do you hear me?" Rebecca screamed, oblivious to the security guard who had stepped inside the room to check out the commotion.

"Save my father."

SHE EXPERIENCED HER grief alone.

Her older brother had died the way too many grown cowboys did. A hunting accident that left his wife, Ann, a widow at the age of twenty-four.

Her mother had run off with a ranch hand shortly after Jimmy's death, leaving Rebecca and Buck Nichols alone. Buck had always been the center of Rebecca's universe, but at the age of seventeen, with the rest of the family gone, her devotion to her father became all-consuming.

Her rebellious teenage days gone, he became her hero, her rock. Her motivation for everything good she did.

Problem was, the not-so-good things Rebecca had the tendency—no, it was more than a tendency, it almost rose to the level of a need—to get into. She'd managed to keep a lot of that side of herself hidden from Buck. She'd even tried to stifle it, kill it, beat it into submission. After all, nothing was more important to Rebecca than pleasing the giant of a man, the giant of a local legend, that was her father.

For as far as Rebecca was concerned, Buck stood for everything good about ranching, and the West. The life he had built for Rebecca and, before they went their separate ways, her brother and mother, was one of hard work, but tremendous satisfaction. And pride. Buck Nichols took pride in everything he did. There were no moral shortcuts for Buck—or for anyone else when they were around him. He lived by a code of ethics and integrity that Rebecca could never live up to. She knew that even as a little girl. Buck would give her chores to do and she'd lie about whether she'd done them. The one time he found out about it, she wanted to die. Right then and there, she vowed that she'd be more careful. She might not be able to live up to Buck's standards, but from that point on, she vowed to at least be more conscientious in covering for her transgressions.

There was one aspect of his daughter, however, in which Buck would never be disappointed, and that was her love for the Double Jump. While other ranchers struggled to understand why their children fled Montana in droves, forsaking family-operated businesses that went back generations, Buck Nichols didn't have that problem.

No, his Rebecca cherished what ranching meant just about as much as Buck himself. It made Buck proud. Rebecca half-suspected this explained why Buck turned a blind eye to her other shortcomings—his gratitude, his unqualified trust in the fact that Rebecca would carry on the Double Jump, come hell or high water. That Rebecca would devote herself to their way of life with the same dedication and passion her father had.

When her brother was still alive, Rebecca used to resent him for his position as undisputed heir to the Double Jump. She loved Jimmy, despite the awful wife he chose, and she grieved him when he died, but having Buck then turn his attention—his tutoring, his confidence—to Rebecca had been a little like the transformation of a little mutt she'd had as a child. Rocky. She'd picked the broken, frightened, and mangy Border collie out at the Humane Society in Butte.

When she got him home, and groomed, and loved, Rocky had blossomed into a sleek, athletic animal, the best and most tireless herder the Double Jump ever had. Buck Nichols loved to show Rocky's skills off to his rancher friends.

"Look at the little son of a bitch," he'd say, laughing, as the streak of black-and-white fur effortlessly rounded up animals fifty times his size and weight, dodging flying horse hooves in the process. "Never seen anything like it."

Buck's faith in Rebecca, the opportunity to work side by side, to plan for the Double Jump's future, did the same thing for the once-rebellious Rebecca. Together they rode the fence lines, inspected cattle, stayed up all night bottle-feeding orphaned calves. Every minute of that time was spent with Buck infusing Rebecca with his love, his knowledge, and his determination that the ranching lifestyle be protected. For ranching was akin to a religion to Buck. A noble way of life that he saw threatened by corporate conglomerates, environmentalists, and rich Californians looking for a new game to play, a new hobby to give meaning to their empty lives and buy the nobility that no other profession offered in today's world. Buck was determined, if not to stop them, then to at least pave a future where family-owned ranches, like the Double Jump, would remain viable.

That became the focus of Buck's tenure as president of the Cattlemen's Association—preserving a way of life.

And now the man who fought so hard to save a way of life that was all Rebecca had ever known was dying, right before his adoring daughter's eyes.

Rebecca would not allow it. On that last day, she'd left Buck's side briefly, headed down to the hospital cafeteria with the ranch foreman, who'd driven to Butte to discuss some ranch problems with her.

A nurse came running in, telling her Buck's blood pressure had dropped.

They were losing him.

Rushing back to his bedside in the hospital's critical care unit, Rebecca negotiated her hands under and around the tubes coming and going from his mouth and nostrils and cupped either side of her father's gaunt face.

"You can't go, Dad," she'd said, tears running down her cheeks. "You can't leave me."

Buck's eyes opened.

At first she didn't think he saw her, but then the pupils constricted, and fixed on his daughter.

"I want to," he whispered. "Let me."

A sob escaped Rebecca's throat. "I can't make it without you."

He spoke slowly, using all the strength that remained in that poor, ravaged body.

"You can do it," he whispered. "I'll be with you."

"No, Dad, no. Please."

"I'll be watching. Show me. Show them all."

Rebecca's sobs rose, blending with the hum of machinery pumping drugs and oxygen, removing urine and fluids, from his body. The sound drifted out into the nurse's station.

"Carry on the fight," Buck said. "For me."

She held his face, kissed him, tears streaking down her face. Behind her, a chaplain slid quietly into the room.

"Will you?" Buck whispered again.

"Yes, Dad," she said, locking eyes with him. "I will."

The tubes made it difficult for Buck to smile, but Rebecca swore he did.

And then Buck Nichols closed his eyes.

And took his final breath.

SHE FOUND ONLY one way to cope with her grief.

She threw herself into working on the ranch. For that was when she felt Buck's presence most keenly. Riding bareback out to look for stray cattle. Ordering supplies. Hiring, firing, supervising the hands who so respected her father and now had no idea how to cope with this new turn of events.

She networked with other ranchers. She attended local functions. She did everything Buck did, only not as well, never with as pure a heart, but always striving to protect the living Buck considered his God-given gift. And right.

Buck had always dealt with a vet out of West Yellowstone, a Dr. Many, but Rebecca had never liked the way Many eyed her.

She'd heard good things about the young vet, the one based in Ennis.

She decided to call him out for spring vaccinations of the horses.

When the big, gentle man stepped out of his truck for the call, Rebecca immediately sensed the similarities—in character as well as physique—between him and Buck.

Jed hadn't ogled her like most men did. She could tell he was keenly aware of her presence, but he was always professional, never an improper glances or assumptions.

It had only taken a week for her to call him back.

He'd acted surprised that her men couldn't handle the mild colic that had her father's mare, Rita, pawing the ground and lifting its upper lip in a Mr. Ed–like smile.

After Jed had tubed Rita with a mixture of warm water and oil and made certain she'd passed stool, Rebecca had invited him in for supper.

He'd stayed after, for several hours, and pleasantly surprised her with his intelligence, and quiet, understated wit.

Still, he'd not asked to see her again.

It was Rebecca who finally made the first move. When she walked him to his truck, he turned to say good-bye and she rose on tiptoe and kissed him.

After all Jed's timidity, she expected at most a peck in

return, but that first kiss had revealed another side to this man who would bring such comfort into her life.

That very night they'd made love. And they'd been together ever since.

If only Jed hadn't come up with that idea for the vaccine.

TWENTY

BECCA'S BETRAYAL HAUNTED Jed. All this time, the months and months that he'd been fighting his suspicions about her, he'd been wrong.

Rebecca wasn't having an affair after all.

He'd never have believed that he could one day find himself wishing that she had been. That Rebecca had been sleeping with someone else. Maybe one of her ranch hands.

Why couldn't that—a fling with a cowboy—have been at the root of Jed's suspicions?

For good people had affairs. Jed believed that. Even people in love had affairs. Jed had known plenty of couples who'd survived infidelities. Charlie Mapson, for instance. Charlie had been crazy, wildly in love with his Annie ever since high school; yet, when he hit thirty-nine, he'd become involved with a waitress at the Rainbow Bar and Grill. It hadn't lasted long—Annie had found out about it almost right away, and Charlie had pretty much lived on his knees for a couple months after that, but they'd gotten past it, even conceived another baby, and now, with that baby due any day, they seemed as committed to each other as they had twenty years ago. People survived affairs. If Rebecca had been having one, it would have been hard to overcome, but they might at least have had a chance.

But this. Who could survive a betrayal of this magnitude? Perhaps even more to the point, how could Jed even have fallen in love with a woman capable of such duplicity? Jed had slept with this person, confided in her, put her well-being above everyone else's. How could he have been so wrong, so utterly taken in?

Was it her beauty? Could that alone have explained Jed's allowing himself to be snookered in? God, he hoped he wasn't that shallow, though he could not deny the power just looking at Rebecca had over him.

No, it had to be more than that. Jed wasn't exactly an Adonis, but he'd had his share of beautiful women come on to him before.

But none like Rebecca.

None with her passion. None with her tenderness.

None with her heart.

Had it all been a game to her? A means to an end?

And just what was the end? Becoming president of the Cattlemen's Association? Could that title actually mean that much to Rebecca? Enough to undermine Jed's research, to sacrifice their future? To kill? For Jed now believed, with little room for doubt, that none of the supposed "accidents"— his, the explosion of the barn, Dusty Harrison's—had been accidental.

And that made Rebecca either a murderer, or an accomplice.

Oddly enough, his anger—it was fast becoming hatred— was what now allowed Jed to carry on with Rebecca. To be in her presence. To pretend nothing had ever happened, that he knew nothing. That a wedding lay in their near future.

He'd surprised himself with how well he did all this. He'd never been a good liar, but his anger, his resentment, had

brought out a new side of him. A side intent on playing this
game of make-believe as well as—no, better than—Rebecca.
Intent upon drawing her out, exposing her, ruining her, just
as she'd ruined him—at least emotionally. Just as she
wanted to ruin his research, and the promise that a brucellosis vaccine held not just to Jed, but to all of Rebecca's fel-
low ranchers, the people from whom she was so desperate to
receive approval.

He'd even begun having fun with this charade.

Tonight, he'd invited her to dinner at the Riverside Hotel.

The Riverside was Ennis's oldest and most refined place to
stay, and dine. People drove from as far away as North Dakota
and Wyoming to celebrate special occasions in the ornate dining room, then sleep it off upstairs in a room that once had
housed the likes of Tom Horn, or Wild Bill Hickock.

"You look incredible," Jed said. He did not have to lie.

She leaned across the table toward him, kissed him on the
cheek. Her slender hands, still tanned, and adorned with
chunks of turquoise and coral, rested on the table between
them.

"So do you. So what's the special occasion? You said you
wanted to celebrate tonight."

Jed pushed back in his chair, slowly sipped his wine, took
his time.

"My research. Remember that cow that I thought I might
lose?"

"The one who got sick after you injected her with brucellosis? Even though you'd vaccinated her?"

"Yep. She's fighting it. Her immune response finally
kicked in. She's turned the corner."

This was all true; however, the cow in question wasn't the
one he'd pointed out to Rebecca on one of her many recent
drop-in visits at the clinic. No, he'd bought that poor, starving
creature from the local feedlot. She'd put on a good fifteen

pounds since, but still looked skeletal. The cow in question, one of his test cows, had been isolated in the barn on the Buffalo Field Campaign property ever since turning ill.

As Rebecca still leaned toward him, Jed saw her relaxed, flirtatious posture stiffen. Light from the candle in the center of the table illuminated her cleavage, tightly packaged in the wheat-colored camisole she wore under one of the many expensive Western blazers that filled her closets.

Before when he'd talk about his research and Rebecca paid such close attention, it had endeared her to Jed. He'd taken her interest as a reflection of her love for him. Now he interpreted it differently. Entirely differently.

It was time to set the trap. Up the ante to where he forced his opponents to make another move.

"I think it might be time for me to contact Manson Cline," he said casually.

Rebecca drew back in her chair.

"Jed, no. You don't want to do that."

"Why not? They'll see that this research is done on the scale it needs to be to get fast approval. And it would give us money to put into the Double Jump." He reached across the table for her hand. "I know you're struggling, Becca. You have to be. Everyone is. Just think what you could do with the kind of money they'd be willing to pay to license this from me. We could get married right away. Why wait?"

"Jed, listen to me. You'll lose all control of the vaccine if you turn it over to them. You don't want that. How many times have you told me you don't trust pharmaceutical companies? That all they care about is profit? That's not what you want for your vaccine. Maybe you should reconsider that scientist from Hamilton."

"No," Jed said, so loudly and emphatically that the couple at the next table both stopped their conversation to look his and Rebecca's way.

Rebecca actually appeared frightened.

Jed reached for her hand.

"What I want is to marry you."

"That's what I want, too," she said, her voice full of emotion. "More than anything in the world. But we have our whole lives ahead of us. This research is important. And it's yours, all yours. It's too important to you to just hand over to some huge faceless corporation."

"Rebecca, I love you, and I respect your opinion. But this is a decision I have to make on my own. And I think I've made it."

As Jed stabbed his first bite of steak with a knife, Rebecca said, struggling to hide her anger, "Well, then I guess I'll just have to accept it."

There, he'd set the trap. Anyone threatened by Jed's work on a brucellosis vaccine would be almost catatonic at the idea that a multinational, heavily funded pharmaceutical company was about to enter the picture.

They finished their meals. Jed could see that Rebecca was agitated by his announcement about Manson Cline, but she realized that to allow Jed to notice it could arouse his suspicions. After all, it made no sense to fight the Manson Cline deal if that's what Jed wanted, since it would stand to do nothing but benefit them financially.

Jed admired her brave attempt at shows of affection, hinting that Jed had a real treat ahead of him when they got back to the Double Jump.

Jed had pulled her chair out for her, and was trying to figure out a way to turn down her invitation to spend the night together without raising suspicion—when had he ever turned down an offer of sex with her?—when he saw Rebecca stiffen in her chair.

She'd turned to look up at him, and in that act, her eyes caught two well-dressed men sitting at a table near the entrance. Jed had never seen either man before, but he could tell from their clothing and demeanor that they were well-to-do out-of-towners, no doubt in Ennis on a hunting trip.

Rebecca rose from her chair and headed straight for them.

"What is it?" Jed asked, grabbing her by the elbow. But she was so focused on the two that she seemed not to hear him.

The men were in conversation. A two-thirds empty bottle of Duckhorn merlot sat on the table.

When the shorter and younger man looked up, he immediately gave Rebecca an appraising, appreciative look, but he did not seem to recognize her.

Recognition darkened the other man's expression the moment he lifted his eyes to her.

In her heels, towering over their table, Rebecca glared at them.

"How dare you show your face in this town?"

Shocked at this attack, the first man looked to the other for explanation.

"Miss Nichols," the second man said politely, squeamishly.

"You're not welcome in Ennis," Becca said, her voice raised almost to a shout.

"Do you hear?"

Jed still had no idea what this was all about. He grabbed Rebecca by the elbow.

"What is it? Who are these men?"

She turned to him. Jed had never seen such grief. Grief and anger. Pure, vicious loathing.

"They're murderers." Jed heard a gasp from a nearby table. "Meet Dr. Simms and Dr. Prigo. They killed my father."

"Miss Nichols," the older, taller man, who clearly had no idea how to handle the situation, repeated graciously.

"Let's go, Becca," Jed said. He felt deeply disturbed. Not by the viciousness he saw in his fiancée's eyes, but by her acute, visible pain, and by his own instinctive protectiveness for her. Despite everything.

Wrapping an arm around her shoulder, he pulled her gently away.

"Come on."

Rebecca did not budge. Instead, she grabbed hold of the table's edge. Her eyes traveled back and forth between the two men, unable to pinpoint the bigger villain.

"My father came to you with mobility problems that a little physical therapy would have fixed and you killed him. All we wanted was for him to get some help walking. He trusted you." Tears dropped from her chin, splashing on the well-polished table. "You put him through hell first. And then you killed him."

The maître d' had now appeared at Rebecca's side. He'd known her since grade school.

"Becca, please," he said. "This isn't a good idea. Please, sweetie. Let it go."

Jed was about to voice his agreement when one of the doctors, the younger one, said, "Get her out of here, will you?"

Rebecca had never, in all this time, discussed her father's death with Jed. Still, some residual feelings of love, of compassion, had managed to survive what Jed had recently learned about her.

Enraged, he reached for the man, grabbing him by the collar, as the maître d' pulled on Jed's shoulders, trying to stop him.

"Apologize to her," Jed ordered.

"Dr. McCane, please," the poor maître d' groaned.

Jed tightened his grasp on the collar, twisted it. The doctor went pale. *"Apologize."*

The frightened eyes—terrified really—quickly found Rebecca's. "I'm sorry," he said. "I'm sorry about your father."

Rebecca leaned toward the man, bored her eyes into his. "Don't ever put anyone else through what you put him through. Do you hear?"

The man nodded his head emphatically.

Jed's grip loosened. Sweat poured down his face.

"Let's go, Jed," Rebecca said quietly.

That night he held her until she cried herself to sleep.

Before dawn, he slipped out.

TWENTY-ONE

JED LIKED WHAT he saw.

The Hereford he'd been worried about—Megan had named her Daisy for the pattern of the faint rings around her eyes, in an otherwise white face—had definitely rallied. He stood outside her stall, watching her munch contentedly on the straw.

She'd been the first to be vaccinated with an aerosolized version of the vaccine. He'd vaccinated six of his herd of ten, five by injection, and Daisy with a spray up her nostrils. The other four would serve as negative controls. He'd waited a month for their immune systems to respond to the vaccine, during which time he'd evaluated antibody responses. Daisy's had lagged behind the others, but shown a definite response.

The real test came when he'd "challenged" the animals by injecting each vaccinated animal with virulent *Brucella abortus*.

The other five animals never faltered. Each day Jed had squeezed a trip down to the Buffalo Field Campaign compound to check on them and record his observations. He'd

run a series of standard tube agglutination tests. The Big
Five, as he'd come to call them, had resisted infection, prov-
ing that his vaccine did, indeed, provide resistance to the
disease.

But resistance would not suffice. Even if his vaccine
proved to provide a higher rate of resistance, as he believed
it would, what would make his vaccine revolutionary, what
would make the greatest difference, especially to wildlife,
like the bison and elk who carried the disease, was a vaccine
that did not result in false positives during later testing, and
one delivered in a more efficient manner. A vaccine capable
of being administered in aerosol form—literally sprayed on
a herd.

Conventional wisdom held that aerosolized delivery
would not be effective. Jed never bought into that wisdom.

Until Daisy fell ill.

A creak of the heavy metal door he'd installed during the
remodel of the BFC barn suddenly turned Jed's head.

"Hey."

Her face hidden by her hair, which the wind had whipped
around her face, Megan stepped inside, wrestling with a gust
of wind to shut the door behind her.

"Hi," Jed replied.

She joined Jed at the stall door.

"She looks great, doesn't she?"

"Yes," Jed said, smiling. "She's finally responded to the
vaccine."

"You were worried, weren't you?"

"I'd be lying if I said I wasn't. The other cows resisted the
Brucella abortus I challenged them with, so I knew my vaccine worked, but after Daisy stopped eating and developed
diarrhea, I'd begun to wonder whether the aerosolized version was just a pipedream."

"I knew you'd be happy," Megan said. "I checked on her
last night. She'd started eating."

"I told you you shouldn't be in here without me," Jed said. "I don't want you exposed to brucellosis."

"Jed, you and I both know I'm not going to get it from standing here."

Jed shook his head in exaggerated exasperation, and reached for the data book hanging by a chain from the stall door. He scribbled an entry under today's date:

Aerosolized version takes longer to enter system and provide adequate immunity.

"So what's next?" Megan asked.

"Next I'll have to challenge one of the pregnant controls mid-gestation. We have to make sure vaccination itself won't cause abortions."

Eyes glued to Daisy, who munched contentedly away, Megan said, "I just know your vaccine's going to be everything we've been praying for."

Jed studied her.

The excitement in her voice was unmistakable.

He had come to enjoy Megan's visits. She dropped in almost every day he was in the barn.

In large part he looked forward to seeing her because of her interest in, and unbridled enthusiasm for, his research. Although they did not see eye to eye on many issues—including ranching—Jed could not help but admire her passion and commitment to her cause. A cause that Jed felt some degree of sympathy for, but definitely only a finite amount. After a lifetime of living among ranchers, and for the past ten years serving them, Jed believed his primary loyalty lay with the people, the industry, that Megan considered to blame for the slaughter of her beloved bison.

Jed's admiration for this quiet, gentle woman had intensified after watching videos of her in the field. The campaign shot footage daily during the winter. There was nothing more powerful, in terms of swaying public opinion, than the sight of a buffalo being hazed by snowmobilers, beaten or shot. Problem was that very few TV stations had the courage or the inclination to subject their viewers to the carnage.

One day several weeks earlier, Jed had climbed the stairs to the little A-frame office. His cell battery had gone dead and he wanted to ask to use the phone to make a call.

He found K.C. in the process of editing footage from the previous winter. NBC *Nightly News* had called and wanted to do a piece on the campaign, and K.C. was updating their old video presentation with footage shot from the previous winter.

K.C. had invited Jed to watch what he'd put together so far.

Jed had been shocked by the strength of his own reaction to what he saw. He'd watched as Megan and half a dozen other motley-looking activists trudged—trying to run— through waist-deep snow, flailing their arms wildly in an attempt to herd errant buffalo back into the park, while dozens of warmly outfitted DOL agents sat watching and laughing on their idling, high-powered snowmobiles.

Jed had watched Megan break down and sob when, after first hazing them with snowmobiles until the creatures appeared ready to drop, a rogue DOL agent put a bullet into the head of a mother and her calf within plain sight of the activists.

Jed felt K.C. observing his reaction closely that day. True to good ol' boy tradition, Jed managed to resist showing the repulsion he felt. Or the gut-wrenching anguish upon seeing the depth of Megan's grief.

But K.C. had sensed it all the same.

"She's seen it dozens of times now," he commented quietly, his eyes fixed on the image he'd frozen on the TV screen—a close-up of Megan's tear-stained face. "But she's never grown used to it. The rest of us don't cry any more. We've developed a toughness. It's pretty thin, but it's there. But Megan, well, she just doesn't have that in her. She cries as hard now as she did the first time she witnessed a slaughter."

Jed had only nodded at these words.

Still, each day he visited the compound, like now, Jed saw ample evidence that Megan's gentle spirit had—thus far anyway—survived intact. Not even the brutality she'd witnessed time and time again could douse her enthusiasm.

It occurred to Jed that those remarkable eyes appeared even more alive today than they usually did. He sensed it wasn't just Daisy's remarkable turnaround.

"You look like the cat that swallowed the canary," he said, eyeing her. She was dressed in sweatpants, covered by a fleece jacket donated by Patagonia—one of the Buffalo Field Campaign's sponsors.

A smile the size of Kansas spread across her face.

"We got wonderful news this morning," she said. "Remember I told you how much all of us at the campaign have been hoping Senator Liddicott would run in the 2004 presidential election?"

Jed nodded his head.

"I remember. All the environmental groups are behind him, but I read that he's reluctant to run. There's speculation he's thinking about leaving politics."

Megan grabbed Jed by the arm.

"Well, guess what? He announced his candidacy this morning! And here's the best part. You know what did it? That *Nightly News* segment on our campaign. This morning he called Colleen Talks to Sky and told her that after seeing what's happening here, he decided he couldn't in good conscience not run. Not with what this administration has done to set back the environmental movement decades. He said even if there's no chance of his winning, someone who will be taken seriously has to run on an environmental platform.

"He's thrown his hat in the ring, and he's making the

slaughter of Yellowstone's bison a symbol of what's wrong with the current administration. He's planning on making the environment the linchpin of his campaign. Colleen said he appeared on all the talk shows this morning, so it's official."

Jed didn't necessarily share Megan's enthusiasm about this highly respected Democratic senator challenging the incumbent Republican president in the upcoming election.

Still, it pleased him to see Megan happy.

"Congratulations," he said.

Just then, another grating groan of strained metal diverted both their attentions away from the topic at hand and toward the open barn door, which K.C. literally blew through with the wind. He clutched a piece of paper tightly in one hand, determined not to lose it to the small tornado outside.

He approached Jed and Megan.

"Wait till you see this."

"What is it?" Megan said, eyeing the paper.

"An e-mail to Cyrus Gibbons."

The mere sound of Cyrus's name made Jed stiffen. "From Rebecca?" he asked.

"No, it's from Bronco. Our mystery man."

K.C. thrust the paper toward the two. "Take a look."

Megan grabbed it and, with Jed watching over her shoulder, read a loud.

"'Trouble. Read the attached article. We better meet. Tomorrow, nine A.M. at the A/S.'"

The message contained a link to an AP site.

K.C. seemed barely able to contain his excitement.

"I went to the link. It's an article from the AP. Basically the same thing Colleen told us. That after watching the slaughter on NBC, Liddicott got so upset he decided someone had to start taking environmental issues seriously. He knows he has enough power to be a strong contender, and that even if he doesn't take the primaries, the votes he'll win will wield a lot of power with the top candidates. He'll cut a last-minute deal if he has to. Throw his votes the way of the most environmentally friendly candidate."

"It's a brilliant strategy," Megan said. "Either way, we win."

"That's right," K.C. answered with a grin.

Megan's gaze went back to the printed e-mail. "Cyrus and Bronco have set up a meeting tomorrow morning."

Suddenly, the significance of this fact dawned on Jed. "That means you can find out who this Bronco guy is. What's A/S?"

"We don't know," K.C. said. "That's not the first time they've met there, but we've never been able to figure it out."

"It's simple," Jed said excitedly. In that instant, Bronco became the focus of all his anger about Becca. "I'll follow Cyrus. I'll find out who this guy is."

When he noticed Megan and K.C. exchanging glances, he said, "What?"

"We've tried that," Megan said. "Twice now. Cyrus lost us both times."

"He knew you were following him?"

"No. We're almost sure he didn't. We think he was just playing it safe."

"How could he lose you?"

The two exchanged a smile.

"You'll see."

AT SIX A.M. the next morning, Jed sat in his idling truck, binoculars trained on the mouth of the long drive that led to Cyrus Gibbons's ranch. He'd parked several hundred yards down the highway, just inside a Forest Service access road, where several cottonwoods offered camouflage.

In cattle country, even the smallest of ranches sported an

arch at the end of the drive to identify the operation. The size and design of these arches were the ranchers' equivalent of Los Angeles's attachment of status to cars. A particularly large lodgepole pine arch with the words "Rebar J" carved across the top crested the road's entrance. That, along with the ornate rock walls on either side, established Cyrus Gibbons as a successful and prominent force in southwestern Montana.

Warm air from the vents blasted Jed from the dashboard, where steam rose from the coffee he'd just poured from his thermos. Wind gusted outside, but the unseasonably early snow had stopped. It was simply a bitter, ugly morning, the precursor to many more, and worse.

Cyrus's meeting with Bronco wasn't scheduled until nine A.M., but Jed knew the ranchers well. They didn't go into town often, and when they did, they made maximum use of the trip. Concerned that Cyrus might leave the Rebar J at the crack of dawn, Jed arrived before dawn.

But after almost two hours, he'd grown concerned. The drive into Ennis took at least fifty minutes. Still no sign of Cyrus's truck. If he didn't leave in the next few minutes, he'd be late for this nine A.M. meeting with Bronco.

Had it been called off? Or might Cyrus have gone into Ennis last night and stayed over?

At the sound of a plane flying low overhead, Jed glanced up briefly from the binoculars. No doubt a local rancher looking for stray cattle. On either side of the road there were thousands of acres of Forest Service land used for public grazing. With a storm on its way, it was imperative that stray cattle—especially the calves born in the spring—not get caught in an early snowstorm.

He turned his attention back to the binoculars.

His anxiety level rose with each passing minute. He had to find out Bronco's identity. An almost overwhelming need to get to the bottom of this gnawed at him. For despite the inescapable evidence that Rebecca had, indeed, betrayed him, Jed still held out hope that at the very least, she was not involved in the plot that had already cost two lives—Clancy's and Dusty Harrison's. In his heart, he and Rebecca were already finished, but he still had a gut-wrenching need to know that he hadn't been *that* wrong about her—so wrong that he'd been able to fall head over heels in love with someone who would willingly be an accomplice in the taking of innocent lives.

At 7:59, out of the corner of his eye, Jed noticed movement in the foothills above the Rebar J. He swung his binoculars west, toward the dark spot moving slowly up the barren slope toward the treeline.

As he adjusted the focus, he quickly made out a horse and rider. He recognized Cyrus's favorite mare, the one he'd treated for colic recently. Her rider had his head down, and a hood thrown over his hat, against the bitter wind.

This confirmed Jed's fear. Cyrus must have spent the night in Ennis, in order to make his nine A.M. meeting with Bronco. Jed had missed him after all.

Jed was just thinking how furious Cyrus would be if he knew one of the hands had taken advantage of his absence by taking his mare out, when the hunched-over figure turned to yell at a black-and-white cattle dog that had come up on him from behind.

He lifted an arm, pointing back toward the ranch, telling the dog to go home.

Jed focused the binoculars on the face.

The rider was Cyrus Gibbons.

THE PLANE HAD already rolled to a stop, its single engine cut. It came as no surprise to Cyrus that its occupant chose to wait for him inside.

Cyrus didn't like the wimpy son of a bitch. Hell, the

pussy couldn't even take a little weather. He was a typical bureaucrat, someone who talked and walked the game but who could never actually make it as a rancher. Didn't have the fortitude, or the character. Still, Cyrus considered their partnership a necessary evil, critical to the future of folks like Cyrus. Hell, critical to Montana itself. Thank God, theirs was a mutually beneficial relationship—kind of like two parasites feeding off each other—because Cyrus had no doubt the plane's occupant would screw Cyrus in an instant if there was something in it for him.

Hoisting himself up on the wing, Cyrus rapped on the door, then opened it and struggled to pull his arthritic right leg up and over the door frame.

"Shut the fucking door. You're letting all the warm air out."

Cyrus settled into his seat and turned to the pilot, who was dressed in his official uniform, on the pocket of which appeared the Montana Department of Livestock logo.

Clay Kittrick reached over him and slammed the door shut.

"Nice to see you, too," Cyrus said, his voice dripping with sarcasm.

Kittrick, clearly in an agitated state, responded with, "I knew that NBC segment was gonna be trouble."

Cyrus grunted his disgust. "Trouble isn't the word for it. The last thing we want is someone like John Liddicott getting all hysterical and posturing for votes over the slaughter. So far we've managed to keep everything pretty much under the public's radar. But if Liddicott means what he says, that he's going to use the slaughter as a way to get people stirred up about the environment . . . hell, that kind of scrutiny would be a nightmare."

"It could jeopardize the whole brucellosis control program," Kittrick agreed.

"You won't be the only one who suffers the consequences

if that asshole starts poking around out here," Cyrus replied, his jaw tight with anger. "You know the impact this could have on public lands ranching? *And* the wolf situation? Just when we're finally close to getting them delisted?"

He glanced outside at his mare, who'd found a patch of grass not yet killed by frost.

"Hell," Cyrus continued, "us ranchers can't survive without cheap grazing fees, or an aggressive predator policy. All those fucking environmentalists need is a voice like Liddicott's. First it'll be the buffalo, then next thing you know, he'll be telling everyone the cattle industry's costing the government a fortune and ruining the fucking environment. It's your job to make sure that doesn't happen. That's what we've been paying you for."

"Don't you think I know that? I'm not about to let it happen."

"Well, far as I see," Cyrus said, "you haven't done much to stop it yet."

"Far as I see, neither have you," Kittrick shot back. "I thought you said you'd get that fucking McCane under control. I hear he's back at his research, that he built a new barn behind his clinic. You call that controlling him?"

Cyrus shook his head.

"We've tried, believe me. I figured with Rebecca Nichols on board, he'd be easy to handle. But the guy's like the fucking Energizer bunny. There's no stopping him."

"Lotta help she's turned out to be," Kittrick replied. "All I know is we can't lose ground on the buffalo. If we lose that battle, it'll be all downhill from then on."

"I agree," Cyrus said. "Which is why the latest news couldn't come at a worse time."

"What?"

"McCane told Rebecca he's planning to sign the vaccine over to Manson Cline."

Kittrick's balled fist shot out and slammed into the plane's dashboard. "Son of a bitch. If they come out with an aerosolized vaccine, we're done for. Brucellosis is the only thing that's given this slaughter program legitimacy. Without it, management of the bison goes back to the Montana Department of Fish, Wildlife, and Parks."

"Which could end up with bison getting priority to federal lands," Cyrus added. "The cattlemen's worst nightmare. It'd lead to the death of public lands grazing. And then ranchers like me."

They both fell silent, each immersed in his own misery.

"We can't let that vaccine get to market," Clay finally said. "Our only hope is to stop McCane."

"Maybe that won't be necessary," Cyrus said.

Kittrick shot him an icy glare. "What do you mean, not necessary? If Manson Cline puts that vaccine out, everything changes. Both of us can kiss all we've worked for good-bye."

"Hell, if Senator Liddicott doesn't shut up, we'll have to kiss it all good-bye a lot earlier than if they get that vaccine on the market. At least the vaccine would take a year or two."

"You're probably right."

"I've been thinking," Cyrus said. "Actually, I can't take all the credit. You gave us the initial idea."

"What the fuck are you talking about?"

"Just that there may be another way. Another way to handle this."

Kittrick had been staring dejectedly outside, at Cyrus's mare, who'd strayed a short distance up the logging road, reins dragging behind her. His eyes widened now, and he turned them on Cyrus.

"What do you mean?"

Cyrus met his gaze. "If what you said before is true, we

could actually pull this off," he said, a note of excitement finally sneaking into his voice. "It's a beauty, Clay. A real, fuckin' beauty."

He broke into a grin, exposing a wad of brown tobacco between his front two teeth.

"A way to make all our problems just disappear."

TWENTY-TWO

THE NEXT MORNING, Jed sat at the same spot on the road, waiting.

This time, he wasn't disappointed. At seven-thirty, Cyrus's white pickup roared down the long drive of the Re-bar J, kicking up a whirlwind of dirt and gravel, turned left onto Highway 287, and headed toward Ennis for the monthly Lions Club breakfast that Jed knew Cyrus never missed.

Jed waited until the pickup disappeared, then he got out of his truck, walked back behind the horse trailer and opened the door.

"Okay, girl," he said to Kola, the paint mare inside the trailer. "Time for a little ride."

Kola's ears pricked with interest as Jed stepped inside the other side of the two-horse trailer, running his hand along her back.

He untied her lead and, walking alongside her, with a palm on her warm, thick chest, backed her out.

"Slow, girl, slow."

Once on the ground, Jed tied Kola loosely to the back of

the trailer, climbed back in and grabbed the Navajo blanket he always used on her.

A Blackfeet client had given Kola to him his first year in practice, when he was still working for Doc Kamus in Missoula, as payment for an overdue bill. Jed had resisted, thinking it too lopsided a deal. Too lopsided in his favor—for Kola was not only a gorgeous Tobiano, but also as skilled a horse as Jed had ever seen. But the man, a tribal elder named Tommy Elk Heart, had insisted. Tommy ran fifty sheep outside of Plains, sold their wool to the Navajo for blankets, and Jed had made the three-hour drive at least half a dozen times in a two-week period that spring, working fervently to save the small herd from hoof-and-mouth disease.

He'd managed to save all but two of the newborns, and hadn't charged for the driving time. When Jed declined Kola as payment, Tommy would not take no for an answer. Besides, he'd pointed out to Jed, he had Kola's two-year-old colt, another strikingly marked Tobiano, whom Jed gelded the day he picked up Kola.

It had been the best trade of Jed's life.

Now Jed threw one of the Navajo blankets he'd bought from Tommy over Kola's back and hoisted himself up. Like Tommy, Jed never rode her any other way than haltered and bareback.

"Let's go, girl."

The cool air, coupled with the anticipation that always accompanied being trailered, energized the mare. Jed held her back as she clip-clopped across the pavement friskily, picking her feet up high. Halfway across, she executed a pretty little side step for Jed's entertainment.

Pleased at the lack of barbed wire along this stretch of federal land, Jed steered Kola down into the dry creek bed—the one he'd rolled the truck into.

Once she crested the other side, Jed gave her her head.

She took it enthusiastically and athletically.

Jed molded his body to hers, his elbows skimming either side of her spine as the mare raced the wind. The circumstances and the weather should, by rights, have taken any pleasure out of this task, but as they galloped across the rocky pasture, grazed to the nub now, Jed could not help but feel the same thrill he'd felt on other such occasions. Kola cleared the occasional brush or downed tree with ease, and as he had before with her, for a moment, Jed experienced the fleeting joy of a oneness with nature and the earth, as though the two of them—this magnificent horse and he—were of another time and place, one where cell phones and DVDs and four-wheel drive did not exist, had not even been imagined.

As they approached the fence line to the Rebar J, Jed pulled back on the lead, slowing Kola. He knew a stream lay up ahead, most likely dry this time of year. With any luck, there'd be a gate near there.

If not, Jed had brought along his wire cutters.

True to his prediction, as he approached he saw what served as a gate in that part of the country: a section consisting of three strands of barbed wire attached to a skinny, loose-standing pole. The pole was fixed to another pole, thicker, and sunk deep into the ground, with a single loop of wire.

Remaining on Kola, Jed unlatched the gate and let it fall to the dirt. He'd felt certain that by now Cyrus would have moved his herd to the inside pasture, but before proceeding, he scanned the pasture to make certain. No cattle. He eased Kola over the gate.

Ahead the land began a barren rise of a quarter mile or so before hitting the treeline. It was this section that he'd worried about the night before in bed. The only place he stood to be seen. He needed to cross to the trees as quickly as possible. There was risk involved—explaining his unauthorized presence on a client's property—but he'd decided he would go mad if he did not get to the bottom of this.

And the best place to start would be finding out just where

Cyrus was headed on horseback the previous morning, when he was scheduled to meet the mysterious "Bronco."

With a squeeze of his thighs and a prompt from his well-worn cowboy boots, Kola took off up the hill at a gallop.

BACK IN HIS truck, instead of heading directly back to Ennis, Jed abruptly turned east on Highway 287.

He had a feeling he'd find Megan inside the park. When he reached Highway 191, he turned north, skimming Yellowstone's northwest border, and began looking for the small red car. He spotted it along the same trailhead where he'd seen it the first time he found Megan in the park.

He pulled over behind it.

It was a two-mile hike in, but not knowing how far he'd be exploring or what he'd find, he'd left his schedule free for the entire morning.

He climbed in the trailer to check on Kola, making sure the windows were open. A cool breeze filtered through. He threw her an extra flake of hay, then, as a reward for the morning, topped it with a handful of rolled oats.

She knickered at the rustling of the paper bag holding the oats.

"I'll be back by noon, girl," he said, patting her rump before jumping down from the trailer.

He followed the trail up over wooded foothills. As he descended the other side, the trees thinned, and when he stepped into the open, just above the valley, the first thing he saw was a distant cloud of dust, covering the western edge of the plateau, on the other side of the river. It moved east, hugging the grassland.

Buffalo—perhaps hundreds of them—on the run.

Within a hundred yards, he picked out Megan, on her rock. She was bent over a spotting scope, motionless, no doubt rapt. Jed stepped up his pace, eager to get a close-up glimpse of the stampede before it became too distant. All those magnificent animals, all that raw power—he imagined the thrill it would be for Megan to watch.

But as he drew nearer, Jed scowled, puzzled.

Megan's scope seemed trained somewhere just behind the mass of fur, and flesh, and dust. Jed quickly decided there must be another group back there, over the ridge, where his position on the lower meadow made seeing them impossible.

When'd he climbed up the rocky hillside to Megan's perch and his head crested the top ridge, he called out, to her back, "What a sight!"

She turned.

Even from a distance of several yards, he saw that something was wrong.

He approached. Both sides of her face bore wet streaks.

She looked away, swiping at them with the sleeve of her jacket.

"What?" Jed asked.

She opened her mouth to speak, then simply nodded toward the scope.

As he stepped to it, Jed's eyes swept the horizon that unfolded like a painting in front of them. Shades of yellow and green and brown, each hill reacting in its own way to the midday sun. To the naked eye, all the action was taking place ahead of where Megan had trained the scope, the great brown cloud that extended along the rolling prairie laid out before them.

As he bent to look through the scope, he bumped it off sight. Closing his left eye, Jed lowered his right eye to the eyepiece and, using the handle on the right, began scanning an area peppered with large rocks and trees, mostly juniper and scruffy lodgepole pines, looking for an answer to Megan's tears.

The round, magnified field of vision skimmed the parched

dry, yellow grasses, hardy wildflowers, and rocks and stumps left over from the great fire of 1988.

At first he swept right over them, then movement drew his eyes back.

So chaotic was the scene, it took him several seconds to realize what he was seeing. Bodies, long and lean—some tan, some gray, one black, one mostly white—swung and lunged.

Wolves, each attached in one manner or another to a downed buffalo, who struggled to get up. The bison tossed its head, trying to dislodge a particularly tenacious wolf hanging from its snout, but rear legs flying, trying to get purchase on the shaggy chest of its prey, the animal hung tight, blinding the bison, both with its own body and by the wounds it inflicted.

"It's Angel."

Jed turned and stared at Megan. She looked so distraught. Still, there was no way anyone could tell that the victim of this feeding frenzy was Angel right now, with five wolves surrounding her.

"How do you know?"

"I've been out here every day, ever since you said she's sick, checking on her." Her voice cracked. She paused, clearly not wanting to give in to her emotion. "She's been getting slower and slower. Houdini's started leaving her from time to time, it's almost the end of rutting season, and she can't keep up with the rest. I'm sure he knows she's not the best choice for bearing a calf. She was back about quarter-mile today, when I first got here.

"I saw the first of the pack—I'm sure they're the Chief Joseph pack—over there." She pointed west. "The herd had already started moving east, and Angel was losing more and more ground. Finally, the pack decided they had a shot at her. The alpha male, the one on her snout, he got to her first. She tried to outrun him, must've run half a mile, but by then the others had jumped her, too, and it was all too much. This has been going on for the last hour. I just want her to go quickly now. That's all I'm praying for."

Jed went to her, put an arm around her, and pulled her head up against his shoulder.

"I'm sorry, Megan."

She began to sob, silent heaves that shook her shoulders, and brought a lump to Jed's throat.

"I just want it to be over for her."

At that moment, a giant bellow floated across the valley until it reached where they stood.

"I can't look," Megan said, pushing away from Jed. "Please, just tell me when it's over."

A new spot of brown had appeared on the distant ridge.

Jed returned to the scope, then moved it just the slightest bit to the west, stopping on the dark mass silhouetted against the blue sky.

"Houdini."

With his majestic head and shaggy robe, there was no mistaking the big beast. He stood ten yards away from the carnage, pawing the ground. When he lifted his head, Jed saw his mouth open.

Another angry bellow wafted across the valley to where they stood.

Angel had stopped moving, stopped fighting her attackers; but now she lifted her head, tried one last time to struggle to her feet, and watched as Houdini charged.

Jed felt Megan's hand on his shoulder. Quickly, he stepped away to allow her to watch the heartbreaking scene unfold.

In his charge, Houdini managed to knock one of Angel's attackers free; but as fast as it rolled to the ground, it sprang back up and returned to the downed animal.

The pack seemed to know that Houdini was too much for them to even try to take down. And Angel had stopped moving. She no longer felt the pain.

Or the fear.

Her Houdini had come to her aid, and at the end, she was finally at peace.

Head down, hiding her tears, Megan turned away.

"I have to ask the Creator to guide her to the other side," she said.

"Would you like me to leave?"

"Either way," Megan answered. "It's up to you."

"Then I'd like to stay."

"Fine."

Each time Jed had seen her, he'd noticed a leather necklace around Megan's neck. It obviously held something of not insignificant weight, which was always hidden beneath her top. Today, a speckled gray T-shirt, covered by a fleece jacket.

Now, Megan reached inside the neckline of her top and pulled out a small leather pouch.

A medicine bundle.

Jed recognized it from one that had belonged to Tommy Elk Heart, the old guy who'd given him Kola. He'd used it when Jed was tending to his sheep. He'd taken something from inside—some kind of leaves or twigs—and, chanting softly to himself, sprinkled them over one particularly sick lamb.

Jed watched as Megan turned her face to the sky.

Her voice came out low and sweet, with that same blend of roughness and honey that had struck him the first time he'd heard it.

"O Creator, guide sweet Angel to the other side with love and warmth. Give her eternal grass to graze, and rivers to sip from, and days with sun and nights with stars. Give her a peace that this life did not always gift upon her. And please, Creator, help her gentle spirit and strength to remain here with us in this world, to make those of us trying to protect her brothers and sisters wiser and stronger."

A tear traced its way down Jed's cheek as he watched her reach inside the tiny pouch and remove a pinch of crumbled green leaves. Jed recognized it—sage. She placed it on her flat palm.

Holding her hand high, to the sky, she continued her prayer as a newly born wind from the west picked it up and carried it in the direction where the wolves now fed on Angel's carcass.

"Thank you for allowing Angel, in her death, to give nourishment and strength to other creatures still struggling to survive in this glorious place, O Creator. Thank you for the circle of life. And thank you, O Creator, for allowing me to witness such a sacred event. I will hold it in my heart forever."

When she finished, they hiked the first mile back to the trailhead in silence.

"Does this change how you feel about the wolves?" Jed asked when they stopped to look back.

"Of course not. Angel was dying. Now, by feeding those young wolves, she's supporting new life. It's how it should be." They started back up the rise, and then Megan added, "If she'd lived till winter, the only way she would've made it through is by going outside the park, where there's less snow. She wouldn't have stood a chance there. Just looking at her, I know what the DOL agents would've done. They'd have shot her on sight, and then later said she tested positive. I know Angel would rather go this way—as part of the natural cycle of life here—than at Horse Butte."

"I'm glad you're at peace with what happened."

Megan stopped. At first, Jed thought maybe she was winded from the uphill trek, that she needed a short rest; but stopping alongside her, glancing sideways at her, he saw that her breath was less labored than his. They'd reached a point that gave them a sweeping view of Yellowstone. A view worth stopping to appreciate.

She stepped up on top of a small boulder, and scanned the horizon.

"It's what makes Yellowstone what it is," she said, eyes roaming to the site where the carcass, and the wolves feeding upon it, all blended together now into one dark blotch on the distant hillside. "One of this earth's last remaining wild places. I don't like seeing what happened to Angel, but I celebrate that it does still happen. That the wolves are here, and the bison. I know this may sound corny, ridiculous even, but for me, I'm not sure I'd want to live in a world without wolves, and grizzlies, and bison. A world without Yellowstones."

She jumped off the rock and started back down the trail. Her healing had already begun.

"You know," she said, glancing at Jed, "I never did ask you what brought you out here today."

"I took my horse and explored that area I saw Cyrus disappear into yesterday morning. For his meeting with Bronco."

"You did? What'd you find?"

"An airstrip. It had just been used. I'm sure that's where he was heading when I saw him. I could really kick myself, 'cause when I was waiting down the road for him to leave, a small plane flew over and I didn't even pay attention to it."

Megan shocked Jed with a giggle.

"That snake. He has Bronco fly in to meet him right there at his ranch!"

"Looks that way."

They parted at their vehicles.

Back in his truck, Jed found himself wanting to turn back and spend more time with Megan.

He believed they'd been brought together by fate. How else to explain an accident that connected two vastly different lives and worlds?

An accident that had turned out not to be an accident.

In the short time he had known her, he'd gone from seeing buffalo through the eyes of the ranching community, to shedding a tear at Angel's death. A lump in his throat at hearing Megan's heartfelt prayer to a deity she knew as the Creator.

She'd said she didn't know if she'd want to live in a world without wolves and bison. A world without Yellowstone.

Headed back to Ennis, Jed found himself thinking that he did not want to live in a world without a woman like Megan.

TWENTY-THREE

Jim Pritchard's bony hand trembled as he laid the two-page document on Clay Kittrick's desk, then pushed it across the pine surface toward the DOL agent.

"I got it yesterday. It's from the bureau chief himself," the Forest Service supervisor said, the strain in his voice raising it an octave.

A pair of bifocals hung from a chain around Kittrick's neck. He lifted them to his nose and he reached for the document, which read:

Memo   Forest Supervisor
To: James Pritchard
From: USFS Chief Terrance Mullen
Subject: Horse Butte allotment grant

In anticipation of a visit at the end of the month from presidential candidate Senator John M. Liddicott and as a result of a preliminary query from Senator Liddicott's office, a field auditor will be contacting you shortly about conducting a review of the granting of the Horse Butte allotment to Jack Hamlin

following the death of his predecessor, Richard (aka "Dusty")
Harrison.

Senator Liddicott's office has expressed concern about the
decision to grant the allotment to Hamlin over the application
of the Cheyenne.

Needless to say, I have assured him a prompt investigation.
I am confident that the USFS's actions will withstand any such
scrutiny. Your utmost cooperation with the auditor in dispens-
ing with this matter swiftly will be appreciated.

Kittrick read it again, then tossed the document back at
Pritchard. "What does this have to do with me? The DOL
isn't involved in granting grazing allotments."

Pritchard looked as though he'd been slapped across his
gaunt face. His mouth opened and shut twice, with no sound
issuing from it. After a short, audible gasp, he finally managed to say, "You're the one who warned me about giving
that allotment to the Cheyenne. You told me not to get on the
wrong side of the cattlemen."

Kittrick maintained a poker face. "We were talking
about who to grant the allotment to after Reed Jones died
then. Not about what to do with that allotment after Dusty
died."

"What the hell difference is there? Both times, the
Cheyenne submitted an application for Horse Butte. They
should've had a shot at that allotment. You made it clear
there'd be trouble if I even included them in the process.
Hell, you even tore up their application."

The crease at the corner of Kittrick's eyes hinted at amusement. "You know, Jim, I'm not sure I remember things exactly
the same way you do. I do remember a visit we had about
Reed Jones's death. But I don't recall ever having a conversation about Dusty Harrison's death, and what your plans were
for Horse Butte after that."

Cracking several times, Pritchard's voice sounded almost prepubescent by now.

"Jack Hamlin came to me. Right after Dusty died. He told me *you* called him into *this* office"—his index finger poked the desk forcefully—"and told him to come talk to me. He told me you said you wanted me to give him Dusty's allotment.

"So that's just what I did. I gave that allotment to Jack Hamlin, even though the Cheyenne had better qualifications, plus they'd applied for it when Reed died."

Clay Kittrick shook his head, lifting the corners of his thin-lipped mouth in a smirk. "I just don't remember a conversation like that with Jack Hamlin. He did come to see me about that allotment, but I sure don't remember telling him to tell you anything."

He removed his glasses, letting them drop back to his chest.

Pritchard leaned his long form toward Kittrick. "You're saying you never told Jack Hamlin that you wanted me to give him the Horse Butte allotment?"

"Without going through standard protocol for making the grants?" Kittrick said. "That'd be in direct violation of federal rules. It'd be illegal, Jim."

Pritchard's face had taken on an unnatural gleam. Jumping to his feet, he stood across the desk from Kittrick and shook his bony finger in his direction.

"You set me up, didn't you? I stood right here after Reed Jones died and listened to you tell me how sometimes, when what's at stake is important enough, rules have to be broken. You told me I'd be in big trouble with the livestock people in this state if I even considered granting the Cheyenne that allotment. You set me up."

Kittrick waved both hands in front of him, saying, "Jim, Jim. Settle down. The last thing I'd ever do is set you up. We've worked together for how long? Twenty-some years? Sit down now. *Calm* down. Let's work through this together.

I'm sure you meant well. You've always done right by me, Jim. Right by the cattle ranchers of this state. I wouldn't let you hang out to dry. You know me better than that."

Pritchard was clearly unable to decide whether to storm out of the office or listen to Kittrick. Apparently realizing his inability to deal with the predicament he'd gotten himself into alone, he finally sank back into the chair.

Kittrick grew pensive.

"Maybe you're right," he said. "Just this once, maybe it was okay to bend the rules a little.

"But what about Senator Liddicott's visit? If he sees the park's bison as a way to stir up voter emotion, someone's gonna come up with some irregularities—either in the way I granted that allotment, or in what's gone on at the Horse Butte facility."

Kittrick's nostrils flared at this statement. "What's that supposed to mean?" he said. "I run a clean operation out there at Horse Butte."

This sent Pritchard to his feet. "A clean operation? Who the hell do you think you're kidding, Clay? It's common knowledge around here that some of those cowboys you hired for the project get their nuts off by torturing those animals. Hell, by the time they're done running them into the ground, those poor beasts are goners before they've even been tested. I've seen men of yours beat a calf to death with a two-by-four."

Suddenly the significance of this recollection flashed across his eyes.

"You were there, too," he said, pointing at Kittrick. "You stood there and didn't say a fucking word. You call that a clean operation? If Senator Liddicott gets wind of how you operate that facility, I won't be the only one whose neck is on the line."

The realization seemed to hit both men at the same time—the instant that Pritchard recalled that day the previous winter when he'd gone to Horse Butte to find Kittrick. He'd needed to discuss the upcoming grazing season with him.

Sickened by the sight of animals being tortured needlessly, Pritchard had turned on Kittrick.

"You have to stop your men. This is outrageous."

Kittrick had spit a slimy, brown wad of tobacco onto the waist-high berm of snow that had piled up around the Horse Butte corrals and snorted a laugh.

"Welcome to the real world, Jim. There's a reason why people like you choose the Forest Service. Protecting goddamn *trees*." This time, his laugh turned the heads of several DOL contractors who'd circled the corral to enjoy the show. "In the real world, it's not so pretty. This'll be good for you. Stick around. You might get a taste of real life. Hell, this is the same thing that happens to cattle every day in feedlots and slaughterhouses across this fucking country. These cowboys are just doin' what they were taught to do. That's all. No reason the fucking buffalo deserve any better."

Disgusted, fighting back the feeling that he was about to be sick, Pritchard had climbed in his truck and left.

The next day he called Kittrick at his office to finish their discussion. No mention was made of the day before, for both men knew the reality: that the politics of both their positions dictated they work together. And that they stay on the good side of the cattlemen.

Each man had forgotten about that incident. Until this moment.

Now both knew that despite Kittrick's earlier, blatant attempt to disclaim any responsibility for any misdoings in the granting of the last two Horse Butte allotments—an attempt that alerted Pritchard to the possibility that Kittrick planned to blame the Forest Service for any problems turned up by Senator Liddicott's inquiry—Kittrick could not afford to double-cross Pritchard.

Like a bad marriage, they were in this together, staring in the face of a nasty storm galloping their way.

For better or for worse.

TWENTY-FOUR

HEY, **PARKER**, **YOU** see where that senator from back East is coming out in two weeks?"

Parker Derkowitz looked up from the slab of beef he'd been quartering and flashed a tobacco-stained grin at a cowboy standing at his meat counter. The stockily built man, in his late twenties, wore jeans and a nicely fitted Western shirt, both coated with dirt. That combination—the dirt and the dress shirt—constituted a sure sign of a rodeo at the West Yellowstone fairgrounds.

Parker himself was covered with blood, which he regularly transferred from his plastic-gloved hands to his apron.

"Howdy, Monty," he said. "Yep, I heard. Everyone's talkin' about it. Most folks around here aren't too happy about it, neither."

"Hell, no. I hear the fool's gonna try to close down the Horse Butte facility. And you can be sure he's got a poker up his butt about the snowmobiles in the park. Hell, son of a bitch oughtta just stay home, if he knows what's good for him."

"Ain't that the truth?" Parker replied good-naturedly.

A half-full shopping cart suddenly appeared from the bread aisle. A moment later, Parker recognized Nada Quinn pushing it.

"Afternoon, Parker," Nada said, approaching with a friendly smile.

"Afternoon, Nada," Parker replied. "You know Monty here? He works for Ozzie Mackie. When he's not rodeoin', that is."

The cowboy removed his felt Stetson, tipping it Nada's way.

"Ma'am."

"Me and Monty was just discussin' that senator who's planning to come to the park," Parker said, adding another bright streak to his once white apron as he bellied up to the glass display case to carry on a proper conversation.

"Nice to meet you, Monty," Nada said, giving the cowboy a friendly smile. She turned back to Parker. "Do you mean Senator Liddicott? Isn't that exciting?"

The cowboy's good ol' boy expression immediately soured.

"Exciting? Hell, he's just comin' to stir up trouble."

Nada's own pleasant façade evaporated as quickly as the cowboy's had.

"Maybe things need to be stirred up a bit," she responded.

"Nada's husband used to be a ranger in the park," Parker offered to the cowboy. "A fine man and a damn good ranger, but 'cause of him, Nada's probably got different ideas than a lot of us down here."

Nada surprised both men with her laughter.

"Stuart was a good man," she said, "but I'll have you know that even when he was alive, I always formed my own ideas. It just so happened we agreed on most issues that dealt with the park. It's a national treasure. One we must protect at any cost. Senator Liddicott coming to Yellowstone is the best news I've heard in a long time."

The cowboy's eyes took on an even harder edge.

"I 'spose when you say we have to protect it, you mean the wolves, too?"

"Of course," Nada replied, the jut of her chin letting Monty know he couldn't intimidate her.

"Tell that to my boss," Monty replied. "Ozzie's lost half a dozen calves this summer. From that damn Swan Lake pack."

Elbows resting on the top of the display case, Parker let out a low whistle.

"Goddamn. No wonder Ozzie's been so ornery these past few months. I heard Cyrus Gibbons has lost a couple calves, too."

"That's right. Triangle C and Cyrus's place border the west side of the park. That Swan Lake pack's been seen on both ranches this summer."

Having heard enough of Nada's anarchical leanings, the two men now seemed to have made some silent decision to exclude her from the rest of the conversation. But Nada would not allow it.

"I read that both men filed claims with Defenders of Wildlife," she said. "And that they were reimbursed for their losses."

"So that makes it right?" Monty snapped.

"Yes," she answered, "I believe it does. The whole point of the Defenders' fund is to compensate ranchers for their economic losses. As long as Defenders makes the payments, I don't understand what the ranchers have to complain about. It's a fair and well-reasoned program, a way to address the concerns of both sides."

Up until this point, Monty's posture indicated he'd been half-enjoying the verbal sparring, but now, with arms clutched tightly to his sides, he looked ready to pounce at Nada.

"You ever see a baby calf that's been ripped to shreds by

one of those savages? Or its mama with an eye gouged out from tryin' to protect it?"

Nada let out a small gasp and stepped back, groping for the side of the shopping cart she'd left standing at the end of the aisle.

At the same time, Parker glanced up the aisle and caught sight of the store's owner, Rudy Simpson, eyeing the three of them from the cash register at the front of the store.

He did not look pleased at what he was seeing.

"Whoa there, Monty," Parker said. "This is getting a little outta hand. Nada here's entitled to her opinion."

He turned to Nada. "Nada," he said, "I want to apologize. You're a good customer and a fine lady, and the last thing I intended to do was get you mixed up in an argument."

The cowboy cleared his throat. Hat now held timidly in front of his crotch, he said, "I'm sorry too, ma'am. I have no business takin' out my frustrations with those wolf people on you."

Nada managed a smile. "I guess it's the differences in this world that make it an interesting place to live." She sighed. "Believe me, this isn't the first argument I've gotten into over the wolves. And I'm sure it won't be the last, either."

Everyone chuckled politely.

"Looks like you're in the middle of your list, Nada," Parker said, "why don't you tell me what you want and I can have it waiting for you when you're done with the rest of your shopping."

"That'd be fine, Parker," Nada replied. Her eyes scanned the glass showcase, which was heavily weighted with Montana fare, primarily beef and pork, but also a section of wild meats: elk, venison, and even bear. "What are you recommending today?"

"Well, we just got some local beef in that looks mighty good. I could cut you a coupla steaks, some ribs, too."

"I like buying local," Nada said. Puckering her lips and twisting them to one side in a manner that made her look like a bird with a lopsided beak, she surveyed her options, then said, "Way the weatherman's talking, we could see snow any day now. Might be a while before I venture back down this way. I'll take half a dozen of your best steaks. And maybe several pounds of ribs. Enough for company, in case I decide to entertain."

"It'll be waiting," Parker replied. "And I'll be sure to package those steaks separately."

"I always appreciate that, Parker. And if you could double-wrap them in plastic first?"

"Already planning to, Nada."

"Well, I'll be back then."

The young cowboy tipped his hat at Nada as she turned back toward her cart. She nodded at him politely, then quickly disappeared down the next aisle.

Parker noticed Rudy, at the front counter, still looking their way.

"How 'bout you, Monty?" Parker asked. "What can I get you?"

"Ribs sound good to me. Maybe 'bout a quarter side."

"Quarter side'll run about eight pounds. Think that sounds about right? That'd feed six to eight."

"That'd do fine," Monty replied. Watching Parker slice a section off the side of beef sprawled across the cutting board on the back counter, he said, "At least there's one thing I agree with the lady about."

Parker tossed the ribs on the scale. Punching the price code into its computer, he replied, "What's that, Monty?"

"Local beef. Them corporate fucks are shooting the cattle full of so many goddamn antibiotics and genetically modified grains any more, it's dangerous not to know where the beef you put on the table comes from. But you can trust local."

"That's for sure," Parker said. He slapped a price sticker on the outside of the brown paper and handed the expertly wrapped package to Monty with a nod.

"Always safe to buy local."

TWENTY-FIVE

HE HADN'T BEEN able to fake it last night.

Despite her attempts at seduction, for the first time, Jed had not even tried to make love to Rebecca. He'd decided he couldn't carry the charade off much longer, regardless of the consequences. He'd heard Rebecca's soft sobs, but had not reached out to comfort her.

His desire, his thoughts, had turned to someone else.

After lying silent, listening to her cry, he'd finally asked Rebecca if she wanted him to leave.

"No," she'd said, sniffling. "Please don't go, Jed."

"I think we should talk."

"No," she'd cried. "I don't want to hear what you'd say. Just go to sleep. Just sleep with me, Jed. Please. I need you here."

It had taken Jed an hour and two glasses of wine to fall asleep. When he did, he dreamed of Megan.

In the dream, Jed was driving his truck—the old one, the one he'd totaled coming home from Cyrus Gibbons's. Megan was seated next to him, in the passenger seat. They were arguing about something, something he couldn't quite put his finger on at first; but he could sense that it was like

their real arguments. Something like whether catch and release made sense.

In her passionate manner, Megan was telling Jed about a
recent study that proved fish do indeed have feelings and are
capable of suffering. Jed had called the study absurd, which
had caused Megan, nostrils flared, to fire back at him that he
was "pigheaded."

Yet, despite the fact that the dream consisted entirely of
he and Megan arguing, several hours later, when the ring of
the phone jerked him abruptly back into the real world, with
a naked Rebecca breathing softly by his side, he felt resent-
ful for having to leave it.

Which might be why he let the phone ring five times before answering.

Groaning, Jed slid his arm out from under Rebecca's head
and rolled onto his side, reaching for the telephone on the
bedside table.

"'Lo?" he muttered.

"Jed? This is Andy Butler. I'm sorry to call you at Rebecca's place, but I'm sure glad I tracked you down."

Andy Butler had attended the University of Montana with
Jed, where, as undergraduates, both majored in biology.
When Jed went off to Washington State University for veterinary school, Andy started med school at the University of
Washington. He'd shown up in Ennis two years after Jed
started his practice, hanging his shingle with a group of family practitioners.

"What's up, Andy?" Jed managed to mutter, wondering
while still half asleep if Andy's call might be some strange
new twist in the dream. He and Andy were always friendly
when they ran into each other in town, but with busy careers,
and Andy the father of young twins, they'd never taken their
friendship back up. A middle-of-the-night call from Andy
was certainly not the norm.

"Can you hurry into the clinic?" Andy asked.

Jed rubbed the back of his free hand over his eyes and tried to read the digital clock on the table.

Four-thirteen A.M.

None of this made sense.

"Nada Quinn's in bad shape," Andy added.

Jed shook his head. This had to be his dream gone bad.

"Nada Quinn? My client? The one who lives down near Reynolds Pass?"

"Yes. She's a patient of mine. I admitted her to the hospital this morning. Thought she had a severe case of flu, but as the day's progressed, she's gone downhill fast." Andy had started out sounding authoritative, doctorly, but the fear in his voice now caused it to break. "I think I may actually lose her, Jed."

By now, Jed had swung his legs over the side of the bed and Rebecca had awakened.

"What is it, Jed?" she whispered, pulling the sheet up over her bare breasts as she stared at him, raised up on one elbow.

Jed silenced her with a quick wave.

"Whoa, Andy," he said into the phone. "Wait a minute. You're losing me. What's wrong with Nada? And why do you need *me*?"

"Because I just got the results from the lab work," Andy replied. "I'd sent blood and urine up to Bozeman this afternoon. I was supposed to get the results in the morning, but when I saw how Nada was declining, I called in a favor. A buddy of mine went in to the lab tonight to run the tests. He just phoned me with the preliminary results."

"I still don't see what this has to do with me."

"Nada Quinn has developed a severe case of encephalitis. I just called Medi-Vac to take her to Missoula General. But the way she's looking, I'm afraid she may not make it."

Instantly, images of Nada from Jed's last farm call sprang to mind.

Images of how thoughtful and concerned she'd been about

his situation. Of her warning that perhaps Jed shouldn't trust all the area ranchers.

Of how much she loved that mare of hers, and the meal she insisted he take with him when he had to hurry off to another call.

The thought that she now lay in the hospital in Ennis, near death, shook him deeply. Nada had always seemed so alone. Jed wondered whether she had any family at her side.

He still, however, did not understand this call.

"That's terrible, Andy. Awful. What's the cause of the encephalitis? Do you know the pathogen?"

Perhaps it was the pause before Andy Butler answered, perhaps some silent, cosmic communication that passed between them in that instant. For before Andy answered, a sense of deep foreboding overcame Jed.

"My friend was able to identify the pathogen in her urine and blood," Andy replied. "But it just doesn't make sense."

"What do you mean?" Jed asked.

"It's brucellosis, Jed," Andy said. His voice dropped to a near whisper. "Nada Quinn's contracted a deadly form of brucellosis."

ON THE DRIVE to the hospital, Jed examined the facts, at least as he knew them, in his mind.

How could Nada Quinn have contracted brucellosis?

Every year, a hunter managed to become infected when he failed to take precautions while butchering a diseased elk carcass.

But both Andy and Jed knew that Nada Quinn did not hunt.

Nor did she keep cattle, another source of possible exposure.

Jed would have given his right arm for Nada to have acquired the brucellosis one of these ways; because if she had not, there was only one other way that Nada could have gotten it. She had to have eaten or handled infected meat, cheese, or unpasteurized milk.

And if that proved to be the case, others might also become ill. Of course, an outbreak of brucellosis did not equate to a medical crisis. Most who fell ill would experience flulike symptoms—muscle aches and pains, fatigue, a continued or irregular fever—that responded to a mixture of antibiotics. Unpleasant, but treatable.

In reality, the consequences of brucellosis were more political and economical than anything else.

Only in the rarest of cases did someone develop any of the serious complications that were known to result from infection. Infective endocarditis, meningitis, encephalitis, chronic fatigue syndrome.

Poor Nada Quinn had apparently been that rare case.

While the rapidity with which her symptoms worsened surprised Jed, he still believed there was no reason to make anything more of Nada's fate than that. He thought Andy Butler's declaration that Nada had come down with a new and deadly strain of brucellosis premature. Perhaps even somewhat hysterical.

The helicopter had put down in the middle of the clinic's parking lot when Jed pulled in to it. It kicked up a storm of swirling dust, candy-bar wrappers, and other litter. Jed shielded his eyes as he climbed out of his truck, just as a team of Medi-Vac personnel, pushing a wheeled cart bearing Nada, exploded out through the clinic's front door.

Andy Butler, running alongside the gurney, shouted orders over the roar of the chopper's blades, which stood his beach-boy-blond hair on end. Silhouetted against the lights of the helicopter, this created a halo affect.

The entire scene had a surreal quality to it—a faint, baby pink ridge above the Madison Range to the east hinted at dawn; headlights of cars that had pulled over on Highway 287 to watch the excitement sent beams of light every which way across the fields surrounding the clinic, and several local dogs had joined a chorus of coyotes. At the center of all this commotion lay Nada Quinn.

She appeared unconscious. But just as the cart passed where Jed stood, feeling helpless and confused, her eyes fluttered open.

She reached for Jed.

Stunned, Jed took her hand.

Nada's lips moved, but the whirling blade and her weakened state made it impossible for Jed to hear her.

He bent low, placing his ear to her mouth. He felt her breath, hot, shallow waves, on his skin.

"Sugar," she said. "Will you take care of Sugar?"

Jed drew back. When he did, what he saw in Nada's eyes caused him to shudder.

Death.

He knew the look. He had, after all, seen it before, dozens—maybe hundreds—of times.

For when it came time to die, Jed suddenly realized that animals and humans were not much different. Both knew when it was their time. You could see it in their eyes.

"Yes," he said, shouting above the din. "I'll take good care of her."

A brief flicker of relief crossed Nada's face. She squeezed his hand, then, exhausted, closed her eyes. When Jed released her hand, the team sprinted back into action, hurtling toward the open door of the waiting helicopter.

Andy Butler already had one leg inside when a medic put a hand on his chest and shouted, "No room, Doc. We'll take it from here."

After the door banged shut, Andy, bent low, retreated to where Jed stood, forearm shielding his eyes from the gale force of the rotating blades.

The two men watched the helicopter lift into the thin morning air.

They stood, silent, for minutes, watching it shrink, until it became impossible to distinguish the mechanical bird from the real thing—the occasional hawk or magpie, out for an early morning hunt over the prairie.

Even then, some force kept the two men standing there, staring at the sky to the northeast.

Dreading what each knew would come.

TWENTY-SIX

NADA QUINN'S DEATH—more precisely, her diagnosis—stunned the community.

Brucellosis did not kill. It caused cattle to abort. It brought short-term misery to the occasional hunter, slaughterhouse worker, butcher, or veterinarian unlucky—or careless—enough to catch it from contaminated carcasses. But it did not kill.

Until now.

Still, for approximately forty-eight hours, the comforting mantra repeated over and over by citizens of West Yellowstone and Ennis held that Nada had died from encephalitis, a rare but not unheard-of complication of brucellosis, and not the brucellosis itself.

The local paper even quoted Jed saying as much. When interviewed because of his expertise on brucellosis, he stated that from what he'd learned, Nada's case appeared to be an isolated and unfortunate example of a normally mild disease resulting in a complication that had turned deadly. It would take medical officials time, Jed explained—perhaps weeks or months—to determine why and how.

Talk understandably turned next to how Nada had become

infected. By the time of her diagnosis, she'd fallen too ill for Andy and his staff to quiz Nada about possible sources of exposure.

Again, rumors ran rampant.

The favorite theory held that someone, a neighbor or former associate of her husband's, had inadvertently given the lonely widow elk meat from a diseased animal. In the West, such generosity remained commonplace. A tradition begun during its settling, when pioneers bonded together in the face of hardship, neighbors today still looked out for one another. While aid in the form of cold hard cash was almost nonexistent, hunters routinely shared the bounty of a good season with those less able or fortunate. It seemed a logical explanation for what had happened, especially in light of the high incidence of *Brucella abortus* in elk.

The sheriff's department quickly initiated a door-to-door survey of Nada's neighboring ranchers, trying to identify who might have given Nada elk meat. No one admitted to having done so. In the same newspaper article in which Jed was quoted, Andy Butler warned local residents to be cautious about the wild game they put on the table—a nebulous enough warning, but it nonetheless sent shock waves through a community in which at least half the households subsisted year round on freezers full of elk and venison.

Immediately after Nada's death, Andy and Jed had formed an unofficial team to deal with the crisis.

Their first move had been to call Sheriff Carroll.

"Henry," Jed said, as he and Andy sat in Andy's office, where they'd been going over Nada's medical records. "We have to get inside Nada's house to look for clues to her exposure. We need to check out her refrigerator, and the garbage."

"That'd take a search warrant, Jed," old Henry had responded.

"Then get one."

"I'll see what I can do." The sound over the line suddenly

grew muffled when Henry placed his hand over the mouth-piece. Jed heard him speaking to someone. "Hold on a minute, will you, Jed?" Henry said, returning to the line. "My secretary says I've got an urgent call on the other line. Every-thing's always urgent 'round here."

Two minutes later, Henry returned.

"Jed, that was a fella named Matthew Hughes. He's with the Center for Disease Control. He said he's sending an in-vestigator up here to check into how Nada got sick."

"Good," Jed replied. "By the time he gets here we'll have gone through Nada's house. Maybe we'll have some ideas for him."

"Uh, Jed . . ." Henry had replied.

"What?"

"This Hughes guy, he says he doesn't want anyone here meddlin' with things. Says they'll be the ones goin' through Nada's house."

"When's his investigator arriving?" Jed asked.

"Within forty-eight hours."

Jed looked at Andy, who must have heard Henry's robust voice from where he sat as his face mirrored the concern on Jed's.

"Did this Hughes guy give you his phone number?"

"Yep, got it right here."

"Give it to me."

Jed hung up and dialed the number.

When a deep baritone with a thick New England accent answered on the first ring, Jed punched the intercom button on his phone.

"Dr. Hughes?" Jed asked.

"Yes," the voice said over the intercom.

"This is Dr. Jed McCane. I'm with Dr. Andy Butler. Andy's the physician who treated Nada Quinn. I'm a local vet."

"War vet or veterinarian?" Hughes replied, with a hint of what Jed took to be humor.

"Veterinarian."

"How can I help you gentlemen?"

"We just got off the phone with Henry Carroll," Jed replied. "Henry tells us you're sending someone up here to investigate Nada Quinn's death."

"That's right."

"Henry also said your investigator won't show up for forty-eight hours."

"It's conceivable Dr. Nguyen will arrive earlier. We're working on his schedule now."

Andy Butler cleared his throat.

"Sir, this is Dr. Butler. We were told you gave Henry instructions not to begin an immediate investigation."

"That's not exactly what I said. What I said was that the CDC will handle this investigation. Anytime we have a death from an infectious disease, it's important that experienced investigators conduct the investigation. Of course, Dr. Butler, Dr. Nguyen will be contacting you immediately upon his arrival."

Jed did not let the obvious slight deter him. "We can't wait forty-eight hours to begin an investigation," he said.

"Er . . . may I ask, Dr. . . . ?"

"McCane," Jed said. "Jed McCane."

"Jed. May I ask what your involvement is in this matter?" Before Jed could reply, Andy piped up.

"Dr. McCane's a brucellosis specialist. Nobody in this part of the country knows more about the disease than Jed. Your investigators will want to speak to him."

"I'll pass that along to Dr. Nguyen," Hughes said. "But I can assure you, the CDC has the world's foremost experts on brucellosis in humans." He stressed the last two words. "Now, is there anything else I can do for you gentlemen?"

Andy looked at Jed, eyebrows raised, to see if Jed wanted to pursue the matter further.

Jed shook his head sharply. *No.*

"We'll look forward to meeting Dr. Nguyen," Andy said before hanging up.

Jed had already stood and reached for the fleece jacket he'd flung over the back of his chair.

"Where are you going?" Andy asked.

Slipping an arm inside the jacket as he strode toward the door, Jed replied over his shoulder, "To Nada's."

As Jed got out of his truck, he heard the anxious knicker. He turned toward the corral that adjoined the barn.

Sugar.

"Hey, girl," Jed called. He glanced toward Nada's house, eager to get to work; but according to Andy, Nada had shown up at the clinic just over thirty-two hours earlier. That meant her mare had been without food at least that long.

Jed headed for the barn. As he entered, Sugar's head appeared over her stall door. She knickered again loudly, hopefully.

Jed climbed to the loft, threw down a bale of alfalfa. Back down on the ground, he opened it, tossing Sugar several flakes.

Entering her stall, he ran his hand along her back, giving her a quick once-over, as he walked to her water trough to fill it.

"Okay, girl," he said when he'd finished. "I'll be back to get you later."

Stepping out of the barn, Jed spied a large green Dumpster—county issue—along the side of Nada's garage. Picking up his pace, he strode toward it.

He had just lifted the lid of the chest-high container when he heard a vehicle approaching.

He turned.

A sheriff's department car eased its way down Nada's long drive.

When it stopped, Henry Carroll emerged.

"Damn it, Jed. I thought I might find you here."

Jed turned his back to Henry and craned to get a look inside the Dumpster.

Empty.

"I checked with the disposal company on the way over here," Henry called from behind him. "Garbage got picked up yesterday."

Jed swirled to face Henry.

"Let me inside, Henry."

"I thought you been tellin' folks there's nothing to worry about, Jed. That Nada's death was a fluke."

"I've been telling people I think Nada suffered a very rare complication from brucellosis. Still, she got infected somehow, and we need to make sure nobody else does. That's why we can't wait forty-eight hours to start tracing Nada's exposure."

"Well, that makes good sense to me, too, Jed, but I can't let you into her house. I got orders. CDC's federal government. I'm local. You know what kind of trouble I'd be getting myself into if I let you inside?"

"Henry, we can't wait forty-eight hours."

"Afraid my hands are tied, Jed. Now go on home."

Jed shot an angry glance Henry's way, then turned and headed back to his truck.

Henry can't stay at Nada's forever.

"Just in case you're thinkin' what I think you might be thinkin'," Henry called after him, "you better know that I got a deputy headin' down here right now, Jed. That Dr. Hughes told me to put a twenty-four-hour guard on this place till his investigator gets here."

WHEN TUCKER MCNAUGHTON fell ill with symptoms identical to Nada's, he happened to be in Missoula, Montana, visiting his in-laws and picking his wife up from a month-long class she'd taken at the university there. Had he been home, and taken to the Ennis clinic instead, Andy Butler, who was already on the lookout for more cases, would no doubt have tested Tucker immediately for brucellosis, then given Tucker the third degree about how he'd been exposed.

But by the time word spread back home that Tucker lay in Missoula's Saint Patrick's Hospital, at death's door, Tucker was already unconscious.

"Two cases in forty-eight hours," Andy told Jed as the two of them stood huddled over copies of Tucker's charts from Saint Pat's. "And not a clue about how either became infected. Still, they have to be connected."

Almost as an afterthought, Andy stuck his neck outside the open door of the impromptu lab he and Jed had set up in the back of Andy's clinic, scanning the short hallway for patients.

Word of Nada's death had spread like wildfire. The news about Tucker, which Andy had received earlier that morning, could result in widespread panic. Fortunately, Andy had met the internist treating Tucker MacNaughton at Saint Patrick's at a medical conference the previous year. He'd called Dr. Singh immediately when word reached him about Tucker. Despite having already passed along all his information regarding Tucker to the CDC, Singh agreed to fax Tucker's hospital records to Andy.

Jed and Andy had no intention of leaving the investigation of the local deaths to the Center for Disease Control.

Andy turned away from the door and back to Jed, who replied, "We don't know it's the same strain. They couldn't possibly tell that already, not from a urine sample."

"I know. We'll have to wait for the histology reports. But the symptoms are identical—fever, excruciating headache, muscle pain, and weakness."

"Urogenital complaints?"

Andy nodded.

"According to Dr. Singh, yes. Same as Nada's."

"Damn."

"And the same rapid deterioration," a voice said suddenly from behind them. It was delivered in a thick New England baritone.

Jed and Andy turned in unison toward the door.

A short, whispish man with thin brown hair and a hook nose strode into the room, hand extended. The man did not match the voice.

"Matthew Hughes," he said. "CDC."

Andy reached for the outstretched hand.

"Andy Butler," he said. "And this is Jed McCane."

Hughes released Andy's hand and grasped Jed's. As he did so, his eyes fell to the papers on Andy's desk.

"I see you've managed to get hold of our latest victim's records," he said. "You Montanans stick together, don't you?"

"I know Dr. Singh personally," Andy replied. "It was only natural that we compare our experiences in treating these two patients."

"I thought you were sending a Dr. Nguyen up here," Jed said, eyeing Hughes, who eyed him back. Each man had already taken an instant dislike to the other.

"That was when we didn't expect much out of this whole situation," Hughes replied. "Before another case turned up. Everything changed when Tucker MacNaughton fell ill. Dr. Nguyen arrived here a few hours ahead of me, but I'll be in charge of this investigation. *The CDC is handling this, gentlemen. Is that clear?*"

"You came all the way over here to tell us that?" Jed asked. "A phone call would have done."

"I came because after only two hours in this town it's already become apparent to me and my team that outsiders are not exactly trusted by the locals."

If the situation hadn't been so desperate, Jed might have smiled. "You're saying you may need us after all?"

"Yes," Hughes replied. "I guess that's what I'm saying. But if I see any evidence of the two of you bypassing me, keeping information from me, I'm warning you now. I'll go after your licenses."

"All we want," Jed said, "is to get to the bottom of this outbreak and stop it in its tracks."

Andy muttered his concurrence.

"You do agree, then," Hughes said, "that the two cases are related?" He addressed the question to Andy.

"We're quite certain they are," Andy replied. "The pattern for Tucker matches Nada's to a tee. According to Tucker's wife, when he arrived in Missoula three days ago to pick her up, Tucker seemed fine. Then the headache hit. Bang. That's what finally brought Nada into the clinic. She thought it was a migraine. Next thing you know, he's in a coma, just like Nada. When I talked to him this morning, Dr. Singh didn't expect Tucker to last the day."

"He didn't," Hughes said matter-of-factly.

Jed and Andy looked at each other.

"Tucker MacNaughton died thirty minutes ago," Hughes announced.

The room fell briefly silent.

"Did he ever come to?" Jed asked. "Did anyone have a chance to question him about how he got infected?"

"No," Hughes replied. "He never regained consciousness. Dr. Nguyen headed directly from the airport to the hospital to talk to MacNaughton's wife, but just now, on my way over here, he called to tell me that she's too upset to get any information out of right now."

"I talked to her earlier today. Singh put her on the phone with me."

This disclosure by Andy clearly piqued Hughes's interest.

"Could she pinpoint any connection between the Quinn woman and her husband?"

Andy shook his head. "Mary MacNaughton didn't even

recognize Nada's name. Tucker taught high school up in Pony. According to Mary, they did all their grocery shopping in Ennis, rarely headed down toward West Yellowstone, which is where Nada's neighbors say she shopped. I couldn't pick up on any connection at all. Nothing."

The three men grew silent again.

"Well, then, I guess we may just have to wait," Jed finally said glumly.

"For my investigators to trace the source?" asked Hughes.

Jed locked eyes with him. "Or for our next victim."

THE KNOCK ON the door startled Jed. He looked up from the DNA tests he'd started running on blood samples taken from Nada Quinn and glanced at the clock.

Seven P.M.

Maybe Andy had forgotten his lab key when he ran home an hour earlier, telling Jed that if he didn't grab a quick bite with his family, his wife would start a meltdown.

It wouldn't surprise Jed. Both he and Andy were operating on no more than a couple of hours sleep a night. They made a point of keeping the door to the lab locked, not just for security reasons, but also so that no one—especially anyone from the CDC, most of whom Jed considered pompous assholes who'd rather hoard information that would be more beneficial shared—would know they were inside, working to identify the particular strain of brucellosis that Jed had isolated from the urine and blood samples Andy had taken from Nada Quinn.

Jed strode to the lab's door and swung it wide, expecting to see a disheveled Andy.

Instead, a man dressed in a pinkish-stained, open-necked, white short-sleeved shirt faced him.

He held both hands unnaturally close to his sides. The fingers of each moved in nervous circles, as though twirling a small, invisible ball.

He looked vaguely familiar to Jed.

"Yes?" Jed asked.

"You're the vet, aren't you?" he said. "Jed McCane. I heard I could find you here."

"Yes."

"My name is Parker Derkowitz. And I have something to tell you."

"YOU'RE CERTAIN? ABSOLUTELY certain you sold meat to both Nada Quinn and Tucker MacNaughton?"

Clearly miserable about the news he'd delivered, the man nodded his head.

"Nada's been buying beef from me for a long time. Made me real nervous when I read what happened to her. Poor lady. I always liked her. She had class, you know? But I was figurin' the same as everyone else—that Nada got sick from wild game. The other guy, this Tucker, I read about him, too, but the name didn't mean shit to me. Actually, when I read his name, I breathed a sigh of relief. 'Cause even though I figured it was wild game did Nada in, I still had the slightest trace of . . . you know . . . doubt. Fear. But I didn't think I'd ever laid eyes on the other fella, the guy who got sick in Missoula. I know most of my customers by name, and the name didn't ring a bell.

"Then I saw an obituary in today's paper. It had Tucker McNaughton's picture. And I realized I'd seen him before. In my shop. He bought meat from me, too."

"You're sure it was him?"

"I wish to hell I wasn't, but I am. He was one of them guys that's goin' bald and instead of just letting nature do its thing, he had all this goopy crap in his hair, to make it seem bigger than it really was. You know the kind. Anyway, soon as I saw that picture, I knew what it meant."

"That your store was the source of the brucella."

"That's what I figured."

"Do you remember what they bought?"

"I been racking my brains 'bout that. I do remember Nada got several steaks, 'cause I always wrap them separate for her, but it's been a while. And Nada comes in regular, so it could've been something I sold her a while back. And I can't remember what the guy bought. Not for the life of me."

"Was it beef?"

"Couldn't say. We sell wild game, too. It's big with the tourists. They like to go home and tell everyone they ate elk or bear while they were out here."

"Where do you get your meat? The beef?"

Parker scratched his head. "California, Canada. A lot of it's local."

Jed had expected just such an answer. Still, his heart sank. "How local?"

"Montana. Most of it within, oh, I'd say maybe a hundred miles."

"Can you get me a list of suppliers?"

Parker shook his head. "That's where we might get into problems. You see, I'm not always the best guy in the world about keeping records. My boss wants me to do it on the computer, and well, . . ."

"Well, what?"

"I can't figger out how to use the fuckin' thing."

"So are you saying you might not be able to produce records tracing the source of all the beef you've sold this past month or six weeks?"

Parker's chest began to rise with each breath.

"Six weeks? Hell, most of my customers freeze half of what they buy. We could be talkin' six months here, and I just told ya, I'm not good at—"

Suddenly, without warning, the door flew open behind them.

Andy Butler filled its frame. Unblinking, he approached

Jed with a wild expression. He stopped when he saw Jed wasn't alone.

Eyeing Parker briefly—and none too happily—he looked at Jed and blurted out, "We've got *more*."

He jerked his head sideways, motioning Jed toward the hall.

"Wait here," Jed told Parker as he followed out the door.

Once out in the hallway, Andy pulled the door shut behind them.

"What?" Jed said. Close up, he noticed beads of sweat lacing Andy's hairline.

"An entire family," Andy answered. His words came in a rush. They almost seemed to be choking him. "They called for an ambulance a few minutes ago. It's on its way down there now. They live out past Yellow Jump."

All Jed could think of to say was, "Damn." But then, grasping for a lifeline, he added, "You can't know for sure that's what it is."

"Same symptoms."

They fell silent, avoiding eye contact—each perhaps afraid of reading the other's thoughts. Despite what he'd just learned from Parker, two incidents still gave Jed room to hope it was a very small, contained outbreak. That hope disappeared with an entire family.

With a sigh, Jed turned to go back inside the room in which Parker waited.

He pivoted to look at Andy. "Do you know their names?"

"Yes. It's Monty Black and his family. I guess all of them—the parents and three kids—are coming in. Why?"

"Come with me," Jed said, opening the door and standing aside to usher Andy back into the lab.

Inside, the West Yellowstone butcher too had begun sweating profusely.

"Parker Derkowitz," Jed said, "this is Dr. Andy Butler."

"Evenin', Doc."

Confused, even irritated that Jed would waste their valuable time right now, Andy nodded curtly without speaking.

"When you said there's more just now," Parker asked, directing the question to Andy, "did you mean someone else is sick?" His fingers rolled imaginary balls as his hands hung loose at his sides.

Unsure of what he could freely say, Andy looked at Jed.

Jed turned and locked eyes with Parker. "Do you know the name Monty Black?"

The second Jed uttered this name, it was as if an invisible fist had lashed out and landed squarely on Parker's chest. He stumbled backward, falling up against the desk where Jed had been sitting when Parker first knocked on the door.

"Holy shit," Parker gasped.

"What? What does that mean?" Andy asked.

Jed's voice came from over Andy's left shoulder. "I think it means we've found the common denominator."

Andy swiveled round to face Jed.

"The link between Nada and Tucker and Monty," Jed continued. "Parker here's the butcher at the West Yellowstone grocer."

"Holy shit," Andy said, wide-eyed. "That's where the contaminated meat came from?"

Jed nodded.

"I think Parker's about to tell us he sold Nada, Tucker, and Monty meat. But there's a problem. He can't remember just what he sold them. And he doesn't keep complete records."

Both Andy and Jed's heads turned at the sound of Parker's voice.

"You won't need them."

"We don't need them?" Jed echoed. "Are you crazy? We've got two people dead, and a family of five on its way to the hospital. Of course we need them."

"No, that's not what I mean," Parker said. "I mean I can

save you the trouble of looking through my records. I can
tell you now, now that I know Monty's sick, too. The last
time Monty came in, it was the same day Nada bought her
beef. I introduced the two of 'em. Then, after she left, me
and Monty talked about it."

"About what?" Andy asked.

"About how safe it was to buy local," Parker replied. "I'd
just bought the beef I sold them, and I remember now, clear
as a bell. I remember who I got the beef from, the stuff that
I sold to Monty and Nada that day."

"Who?" Jed and Andy spoke in unison.

A nervous tic played at the corner of Parker's left eye, but
in his face there also resided just a trace of excitement at being the focus of attention in the unfolding drama.

He lifted both hands in the air, in the style of a Pentecostal
preacher enjoying his control over a rapt audience. The
creases in his palms carried red stains.

"I bought that beef from Rusty Wallace," he said.

The name did not ring a bell with Jed. He looked at Andy
and saw that it failed to register with him, too.

"You know," Parker said, "Jack Hamlin's foreman."

AFTER THEY'D QUIZZED Parker thoroughly, and left an urgent
voice mail for Matthew Hughes, Andy and Jed gave Parker
enough money for a night at the Madison River Motel next
door and told him to stay in his room, by the phone.

By the time they'd closed the door behind the butcher, the
energy level in the lab had risen to a palpable level.

"I tested Hamlin's cattle," Jed said as the two men alter-
nately paced the small room. "I *know* I tested them."

"When?"

"This past spring."

"And?"

"And of course they tested clean. The state of Montana

hasn't had a case of brucellosis in cattle for almost twelve years."

Andy stuck a finger through his disheveled hair and scratched his scalp.

"Then—assuming that guy's right, about the infected meat coming from Hamlin's—how the hell did Hamlin's cattle get infected? Elk?" His face screwed up in confusion. "Just where is this Hamlin guy's ranch?"

"It's up near Pony, along the Tobacco Roots," Jed answered. Even as he said it, the conversation he'd had with Megan about Jack Hamlin came back to him.

"Sweet Jesus," he said, freezing in his tracks.

"What?"

"When Dusty Harrison got killed, they awarded that grazing allotment to Jack Hamlin."

Andy's patience had worn thin. "*What* grazing allotment?"

"The Horse Butte allotment," Jed replied.

"The allotment outside Yellowstone, the one that's caused so much controversy?"

"Yes."

Andy let loose with a low whistle. "Then the infection had to have come from park bison," he said.

"I've tested those bison," Jed snapped at him.

Involuntarily, the image of Megan, tears streaming down her face as she watched her beloved Angel die, came to mind. He shut his eyes, willing it away.

If what Andy said proved to be true . . . Jed couldn't even allow himself to contemplate that possibility. His primal instinct was to squelch it, kill it, right here and now.

"The ones who do test positive for brucella carry *Brucella abortus*," he said. "The most it could do is make a person sick. Plus the bison are only on that land in the spring. Hamlin's cattle weren't moved there till late summer. It can't be the park bison. It can't."

Andy eyed him, clearly puzzled about the intensity of Jed's reaction.

"If the chain turns out to be what Parker said," Andy replied, "that Nada and Tucker and Monty all ate Jack Hamlin's beef, and Jack Hamlin's cattle weren't infected before they moved to Horse Butte, but now they are—how else can you explain it?"

"I don't know," Jed said testily. "But you can be damn sure of one thing."

"What's that?"

"I intend to find out."

TWENTY-SEVEN

As Jed's headlights swept the parking lot, he thought he saw something—a figure, slight, fluid, and decidedly unthreatening—dart back into the shadows surrounding the veterinary clinic.

He didn't notice the car parked at the end of the sidewalk until he'd pulled to a stop. A Subaru, its dangling muffler visible in the light from the street lamp.

Just as he recognized it, Megan stepped out of the shadows.

Jed climbed out of the truck and met her on the sidewalk. "What are you doing here?" he asked.

She'd twisted half her hair into a knot on top of her head, while the rest swirled around her face like a small storm, at the center of which lay those eyes.

In the harsh light of the street lamp, she looked almost like a wild animal.

"I heard what they're saying," she said, her voice breathless, though she had apparently been waiting there for some time for him to return. "That the brucellosis came from the park buffalo."

"I've heard the same thing."

"You know it's not true. You've told them that, haven't you?" She grabbed Jed's arm. "You're telling them that, aren't you?"

"Megan, calm down. Yes," Jed said. "I mean, no. I can't say anything definite at this point, but I've told everyone who's asked that I don't see how it could come from the park bison." He fingered his key ring, looking for the key to unlock the clinic. "By tomorrow, I'll be able to tell them with certainty, though."

"How?"

"I came back to get some of the samples I took for my research. The ones from the Yellowstone herd. Back at the lab we've set up at Andy Butler's clinic, I've got the brucella we isolated from Nada Quinn's blood. I'll do DNA tests to see how the two compare."

"Tonight?" Megan asked. "You're doing these tests tonight?"

"Actually, I was planning to get some sleep tonight, and then do gels first thing tomorrow."

"You mean DNA fingerprinting?"

"Yes. I'll be able to compare the bacteria that infected Nada and the others with the brucella I sampled from the park bison last spring."

"So you'd be able to prove that the brucellosis those people died from isn't caused by the same brucella strain the bison carry?"

"Yes," Jed said, wearily. "If that's how it really is. This test could prove that, once and for all."

"Please, Jed, please, can't you do the tests now?"

Jed studied her. For a moment, looking at the abject torment in her eyes, he vacillated, but then he said, "I have to get some shut-eye. I won't be any good until I do and this is too important—to you, to me, to the community—to take the chance I'll screw it up. Just a couple hours. Give me two hours, okay? Then I'll do the gels."

"Can I stay with you?" Megan replied. "Can I go with you when you run the tests?"

Jed and Andy had agreed to keep their work as hush-hush as possible. After Matthew Hughes and his CDC team learned that Parker Derkowitz had gone to Jed and Andy before contacting the official investigators, Hughes called Jed, telling him he'd be treading on dangerous ground if he did anything to "interfere" with the CDC's work. Andy and Jed both believed that Hughes's response—and the CDC team's obvious determination to minimize the involvement of the local men—stemmed more from egos than from any legitimate concerns about "losing track," as Hughes had put it, of valuable information.

Jed and Andy had no intention of backing off on their own investigation. Still, they'd decided that keeping a low profile would be wise, and to limit what information they shared with any outsiders. Knowing Andy wouldn't want Megan, of all people, to be privy to the test results before he and Andy decided to make them public, Jed knew he should refuse her request to observe his testing of both brucella samples, but instead, he replied, "Yes. You can watch."

She followed him inside. They walked in silence through the clinic, entering his apartment by way of the unmarked door at the end of its central hallway.

A single light from the kitchen spilled down another short hallway that led to the living room, bathroom, and Jed's bedroom.

At the arched doorway to the living room, Jed stopped. "You can rest there, on the couch. I'll get you a blanket."

Behind him, Megan said, without hesitation, "Can I go with you?"

He turned to study her.

"I'm scared," she said.

Jed knew that the fear she spoke of had nothing to do with fear for her own safety or health. It was strictly fear for her beloved buffalo, for the possible repercussions if the tests he was about to run revealed the two strains to be the same.

He reached for her hand.

"Me, too," he said. "Come on."

LATER, JED WOULD think back and marvel at the fact that there was never an awkward moment between them.

Standing beside his bed, he shed his flannel shirt and boots, also his leather belt. He kept his Carhartt jeans on. Without hesitation, fully dressed, Megan climbed under the covers with him. They lay facing each other in the dark, and she held him, cradling Jed's head between her slender arms.

Jed had never felt such comfort.

Nor had he realized how badly he needed it.

For the first time in many months, bizarre dreams and violent images—pieces of his barn exploding into the night air, the bloated cow's carcass on the side of the road the night he drove home from Cyrus Gibbons's, the sound of the semi's trailer crashing down Beartooth Pass, all part of the repertoire of torment that haunted him nightly—did not torture him as he slept.

He dozed, aware of Megan's breath, soft and steady, against his neck. He had just the vaguest conscious thought that she too seemed to take comfort in their physical contact; but it did not last long because sheer exhaustion—both physical and mental—caused him to fall asleep almost instantly.

Still, precisely two hours later, Jed awakened to Megan shaking his shoulders softly.

"It's time," she said. "It's time to run those gels."

TWENTY-EIGHT

JED TRIED TO keep his expression neutral, but that didn't help. Megan sensed it, almost before he'd allowed himself to form the thought.

"What?" she asked.

She'd patiently stood by his side as he ran the gels that would enable him to compare the DNA of the brucella he'd extracted from blood samples of the park bison early in the spring to the brucella DNA isolated from Nada Quinn's blood.

Using restrictive enzymes, he'd cut both DNA samples into thousands of pieces that, when applied side by side to an agarose gel and stimulated by an electric pulse, migrated across the plate. Depending upon their size, the pieces moved at different rates, and once they'd spread out—with the longer pieces lagging behind—Jed stopped the electricity, applied a dye, then photographed the two patterns left by the samples. In all, the gel electrophoresis process had taken seven hours, during which he and Megan barely spoke. She'd made good on her promise not to get in the way, spending most of her time perched on a stool at the end of the long counter upon which the gels were set up.

But ever since he'd walked back into the room with the photographs, Jed felt her studying his face, watching for any hint of a reaction as he studied them.

"What?" she repeated.

Jed had trouble taking his eyes off the photos. Whether it was because of what they told him, or because of what he knew he'd see in Megan's face when she learned the results, he did not know.

Slowly, he lifted his gaze to meet hers.

"They're the same organism," he said. "The brucella from the park bison. And the brucella that killed Nada and the others."

Megan's gasp was more visible than audible.

"That can't be!"

"It's true," Jed said, making a conscious effort to hold his voice steady. He had to stay in control of the situation. "This is just preliminary. More tests will have to be run, but from what I've seen today, I'm certain it's the same strain. The DNA patterns are basically identical."

Megan jumped on this.

"*Basically*," she practically shouted. "That must mean you see some differences. Don't you? *Don't you?*"

Jed's eyes fell back upon the photos in his hand. She'd picked up on it. On the one note of confusion in Jed's mind, and apparently, his voice. While the patterns created by both samples virtually guaranteed they'd come from the same organism, there were variations between the two that Jed could not explain.

"Yes," he replied. "There are also some differences. That's why we'll need more testing. I'll turn these results over to the CDC team, and let them conduct the rest. This lab Andy and I set up isn't equipped to go to the next level."

Megan's hand shot out and grabbed him by the arm.

"No," she cried. "You can't do that. You can't turn them over to the CDC."

"Why not?"

"Because you can't tell *anyone* about this."

Jed pushed out of her hold.

"How can you even suggest that I not tell?"

Jaw set, Megan answered, "Because it's impossible. And we both know it. Bison don't transmit brucellosis to cattle. There's never been a documented case. Never."

"There's always the first."

"No, Jed. That's not what this is. *They* did this."

"Who?"

"Who do you think? Cyrus, and Bronco, and your girl-friend. They're behind it, Jed. They have to be."

"What are you saying?"

"I'm telling you, somehow they're responsible."

"Megan, you're not making sense. I guess you just can't be rational about this."

She grabbed him again. "You're the expert on the park bison and brucellosis. If you tell everyone it didn't originate there, they'll believe you. They'll stop pursuing that angle right then and there."

Jed stepped up to her, facing her squarely. "Megan, stop. Listen to yourself. Of course I have to reveal the results of these gels. I have no choice."

"You *do* have a choice. You can choose to be manipulated by them—by *her*—to be their pawn, or you can save the bison."

"Rebecca isn't behind this. I promise you. Neither are the others. No one in their right mind would do this deliberately. People are dying! For God's sake, think about what you're saying."

With a suddenness that left Jed speechless, Megan stepped into Jed, wrapping her arms around his waist, burying her face in his shirt, like a child clinging to an angry parent.

She shook with sobs.

"Please, Jed. I beg you. Don't tell anyone the results. I'm begging you."

Jed stroked her hair, pulling her closer.

He realized at that very moment that he'd fallen in love with her.

"I'm sorry," he said. "I can't do that."

Without another glance his way, Megan pushed out of his arms, then turned and walked out the door.

TWENTY-NINE

AT ONE TIME, Jed's heart would have skipped a beat at the sight that met him when he turned down the drive to the Double Jump and saw the two figures in the distance.

Rebecca, blond locks flowing behind her, galloping across the meadow of the Double Jump at a speed only an expert, and fearless, rider would dare. Neither she nor the horse—a sorrel, he couldn't yet recognize which since Rebecca owned several—had noticed the truck yet.

Jed slowed the truck, watching. He could not help but admire her skills as a horsewoman.

As they approached a downed tree, Rebecca actually spurred the horse, demanding more speed. Then, with Rebecca bending at the waist to become one with the animal, they soared, suspended in air, until they'd cleared the thick debris with yards to spare. Jed saw Rebecca bend even lower, hugging the horse, no doubt thanking it for its performance.

He gave the truck more gas.

This finally caught the sorrel's attention. It turned its ears back, ever so slightly, but enough for Rebecca to turn, too, waving gaily when she recognized Jed's truck.

As Jed approached, she trotted across the gravel road in front of him, then circled round to ride alongside him.

Now Jed recognized the mare.

After Nada Quinn died, Jed had pick up her beloved mare. Jed knew that horses grieved just like their human counterparts, and he'd also known that at that time Sugar needed more attention than he could give her. When he'd called Rebecca, she'd insisted that he bring the mare to her. Just until things settled down a little for Jed.

Rolling alongside the twosome, he lowered his window.

"I see you and Sugar are getting along just fine."

A huge grin split Rebecca's face. She was one of those women who people assume only looked good with the right makeup and hair, but the truth was that Rebecca's beauty only grew when she went natural, like today. No makeup, worn jeans, a down vest, and cowboy boots. Hair ungroomed and wild.

"She's a sweetie," she said, wrapping both arms around the horse's neck as they trotted alongside the moving truck. "I may not let you have her back. Did you see her clear that log?"

Jed nodded. "It was a pretty sight."

Rebecca's grin grew wider still. "You *do* still care for me."

Jed did not look her in the eye. "Of course I care for you," he said.

Rebecca was still lying against Sugar's neck, her face pressed to its warmth, her eyes studying Jed.

"Then why is it that things just haven't felt the same, Jed? Not for a while now."

Jed loved the sound of Sugar's shoes on the road, the smell wafting toward him. He loved this world he and Rebecca had inhabited together. For a moment, a sadness, a sense of profound loss, washed over him at the knowledge that it had fallen apart.

"It's been a stressful time," he replied.

"I hope that's all it is," Rebecca said, in a voice so sincere that Jed could not resist looking at her. How could it be that this day he had come to confront her—the same woman he'd loved so wildly just a few short weeks ago?

Rebecca seemed to sense his melancholy.

"I love you," she said, her smile turning sad.

He did not respond.

She trotted alongside his truck the rest of the length of the drive. When they reached the barn, she jumped down to the ground. Jed watched as she slid the saddle off Nada Quinn's old mare. He watched as Rebecca stroked and talked to Sugar, soothing her, sensing the mare's loss as clearly as she seemed to sense hers and Jed's.

Jed had never seen anyone more gentle with horses than Rebecca. Bringing Sugar there had been the right thing to do.

Once she'd brushed the sorrel down, delaying the inevitable, Rebecca turned to Jed.

"This isn't a social visit, is it?"

"No. It's not."

"So tell me, Jed. Tell me what brought you here today. Tell me what's happened to you. To us."

This time Jed did not avoid her eyes.

"Did you have anything to do with those people who got sick and died?"

"*To do* with it? You mean, did I know the people who died? What the hell *do* you mean?"

"I mean are you in some way responsible for the brucellosis outbreak?"

Rebecca looked like she'd just been slapped across the face.

"You son of a bitch. How dare you?"

Every frustration, every hurt, came boiling up in Jed at that moment.

"How dare I?" he said. "I'll tell you how." He pushed his index finger into Rebecca's chest. "I know about you and

Cyrus. I've seen the e-mails. I know that you were feeding him information about me. About my research."

At first, Rebecca fell back, gasping at the disclosure. Then, desperate, she closed the distance between them, trying to put her arms around Jed.

He pushed her away roughly. She had never seen this side of Jed—anything short of gentle. It clearly frightened her.

"I'm sorry, Jed. I'm sorry."

"It doesn't even matter any more. All I want now is the truth. Lives are at stake, Rebecca."

Still shocked to learn that Jed knew of her betrayal, Rebecca pawed at him.

"Maybe I shouldn't have. But Cyrus convinced me that . . ." Her words drifted off.

Jed grabbed her shoulders, holding her at arm's length.

"Convinced you *what?*"

"No." She shook her head. "I can't say. All I can tell you is that Cyrus promised he'd never do anything to hurt you. He promised he was only looking out for ranchers like him and me."

Disgusted, Jed dropped his hands.

"You were willing to kill people in some misguided effort to protect the ranchers?"

"Kill people!" Rebecca cried. "You're out of your mind. I'd never allow anyone to be hurt, much less killed."

"What about Clancy?" Jed replied, glaring at her. "And Dusty Harrison? What about *me?*"

Refusing to let him push her away again, Rebecca fought Jed. She reached for his face, pulling him roughly toward her, giving him no choice but to look into her eyes.

"Jed McCane. You listen to me and listen good. I'd never do anything to hurt another living soul. I give you my word. It hurts more than you could know to think you'd even think that was possible." Her expression softened, and Jed knew she was about to cry. "But most of all, Jed, I'd never do anything to hurt you. Don't you know that? I love you. You're all I have."

Jed slapped her hands away from his face.

"Why shouldn't I tell the CDC you're involved in some way in those people's deaths?"

"Because it's not true! How can you think I'd do that? How can you? You're losing your mind, Jed."

"Maybe I am," he answered. He turned, and walked toward the parked truck.

"Don't go," she cried, running after him. She grabbed his shoulders from behind. "It's okay, Jed. I'll stand by you. We'll get you help. I love you, Jed. I'll do whatever it takes."

Jed could hear her sobs as he reached frantically for the key in the ignition. Turning it, he exhaled a sigh of relief when the motor finally drowned them out.

THIRTY

THE SIGNS POSTED at every grocery store and gas station throughout southwestern Montana called it an "informational meeting."

In response to the recent deaths of six locals from brucellosis, the Montana Department of Livestock, in combination with the CDC and Ennis County health department, will be presenting information and answering questions at the West Yellowstone High School gymnasium from 7 to 9 P.M. on Wednesday, October 19.

By six forty-five, all the seats that had been set out earlier in the day—120 to be exact—in the center of the auditorium had been taken. Several of the local men had begun pulling out the stadium bleachers, over the protests of the high school custodian, who claimed that the bleachers had been declared unsafe and were due for repair before the start of basketball season.

By the time Jed strolled through the door at five minutes

before the hour, a noticeable degree of chaos had taken over. The buzz of nervous, angst-riddled voices mixed with bleachers thundering down from the wall. The cool fall temperatures outside instantly gave way to the sweat- and tension-filled air inside the gymnasium.

Jed spied Andy at the front of the room and made his way to the long table that had been set up for the panel of experts assembled to reassure the community.

"Quite a turnout," Jed said, eyeing the crowd.

"Those kids' deaths scared them all shitless," Andy replied. "Can you blame them? Recognize her?"

Jed followed Andy's eyes to a stately woman standing to the side of the table. Tall, thin, with short, graying hair, she looked the part of a corporate executive.

She stood at the center of a group of three men, two of whom Jed recognized. Clay Kittrick and Cyrus Gibbons. The attire of the other—an expensive dark suit—declared him an outsider.

Several yards away, a group of CDC people—Matthew Hughes at its center—huddled in discussion.

"No," Jed said. "Who is she?"

"Jo Chandler. Superintendent of the park."

Jed's eyebrows shot up. He'd corresponded with Chandler, even had phone conversations with her, but had never actually met her. He'd always liked her and respected what he knew of her.

"Who do you suppose invited her?" Andy said.

"My guess is she wasn't invited," Jed replied. "But I know she's a dogged protector of the park and anything to do with it. I'm sure she realizes the potential this outbreak has to affect that."

"Probably. Still, it's a gutsy thing to do. She's none too popular in these parts. And what's happened recently can't have helped."

As they talked, Clay Kittrick left the group to stand at the center of the table. He reached for a wooden gavel and pounded it three times.

The microphone emitted an excruciating screech as he spoke into it. He tried again with the same result. Finally, he ditched the mike, cupped his hand to his mouth and shouted.

"Everyone take your seats."

The groups assembled at the front of the room immediately disbanded, heading for each person's designated seat at the long center table.

It became apparent immediately that one had not been provided for Jo Chandler.

Jed stood and offered her his chair.

Determinedly, she nodded and thanked him, slipping into his seat. As she did so, she touched his forearm, giving it a light squeeze of thanks.

Jed had turned to head for the bleachers when Matthew Hughes materialized beside him with an extra chair. Jo Chandler immediately scooted over to make room for Jed, and in a ripple effect, the rest of the panelists slid their chairs noisily in each direction to accommodate the extra chair.

While all this was going on, the school custodian appeared and began tinkering with the microphone.

"Testing one two three," he said, adopting the hushed tone of a golf announcer. "Testing."

When his voice came through loud and clear, Clay turned the portable microphone in his direction. "Everyone please settle down so this meeting can get started."

Latecomers began scrambling into the stadium bleachers, and within a minute or two, the room fell silent.

Clay cleared his throat.

"We're here tonight to reassure you about recent events in this area. As you know, we've had several locals contract brucellosis. Not only are the people in this area concerned about their own health, this is ranching country and you cattlemen are understandably concerned about if, and how, your herds and businesses will be affected. This team of panelists here has been assembled to answer your questions and put your minds at ease."

"At ease," a man from the back of the room shouted. "How the hell can you put us at ease? Folks are dying right and left."

Jed had been skimming the handwritten notes he'd prepared for the meeting throughout Clay's introduction, but at this angry protest, he looked up. As he eyed the audience, trying to pinpoint the person who'd shouted out, a wild mane of jet-black waves caught his attention.

Megan.

She sat about two-thirds of the way back, in the rows of chairs on the floor. K.C. sat by her side, eyes darting among the crowd like a hunted prey. An attractive Native American woman on Megan's other side whispered in her ear. When she lowered the hand cupped to Megan's ear, Jed recognized her as Colleen Talks to Sky. He'd seen her picture in the paper numerous times.

Suddenly, another head of hair caught Jed's attention; only this time, it was strawberry blond in color.

Just two rows in front of the Buffalo Field Campaign activists, Rebecca Nichols stuck out like a rose in full bloom in a vase of wilted geraniums. She'd apparently noticed Jed eyeing someone behind her, for she'd turned, and now studied Megan, wearing an expression that Jed knew meant trouble.

Clay had introduced Matthew Hughes.

"We've traced the brucella that caused the outbreak to beef sold at the West Yellowstone grocery," Hughes announced. "We believe we've been successful in removing all that beef from the market. We have every reason to believe we've seen the worst of this outbreak."

"Is it true that the beef came from Jack Hamlin's herd?" someone shouted.

"We believe so, yes."

Another anonymous questioner called out, "How the hell did Jack's herd get infected?"

"We're still investigating."

Another man jumped to his feet. Jed recognized him as Jack Hamlin. "There's no need to investigate. I'll tell you how my herd got infected. They got it from the park bison."

The CDC investigator glanced Jed's way. "That's a possibility we're looking into."

"Looking into?" Hamlin, red faced, shouted. "I lost my whole goddamn herd. Every penny I invested when I moved up here. Looking into it isn't enough. Those buffalo should be killed. Every goddamn one of them." He held his arm out, finger pointed, and swept the audience with it. "Or you'll all end up like me. With dead herds and filing bankruptcy."

A roar greeted these words, and several shouts of "Kill 'em."

Colleen Talks to Sky had been waving her hand in the air and shouting, trying to be heard. Now, she stood, mowing her way across an assortment of knees to reach the center aisle.

"Stop. Listen to yourselves. These are America's last free-roaming buffalo and you're suggesting we wipe them out. Over a myth. A myth that they can transmit brucellosis to cattle. Well, they *can't*!"

This only agitated the crowd more.

"Sit down."

"Shut 'er up."

"Fuckin' radical Indian."

This rough Montana talk made Hughes decidedly nervous. "Now we're getting a little out of my area of expertise," he said. "We've asked a local veterinarian who's an expert on brucellosis to be on the panel tonight. I'm going to ask Dr. Jed McCane to address the transmission issue."

Jed cleared his throat and stood, declining the microphone Hughes passed his way.

"Preliminary tests have indicated that the *Brucella abortus* strain that killed Nada Quinn and the others is related to the strain carried by the park herd."

This time the response that issued from the auditorium amounted to nothing less than a roar.

"But wait," Jed yelled over the uproar, holding up his hand. "There are distinct differences between the two strains. A mutation's taken place. It's premature to blame this outbreak on the park bison. The brucella carried by the park bison is not deadly. And, as most of you know, there's never been a documented case of transmission of brucellosis from bison to cattle. Never. Now, I realize there's always the possibility that this is the first. But scientific logic argues against it."

"Why?" someone yelled out.

"For one thing, we know with absolute certainty that the time lapse between when the park bison occupied the Horse Butte allotment and when Jack Hamlin's herd occupied it was over a month. The *Brucella abortus* organism can only survive ex vivo—meaning outside the body—for hours. Not days. And certainly not weeks."

A man rose from the front seat. It was the guy Jed had seen talking to Cyrus Gibbons before the meeting was called to order.

"But you've reported that this new strain is a mutated version of the strain you isolated last spring from the park bison."

In addition to the quality and cut of his custom-tailored gray suit, his midwestern accent set him miles apart from the rest of the group.

"Yes," Jed answered. "But we don't know where that mutation took place. It's possible it mutated in the bison; but I believe it's more likely it mutated in Hamlin's cattle, or even in Reed Jones's."

Jack Hamlin jumped back up, but the man who'd just spoken had moved to the center aisle now, and all heads had turned his way.

"You believe the mutation is what transformed the bru-cella from a nonfatal disease to a fatal disease, do you not?"

"That's the current theory, yes."

"Well, what's to say that same mutation doesn't allow the brucella to survive ex vivo for weeks? Under that scenario, the park bison could very well be responsible."

Jed felt Jo Chandler's touch on his arm.

"Ask him to identify himself," she whispered.

Jed stared at the man.

"Would you like to introduce yourself? I don't think I've seen you around here before."

"Gladly. My name is Stanley Kemper. Dr. Stanley Kemper."

"Are you a physician?"

"No. I'm a veterinarian."

Jed realized what Jo Chandler had been getting at.

"Do you have an affiliation with someone here?"

Kemper looked to Cyrus Gibbons. "I work for the Na-tional Cattlemen's Association," Kemper answered.

Jed tried to hold back his temper. "And just where are you from, Dr. Kemper?"

"Denver."

"I assume then that you're here in your official capacity."

"That's right. It's been the National Cattlemen's Associa-tion's position all along that the only way we're going to eradicate brucellosis in this country once and for all is to wipe it out in Yellowstone's bison."

Jo Chandler couldn't restrain herself. She grabbed the mi-crophone from Jed.

"The only way that's going to happen any time soon is by slaughtering all the park's bison."

"If that's what it takes," Kemper replied calmly.

Colleen Talks to Sky had jumped back to her feet and now she too stepped into the center aisle.

"What about elk?" she called. "They carry brucellosis, too. Are you going to wipe them out? No, of course not. Because the hunting and guiding lobby's almost as strong as the cattlemen's lobby."

Several people in the audience had jumped up and were waving their hands madly, trying to get Clay Kittrick's attention.

He pounded his gavel three times.

"That's enough speaking out of order," he said, glaring at Talks to Sky.

He pointed at a man at the back of the room.

"Harold, go ahead."

A man in a green plaid shirt rose to his feet.

"Them fuckin' buffalo been threatenin' our cattle for years. Now they're killin' our neighbors. It's time to get rid of them."

A chorus of voices indicated the crowd's growing interest in this plan.

Instinctively, Jed looked at Megan. Her face revealed an unspeakable horror. She suddenly realized he was staring at her and locked eyes with him. Jed flinched at the memory of her begging him not to disclose the fact that the strain of brucella that killed Nada and the others was the same as that isolated from the park's bison.

She jumped to her feet and spoke without waiting to be recognized.

"The park bison have nothing to do with what happened. Nothing. Let Jed McCane prove it."

Jed's eyes had fallen on Rebecca. He saw her nostrils flare with anger at the familiarity of Megan's reference to Jed.

"She's another one of them hippie buffalo people," someone called. "Shut up and sit down."

Jed held his voice steady as he spoke into the mike.

"She has as much right to be here as the rest of you. And she's right. We can settle the question of where the mutation took place once and for all."

"How?"

"By testing the park bison again."

Cyrus didn't wait for the microphone to be passed down to him.

"Tests take time," he said. "Weeks. We can't let this deadly disease spread and kill more innocent people."

"But as Matthew Hughes just said," Jed replied, "the disease has been contained. As long as that's true, we have time."

Kemper had never left his spot. He waved a hand in the air, trying to get Clay's official recognition.

"Kemper," Clay said, nodding at him.

"Even if you do some sampling and only find the strain that hasn't been mutated, you'd have to test every animal in the park to be absolutely certain this new, deadly strain didn't start somewhere in the park herd."

Things had gotten so rowdy that no one had even noticed several minutes earlier when the doors at the back of the gymnasium opened and a group of five men and one woman had entered. All of them, including the woman, wore dark suits easily as expensive as Kemper's. One man strode down the center aisle toward the front of the room, brushing by Kemper as he did so.

Jed recognized him instantly. John Liddicott, senator and presidential candidate.

Murmurs of recognition rippled through the crowd.

"May I address the panel?" he said, speaking to Clay Kittrick.

"Of course, Senator."

He looked immediately to Jo Chandler.

"Good evening, Ms. Chandler," he said. "It's nice to see you again."

"It's nice to see you too, Senator, though I wish it were under different circumstances."

"I agree," he said solemnly. "Ms. Chandler, as superintendent of Yellowstone National Park, one of this nation's greatest treasures, I'm sure you appreciate the need to protect the park bison."

This drew loud boos from the crowd.

The senator held his hands up, asking for silence.

"Of course," Chandler replied when it quieted down.

"But I'm equally sure you understand that human health and safety is paramount."

"Yes," she replied. "I agree."

"With that in mind, Ms. Chandler, would you approve of a sampling of the park bison to resolve this issue once and for all?"

Chandler was quick to respond. "Yes, of course," she said. "I would, however, have to get approval from the Department of the Interior before we actually commenced any new project to sample the bison."

Kemper shouted out, "I stand by my assertion that all the park's bison would have to be tested. There are lives at stake here."

Jed was on his feet now.

"It's ridiculous to claim that you have to test every animal. Scientific sampling has been the basis of sound research for decades. It's a known discipline."

A small cluster of cheers from the vicinity of the BFC members greeted Jed's words.

Clay Kittrick pounded his gavel again.

"The only way to resolve the issue of whether or not to sample the park bison is to put it to a vote and see what the consensus is. Everyone on this panel will have one vote. Let's just see where the panel stands, then go from there."

He looked both directions for approval of his proposal. Several heads nodded.

"Okay, now," he said, "everyone who agrees the park bison should be sampled, raise your hand."

Jed and Jo Chandler each lifted their right arm in the air.

Jed glanced to his left and saw that Andy did not.

"Everyone who thinks they should not?"

Four other members of the panel raised their hands. Clay Kittrick did not vote.

He appeared somewhat shaken as he announced, "It appears the majority of this panel does not think a sampling is adequate protection for this community."

"What'd I tell you?" Cyrus said, pulling the microphone his way.

Colleen Talks to Sky shouted to be heard over the cheers that met his proclamation.

"Then we must test all the park's bison. If that's what it takes."

Senator Liddicott saw this as a way to get back into the fray.

"Ms. Chandler," he said, striding front and center again. "How feasible do you think it is to test every bison in the park?"

The crowd grew silent.

Jo Chandler did not respond.

"Ms. Chandler?"

Sitting next to her, Jed could see Chandler's hands shaking; however, when she answered, she held her voice steady

"In my opinion, it would be impossible to test every bison in the park."

"Thank you, Superintendent Chandler. I was afraid that would be your answer. Like you, I believe that we must put human health and safety above all other priorities. I appreciate your candor."

Jed felt an acute disappointment at how the superintendent had responded. Why had this champion of the park and all its inhabitants not fought harder to clear the name of the bison?

K.C. was back on his feet, shouting, "You've been relying

on sampling the bison for years now, when it suits you. Why stop now?"

Cyrus jumped to his feet.

"We've already heard, testing just a few of the park bison won't prove anything. And the superintendent herself says we can't test them all."

Kemper too decided to make the most of the growing hysteria.

"Even if it was a theoretical possibility to test them all, we can't afford the time it would take. Like the superintendent herself said, those park bison are under the jurisdiction of the federal government. There's a process that has to be followed to get approval to sample them. That could take weeks. And I guarantee you, during those weeks, there'd be some lawsuits filed and injunctions slammed on the sampling. Add to that the time it would take to actually do the sampling. We don't have that kind of time to get this situation under control. People are dying. Your friends and neighbors are at risk. Your children."

"What then?" someone in the audience called out. "What're you gonna do to make all of us here safe?"

"I say we slaughter them all," someone else yelled.

"I agree," Cyrus said. "That's exactly what we need to do."

For once, the Buffalo Field Campaign activists were not alone in their protest. Despite the antienvironmental leanings of most the crowd, talk like this did not sit well with many of those in attendance, especially those whose livelihoods depended upon visitors to the park. Hundreds of thousands of visitors each year came to see the bison and more than a few in the audience made a living from those visitors.

"You can't do that," K.C. shouted. He turned to face the crowd. "Can't you see? They're just trying to use this unfortunate tragedy for their own political motives."

Shouting and name-calling erupted from both sides.

Senator Liddicott raised both arms in the air and slowly circled, making a patting motion with his hands.

"Calm down. We cannot allow our fear to create a mass hysteria. There has to be a solution that balances human health with the safety of the park bison and I pledge to help this committee find it."

"Go back home," someone shouted. "You're just a bleeding-heart liberal, trying to get the environmentalists' votes."

This didn't daunt the senator.

"If the definition of an environmentalist is someone who wants to avoid squandering the resources and natural beauty of this earth, I am an environmentalist," Liddicott said, "and proud of it. But I give you my word here and now. I will not put the health and safety of park bison over that of this country's constituents."

It surprised Jed to see how quickly Clay Kittrick piped up.

"I agree with the senator. There have to be other solutions. I say it's premature to discount the possibility of testing all the park bison. We've got the best medical minds in the world working on this. There've been no new cases. This talk of slaughtering all the bison is too radical. I think maybe we need to talk more about whether to proceed with testing the park herd. I propose a meeting of this panel in four days. Sunday afternoon. Two P.M. That will give us all time to get our facts straight. Dr. Hughes, would you make certain you have the timeline required for definitive test results?"

Hughes nodded his assent.

"And I'd like to invite Senator Liddicott to join us. Also, Superintendent Chandler."

"I'd be honored," Senator Liddicott called from the back of the room.

At the opposite end of the table, Cyrus Gibbons leaned

forward, his bloated stomach resting on the tabletop.

"What the hell you doing, Clay? We voted fair and square. We're not gonna test all the bison. Period." He glared at Clay. "I'll get you fired for this."

Kittrick ignored him.

Clay's proclamation, coming as it did from a professional who'd devoted his life to an industry directly at odds with the bison, a man respected and needed by the entire ranching community, carried considerable weight and managed to bring some degree of order back to the meeting.

Seeing that, Clay decided to cut the meeting short and eliminate the chance for further eruptions.

"And now I'll call for a motion to adjourn."

The motion was made and seconded, and Clay struck the table one last time, disbanding the group.

Troubled, Jed pushed through the crowd to exit the gymnasium. He saw Andy making his way toward him and tried to avoid him, but just as he reached the exit, Andy stepped in front of him.

"What's the hurry?" he said.

Jed stared at him several seconds before answering.

"You just voted to wipe out the entire herd of buffalo in the park."

"Jed, what's gotten into you? You've seen what this disease can do. Protecting local ranchers' cattle should be your top priority. Mine is to protect the people of this area. I love those bison, too. But not at the expense of human lives."

"It's too early to start blaming the park bison and you know it. They're being tried and convicted when a simple test can tell us if they have anything to do with the outbreak."

"Even Superintendent Chandler admitted testing all the bison is impossible. And the issue isn't dead anyway. We'll revisit it on Sunday, when we have more facts. And when emotions aren't flying quite so high."

"I don't believe this," Jed muttered. He saw no point in arguing with Andy. He pushed past him, only to come face-to-face with someone else he'd hoped to avoid.

Rebecca.

"We have to talk," she said. "I'll stand by you, Jed, if you let me."

Almost immediately, Jed felt someone grab his arm from behind.

"Jed."

He turned to see Megan standing behind him. Her face held utter despair.

Instinctively, he reached for her, putting his arm around her shoulders. "It'll be okay," he said.

Rebecca stood there watching. Then, eyes glued to Jed, she stepped forward and, without warning, delivered a stinging slap across his face.

Several gasps escaped from the exiting crowd, most of whom recognized both Jed and Rebecca.

When Jed saw Rebecca turn her attention to Megan, he stepped between them.

"That's enough," he said. "Go, Rebecca. Go home. Before you do something you'll regret."

"Is it *her*?" Rebecca cried. "Is *she* what happened between us?"

Jed put a hand on her shoulder and, more gently now, said, "Go home, Rebecca. Please."

Slapping his hand away, Rebecca turned and walked through the crowd of stunned onlookers.

Like the Red Sea dividing for Moses, they parted as she passed.

THIRTY-ONE

THE VAN CRUISED slowly along the narrow two-lane road. K.C. sat at the wheel, negotiating its curves, using utmost care in light of the fact that the vehicle's tires were bald, and a thin coat of ice had formed on the road overnight.

Just before the turnoff to Virginia Cascades, along the Norris to Canyon road, their headlights picked up a black form, moving low and fast—so fast that in the darkness just before sunrise they might well have thought it a mirage if it weren't for the fact that it paused on the other side of the road and looked the van's way. For one fleeting moment, the headlights caught those hauntingly beautiful gray eyes before the creature disappeared into brush at the side of the road.

"A wolf," Megan said quietly, reverently.

Jed's breath caught. As much time as he'd spent in the country, he'd rarely seen a wolf. He had, however, on several occasions, seen the carcasses of calves taken down by a pack; and before this instant, Jed had even questioned the wisdom of Yellowstone's reintroduction of the wolves in 1995.

But in that fleeting moment when the wolf's eyes turned

their way, the sight—the magnificent wildness of the animal—instantly banished any doubts he'd previously had.

It also bolstered his sense of purpose.

So little wilderness remained on this planet. Yellowstone and its wild creatures—especially its magnificent bison—had to be protected. At any cost.

They drove on in silence, to the Chittenden Bridge.

"There," Megan said. "Up ahead."

The van pulled over and Jed and Megan stepped into a bitter wind that rushed down upon them from the north.

They moved quickly. Law-enforcement rangers patrolled the roads regularly. They'd strapped their backpacks on before climbing into the van. Jed nodded at K.C as he slammed the door shut.

"Good luck," K.C. called.

Three herds of buffalo roamed freely in Yellowstone. The Pelican Valley, the Mary Mountain, and the Lamar. It was members of the Mary Mountain herd who wandered onto the Horse Butte allotment in search of food in the late winter months. Jed had tested them there the past spring, during the DOL testing.

The Mary Mountain bison summered in the Hayden Valley, where tourists could spot them from their cars. Now, many of the herd were making their way back across Mary Mountain. They'd winter near Mary Lake.

The night before, after the town meeting, Jed, Megan, and K.C. had mapped the course Jed and Megan would follow. From the bridge, they would head southwest, into the woods, and hike several miles before connecting with the Mary Mountain Trail. They had to reach backcountry, and be out of sight, by daybreak. All in all, they anticipated a ten-mile hike to find most of the Mary Mountain herd, on its way to wintering grounds.

The wind, howling down from the Canadian Rockies, dropped temperatures that registered in the twenties on the thermometer to less than ten degrees. It also made talking impossible; but as snow began to fall, Jed welcomed it for the simple fact that it obliterated their old footprints as quickly as they made new ones.

As day broke over the Absarokas, a dense fog rose from the Yellowstone River, giving the majestic landscape an even more mystic quality. Fleetingly visible through the steam rising from the water, a herd of bison grazed.

When they reached Otter Creek, Jed and Megan stopped to put on waders for crossing. Bent at the waist as he wriggled his boots into the waders' rubber feet, Jed looked up. Just on the other side, through a veil of steam, a huge bull stared at them. Already sporting a thick, ragged winter coat, its broad shoulders and massive hump declared its readiness for the upcoming winter—a war it had obviously survived for many years now.

A chill ran through Jed.

"These are just the slow ones," Megan said as they trudged across the creek. "The others are already up there, near the lake."

The bison paid them little heed as Jed and Megan climbed out on the other side, removed their waders and stashed them back in their packs, and continued on across the open land.

The night before they'd agreed that they needed to go deeper, into the backcountry, before beginning their clandestine mission—back where they were certain not to run into hardy hikers or, worse, rangers.

They would not stop until they'd traveled miles from any roads, and had reached the shelter of the forest surrounding Mary Lake. The rest of the Mary Mountain herd should be found there.

Jed had trouble keeping up with Megan.

He had known plenty of stubbornly determined people in his life. Rebecca could certainly be counted among them, but over the past ten hours, since the town meeting, at which the

threat of a bison slaughter more horrific than anything anyone had imagined in their wildest dreams hung heavy in the
air—like smoke from a summer wildfire—Jed had witnessed
a level of determination in Megan that he'd never before
known.

Megan had been the first to put it in words. Jed later told
her that sitting there the night before, observing the direction
the meeting had taken, he'd already made the decision.

*I'll sample the park buffalo, with or without permission to
do so.*

Jed knew that sampling done correctly carried scientific
weight. More important, it represented the only constructive
course of action he could take at the moment. He'd conduct
his own tests on the samples and also send them off for further testing, and then do everything in his power to force officials to take the results seriously. Of course, it had become
clear the night before that Cyrus Gibbons and his hired gun,
Kemper, would just as adamantly insist that all the park's bison had to be tested in order to ensure public health and
safety—an impossibility that meant the park bison could not
be cleared. And Cyrus had pull, no doubt about it. As a big
player in the Montana Cattlemen's Association, he had many
of the state legislators in his pocket, as well as an able side-
kick in Kemper.

But now a new wild card had entered the picture. John
Liddicott. Jed sensed that the senator and presidential candidate's position the night before had been calculated to appease both camps—the environmentalists, as well as citizens
concerned about the genuine risk of brucellosis. Still, Jed
felt hopeful Liddicott would get behind Jed's crusade to allow scientific sampling to determine whether the park bison
presented a threat.

At any rate, Jed simply could not sit idle until three days
from now, when the assembled experts debated the issue of
whether to sample the park bison. And he knew that any

formal action would take days, if not weeks, to be run through proper park channels, time they might not have.

If things went well, he would get a head start on the process, and save valuable time. Perhaps his preliminary results could stave off something drastic.

"Wait up," he finally called, his words forming clouds that lifted into the frigid air.

From behind, with her bulging backpack—she'd insisted on carrying the same weight, pound for pound as Jed; veterinary supplies, water, food, and sleeping bags; all necessary for their projected two-day sampling spree—the only thing that gave away Megan's frail build were her pencil-thin legs, clad this morning in wool pants instead of the usual blue jeans.

She turned, and flashed him a smile. This mission had given her hope.

"Come on, slow poke," she called, not daunted by the falling snow, or the fact that they'd entered prime grizzly country.

The grasslands had given way to thinly forested hills. Skeletal reminders of the fire of 1988—which had swept through part of Yellowstone, burning almost eight hundred thousand of the park's 2.2 million acres—stood black against the falling snow.

The burned-out forest finally led to an area unscarred by the fire, and on top of the Yellowstone plateau, they came across a small, high-country lake.

Continuing on, they hiked up and over ridge after ridge side by side, each ridge becoming more rocky and precarious, with Jed making a determined effort not to lag behind.

As they crested another, Megan suddenly stopped.

"There they are."

Below, snow coating their massive heads and backs, a herd of almost three hundred bison grazed in an area of burned-out trees.

They stood silently, staring in awe.

"Look," Jed finally said, "stragglers, over there. Let's start with them."

He scanned the scene below.

"That rock," he said, pointing to a VW-sized boulder sitting behind the main herd but within a hundred yards of the strays. "It's perfect."

As they scrambled down the rocky hillside, patches of ice caused them to slip several times on the rhyolitic surface. Each slip sent torrents of smaller rocks and gravel raining down below.

The bison paid them no heed.

When they crossed the thinly treed field and reached the rock Jed had pointed out, he dropped to one knee and slipped out of his backpack. Reaching inside, he withdrew a dart gun that looked like a pistol, then a bottle of Telazol, which he steadied by pushing it into two inches of fresh snow.

As he used a syringe to remove the fluid from the pharmacy bottle and inject it into the darts, he said, "The wind will help. The rest shouldn't even hear."

He loaded a dart into the gun.

"You're sure this won't hurt them?" Megan called over the howling wind.

"It'll just knock them out for a few minutes. We'll have to act fast."

"I'm ready."

"That one," Jed said, pointing to a big bull grazing some twenty yards away.

Megan lifted binoculars to her eyes and said, "I've got him in my sights."

Jed took aim and fired.

"You got him!"

Right when the dart hit, the big animal, a bull, started. He glanced over first one shoulder, then another, but then, as if he were accustomed to projectiles puncturing his hide, he soon returned to grazing, swinging his head like a pendulum from side to side, brushing through the light layer of snow hiding the grass.

Even from twenty yards, Jed could hear his breaths, expelled in snorts. The tranquilizer should have caused them to grow slower, longer.

"Damn," Jed said after a couple minutes had passed. "Maybe I didn't load enough of the Telazol. That dose would've brought a Brahma bull to its knees by now."

"No, look," Megan said, handing Jed the binoculars.

The animal took two steps forward, wobbling first left, then right. Suddenly, it toppled to the ground, sending snow and dirt flying into the air.

Just ahead, two other bison grazed undisturbed.

"Bingo," Jed cried. "I'll hit the others now, too. Then we can sample all three at once."

This time the first dart missed. The second one hit its target, but this bison didn't share the first bull's laid-back disposition. It turned, looking for its attackers. Seeing Jed and Megan standing, watching, five or six feet from the rock, it began running toward them. Its companion joined, lumbering behind.

"Get behind the rock," Jed ordered while he lifted the gun and fired at the second animal.

"Look out, he's charging," Megan cried. However, halfway through the charge, the first animal began to stumble.

The second one kept coming at Jed.

"Jed," Megan screamed, "get back here."

Jed stood his ground, reaching for another dart.

"Jed!"

Just as Jed slid the dart into the gun, the bison's head swayed left, then right. Then the giant form crashed to the ground, less than a dozen feet away from where Jed stood.

"Quick, my pack," Jed yelled as he ran past the two that had just charged toward the first animal he shot, thirty yards away. He would be the safest to sample.

They'd let the sedative do its work on the others before approaching them.

Megan followed behind, keeping an eye on the other two forms, both of which still twitched. One bellowed weakly as she passed, its legs, moving in useless circles, kicking up snow.

She caught up with Jed, who kneeled beside the first animal, and handed him the sampling kit. They both made certain to position themselves so they faced the two other bison in case one were to charge.

"Jed . . ."

Jed felt Megan nudging his arm, but he'd just begun probing the thick mat of fur on the bison's foreleg and did not want to look up.

Another voice, however, stopped him cold.

"You could go to prison for this."

Jed's head snapped around to look over his shoulder.

Megan had apparently already noticed the approaching rider, who sat tall on a gelded paint, head covered with a hooded parka.

The crest plate on the horse's harness bore the insignia of the National Parks.

Law enforcement, Jed thought, taking a deep breath.

He looked over at Megan, and could not tell whether she was more frightened or grief stricken. They'd just lost their only hope to clear the park bison of suspicion.

"She has nothing to do with this," Jed said, nodding to Megan. He still held the front leg of the bison in his left hand. "I lied to her. I told her we had authority to be here."

Megan stepped toward the horse. The wind plastered the hood against the rider's face, shielding it.

"That's not true. It was my idea. This is Jed McCane. He's a vet. An expert on brucellosis. He's only trying to prove that the park bison didn't cause those deaths."

"I know Dr. McCane," the rider said, throwing the parka's hood off.

Jed and Megan gasped simultaneously when they saw her face.

Jo Chandler, superintendent of Yellowstone.

"Ms. Chandler," Jed said.

"Dr. McCane."

In that moment, Jed knew he'd put his reputation—his entire career—in jeopardy.

"I know we're not supposed to be here," he said. "But you were at the meeting last night. If we wait for the committee to make up its mind, then for the park bureaucracy to go through the approval process, you and I both know these bison will be in grave danger. I'm willing to go to jail for this, but please, just allow me to take these samples first and send them off. Please."

"Why are you doing this, Dr. McCane?" Chandler shouted over the storm. "Your business is with cattlemen. You know how cattlemen feel about these bison."

Jed glanced over at Megan before answering. His feelings for her no doubt helped explain it, but it was more than that. He stepped close to Chandler and her mount, wanting to make certain he was heard.

"I took an oath never to do harm to animals. I can't allow my loyalty to the cattle ranchers to compromise that. If these bison are responsible for the deaths that took place, I'll have to make a very hard decision. But my experience and gut tells me they're not. I think finding the truth is what matters here. To the cattlemen, to the bison, and to the public. And the only way we're going to do that is by sampling these bison."

Chandler studied him long and hard.

"I agree with you," she responded.

As she turned her horse's head to go, Jed and Megan exchanged confused glances.

"What?" Jed shouted. "But at the meeting last night . . ."

Chandler jerked back on the horse's reins, bringing it to a stop. She turned back, slowly, to meet Jed's gaze.

"My job is a very political one, Dr. McCane. I've learned that sometimes the best way to protect this park, and all its animals, is by playing games I don't much like playing."

"Are you saying you're not going to stop us?"

For a moment, a gleam brightened the superintendent's otherwise sad eyes.

"Stop what?" she answered. "I'm just out for a morning ride."

She pressed her knees to the animal's belly. As it broke into a run, she called over her shoulder. "I didn't see a thing."

"I GUESS WE DIDN'T need the cooler after all," Jed said as he gently packed plastic pouches filled with air around the vials of blood nestled in the small Coleman cooler he'd carried in his pack.

"I guess not," Megan replied cheerfully, though from all appearances, the day had exhausted her. Mud coated her clothing, and face. "Do you think we need more?"

"No," Jed replied. "We sampled twenty-seven. Cows, bulls, and calves. That should be enough." His eyes scanned the scene before him. The wind had finally let up. As the light faded, with snow still falling, adding to seven inches on the ground, he could just make out the outline of the Gallatins—a mountain range to the west. "Do you want to try to hike a while before we bed down?"

Megan shook her head. "I don't think I have the energy. And there's no moon. Or if there is, the snow's hiding it. I think we should stay right here."

"Okay, then," Jed replied.

Silently, with the same teamwork that had seen them

through a day of stalking, tranquilizing, and once, even wrestling a half-sedated bison, they set about making camp. Once the tent was up—a two-person backpacking tent that measured three feet in width by seven feet in length and three feet high—they lit the small backpacking stove and cooked a meal of dehydrated lasagna, which both wolfed down hungrily.

"I'll hang the packs," Jed said, leaving Megan to stuff the two sleeping bags inside the tent.

Backcountry camps in Yellowstone always sported bear poles from which campers hung their food out of reach of marauders, but this was not an authorized camping spot. Still, it was definitely bear country. Jed had trouble finding a lodgepole with branches thick enough to hang the packs the requisite ten feet from the tree's trunk. Finally he settled on two-thirds the distance.

As he stepped back out of the thicket of trees into the clearing in which they'd set up the tent, Jed stopped and stared, a sense of wonder suddenly flooding him.

The bison, mere shadows now, still swung their massive heads from side to side, sweeping away the accumulating snow to graze. Flakes the size of cotton balls drifted almost aimlessly before settling on the animals' thick fur.

Megan had lighted a small lantern, giving the tent a warm glow under its thin winter coat.

Jed could not wait to get inside.

Still, when he stuck his head between the flaps and saw Megan cocooned in her down bag, he felt obliged to offer, "I could sleep outside."

In the glow of the lantern, he could not read her smile.

"Don't be silly. Get in your bag before you freeze."

As Jed did as she ordered, removing only his boots to slip inside the bag, Megan produced a flask.

"Here," she said. "This will warm you up."

Jed took the flask. The whiskey burned his throat. He

handed it back to Megan and settled down deeper, watching as she threw back her head and sipped from it.

After several minutes, the heat from his body had warmed the bag and he slipped out of his jacket. They lay on their sides, face-to-face, too exhausted for all but the most essential conversation.

"I don't think I've ever been happier," he suddenly said.

Megan's laughter brought color to his face.

"What?" he asked. "What's so funny?"

"It's below freezing, and we're both filthy and exhausted."

"I can't explain it," Jed replied.

She reached over then, and placed a mittened hand against his cheek. "You don't need to," she said. "I feel it, too."

During the night, when the temperatures dropped to zero, they unzipped their bags and slid next to each other. Jed tucked Megan's bag around her thin frame, pulling her close to warm her. And then they made love.

Neither one of them felt the cold.

After, they dozed off, with Jed's arms encircling her. He listened to each of her breaths, awed by what he felt.

A wolf's howl signaled the coming of a new day.

"Do you think we can save them?" she whispered.

Jed thought she'd been sleeping.

"I hope so," he said. "I hope so."

THIRTY-TWO

THE COW BELLOWED its greeting as the squeaky barn door signaled Jed's entry.

"You've put on weight," Jed said, laughing as the Hereford stuck her head between two rails to contemplate his approach, her jaw grinding on alfalfa all the while.

She had been near death when he purchased her as one of a dozen cows and bulls that he led everyone to think were the animals he'd been conducting research on in the barn behind his clinic. He'd felt guilty purchasing these animals, knowing as he did the danger it put them in.

It cheered him to see them thriving now in a warm and clean environment, with enough good hay to fatten them.

"Hello?" someone called from behind him.

Jed turned. Andy Butler stood in the half-open door.

It had taken a minute for Butler to adjust to the lighting of the barn, but seeing Jed now, he strode his way.

"Jed, we need to talk."

A sense of dread ran through Jed. Had Andy and the rest of the CDC team learned about the samples he'd sent to the lab?

Jed watched Andy approach.

Definitive test results were still a week out, but at tomorrow afternoon's meeting of the advisory committee, he was looking forward to presenting Andy and the others with initial tests Jed had run, which indicated that the *Brucella abortis* he'd taken from the bison had not been the source of the deadly strain.

He expected the disclosure that he and Megan had made the illegal trip into the park to sample bison to cause a commotion. Still, when emotions died down, he'd been feeling confident that the levelheaded members of the board—the CDC investigators, Senator Liddicott, Jo Chandler, and perhaps even Clay Kittrick—would give more serious consideration to sampling all the park bison.

Now, watching Andy approach, for some reason, that confidence wavered.

"What is it?"

"The worst possible news," Andy said. "Two more people have taken ill. One of them died half an hour ago, before Life Flight could arrive."

"God, no," Jed cried.

"Jed . . ."

With that, a loud creak turned both men's attention toward the barn door.

Three men and one woman entered. Cyrus Gibbons, Matthew Hughes, Stanley Kemper. And Rebecca.

They strode toward Jed and Andy, determined expressions on each face. Rebecca trained her eyes on Andy, not Jed.

"I just told him," Andy said.

"You know what this means," Cyrus said brusquely.

"No," Jed answered. "I don't."

"The park bison have to be eliminated," Kemper said. "All of them."

"You can't do that. We don't know that the bison are the source of the infection."

"I think we do," Cyrus said. He looked at Andy. "Tell him."

Rebecca hadn't made eye contact with Jed yet.

"The woman who died got the beef at West Yellowstone grocery. Parker Derkowitz already confirmed that it was the same beef that killed the others. From Jack Hamlin's herd."

Cyrus added, "The only way Hamlin's herd could've got it was from the bison that grazed there earlier. We all know that. You said yourself it's the same strain."

"The same strain, but it's mutated. That's the whole point. We don't know when and where it mutated. It could just as easily have been in Hamlin's herd, not the bison."

"Only tests will tell that, and time for dillydallying has run out."

"I already have preliminary test results."

Every face staring at Jed transformed with a confused scowl.

"How?" Andy asked.

"I did a sampling. I drew twenty-seven samples two days ago and ran gels. There's no sign of the mutation."

This news sent Cyrus through the roof. "How dare you sample without this committee's knowledge?"

"What does it matter, Cyrus?" Jed looked from one to the other. "I can show you the results. It's a strong indication the mutation took place within the cattle. Not the bison."

Kemper grabbed Cyrus by the arm, calming him.

"It won't make a difference, Cyrus. No one will take twenty-seven samples seriously."

He turned to Jed, eyes alive, and said, "The governor of the state of Montana is insisting that the buffalo be killed."

Jed groaned. "What about Senator Liddicott?"

Cyrus blurted out a laugh. "Senator Liddicott's gone. He left the state. Said he had urgent business back in D.C. But we all know the truth. The new death makes this thing too hot a potato, even for Liddicott. He's already issued a statement saying he's dropping out of the presidential race."

"The governor of Montana doesn't have the authority to authorize this insane plan," Jed argued fiercely.

"He's put a call in to the president," Kemper replied. "He's asking for an executive order."

"All we need are a couple more days. We'll have definitive lab results soon. We have to hold off until we do."

Matthew Hughes finally cleared his throat.

"Dr. McCane, twenty-seven samples will not persuade anyone, including the committee, to hold off. Not when we're seeing new cases.

"We need you on board with this. The locals consider you an expert. They've quoted you in national newspapers. There will be a national outcry. We need to nip it in the bud, before it gains momentum. Your authority may make the difference. We need to do this swiftly, Dr. McCane, before more people die. If Senator Lippicott saw the futility of fighting this, surely you must."

When Jed's only response was a defiant glare, Andy spoke his turn.

"What's come over you, Jed? They're animals. Animals." He spoke with disdain. "These are people we're talking about. Real people. The woman who died was a thirty-seven-year-old mother of two children. Are you willing to tell her husband and kids that you consider the lives of a herd of wild animals more important than their wife and mother?"

"There'll be no holding off," Cyrus declared. "We already went over this. Whether Jed likes it or not, those bison are going to be killed. It all starts tomorrow. Like the doc here says, we were hoping that since you're known as an expert on brucellosis, you'd stand with us on the issue. There's gonna be a lot of hell-raising, and you could minimize that. Besides, we need your help. Hell, you can imagine how many cowboys we're gonna have to recruit, and how much they'll get off on this whole thing." He threw his head back and laughed. "It could be a new reality show. Rambo meets Bambi."

"You scum," Jed said, lunging at Cyrus. His fist caught the paunchy rancher squarely under the jaw.

Cyrus fell back, swearing and kicking at Jed to keep him away.

Kemper and Andy jumped Jed simultaneously, wrestling his arms behind his back.

Instinctively, Rebecca ran to Jed's defense.

"Let him go," she cried. "Let me talk to him."

When they did not do as she ordered, she began to scream. "All of you, get out. Now. Leave us alone."

The men looked in unison at Cyrus, who'd picked himself up off the ground and now swiped at the dust on his pants.

He straightened, studied Rebecca momentarily, then nodded toward the barn door, motioning them out.

Jed stood with clenched fists, blood pounding in his temples, as he watched them go.

Rebecca swung him around with a hand on his shoulder.

"Jed, please, listen to reason. You are not going to stop this. Can't you see? It's going to happen. With or without you. The governor, the Cattlemen's Association, the CDC, everyone is behind this now. Your only ally with any influence has just left town. Can't you see? Having you there would at least ensure that those poor animals die humanely."

Jed closed his eyes against the images already running through his mind.

"Are you going to leave their final moments in the hands of men like that?" Rebecca pressed when he finally opened them. She nodded toward the door where Cyrus Gibbons stood, peering inside.

"Make sure they do this humanely, Jed. Please. *You cannot stop it.*"

Jed opened his eyes and took a deep breath.

He looked at Cyrus Gibbons and saw a man who personi-
fied hatred and cruelty.

"All right," he finally said. "I'm on board."

THIRTY-THREE

HE **FOUND HER** where he knew he would.

He trudged through the snow to where she was seated.

When she saw him coming, she stood and waved.

Her smile—the purity of it—broke his heart.

"Did you get the results?"

"No."

"What? What is it?"

"There's been another death. And two more sick people."

"That's terrible. Awful."

She fell to her knees, then slowly looked up at him.

"That's not all, is it? That's not what you came here to tell me."

"This is the hardest thing I've ever had to do."

She looked at him, studied him.

She lifted her face to the sky then, closed her eyes. Her scream of anguish echoed across the draw and back. It seared through Jed's entire being like a bolt of lightning.

"No!"

When she turned to him again, her cheeks were streaked with tears.

"You said you didn't get the results yet."

"I didn't. But they're not waiting. I don't know how to tell you this. They're going to do it. They're going to kill all the park's bison."

"How can they do that? How can they . . . ?" She grabbed him, her gloved hands grasping the collar of his jean jacket, and shook him. "How can you let them? Those deaths have nothing to do with the bison."

"You can't know that."

"Tell them it might be the elk. You know that's every bit as likely. More likely! *Tell them!*"

"It doesn't matter to them, Megan. Don't you see? Even if it weren't for the fact that the hunting and outfitter lobbies wouldn't allow it to happen, there's no way in hell they can slaughter all the wild elk in this country. The bison are a different matter. If there's a chance the disease started in them—"

"Those tests will tell. You said they would."

"They're not going to wait, Megan."

"You have to stop them."

Jed wanted to look away. He could not bear to look into her eyes. But he owed her that much.

"It's not 'they.' "

Her fingers froze in their grasp on his coat. Slowly, as if poisoned by touching any part of him, she opened them and stepped back.

"Megan, please."

He reached for her. She stepped toward him, and for a moment, he thought she might be willing to forgive him. But instead, she spit on the ground in front of him.

"I can at least make sure they don't suffer," he said. He was pleading now. "And if it's a matter of human lives versus the bison, I have to do what I can to protect human life."

"We have no more right to be here than they."

She stared at him, as if she no longer recognized him.

"And I thought I loved you," she said.

Then she turned and walked away.

THIRTY-FOUR

THE MOOD IN the truck was grim.

Andy Butler and Matthew Hughes sat in the front seat, Jed in the back. He and Andy were barely on speaking terms.

As the Jeep approached the park, they saw flashing lights ahead. A roadblock.

As they waited in a long line of vehicles, a string of moving lights to the left caught Jed's eye. He turned to try to discern what they were. An ATV. Behind it another, then another. He looked right. The same scene met his eyes.

Patrols.

For the first time in its 130-year history, Yellowstone National Park had been closed. Not only closed, it had become a guarded fortress. No visitors would be allowed in. All borders were being patrolled.

Even air traffic had been forbidden.

No video footage or photographs of what was to take place could be leaked to the public.

In silence, they drove under the stone arch and drew nearer to the north entry gates. The booths were now manned by police and National Guardsmen.

When it came their turn, Andy stopped and handed over credentials.

They were asked to get out of the Jeep. It was searched.

Not for guns. For cameras.

A row of pickup trucks waited in the next line. As Jed stood waiting for the uniformed soldiers to finish searching the vehicle, he heard one after another of the pickups being turned away.

"But I heard they're hirin' wranglers for the roundup," one particularly youthful cowboy complained.

"They've got all they need," a Montana state patrolman responded.

Back inside, as the Jeep climbed the highway leading to the Mammoth visitors' center, which had been designated headquarters for "Operation Roundup"—which was what they'd termed it—Jed saw a lone bison grazing up ahead, fifteen yards off the road.

He pressed his eyes closed until they'd passed it.

The scene at Mammoth resembled something out of a movie. Trucks everywhere. Jed counted over a dozen horse trailers, all full. Cowboys milled about in their hats and boots and chaps, drinking coffee and talking in small clusters. Park Service vehicles were parked at every angle.

Uniformed rangers, most looking numb but some looking ready to mutiny, walked silently by on their way to the visitors' center, where the briefing would be held.

As the CDC man maneuvered the car up onto a cement sidewalk, Jed spotted the SUV. It was marked "Park Superintendent."

When the driver's door opened, Jo Chandler emerged. Immediately she became engulfed by uniforms—Park Service, police, National Guard. They moved en masse along the sidewalk outside the Albright Center.

As she passed Jed, her eyes briefly rested on him.

He nodded to her.

She looked away quickly, but it was long enough for Jed to see the terror in her eyes. The group proceeded up the cement stairs and disappeared inside.

It took half an hour for everyone to squeeze into the theater where, during the summer, visitors watched films shown at half-hour intervals throughout the day. The seats had already filled when Jed stepped inside. Along with fifty or more others, he stood in an aisle, pressed against the wall.

The meeting was brief. Jo Chandler handled it with utmost professionalism, giving clarity to the murky instructions that, until now, had been passed by word of mouth, like some dirty secret. These instructions were now enumerated behind her on a screen normally used to show films about the grandeur of the park and its wildlife.

"We will form three teams," she announced, eyes always cast on the screen behind her, avoiding meeting the eyes—especially those belonging to the park rangers—in the audience. "One for each herd of bison."

"Death squads," Jed heard one ranger behind him whisper to another.

"Please find your name and report to your designated team," Chandler continued.

Jed looked for his name. He had been assigned the Lamar Valley herd. He was surprised to see he'd been put in charge. Did he have Jo Chandler to thank—or curse—for that fact? Andy Butler would be the physician.

"I will at all times remain here at the Albright Center to coordinate the operation," Chandler said, "which we expect to complete in three days."

With cool precision, she laid out the plans.

The bison, numbering in excess of three thousand, were to be herded into round pens where they would then be led, one by one, through a chute. At the end, out of sight of the others, and most workers, each would meet its death.

"Each team will be given a two-way radio," Chandler

explained. "Please listen closely. Because it is impossible to ensure privacy for communication over a two-way, they are to be used only for emergencies. I repeat, the only use of the two-way radios that is permissible will be for emergencies. Two-way communications can be—and we are most certain that under these circumstances, they *will* be—intercepted.

"Also, to ensure the authenticity of any communication, any radio transmissions taking place during the operation shall begin with the words 'Code Sienna.' I repeat, if you have an emergency and you need to communicate with headquarters here, any transmission must begin with the words 'Code Sienna.' Any communications that do not begin that way will be considered from outside, unauthorized sources and will be disregarded as such."

As the meeting ended and the crowd dispersed, Jo Chandler strode down the aisle, her pace making it clear she had no intention of engaging in further discussion.

Still, this time when she recognized Jed, she stopped. Jed had been standing with arms folded in front of him. She reached out, and clasped one of his hands.

"We tried, didn't we?"

A lump formed immediately in Jed's throat.

"Yes," he said. "We did."

Back in the Jeep, Jed and Andy drove in silence, having parted with Matthew Hughes, who had been assigned to the Pelican Valley herd.

They were third in line in a procession of cars, trucks, and trailers that extended half a mile. Still, Yellowstone seemed to Jed empty and surreal. Gone were the usual crowds, lines of cars with windows rolled down and fingers pointing. Bear jams and buffalo jams and elk jams, the park terminology for drivers who stopped traffic at the sight of wildlife. No amateur photographers slinking their way too close to the animals, no children calling excitedly to a mother or father. Just this procession of death.

The line headed east, toward the Lamar, passing the horse corrals, then the Roosevelt Lodge.

A short distance later, it rolled past the Yellowstone Institute, where staffers of the Yellowstone Association lined the way for several yards, staring inside the passing vehicles. Accusing stares, stares filled with hatred. Despair. Oddly, there were few tears. Perhaps after the anger died down.

Jed could not meet their eyes.

When the rolling meadows of the Lamar Valley, bisected by the river of the same name, came into sight, a dread like nothing Jed had ever experienced took hold of him. The cloud of dust sickened him. Where there was dust, there were bison. Herds of them.

The procession slowed, pulling over alongside the road.

An eerie silence before the storm.

When the horse trailers and cowhands came to a stop, that changed. The sound of horses neighing, trailers opening, hooves on metal floors and ramps. Cowboys' voices started out low and subdued, but the chatter built as Jed watched, mute, letting the designated roundup supervisor bark out orders.

Jed's job didn't start until the bison had been herded into the round pens, which he could see being built on the other side of the river. Even now, as the herd eyed them, workers put finishing touches on the structures.

"Here ya go, Doc," the supervisor said, leading a sturdy bay quarter horse Jed's way.

Jed let the stirrups down to allow for his long legs, swung up on to the horse and joined a group of more than a dozen riders, mostly park personnel. They rode north, toward the herd, in silence.

Halfway to the river, a trio of cowboys roared by, crashing into the Lamar's frigid waters with shouts of nervous anticipation.

By the time Jed's group arrived, the first bison had been herded into one of five enormous round holding pens.

Still mounted, Jed circled the scene slowly, observing, delaying as long as possible the inevitable.

Grunts, snorts, and groans filled the air as bison charged the heavily reinforced fence. Calves snorted, crying for their mothers who, in those instances where they'd been separated, bellowed back.

Each holding pen connected to a long chute.

"Ready to go, Dr. McCane?"

Jed tore his eyes from the sight of the chute and laid them upon a young man wearing a Yellowstone County Sheriff's Department uniform.

Seeing the distress of the fenced animals, Jed took air deep into his lungs.

"Yes," he said, "I'm ready."

He dismounted, following the deputy toward the platform at the end of the first chute.

As he walked, his gaze fell upon Andy Butler, who'd been standing beside the half-filled pen, talking to two senior DOL officials. Mid-conversation, Jed saw Andy reach for his cell phone. As he stood, a finger pressed to his free ear to drown out the hellish sounds all around him, Andy's expression went from dulled to one of horror.

"I'll be right back," Jed said, turning away from the deputy.

He strode to where Andy stood, eyes downcast, shaking his head.

"Keep me posted," he heard Andy say. "I can drive up there as soon as we're done here."

Andy slapped his cell phone shut, and stood there, his expression eerily blank.

"Who was that?" Jed asked, alarmed.

"The Missoula hospital. They've been treating another victim."

Jed had never understood why the people who'd fallen ill

had come to be known as victims. His heart went out to them, but he suspected there was a political agenda behind the term. Still, this news triggered a strange reaction in him.

A sense of relief flooded him.

It wasn't due to any lack of caring on his part. But the people who'd just fallen ill were still nameless to him at this point. The animals who would soon die as a result of those illnesses, they were right there in front of Jed's eyes, in flesh and blood. Grunting and calling. Mothers frantically bellowing for their calves.

Ironically, Andy's news conveyed upon Jed a sense of confirmation, a cleansing of sorts. A pardon. Perhaps this hideous, cruel task had become necessary after all.

Until this very moment, he'd wondered if he had the strength to do what he had to do.

Perhaps now he would find he did.

Jed suddenly realized that Andy's expression hadn't changed. The sense of shock from the news he'd just received had apparently not dissipated.

"Did he or she die?" Jed asked.

"He," Andy answered. "They're sure he will. They think maybe he already has."

"They *think* he may have died?" Jed parroted. "How can they not know?"

Andy's eyes finally met Jed's.

"Because he's disappeared. He came in yesterday afternoon, but during the night, they found his room empty."

Jed stared at him, uncomprehending.

"That makes no sense."

"They're looking for him now. They had the police put out an all-points bulletin. They've got a car heading down to Hamilton now."

That one word took the breath right out of Jed's lungs, as surely as if someone had just sucker-punched him in the gut.

"What did you say?"

"I said they even have the police looking for this guy."

"Not that," Jed said impatiently. "Where? Where did you say they sent a car?"

"Hamilton. That's where the guy was from. They figure he may have headed back there to die."

Reaching for the two-way radio attached to Andy's belt, Jed said, "Give me that."

At first, Andy clasped his hand over it, as if to stop Jed.

"What's up, Jed? What's going on?"

Jed wrenched the radio out from under his grasp.

With his heart hammering against his ribs, he held it up to his mouth and pressed the red button on its side.

"Code Sienna. Code Sienna," Jed said. "This is Dr. Jed Mc-Cane."

Jo CHANDLER HAD slid out of the operations room, excusing herself to go to the restroom.

But instead, she'd headed to her office. She shared a restroom with others in the complex of offices on the third floor of the Mammoth headquarters building, and right now, she needed to be alone.

Inside the office, she stood, hands grasping the edge of her desk. She'd lost the ability to breathe, to even think clearly.

She felt certain she would pass out any second now.

She went to the minirefrigerator in the corner and grabbed a bottle of water. She opened it and drank it slowly, trying to calm herself. Telling herself this had to be done. She was powerless now to stop it.

I have no choice.

A knock on her door startled her.

"There you are," Bob Franks, the Mammoth District's head ranger, said. Bob had been working in Yellowstone for thirty-two years.

He and Jo had started out together as interpretive rangers at Mammoth. But Bob was not a political creature and promotions had passed him by.

He too appeared shaky and chalky white.

Jo suddenly saw that he held a two-way radio.

"What?" she said.

Bob extended his hand.

"It's a Code Sienna. Dr. Jed McCane wants to talk to you."

Jed McCane.

Her own hand trembling now, Jo reached for the radio.

"This is Jo Chandler," she said, pressing the red button on its side. Amazingly, her authoritarian bearing returned instantaneously. "Go ahead Dr. McCane."

The response came in amid a clatter of static.

"Ms. Chandler, Operation Roundup must be stopped. Immediately."

The hair on the back of Chandler's neck stood straight.

"Please repeat." She was yelling now into the radio. A group had gathered at her open door. Rangers who'd devoted their lives to Yellowstone and its animal inhabitants. "You're not coming through clearly."

"Operation . . . Roundup . . . must . . . be . . . stopped . . . NOW."

They'd all heard it. Gasps gave way to air thick with silence.

A glimmer flickered in Bob Frank's eyes as Chandler's met them. She pressed the button again.

"Dr. McCane," she said slowly, enunciating every word to perfection. "You of all people know what an extraordinary request that is."

Now Jed's words came faster.

"It's not a request, Ms. Chandler. I'm telling you. You must stop the slaughter."

When Chandler did not respond, the radio crackled again.

"Give me forty-eight hours."

Jo looked up at Bob again.

He'd pursed his lips tight, in an effort to control his emotion. Chin quivering, parched skin wrinkling with the strain of holding back tears, he nodded at her.

"Do it," he whispered.

Suddenly Cyrus Gibbons appeared behind Franks in the doorway.

Right after the meeting, during the commotion that ensued, Jo had heard Cyrus tell Clay Kittrick he would stay behind at the headquarters. She did not understand why at the moment.

Now she did.

Red faced and clearly seething, Cyrus said, "You can't call it off. You have no authority."

Jo dropped the hand holding the two-way to her side and, in two strides, came face-to-face with him.

"I'm the only one here who *does* have authority."

"We won't stop," Cyrus declared. "I'm telling them to go ahead. They'll listen to me."

With great deliberation of movement, Jo lifted the two-way to her lips. Locking eyes with Cyrus over the radio, she delivered her words with even greater deliberation.

"If your men shoot so much as one hair on any of those buffalo, I'll have your neck. Do you hear? I'll make sure you are prosecuted for a federal offense and put away so long that no one in this state will even remember your name."

She pressed on the radio's button.

"Very well, Dr. McCane," she said calmly. "You have forty-eight hours."

THIRTY-FIVE

DID YOU HEAR that?"

A whooping cry echoed down the hill and across the draw as K.C. sprinted toward Colleen Talks to Sky, his two-way radio held high in the air.

"Did you hear?" he screamed again, looking for others with radios, others who had heard.

The scattered group of Buffalo Field Campaigns activists turned in unison to look at him. They'd been standing high on the hill, watching the procession of trucks enter the park. Videotaping.

Earlier, they'd seen dozens of horse trailers pulled behind pickups filled with cowboys. But the huge vehicles that had rolled in just minutes earlier, dozens upon dozens of them, were a new kind of truck.

Haulers.

Each person knew what they would take back out through the arch. And each was prepared to go to jail to stop that from happening.

But timing would be critical.

Colleen Talks to Sky had received a warning from

a buffalo-friendly dispatcher at the sheriff's office. Word had it that if the Buffalo Field Campaigners turned the operation into a media frenzy, they would be immediately classified as domestic terrorists under the Patriot Act and arrested en masse. They suspected their communications from the compound were already being monitored.

In order to retain as much control as possible until the last minute and minimize the chance that the media would be turned away and prevented from covering the slaughter, a team of activists had been sent to Butte to secretly put buffalo-friendly media on call. Since dawn, reporters and cameramen had been migrating toward a secret meeting place thirty miles north of Yellowstone. At the critical moment, Megan, K.C., and Colleen would make the call. Until then, they would monitor the situation from the hilltop, where they would record what little videotape they could from the perimeter of the heavily patrolled off-limits zone.

"What?" Colleen Talks to Sky shouted now, running to meet K.C.

"Listen," K.C. cried. By now the crowd had gathered around him.

The transmission, faint and filtered through a storm of static, was far from perfect; but the words were unmistakable.

A woman's voice saying, *Please repeat. You're not coming through clearly.*

"That's Jo Chandler," K.C. explained.

A collective gasp issued from his audience. K.C. shushed them.

The next voice was that of a man.

Operation . . . Roundup . . . must . . . be . . . stopped . . . NOW.

Stunned silence followed as the group crowded in closer, waiting for the response.

When the radio remained silent, K.C. shook it. Finally, after what seemed an eternity, it crackled to life again.

Very well, Dr. McCane, you have forty-eight hours.

Chaos broke out on the hill.

Amid the shouts and cries of celebration, a tearful Colleen Talks to Sky—at the group's center—circled, searching for one particular face.

"Where's Megan?"

Only K.C. heard her over the jubilation of the others. "She'll be back. She went to offer one last prayer."

Talks to Sky broke into a serene smile. "It looks like the Creator may have heard."

SHE HAD PRAYED and cried herself into a state of exhaustion.

Now, she sat cross-legged in the teepee that looked down upon the Buffalo Field Campaign compound, wrapped only in her misery and a wool blanket.

Like the wild places that gave Megan comfort, the teepee had always been a place where her spirit could find peace. But right now she feared peace would elude her for the rest of her life.

She'd lost everything that mattered to her. Her beloved bison.

And Jed.

No more hope, or prayer, or strength remained in her frail body.

She lay back, reclining on the cold ground, and closed her eyes.

THIRTY-SIX

AT A RUN, Jed followed the prints left by her boots in the snow, from her Subaru, up the steps to the A-frame Buffalo Field Campaigns office, and then beyond, along a path up the hill. Thick foliage had hidden the buffalo-hide teepee on his previous visits, but the early cold had finally robbed it of its last vestige of camouflage.

K.C. had told him he'd probably find her there.

Jed didn't understand teepees, and medicine wheels, and prayers to the Creator. When he prayed, he prayed to God, in an old-fashioned church. But in the past few months, he'd learned to accept—if he were honest, at times even embrace—attitudes and ways he might once have derided. And right now, all that mattered to him was finding Megan.

Out of breath, he raced up to the teepee, and pushed aside its flap.

He cried out at the sight that greeted him: Megan sprawled across the floor.

"Megan!"

She opened her eyes, then bolted to an upright position, still seated on the ground.

"Jed."

Shaken, Jed found himself yelling at her.

"Dammit, Megan. Don't ever do that again. Do you know how much you just scared me?"

His reaction did not move her. Her eyes still held too much hurt and anger—but mostly, they held grief.

"Why are you here?" she said, pulling her knees to her chest self-consciously.

Jed stood above her, towering there, looking down.

"I came to tell you I won't let them do it. I'm going to stop the slaughter."

Megan's entire demeanor transformed with those words. She jumped to her feet, and grabbed Jed's arms.

"How, Jed? How can you stop them?"

"I think I know where the mutated brucella came from. I'm going right now to find out."

Megan's grasp on him tightened. "Where?"

"I can't take the time right now, but I promise I'll tell you as soon as I get back."

"Get back from where?"

"Hamilton."

"Take me with."

"It could be dangerous, Megan."

She looked at him with eyes so haunting they sent shivers down his spine. "I was just asking myself if I really wanted to live, Jed. What could be more dangerous than that?"

He studied her for a second.

And then he said, "Come on. I'll explain on the way."

THIRTY-SEVEN

ICE COATED THE highest stretches of Interstate 90, over the Continental Divide, but Jed did not allow it to slow him. They stopped once, for gas, in Butte.

They pulled into Missoula's Saint Patrick's hospital at just past six.

Once on the road, Jed had called Andy from his cell phone. Andy, who'd left Yellowstone two hours after Jed, announced that he was already on the road behind Jed. He'd called ahead to the hospital, directing them to release all the patient information they had to Jed.

He'd resisted at first.

"Before I do that, I want to know what you're thinking, Jed. Do you realize what you just did? Calling off that roundup will turn this whole situation upside down. The media will be all over it, and you know who's going to pay. For starters, *you*."

"You'll just have to trust me, Andy. Now will you do it? Will you make sure Saint Pat's has that information ready for me?"

The phone went silent.

"Yes," Andy finally said. "I'll do it. I just pray to God you know what you're doing."

"So do I," Jed said.

He looked over at Megan. She gave him a half-smile.

Andy had arranged for the director of Saint Pat's to meet with them. He'd stayed late. A tall, dark-haired man in his forties, he hurried out the front door when he saw Jed's truck pull in to the hospital's lot.

He introduced himself as Joe Utzinger.

Utzinger ushered both Jed and Megan into a small conference room. In his hand, he carried a manila file.

Once seated, he slid the file across the table to Jed.

"We don't really know what we're dealing with here," he said. "The situation grows more bizarre by the hour."

"How so?"

"This guy comes in to the ER yesterday afternoon, obviously in very bad shape. We were lucky we'd been the hospital to treat that other fella from down your way."

"Tucker MacNaughton?"

"Yes. If it hadn't been for that, we might not have recognized the symptoms right away, but our chief ER resident called in Dr. Singh, who treated the other brucellosis patient and he ran tests for *Brucella abortus* immediately. Urine came back positive. We began treating him with massive doses of a broad spectrum of antibiotics, and fluids.

"The fluids seemed to help at first, but then he began crashing. As you no doubt know, they haven't found an antibiotic that works with this new strain. By late last night, Singh gave orders to move this guy to the critical care unit for supportive care. When staff went to do that, he was gone. His bed was empty, he'd taken everything with him. Just disappeared."

"Because we were dealing with this new strain of brucellosis, and as far as Singh knew it hadn't been determined yet whether human-to-human transmission was a possibility, we immediately contacted the police and asked them to start looking for him."

"He sounds pretty sick to get up and get out of here on his own," Jed said.

"He may not have been on his own. Just a short while before they found his bed empty, one of our security people had noticed a truck out in the parking lot. The motor was running but no one was in it. At the time, he didn't think that much of it 'cause we see that type of thing fairly often. You know, when people are rushing to the ER in the middle of the night."

"But when they started looking for this guy, the same security person noticed the truck had disappeared. And no new patients had come in during that time frame." His eyes moved from Jed to Megan and back to Jed as he talked. "We think someone sneaked into the hospital and got him out."

Jed wondered why Utzinger kept referring to the patient as "this guy" when they obviously had an entire file on him. "You keep saying 'him,'" Jed finally said. "Does the patient have a name?"

It startled Jed when Utzinger laughed.

"That's where it gets even stranger. He registered as a Muhammad Farouk. From Hamilton, Montana. That's the information we gave to the police, but the Montana driver's license the police pulled up had a picture of a Middle Eastern guy on it, which shouldn't have surprised anyone, since he had that name. He had a Hamilton address. I can tell you, the guy who checked into Saint Pat's wasn't from the Middle East. According to the staff who attended to him, he was American as applie pie.

"I just got off the phone with the police and they confirmed that this guy checked in using a fake ID. At this point, we don't know who the hell he was. And apparently the police have had no luck finding Farouk."

Jed and Megan exchanged glances.

Utzinger tapped the file. "All the information we do have

on this Farouk guy is in there, but it's probably worthless." He cleared his throat. "You know, I'm really sticking my neck out giving you that, you not even being a medical doctor."

Jed had already pushed back from the table to leave.

"I appreciate what you've done. I'm sure you know Andy Butler well enough to trust him."

Utzinger nodded, clearly uneasy now about his actions.

Still, as Jed and Megan strode out of the room, he called after them.

"Oh, and one more thing. We also just got preliminary blood work back on this guy. It showed traces of rifampin and doxycycline."

Jed stopped dead in his tracks and pivoted to face him again.

"Those are the antibiotics that have traditionally worked against *Brucella abortus*. But we've seen from the other cases that they're not effective against this strain."

Utzinger shook his head. "Well, apparently this guy didn't know that. Looks like he'd been trying to treat himself." He stood, looking exhausted by the unfolding drama, and no doubt, the hospital scrutiny that would follow. "Guess he was grasping at straws."

THIRTY-EIGHT

YOU THINK IT'S Nicolas Sandburg, don't you?" Megan said once they were back in the truck. "That scientist you told me about. The one who works at the lab in Hamilton."

Jed sped down Reserve Street—Missoula's strip-mall-congested main drag and one of only two routes to Hamilton—dodging in and out of thick traffic while Megan reviewed the file given them by Joe Utzinger.

"It's only a hunch, but all along I've realized there are only two possibilities to explain the *Brucella abortus* suddenly turning deadly. That it mutated spontaneously, either with the bison as hosts or Jack Hamlin's herd. Or that someone genetically engineered it. I didn't want to think the latter was possible. Even when you told me you suspected Cyrus was behind it. I guess I didn't think anyone could be that evil. Or that desperate."

"Way I see it," Megan said, bracing an arm against the dash as a Land Rover cut suddenly in front of them, causing Jed to swerve briefly into oncoming traffic. "Anyone heartless enough to want thousands of bison killed would have no trouble with the idea that a couple people might have to die, too."

"I guess I never thought of it that way."

"Jed . . ."

She did not finish.

"What?"

He glanced over at her. Megan was staring at him.

She did not respond.

"What?" Jed pressed. "What were you going to say?"

"I'm just wondering how you'll deal with it if Rebecca's somehow involved."

"Rebecca?" He shook his head. "She's not that bad, Megan. Honestly. Yes, she did betray me in passing along information about my research to Cyrus. But you have to understand something about Rebecca. Her father had this incredible hold on her. She'd do anything to win his acceptance. And ranching was his life, so she made it hers. After I thought about it, I realized that she just didn't have it in her to resist Cyrus, especially his promise to get her elected president of the Cattlemen's Association.

"Rebecca wouldn't hurt anyone, Megan. She's a good but misguided person. I pity her, but I've finally let go of my anger."

He glanced Megan's way again, fearful that his words had made her jealous. But she just continued to look at him, concern darkening those eyes.

"I guess we won't know anything for sure until we find Sandburg."

"No," Jed replied, "we won't."

"How are we going to do that? Find him?"

"First, we find Farouk."

"But where?" She sifted through the file, then pointed to a preprinted form. "He left the employment section in the insurance form blank."

Jed's expression made clear he didn't consider the omission an obstacle.

"Where do you suppose a guy from the Middle East would find work in a little town like Hamilton?" he asked, glancing her way.

"Rocky Mountain Labs?"

"Bingo. Those research institutions hire the best scientists from around the world. I'd be willing to bet that that's where Farouk works."

As they drove south, heavy storm clouds parted briefly to the west and the Bitterroot Mountains sprang to life, magnificent with the sun setting behind them. Jed hadn't driven Highway 93 in years, since his college days. The fields and ranches he remembered, an impossibly idyllic valley between two glorious ranges, had turned into mirror-image subdivisions. Even ten miles outside Missoula, traffic hardly let up.

Forty minutes out of Missoula, a sign welcomed them to Hamilton. Jed drove straight to Rocky Mountain Labs.

By now darkness had descended. Still, most the windows of the two-story brick buildings blazed with light, and inside, Jed saw several figures moving about and hunched over lab tables.

As Jed pulled the truck up to the entry gate, two uniformed guards approached. Both wore highly visible gun holsters.

"ID please," the one who approached Jed's door said.

The other shined a flashlight into Megan's side of the car.

Jed pulled out his wallet, and withdrew his driver's license and a business card.

"I'm Dr. Jed McCane," he said.

"Dr. McCane, who are you visiting tonight?"

"Muhammad Farouk."

Jed noticed the two guards exchange glances.

"Do you have an appointment with Dr. Farouk?"

"No."

"I'm afraid no one gets inside without an appointment. Please back up and depart the premises, Dr. McCane."

"What about Nicolas Sandburg? Is he available?"

At this, the guard drew his gun, holding it barrel aimed skyward, but he'd made his point.

"I'm afraid I'm not making myself clear. Either you leave, *now,* or we'll have to arrest you for trespass. Got it?"

"Got it," Jed replied, shifting into reverse.

They did a three-point turn, waited for an opening in traffic, then pulled back onto Highway 93.

The moment they did, Megan turned to Jed. "You were right. Farouk works there!"

"Looks like it. Did you notice the guards' look when I said his name?"

Megan shook her head from side to side slowly. "What the hell's going on in that place?"

"I'd usually say you don't want to know, but I'm afraid that's not true right now," Jed answered. "RML will soon be one of only three Biosafety Level 4 research centers in the country. That means they'll be researching the most deadly pathogens known to man. Which means the security is actually a good thing."

"If they have so many security precautions in place, how could your theory be true."

"I don't know. It may not be. But if someone genetically engineered the new strain, it took a lab and someone with know-how. Sandburg has both."

"Plus he knew about your research."

"Exactly."

Jed had noticed a café directly across the street from the RML compound. He made a U-turn and headed back toward it. Cruising by, he noticed half a dozen people sitting inside.

Two wore white lab coats.

He pulled in.

Inside the café, Jed and Megan settled at a table next to

the man and woman wearing lab coats. The quiet café allowed Jed and Megan to hear the conversation taking place—a meeting they were preparing for the next day—and immediately confirmed what Jed had hoped. They were employees at RML.

As the two got up to leave, Jed leaned their way, smiled, and said, "Pardon me. You work with Muhammad Farouk, don't you?"

The man look startled.

"I don't exactly work with him. But I serve on the QC advisory board with him."

QC. Quality Control.

"Do you know if he's working tonight?"

"He's been out of the country for weeks now. His wife is ill, back in Saudi Arabia."

That explained why Sandburg had used Farouk's identity in checking in to the hospital. With Farouk out of the country, he'd be less likely to get caught. Perhaps he'd even broken into the missing man's residence to get his insurance information, which he'd presented to the hospital upon checking in.

"Oh, that's too bad," Jed said. "Thanks for the information."

The two nodded and smiled, then headed toward the cash register.

"Oh, one more thing," Jed said, getting up to follow them. "I'm trying to reconnect with Nicolas Sandburg. We went to undergrad school together. You wouldn't know where he lives, would you?"

On the way down to Hamilton, Jed had tried directory assistance for a listing for Sandburg. He'd been told the number was unlisted.

"Nick's been gone for the last week or so."

"Vacation?"

"I don't think anyone's really sure."

Jed scratched his head. "Maybe I'll just drop by and see him in the morning. Does he still live down in Darby?"

It was a guess, a shot in the dark; but Sandburg had set the meeting in Darby, and the waitress at the café had seemed to know him.

"You know, I thought he lived up on Sweat Hut Creek somewhere," the man said. "But I've never been there."

The woman nodded.

"He's got a ranch up there. He raises llamas."

"That's right," Jed said. "He mentioned that to me last time we talked. Well, thanks again, folks. Good night."

"Night," they said in unison.

THE GAS STATION attendant was just flipping the Open sign to Closed when Jed stuck his head in the door.

"Can you give me directions to Sweat Hut Creek?"

The attendant pointed north, the direction Jed and Megan had come.

"Up that way, 'bout ten miles. Just before Florence. I think there's a sign that marks it."

"Thanks," Jed said.

He'd left Megan in the idling truck.

On the way back to her, Jed broke into a run.

THIRTY-NINE

THE COMMENT ABOUT llamas saved them.

They had trouble finding Sweat Hut Creek. Contrary to the gas station attendant's belief, no sign along Highway 93 distinguished it from any of the dozen or more other rivers and streams the highway crossed. However, once they got off the main highway and found their way to an access road that paralleled 93, they saw it. A sign.

Sweat Hut Creek.

Sweat Hut ran east and west. But Jed and Megan soon discovered that small ranches and large estatelike homes, none of which bore names on the mailboxes, lined it in either direction.

They'd driven several miles east of Highway 93 with no luck, then headed an equal distance west of 93. Again, nothing to help them identify Sandburg's residence. Old and new intermingled; rundown ranches, with horses held back by little more than two strands of barbed wire, neighbored six-thousand-square foot Tudors with immaculate lawns and long, gated driveways.

They'd almost decided it was hopeless to keep searching

without an address when Megan's voice pierced the dark, silent cab of the truck.

"Look, llamas."

Jed pulled the truck off to the side of the road.

"Back up," she said. "We just passed them."

Jed backed the truck up twenty yards. Silhouetted against a half-moon trying to break through rolling banks of clouds, Jed had to strain at first to see them.

Then movement caught his eye. A small herd of llamas ran nervously back and forth along a white three-rail fence. Backing up even further, Jed saw that the fences surrounding the pastures to the north and south of the driveway met at an arch that read RANCHO DURMIENDO. Sleeping Ranch.

Jed hit the lights on his truck and pulled into the long, paved drive.

The top branches of the cedars, Tamaracks, and naked cottonwoods that lined the long drive waved eerily in the gusty wind.

"You sure we should be in the driveway?" Megan asked, fear tweaking her voice for the first time.

"If Sandburg's the one who checked into Saint Patrick's, you can be sure he's not outside where he can notice us."

"But Joe Utzinger said he may have had someone else with him . . ."

"You're right. I'll pull into the woods before we get within sight of the house."

They crept forward until light began flickering through the dense stand of trees ahead, where the driveway curved left, apparently just before reaching the house.

Jed backed the truck onto the lawn, tires crunching its frozen grass as he eased it back far enough between the trees to be hidden from sight.

They moved side by side across the lawn, bent low and in silence, maneuvering around a pond with a waterfall.

The house came into view. A long cedar rancher. Lights

blazed above the front door and each door of the three-car attached garage, but inside, only two windows, at the far end of the house, were lit.

Jed reached for Megan's hand.

Sheltered by several rows of neatly planted shrubs, they worked their way around to the back of the house.

"You stay here," Jed Whispered, pressing his lips to Megan's ear in order to be heard over the wind.

He crept toward the house. The door to screened-in porch suddenly clapped noisily, opening and closing in a gust. Jed slid inside and moved to the row of windows encased by it.

He rose up to get a look inside the small window to the right of a door that led inside the house.

The kitchen.

A light from down a hallway to the left threw a pale shaft across the floor, enabling Jed to see inside. The counters were littered with food items and no less than eight or ten empty plastic bottles that appeared to have held drinking water. Jed's eyes stopped when he noticed a clutter of syringes strewn haphazardly across the counter in front of the microwave. Small glass vials lay everywhere.

He tried the door.

Locked.

Returning to the double-hung window, he pulled his car keys out, clasping the keys tightly to avoid making any noise. Using the longest as a tool, he priced it under the bottom window. It budged.

Once he broke its vaccumlike hold on the sill, he was able to slide his fingers underneath and raise the window. With a quiet grunt, he hoisted himself up, forearms poised on the sill, and stuck his head inside.

It immediately became clear he could not fit through it.

"Let me."

Jed jumped down and whirled around.

"I told you to stay back there."

"Just give me a boost," Megan said. "I'll open the door for you. Hurry."

Wondering if it was against his better judgment, Jed put a hand under each of Megan's arms and lifted her up to the window. She slid inside on her stomach, onto the counter, pulling her legs in behind her and disappearing from sight.

Several seconds later, Jed heard the dead bolt slide clear. The door squeaked softly as Megan opened it.

He slid through it.

Inside, they stood, listening. Outside the wind continued to howl, but inside, only silence greeted them.

Jed moved to the counter, where he grabbed one of the empty vials. He lifted it, holding it at an angle in the dim light, and read the label.

Doxycycline.

The lab reports had detected its presence in the blood of the man who checked in as Muhammad Farouk.

Suddenly, the logo above the word caused Jed to bring the bottle even closer to his eyes.

Manson Cline.

Brow furrowed, he grabbed another empty vial. And then another. Surely it was some mistake. A fluke.

But each label bore the same symbol.

A veterinary-medicine symbol, with an *M* and a *K* transposed over it.

Nicolas Sandburg had been treating himself with antibiotics intended for veterinary use.

A sense of heightened dread filled Jed as he crept down the hallway, hugging the wall. Megan moved in unison with him, directly behind. He must focus on the job at hand, not on the myriad thoughts—really just impressions and impulses, nothing that made any kind of sense—assaulting his brain.

They'd taken only a few steps when he froze.

He turned, holding a finger to pursed lips to signal Megan that they were not alone.

It came from the lit room at the end of the hall.

A deep, labored wheezing.

Jed recognized it instantly. The sound of lungs filled with fluid.

"Please."

Jed felt Megan grasp his elbow. They stood, frozen with terror.

Had they been detected?

Again, a man's voice, weak, desperate.

"Please," he begged, "take me back to the hospital. I'll die."

Jed turned to look at Megan. She too appeared not to know whether the words were intended for them, or whether someone else—someone besides the person in the room ahead, who was obviously on death's edge—was present in the house.

The sob stunned Jed.

Like a lit fuse, it sizzled through his body, raising on end the hair on the back of his neck and on his arms, permanently embedding itself in every cell of his brain, where he had recently buried it.

He staggered backward, into Megan, who looked confused by his reaction.

And then the voice, spoken through more sobs, but clear as a cow bell on a crisp Montana morning.

"I don't know what to do."

A voice Jed knew as well as that of his mother or father. His brother. A voice he could never mistake.

It belonged to Rebecca.

JED INCHED FORWARD, straining to hear more.

"You promised you wouldn't go to the hospital if I brought you the antibiotics," Rebecca said, her tone quickly changing from contrite to angry.

"They weren't working," Sandburg replied, "can't you

see? I took them, all of them, and look at me. The new strain is resistant."

"Whose fault is that? Maybe you should have thought about that."

"You told me that's what you wanted. You wanted brucellosis to start killing people."

"Well, I would've thought you'd at least be careful not to get it yourself."

When he responded, Sandburg's voice was filled with equal parts disbelief and anguish.

"It had to be the centrifuge," he said slowly. "It made this rattling noise when I was purifying the tissue culture fluid. When the unit stopped, I opened the chamber and removed the bottles from the rotor. That's when I noticed that one of them had leaked some of the infected culture into the rotor. I must have been exposed to aerosolized brucella when I first opened the chamber."

The laughter stunned Jed.

It was Rebecca's laugh, no doubt about it, but there was an eerie quality to it, a callousness.

A lack of sanity.

"So much for all the safety they've been touting at that place," she said casually. "See, I'm doing you and your scientist friends a big favor. The press would've had a field day if they knew about that accident. Those people who are fighting against RML being turned into a Level 4 facility would've used it to make sure it doesn't happen. And our country would be less safe because of it."

She fell silent for a moment.

"See, we actually did a service to the whole damn country getting you out of that hospital. 'Cause once they figured out who you were, they would've known how it happened."

"Please, Miss Nichols, please."

"Shut up!" Rebecca shouted.

Suddenly, as a huge gust of wind rattled the windows, the

lights flickered off, then on again. This seemed to be the last straw for Rebecca.

"Where the hell is Cyrus?" she screamed.

Jed heard the scrape of a chair against the hardwood floors and, with a start, realized that she was leaving the room.

He spun around, instinctively shoving Megan into the darkness of the next bedroom. She struggled against him briefly.

"Jed! Oh, my God."

He turned.

Rebecca stood in the doorway at the end of the hall.

"What are you doing here?"

She said it as if he'd come home early from work.

"Becca," Jed said, approaching her, wanting to keep her away from the room into which he'd pushed Megan.

Rebecca tilted her head to the side. She held a small Colt .45 in her hand, loose at her side. Her father had given her the gun for her twenty-first birthday.

She simply stared at him, an amused expression on her face.

"What are you doing, Becca?"

"Did you discover I'd been taking your supplies?" she asked, clearly intrigued by the situation. "Is that it?"

"No," Jed replied. "Not until I saw them on the counter just now."

"Then how did you know to come here?"

"When I heard someone from Hamilton got sick, I guessed it," he said. "Until just now, I forgot that you knew about Nicolas Sandburg. So *you're* the reason he called me about my research."

She laughed.

"No, I can't take credit for that. That was Clay Kittrick's idea. Clay and Sandburg are second cousins, or something like that. Cyrus only told me about Clay's plan so I'd encourage you to work with Sandburg. Clay had something else in mind. He just wanted Sandburg to sabotage your work, to make you believe there was no validity to your research so that you'd drop the whole thing.

"The idea to contact Sandburg this last time was all mine." She leaned against the doorway, lazily crossing one booted ankle over the other. They could have been reminiscing about their childhoods. "Remember, you told me how you worried that one day *Brucella abortus* would mutate, and become more deadly? That was one of the reasons you thought it was so important to wipe it out now."

Jed's mind raced. All he could think about was Megan in the room behind him and how to keep her safe. Maybe if he gave her time, she could find a way out a window.

"I remember."

"Well, it gave me the idea. If it could mutate on its own, someone like Dr. Sandburg should be able to help it along. I'd mentioned it to Cyrus a while back, just in passing, kind of as a joke, and then when Senator Liddicott decided to turn the spotlight on the bison issue, Cyrus and Clay decided it'd be the perfect solution. What better way to turn public sentiment our way than for people to start dying from brucellosis?"

"You wanted people to die?" Jed cried, unable to contain his incredulity and disgust.

"We didn't know whether it'd actually be deadly. Sandburg was pretty sure he'd succeeded in making the new strain a lot more dangerous than the brucella the park bison carried—the strain I gave him—but there was no way to know whether it would kill anyone until it actually did."

"*You* gave him the original strain?"

Rebecca laughed, her eyes gleaming at the memory.

"Remember the night you had your little 'accident'? You asked me to put the samples you'd collected from the park bison in the refrigerator. I kept two of them. You were so shaken, so obsessed with the idea I'd been cheating on you that night, that I figured you wouldn't notice. You know, it was just instinct. The idea hadn't fully formed in my mind yet. But something just told me those samples might come in handy sometime."

Jed groaned as the realization of his own role in the hideous chain of events sank in. "Sandburg used samples I'd taken from the bison," he mumbled hollowly.

"Yes. Isn't that ironic?" Rebecca replied, grinning. "We had to make certain everyone blamed the park bison for the new strain, so it was imperative that Sandburg start with that strain. Then Cyrus heard that Jack Hamlin had just arranged to sell half a dozen head of his Horse Butte herd to Parker Derkowitz, so it gave us the perfect opportunity. We injected the new strain in Hamlin's herd while they were still on Horse Butte. A week later they went to slaughter. The rest is history.

"You should be thanking me, Jed. What's happened will make you a rich man. Your vaccine will be more important than ever." Her smile vanished. "I'd hoped it would make me your rich wife. But I realize now that's not going to happen."

Suddenly a door down the hallway, behind Jed, creaked.

Rebecca's relaxed posture went stiff.

As skilled a marksman as a marine trained for combat, she planted herself on both feet and raised the gun.

"What's that?" She shook the gun, barrel first, at Jed. "Back up. Get out of my way."

She started down the hall, but Jed reached for her and she drew sharply back, out of reach.

She began to scream.

"*Who's with you?* Is it *her?* Is it that buffalo bitch?"

Jed heard the click of the gun cocking.

"You son of a bitch," she said. "I should kill you right now."

Suddenly he felt movement behind him.

"Don't," Megan said quietly. "Please. Don't hurt Jed."

Jed saw the look of absolute insanity in Rebecca's eyes when they traveled from where he stood to just behind him.

Knowing time had run out, he lunged for the gun.

In the same instant, as if in slow motion, he saw its barrel swing toward Megan.

And then he heard it explode.

"No," he screamed.

Behind him, he heard a groan.

FORTY

REBECCA STOOD, STARING blankly at Megan's crumpled body, gun dangling loosely from her hand. Pushing her aside, Jed rushed to where Megan lay curled on her side, clutching her chest.

He rolled her over gently.

The bullet had entered on the left, just below her rib cage, but she was still breathing, and alert.

He scooped her up, and carried her into the lit room at the end of the hall.

Nicolas Sandburg, obviously near death, lay on a king-sized bed, his eyes closed.

Jed lowered Megan onto a red velvet settee situated at the foot of the bed to examine her more closely. Her coloring and vitals told him she was going into shock.

Her eyes followed his, but she could not speak.

"I'll call an ambulance," he told her, gently brushing the hair back off her forehead.

"No you won't."

Rebecca's voice was determined and steely.

Once again, she'd trained the gun on them, and Jed instantly regretted not fighting her for it.

"Rebecca, please. Let me call for help."

"No," she said. "No calls. No help."

"She'll die, Becca. Can't you see?" He waited for a response. When none came, he said, "Becoming president of the association can't be worth killing for."

Rebecca's brow furrowed in momentary confusion.

"This isn't about becoming president of the association," she said.

Jed turned to study her. Did he dare risk her using the gun again? If she used it on either one of them—him or Megan—it would practically ensure Megan's death.

"It isn't?"

"No, it's never been about that. It's about my daddy. His name. I had to do it, Jed. I had to do it. Otherwise everything Daddy worked for would have been lost. He was a hero in this country. He would have lost that. Once the press got wind of it, he would have lost everything that mattered to him. Just like he lost my brother and my mama."

"What are you talking about?"

"Daddy killed a man. It was Daddy who killed Running Wolf over that buffalo, way back then."

"Rebecca, that's not true."

"It *is* true. Cyrus told me. He's protected Daddy's name all along. Cyrus had the casing, the one they've looked for all these years. He gave it to me. He hid it to protect Daddy. That's why I had to go along with Cyrus. He said it was what Daddy would've wanted. To get rid of the bison once and for all. Cyrus said if I didn't find a way to do that, he'd turn that casing over to the authorities.

"I couldn't do that to Daddy, Jed. You know I couldn't." She actually smiled then. A sweet, desperate appeal for understanding. "Plus I thought I was helping you, Jed. Helping us. I thought if the brucellosis scare got big enough, some company would offer you a fortune for your vaccine and we'd get married and have a bunch of kids. I was sure you'd come back to me once all this died down. A family with me was everything you ever wanted. You used to say that. Do you remember?"

Jed nodded.

"Yes, I remember." He locked eyes with her. Time was running out. "I'm going to lift her up now, Becca. I'm going to take her to the hospital. You'll have to kill me to stop me."

A mournful sob escaped Rebecca's lips.

"How could you love someone like that?" she cried.

Jed slid his arms under Megan's torso, cradlelike, and stood.

He'd turned and taken one step toward the door, when a large shadow suddenly filled it, blocking his way.

"You'd better think again, Jed. I'm afraid it's a little late for you to be going anywhere."

"Cyrus."

The rancher held a hunting rifle at his side. The wind had left what little hair remained on Cyrus's head standing on end. That, combined with the gleam in his eye, lent him an especially wild look.

"You know you can't get away with this," Jed said. "Let me take her to the hospital. It'll be one less death on your hands."

Cyrus snorted a laugh.

"Hell, Jed, I agree that this thing has gotten way out of hand but I'm so deep in shit right now that I'm already as good as swinging by the neck. There's only one way out of this now. You *all* gotta go." His sweep of the gun included Rebecca. "You too, sweetheart. Drop that little thing and get with the rest of them."

Rebecca did not move.

"Now, Rebecca, if you don't drop that thing, I'll just have to put the first bullet through your man here. I know you're mad as hell at him, but I still don't think you wanna watch him die."

When she did not respond, Cyrus raised the gun several inches higher, so that it lined up directly with Jed's forehead.

"Okay then," he said, tensing his forefinger on the trigger.

Rebecca fired first, before Cyrus had a chance to.

With a shout, Cyrus folded to his knees, clutching his chest with his free hand. The rifle clattered to the floor.

His eyes opened fully in shock, two white orbs in a face turned instantly pale.

Still balancing Megan in his arms, Jed turned to look at Rebecca.

"Rebecca, no."

He screamed, bolting toward her clumsily.

But he was already too late.

Head tilted back, mouth wide, eyes placid, Rebecca stared at him from over the butt of the gun. The barrel had disappeared inside her mouth.

Jed swore she smiled at him before she pulled the trigger.

FORTY-ONE

HELL, JED," HENRY Carroll said, "there's no way to solve that crime now. And I see no reason to start digging it back up."

Jed sat opposite the sheriff. With each impatient tap of his foot, the cowboy hat resting on his lap bounced as if it had nerves of its own.

"A man died, Henry. Fact that he didn't have white skin, or see eye to eye with the cattlemen in this state, doesn't make that okay."

"No, I guess not. But I can tell you, that casing you found in Rebecca's jewelry box, the one you say Cyrus gave Rebecca, it wasn't the one that killed Running Wolf."

"You've run tests on it?"

Carroll nodded.

"Sent it up to the state crime lab. That bullet came out of a Winchester model that wasn't even manufactured till the mid-eighties. Running Wolf was shot in seventy-nine." He rocked back in his chair, eyes straying to a photograph on the opposite wall, which featured a youthful Henry, right hand over his heart, left in the air, being sworn in by the governor. "I remember' cause it was my first year in office."

Jed refrained from voicing the sarcastic thought this prompted.

"Well, what about Clay Kittrick?" he said instead. "Surely you're planning to bring charges against him."

"For?"

"For all those people dying from brucellosis. And for almost causing the slaughter of every bison in the park."

"We don't have any proof that he was involved."

"Hell you don't. Nicolas Sandburg was his cousin."

"That's the point. *Was.* Sandburg's dead, and he never implicated Clay before he died. Couldn't, considering he never regained consciousness after the night you found him."

"What about payments? Sandburg didn't just do what he'd done out of a loyalty to family. He has to have been paid."

"We're looking into that, Jed. I know you think I'm not good for much, but I've got it covered. Believe me. But without solid evidence indicating Clay had something to do with what happened, with the brucellosis deaths, we wouldn't stand a chance in hell of getting him convicted. This is cattle country, Jed. I arrest Clay, he's gonna ask for a jury. And you really think there's a jury within five hundred miles of here that'd convict him? He's a hero to these people."

"Well, then what about conspiring with Cyrus to murder Clancy? And Dusty Harrison?"

Jed still refused to believe Rebecca had anything to do with either death.

"I'm investigating, Jed. But it may just turn out that only three people knew the real story about what happened. Rebecca, Cyrus, and Clay. And two of them are dead. That leaves Clay to tell us his version. And Clay's version so far is that he and Cyrus did have that meeting you told me about, the one above Cyrus's ranch. After I told him a local rancher had IDed his plane—which was a damn lie, but it worked—Clay admitted that he'd flown in to talk to Cyrus

that morning. Clay says that's when Cyrus told him about
the plan to unleash a new, deadly strain of brucella. But Clay
swears he told Cyrus he wanted nothing to do with it."

Jed shook his head.

"I feel like I'm living in the old West. The Tom Horn
days, when cattlemen could get away with anything, so long
as it was in the best interests of ranching."

"Well, if it cheers you up any, after poor Jim Pritchard
confessed to irregularities about the Horse Butte allotment
and implicated Clay, Clay all but admitted he'd been skimming money off the DOL testing and slaughter program,
too. That's got to be the reason he didn't jump on the band-
wagon to kill the whole Yellowstone herd. I do remember
that, Jed. Remember the town meeting where Clay and
Cyrus butted heads over wiping out the whole bunch of 'em?
My guess is Clay's had a nice little pipeline of income coming in from that operation. Wiping out the herd would've
wiped that out, too. For that reason, his denial about the new
brucellosis strain makes sense to me, Jed. In fact, I think
Clay might just enter a plea on the embezzlement charges, if
I agree not to bring charges against him for any of the other
stuff."

Jed jumped out of the chair he'd been sitting in opposite
Henry and pounded a fist on the sheriff's deak. His hat hit
the floor softly.

"You can't do that, Henry. You can't agree not to prose-
cute him for what happened to Clancy and Dusty Harrison.
Whether or not he went along with the plan to unleash the
new strain of brucella, Clay Kittrick was deeply involved in
the earlier incidents. I've shown you the e-mails he wrote. I
told you, Kittrick is Bronco."

Carroll appeared unimpressed.

"I'm still waiting for the results of the trace the FBI's doing
on those e-mails. Without proof that Kittrick's this Bronco
character, I'm not sure we'll have a case against him."

Jed reached for his hat. Straightening to his full height, he locked eyes with Carroll.

"I'm not going to rest until someone pays for Clancy's and Dusty's deaths."

Carroll fingered the badge on his shirt pocket absent-mindedly.

"Well, now, Jed, I guess you're free to do all the investigating you want. I'm not gonna stop you. I understand why you're upset. Especially with Rebecca gone now. She was a fine woman. A man needs to do something to deal with the grief."

Thoroughly disgusted, Jed turned and, without a good-bye, walked out of the sheriff's office.

He headed for the hospital.

His spirits lifted immediately when he entered Megan's room to find her nose buried in a vase overflowing with flowers. She looked up and smiled at him.

"Who sent those?" Jed asked, bending to kiss her and then taking a sniff himself.

Megan laughed. "I like that."

"What?"

"That you want to smell them. Most the men out here don't exactly take pleasure in the smell of flowers." She held up the card that came with them. "They were from a group of ranchers. Tom Barton, Dutch Marsh, Frank Thompson, and half a dozen others."

Jed thought back to the day he'd stitched up Dutch Marsh's bull. That same day, Frank Thompson had blamed Jed for his gelding's death from colic.

"You're kidding."

"No, I'm not. They were hand-delivered by some of the most uncomfortable-looking cowboys I've ever laid eyes on. They just stood there, not a one of them would sit down. They said their bosses wanted me to know that not everyone in these parts wants to get rid of the buffalo. They said they hope we can find a solution that respects both the bison's right to be free, and the ranchers' rights to ranch. They apologized for what happened to me."

"I guess their bosses didn't think it was such a smart thing to come here themselves," Jed said, still thinking about the gelding.

"It's no wonder. Too many ranchers are furious that the bison slaughter was called off. Can you believe some people are actually so threatened that the only way they'll feel secure is to wipeout every last buffalo that roams free in this country? It still blows me away."

At one time Jed would have defended the ranchers, denied anyone actually felt that way. But he knew better now. News that the bison slaughter had been called off, and the bison cleared of any blame for the brucellosis deaths, had been greeted with jubilation by most of the country—indeed, Jed had read in *USA Today* that not only had Americans rejoiced, but the rest of the world as well—but in cattle country, many had deemed it a dark day.

"What did you tell them?"

Her slender lips turned up in a wistful smile.

"I told them I hope for the same thing. Do you think it's possible, Jed? There are so many good people in this state. So many honest ranchers, just trying to make a go of it. I really think they don't know who or what to believe. If only we could all be left to work it out together, person to person, without the lobbies and state agencies and the pressure from faceless corporations. Without political agendas."

Jed reached for her hand.

"You know that'll never happen, Megan. But I think the public outcry we're seeing from the news reports that a former president of the Cattlemen's Association was behind the brucellosis outbreak, and the fact that we almost lost something as important to this country as our last free-roaming buffalo, is going to protect the animals you love. The word is that the Forest Service is going to stop leasing out the Horse Butte allotment."

Megan's face brightened in a smile that faded quickly.

"That's what Colleen said when she called me a little while ago. And it's wonderful, Jed. But it's not enough. Not when the state of Montana's just approved a buffalo hunt for next fall. Not when the most powerful lobby in this state is determined to make the bison scapegoats for every cattleman's problems."

"I was hoping you hadn't heard about the hunt," Jed replied, shaking his head. "Horse Butte's a start, Megan. It's better than nothing. It's better than what we were looking at ten days ago." His voice grew thick as he added, "And it's a helluva lot better than if I'd lost you."

Megan studied him. "You still look so sad."

One thing he and Megan had going for them was complete honesty. He wouldn't insult her now by changing that.

"I am. In some ways, Rebecca was a good person, Megan. I know that's hard to believe, but she was. I wish I'd seen how disturbed she was deep down. I should have tried to help her." He sighed before adding, "I'll miss her."

"No one can know with absolute certainty what goes on in another person's mind, or heart. Don't blame yourself, Jed. And I *expect* you to miss her."

Jed squeezed her hand, grasping it in both of his.

"So what do you think the future holds for us?"

Megan laughed softly.

"For a country vet and a radical animal rights activist?"

For the first time in what seemed forever, Jed smiled.

"I don't know, Jed," she answered. "I think we should take it slow. Don't you?"

"I guess with this new deal I have with Manson Cline, I won't have much choice. It's going to keep me pretty busy till we get the vaccine into production."

"Do you think it'll work against the new strain?"

"We're going to make sure it does. Sandburg's work was pretty bold. And brilliant. Basically, he used the bison strain of *Brucella abortus* to create a hybrid pathogen that can cross species lines. That means Manson Cline's also going to have to work on that aspect of the vaccine, while I fine-tune the animal end."

Jed's voice filled with dread.

"Moving to Indiana to work at their research facility is gonna just about kill me. Leaving this country"—his voice grew thick again—"and you."

She raised his hand to her lips and kissed it.

"I'll be here when you get back. Just me and the bison. Waiting for our hero to return."

"That's what'll keep me going. Knowing that if my vaccine works, it'll put you out of a job."

Gently, Jed leaned toward her, and kissed her. They did not stop when the nurse came in. She mumbled, "I think I'll just come back," and slipped back out of the room, a rare smile on her normally tight face.

As Jed finally started pulling away from her, Megan put a hand on each side of his face and held his gaze.

"Do you think the new vaccine might actually make it possible for everyone to live in peace?"

He thought about it, long and hard, wanting to remember her touch, to catalog it for recall when he was a thousand miles away.

Finally, he gave her the only answer he could come up with.

"I guess we'll just have to wait and see. Won't we?"

He could tell it wasn't the answer she wanted; but still, it hadn't extinguished the hope in her eyes.

"I guess so," she replied.